Chrissy,
Best wishes!
W

CROSSING DAY

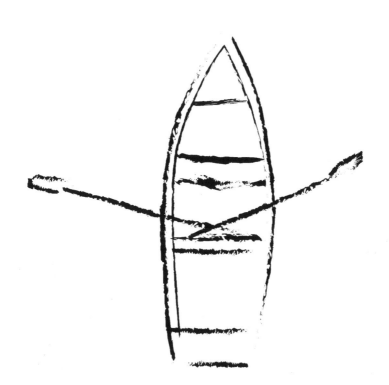

William A. Glass

Crossing Day © copyright 2024 by William A. Glass. All rights reserved. No part of this book may be reproduced in any form whatsoever, by photography or xerography or by any other means, by broadcast or transmission, by translation into any kind of language, nor by recording electronically or otherwise, without permission in writing from the author, except by a reviewer, who may quote brief passages in critical articles or reviews.

Publisher: William A. Glass, Author LLC
williamaglass.author@gmail.com

ISBNs: 979-8-9898175-1-1 (paperback) 979-8-9898175-2-8 (hardcover)
979-8-9898175-0-4 (ebook)

Cover art by Natalia Matuszewska
Author headshot by Daniel McDonald Johnson
Cover and book design by Mayfly book design

Library of Congress Catalog Number: 2024905526
First Printing: 2024
Printed in the United States of America

This book is dedicated to my grandmother,
Ethel Gorman Lansdale

CONTENTS

CHAPTER ONE

POP QUIZ

T he referee blows her whistle and points to the Joseph Johnston High School goal. It's a foul, just outside the penalty area. Hastily, several defenders form a wall. Liam Larsen, the goalkeeper, shouts directions.

"Block that kick, block that kick," the Johnston cheerleaders yell.

Melanie Montgomery, wearing her purple and gold cheerleader outfit, catches the eye of one of the boys on the squad. He nods as she runs toward him and then leaps, placing her foot into his waiting hands. Melanie's world dissolves into a swirl of color. She comes to earth with a thud.

"Nice landing," the boy says.

"Thanks." Melanie glances at the scoreboard and sees that despite their efforts, another goal has been added to the visitor's tally. "I hate these German schools," she pouts.

"Yeah, they act like they invented the game," one of the other cheerleaders exclaims.

There's no injury time added in high school soccer, so the match comes to a screeching halt when the clock winds down and the buzzer goes off. Most players line up to shake hands, but three of the Germans laugh and walk off. Their coach gives a Hitler salute to the Johnston stands. A chorus of boos greets his gesture.

"Everyone on the line," Sam Gorman, the Johnston soccer coach, shouts. He crosses his arms and glares at his players threateningly until the whole team is on the touchline. "All right, Ryan," he says to the team captain, "cool down."

"High knees," Ryan Walters shouts, and the JHS Rebels half-heartedly begin their after-game cool-down routine. Afterward, they form a circle to stretch.

"Why didn't you let Gerry take the penalty kick?" one of the boys asks Ryan. "She never misses."

"Sean's the one who got fouled, so he took it," Ryan answers. "Now grab a partner and do your hamstrings. One, two, three . . ."

"It was a good try, Sean," Liam grunts. He's standing on one foot with his hand on Ryan's shoulder. Liam uses his free hand to bend his other leg so the heel touches the back of his leg.

"Thanks," Sean smiles. "Their keeper just guessed right."

Coach Gorman approaches and hollers at the team. "If you don't all count together, we're going to start at the beginning. Only this time, I'll take the lead."

"Four," the players all shout in unison, "five, six, seven . . ." None of them wants to have one of Coach's lengthy stretching sessions.

Once the final stretch has been completed, Gorman calls the team together. Fortunately, he's not given to the lengthy post-game analysis many soccer coaches inflict on their teams. He says a few words of encouragement and cuts the players loose. Soon, they're drifting across the field toward a stadium exit.

The cheerleaders have gotten a head start, so Ryan must run, carrying his bag, to catch up with Melanie. "Let's go," he says.

"Where to?"

"Jaybird's, I'm starved."

"It'll be packed."

"So what?"

Melanie and Ryan join the throng leaving the stadium. Gray-clad Confederate soldiers discourage those who try to shortcut past the cameras. "I forget where we parked," Ryan says once they're outside.

Melanie looks out at the sea of cars. She can't remember either. From the corner of her eye, she spots a middle-aged Black woman rushing over. "Oh no," she says, but it's too late.

"Law, Mel, what'd I tell you 'bout those backflips?" the woman says.

"Sorry, Versa, didn't think you'd see it from over yonder."

"See? Why, the whole town got a look at those purple bloomers."

"They aren't underwear; they're part of the uniform. I've told you."

Versa shakes her head disapprovingly. "Girl, you're goin' to put me in an early grave."

"You'd better hurry," Ryan tells Versa. He points to the slave entrance to the stadium, where several buses are rapidly filling. "You don't want to walk back to the quarter, do you?"

Versa gives a start, then turns to go. "We'll sort you out in the morning," she says over her shoulder.

By the time Melanie and Ryan arrive at Jaybird's, a line of cars is waiting to get into the drive-in. The two teenagers listen to the radio, and Melanie gets lost in her phone as Ryan inches his pickup along. Eventually, they reach the head of the line but must wait until a sports car backs out of a place and rumbles off. "Hallelujah," Melanie sighs as Ryan slides them into the spot. She puts her phone down and looks out her window at the menu.

Moments later, a slave girl roller-skates over. "Hi, Ryan," she says. "Let's see if I can guess. Two double cheeseburgers, a large chili fries, one cherry limeade slush, and a pineapple milkshake."

Ryan laughs and looks at Melanie. "We're in a rut."

"Then let's live dangerously and get onion rings instead of fries."

"No way," Ryan laughs. He turns back to the window. "Don't pay any attention to her, Mish. Get us what we always have."

Melanie picks up her phone again, and now Ryan takes his out. Soon, he's texting with some friends on the team, trying to cheer them up after the loss. Glancing up again, he sees a school bus enter the drive-in and park in the back. It belongs to Erwin Rommel Gymnasium. "Uh-oh," Ryan says as the German soccer players begin getting off.

"Relax," Melanie says. "The game's over. You know the rule, 'What happens on the field, stays on the field.'"

"Yeah, sure," Ryan says doubtfully. He watches the Germans line up at the take-out window. They smile, laugh, and gaze at their phones like normal kids. Ryan relaxes again and checks to see if his latest text to Liam has been answered.

It doesn't take long for Mish to return holding a platter. She pirouettes skillfully and then places it on the car tray. "Thanks," Ryan smiles, and now the food commands his undivided attention.

After wolfing down the meal, Ryan decides to stretch his legs. "I'm going to see who else is here," he says, opening his door. Melanie nods distractedly. She's in a group chat with other cheerleaders, discussing one of the boys on the team. "With Stan, it's all about Stan," she types, fingers moving too fast to see.

As Ryan strolls through the drive-in, he passes several vehicles filled with Johnston soccer players. They wave but aren't in any mood to socialize after the loss. Ryan loops around the restaurant's rear to complete the circuit. Through a kitchen window, he sees the staff bustling to get orders ready. The door opens, and Mish skates out with a tray. She delivers it to one of the German soccer players seated at an outside table. "What took so long?" the boy asks.

"We're a bit overwhelmed," Mish admits.

"You're cute for a *Schwarze*. My name's Dieter."

"I've got to go and get another order."

"What's your number?"

"That's not allowed." Mish spins on her skates, but Dieter is too fast. He jumps up and seizes Mish's wrist, twisting it to read the number tattooed on the inside of her arm.

Ryan sees what's happening and comes over. "Let go of her," he demands.

"Make me," the German sneers. Slowly, he increases the pressure on Mish's wrist. She gasps and her knees buckle.

Pulling out his phone, Ryan snaps a photo. "Fraternizing with slaves is illegal," he says.

Angrily, the German releases Mish and lunges at Ryan, knocking the phone out of his hand. As the two boys ball their fists and circle each other, vehicles throughout the drive-in empty. Instantly, the German soccer team is surrounded by a crowd of irate Southerners. Dieter drops his hands and backs away. "Ha-ha, I was just joking." He smiles, but there's no laughter in his eyes.

"What's all this?" the German coach bellows, bursting through the crowd. "I'm a party member." He holds out his hand to show the

4

Confederate swastika on his ring. The crowd grows quiet. "We are allies after all," the Nazi says. "Let's act like it."

Muttering among themselves, the crowd breaks up, and people return to their vehicles. As Ryan bends to pick up his phone, Dieter taunts him. "I've got her number," he says. "Dad will buy her for me."

Ryan turns only to see Dieter and his friends jogging toward their bus. Melanie comes up beside him and takes his hand. "You OK?" she asks.

"Sure, nothing to it," Ryan lies. He and Melanie kiss briefly and then return to where the pickup is parked.

Knowing Mish is busy, Ryan returns the tray to the restaurant. He pays the check inside. Afterward, Ryan drives Melanie to the gated community where she lives. They hug and share another, more passionate kiss before Melanie jumps down from the truck holding her bag. With a disconsolate feeling, she watches Ryan drive off. *He hasn't even reached the end of the street, and already I miss him*, she marvels.

Melanie goes inside the darkened house and takes her things upstairs. Passing her parents' bedroom, she hears canned laughter from a TV sitcom. Her room is at the end of the hall. Once inside, Melanie changes into a nightgown. Then she gets out her phone. Hours later, she goes to brush her teeth before finally getting under the covers.

The following morning, Melanie's up early to get ready for school. When she goes downstairs to the kitchen, Versa is at the stove. "Smell's good," Melanie says, sniffing the air.

"That's what you say every morning," Versa smiles.

"Still mad at me?"

"No, I heard how y'all took up for Mish last night."

"Ryan was the hero; the rest of us didn't do much."

"It was enough. Now, go sit down."

Melanie wanders into the dining room and finds her parents already seated at the table with their personal slaves standing behind them. Her mother, Dorothy, takes a sip of orange juice and replaces the glass on the lace tablecloth. Her servant, Natty, immediately gets a pitcher from the sideboard and refills the glass. Meanwhile, James is smiling at Melanie. "Morning, Miss," he says. The white-haired Black man pulls out her chair. Once she's seated, he spreads a cloth napkin over her lap.

"What was all the ruckus at Jaybird's last night?" Dan Montgomery asks. He's the mayor of Huntsville and knows everything.

"A German boy started it," Melanie says defensively.

"Yes, and his father already called me to complain. He's a big wheel at The Space Flight Complex."

"Sorry!"

Montgomery points to the syrup. His slave, Parker, reaches for it and then pours. "Enough," Montgomery snaps. He turns back to Melanie. "You and all the others will have a week of detention."

Melanie gasps. "What about cheerleading practice?"

"You should have thought of that before you went to the drive-in. That's where all the delinquents hang out and you with them."

"I won't go anymore. Please." Melanie bats her baby blues at her father. His expression melts. "Go to detention after school today, and maybe we'll see about tomorrow."

"Thanks, Dad."

Montgomery cuts off a bite of pancake and pops it into his mouth. That reminds Melanie to eat as well. It's almost time for the bus.

It's a short ride to Joseph Johnston High School. Melanie uses it to put the finishing touches on her calculus homework. She has it ready to turn in by first period when class begins. Over the next hour, Mrs. Carter, the teacher, reviews each problem. Time flies, and before she knows it, the bell rings. Melanie stuffs her bookbag and then goes out in the hallway to fight through the two-way stream of students to her locker. Moments later, Ryan comes over. "Hey," he smiles.

"What are you so happy about?"

"I'm always happy to see you."

Melanie puts her math book away and gets out the one for chemistry. "Dad's mad about what happened at Jaybird's yesterday."

"Yeah, I heard. See you in detention hall."

"He thinks we should be nicer to the Germans."

"Most of the Germans are OK," Ryan shrugs. "Except the Nazis."

The bell rings, and footsteps quicken in the hallway. "Got to go," Melanie says.

"Me too."

Ryan goes down the hall to his "Confederate History after 1865" class and gets there before the teacher. The boy at the next desk is folding a paper airplane. He makes a slight adjustment to the nose, then shows it to Ryan, who gives the thumbs up. "I'm saving this baby for after school," the boy says.

Just then, Mr. Dickens comes in wearing a harried expression. "Quiz today," he announces. "Put away all your books and study materials." Ryan experiences a momentary panic attack. He forgot all about the quiz. Still, history is his best subject. His pulse returns to normal as Mr. Dickens goes to his desk and taps on the keys of his laptop. Moments later, Ryan's phone vibrates, and he finds a text with a link to the quiz.

The first half of the test is all multiple choice, and Ryan breezes through it. The next part is matching. That's also easy. All Ryan must do is match the correct answer with the corresponding question. Before beginning, Ryan looks over the entire section:

SECTION II: MATCHING

_____ Designer of Confederate Capitol	A. Cuba
_____ Name of first Confederate nuclear-powered submarine	B. Albert Speer
_____ Location of Confederate atomic research laboratory	C. Kings Bay
_____ Only Confederate leader to be assassinated	D. Werner von Braun
_____ Reason martial law was declared in the CSA	E. Erwin Rommel
_____ Father of Confederate space program	F. Hunley
_____ Home of Confederate submarine fleet	G. Huey Long
_____ First Chairman of the Combined Military Staff	H. The Resistance
_____ Last Confederate colony to gain independence	I. Oak Ridge

It takes several minutes for Ryan to feel comfortable with his answers in the matching section. Finally, he taps "SAVE" and continues to the last part. It's an essay question :

SECTION III: DESCRIBE THE ORIGIN OF THE CONFEDERATE NAZI PARTY (CNP)

Ryan stares at his phone for a moment and thinks about his answer. Then, his thumbs begin to fly over the keyboard.

"It started in 1933 when the Nazi Party took over Germany and signed a treaty with the Confederate States of America (CSA). Eight years later, the Nazi leader, Adolf Hitler, asked the Confederacy to help in his war against the United States. The CSA agreed but couldn't spare troops from defending its borders. Instead, the South provided Germany with military bases and manufacturing facilities. Confederate shipyards were used to build a fleet of speedy transports that became famous when they rescued the Afrika Korps from Tunis. With defeat looming, Hitler sent Field Marshal Rommel and his soldiers to bases in the CSA. The ships continued bringing Nazis plus loads of manufacturing equipment to the South until the war ended. The United States and its allies won, but today the CSA is home to many German manufacturers. German scientists have made the Confederacy a nuclear power and designed missiles for defense and exploring outer space. The German population of the South has grown but never assimilated. They maintain a separate school system and have their own housing compounds, clubs, and associations. In 1946, Nazi leaders were included in the CSA's ruling coalition. Today, the Confederate Nazi Party governs the CSA. Still, many Germans dream of leaving the heat, mosquitos, and ignorant farmers of the South to return to their European homeland. This is unrealistic since Germany is now a Federal Republic allied with Great Britain and the United States. It has repudiated fascism, made restitution for war crimes, and the government refuses visas for Confederate Nazis who wish to immigrate."

Ryan scans what he's written and thinks about deleting the last few sentences. *Nah, I'll leave it,* he says to himself and clicks "SUBMIT." Now he can check for messages and then scroll through his Instagram while waiting for class to end.

After school, Ryan joins the soccer team in detention. Several goths whistle as the clean-cut athletes come in. "Hi, Jeff," Ryan says to a boy with fluorescent-green spiked hair.

"What are you goody-goodies doing here?" the goth answers. He's rebelling against Confederate culture and his name—Jefferson Beauregard Perkins.

Ryan grabs a desk near the door and stows his bookbag. "We had a little go-round with some Germans after yesterday's game."

"Yeah, I heard."

A gaggle of cheerleaders comes into the classroom, gaily chatting. The teacher hasn't arrived yet, so they stand uncertainly at the front. "Come sit on my lap," one of the goths calls out.

"Down boy," Ryan growls. He's a tall, sturdily built athlete, so the goth backs off.

"What's all the racket?" Mr. Siren hollers, coming into the room. He's the basketball coach.

Melanie leads the cheerleaders to a back corner, and they settle behind desks. "Get out your books and study materials," Siren demands. "I have papers to grade, and you can work too." The coach glares at the students until some get textbooks out and bury their faces in them.

An hour later, detention is over. "Want to go for a milkshake?" Ryan asks Melanie.

"No, thanks. I'm going home to see if I can get Dad to call off the rest of our punishment."

"Good plan. I'll give you a ride."

After dropping Melanie off, Ryan goes to Jaybird's and finds several friends there. The soccer team members are in a better mood, so Ryan hangs out with them. Meanwhile, Mish glides back and forth across the pavement, gracefully delivering meals. It's as though she's floating.

Daylight is fading by the time Ryan leaves the drive-in. As he heads out of town, vast plantations, white with blooming cotton, line the highway on either side. In the fields, slaves wearing ragged overalls drag sacks full of the South's cash crop. Overseers on ATVs race up and down the rows, sometimes stopping to prod a slow-moving field hand. Ryan glances at the dashboard clock. *Almost seven and they're still at it,* he thinks to himself, shaking his head.

A sign for Ryan's turnoff appears, followed by another showing nearby options for refilling empty stomachs and gas tanks. Ryan takes the familiar ramp and then goes less than a mile up a secondary highway before turning onto the dirt road that leads to the tenant shack he and his father call home. In the fields on either side, stubble from the just-picked cotton crop is decorated with bits of white fluff left by slaves. *Seems like a waste,* Ryan thinks. But it's not his concern. The land no longer belongs to his family. An agribusiness now owns it.

Inside the shack, Ryan drops his bookbag onto the kitchen floor. Peering into the small living room, he sees that the door of the wood-burning stove is open. Flames flicker while Ryan's father, Bryson Walters, sits in an easy chair nearby. He's peering intently at his phone and doesn't notice his son come up from behind. Ryan looks over Bryson's shoulder and sees a man dressed in body armor throw an oddly-shaped ball. Another much larger individual knocks him down. "What in the world is that?" Ryan asks.

Hastily, Bryson pockets his phone. A quart of Tennessee whiskey is nearby, and he reaches for it. Ryan watches his father's Adam's apple dance as bubbles fight their way to the surface of the inverted bottle. He shudders as he replaces the cork. "You need to make yourself something to eat," Bryson belches. "I'm going out."

"With The Resistance?"

"Yeah."

"Can I go?"

"Better not."

"Why? I mean, if you're caught, they'll punish me as well. So, I might as well go."

"Not 'til you're done with high school."

"Oh, come on."

Bryson rises from the chair. "Did you put any fuel in the pickup?"

"Yeah, she's full." Ryan watches his father put on a ragged Carhartt and open the door. "Don't wait up for me," the old man says over his shoulder. A moment later, the pickup's diesel motor clatters to life. The sound slowly fades as Bryson drives off. With a sigh, Ryan goes into the kitchen and gets his bookbag. He sits at the table and reaches for a textbook. That's optimistic since it's difficult for him to concentrate when his father's out with The Resistance.

It snows overnight, but snow in North Alabama is not all that rare. A dusting of the white stuff fails to generate much conversation among The Resistance members who greet the dawn at Hardee's the following morning. "They call this good soccer weather," a heavy-set man named Harper says.

Bryson blows on his coffee to cool it. "Guess playing in the snow beats battling the heat in August," he comments.

"And the gnats," Harper laughs.

"I ain't innerested in seein' a bunch of grown men kick a ball around in their underwear," Gary Wright says. "Even if it's Clemson coming to play 'Bama." Gary raises horses when he's not out with The Resistance.

"Keep it down," Bryson whispers. He looks meaningfully at one of the cameras mounted on the wall. "You're talking about our national game. The Leader loves it."

"I've got to go work on my hay baler," Gary says loudly. He gets up and pops a toothpick into his mouth. The others hurry to finish what's left of their breakfast.

Soon, the men are all gathered behind the restaurant next to their trucks. "You've got to watch every dadgum word nowadays," Harper complains. He shields his mouth to prevent a light pole-mounted camera from reading his lips.

Bryson reaches into his pickup to turn on the radio. "Pittsburgh's on the way to another Super Bowl." He grins as a country song partially drowns out his voice.

"Now that's real football," Gary mutters.

"Best not get caught on the dark web watching it," Harper warns.

"What're they gonna do to me they ain't already done?" Bryson shrugs. "Put my wife in a labor camp, took my farm. What else is there?"

"What about Ryan?" Gary whispers.

"That's all I think about," Bryson nods. "Onliest thing that keeps me goin'." Abruptly, Kenny Chesney's voice is cut off to be replaced by that of The Leader. "Fellow Rebels," General Van Dorn intones, "our glorious cause continues triumphant. Yesterday, SS agents foiled an assassination plot against me. Rest assured that the scum behind it are on the way to Andersonville."

"Oh, too bad," Harper whispers.

Bryson switches the station, and more music comes on. "Probably another Resistance cell," he comments. "Mighty ambitious of them."

"We'd better keep 'em in our prayers," Gary says, "where they're headed."

"I don't want to think about it." Harper shudders. A momentary silence ensues as the three men reflect on what they've heard about Andersonville Death Camp. "Well, so long," Harper finally says.

"Same time, same place, next week?" Gary asks.

"You got it." Bryson watches his friends climb into their vehicles. Out of habit, he waits for them to depart, checking to see if anyone is taking undue interest. *I'm gettin' too old for this*, he thinks, opening the door to the pickup.

While Bryson and his colleagues head home to rest, most people in Huntsville are on their way to work. At Johnston High, the teachers' parking lot slowly fills. Buses line up to disgorge students into the early morning chill. Groups form as friends who ride different buses find each other to hang out until the bell rings. Melanie, who comes from the rich part of town, looks for Ryan who normally approaches from the student parking lot. Instead, she sees him among some kids emerging from a bright yellow school bus. She waves and he hastens to her. "Hey, good morning."

"Hi, Melanie."

"Where's the pickup?"

"Did you forget? It's Friday."

"Oh, that's right, so your father is using it."

"Yep."

"Well, I've got news. We don't have any more detention. Dad fixed it."

"Great, we can have soccer practice today."

"Cheerleaders, too," Melanie smiles.

Because winters are mild in Alabama, the snow doesn't take long to melt. By noon, the Johnston students have shed their coats and left them in lockers. As the school day drags on, they gaze longingly out the windows at the cloudless sky. Then the final bell rings and it's like a jailbreak.

In the soccer locker room, several phones blare competing tunes as athletes get into their training uniforms. "Move it," Ryan yells. "If we're late, Coach will double the run." He heads for the door, followed by the others.

Before long, the soccer players are warming up. Meanwhile, Coach Gorman uses a stack of plastic cones to mark places on the field. Once the athletes have stretched, he has them dribble balls from one cone to the next. "Keep your head up," he hollers. "Right foot only. Use inside and outside touches."

The players begin to breathe heavily as they make repeat trips through the dizzying array of red and yellow cones. "I wonder if we'll get to scrimmage today," Ryan pants as Gerry crosses his path. She's the only girl on the team and wasn't allowed to play until her parents sued. "Hope so," Gerry exclaims.

"Water break," Coach Gorman hollers, but the players know to keep going until they reach the end. Then they jog over to the Igloos. Immediately, competition develops to see who can be first in line to get water. Elbows and insults fly as the players jostle for advantage. Size matters in the melee, so it's no surprise when Liam stakes his unshakable claim to the spigot. As the goalkeeper fills his water bottle, he sees Gerry waiting nearby. "Come on, Gerry, I'll hold it open for you," he offers.

Gerry blushes a bright red. Hanging her head in embarrassment, she walks away. Ryan leaves the line and follows. "Hey, are you OK?" he asks.

"Yeah, I guess."

"Liam was just trying to be nice."

Gerry kicks the ground, taking a divot with her cleats. "I know," she says. "But I wish he wouldn't treat me like a girl."

"Why? I mean, you are a girl, right?"

"Wrong!" Gerry exclaims. She glances around nervously and then shields her mouth. "I may look like a girl, but that's it." The shrill blast of a whistle interrupts. On the field, Coach Gorman beckons the team to a new cone array he created while the players were on break.

After another hour, soccer training is over. The cheerleaders have already gone in and only a few track and field athletes are still practicing. With the sun now low in the sky, most soccer players quickly return to their warm locker room. However, Liam and Ryan stay behind to help Gorman pick up cones. Afterward, Liam takes the ball bag and goes toward the gym. Ryan strolls beside him. "I wonder where Coach Gorman finds all his drills," he muses. "Seems like he has a new one every week."

"I asked him that once," Liam says. "Coach told me he gets ideas from other coaches. If he sees one doing something he likes, he makes notes and then uses the drill with us."

"In other words, he steals from other coaches."

"Coach said it wasn't stealing. He called it 'adaptive creativity.'"

Everyone else is gone when Liam and Ryan get to the locker room. Liam puts the balls away and then starts to change out of his uniform. "Sometimes I wish I could just stay here and not go home."

"Are you kidding?" Ryan asks.

"Yeah, in a way. But you have no idea what it's like at the orphanage."

"That bad, huh?"

"I mean, they try, but it's four of us in a small room, long waits for a shower or to use the toilet, meals that make the free and reduced-price lunches here seem tasty . . . well, you get the picture."

"Yeah, sounds grim." Ryan throws his sweaty training uniform into his gym bag, then laces up his sneakers. "What happens after you graduate?"

"I'll have thirty days grace, then have to move."

"Where?"

"No idea," Liam shrugs.

The locker room door opens, and Gorman sticks his head inside. "Security will be around in a minute to lock up," he says. "You guys need to git."

Outside the school, Ryan is gratified to see the pickup waiting in the mostly empty parking lot. Bryson is standing outside talking on his phone. He pockets it as the boys approach. "Can we drop you?" Bryson asks, even though it's become routine to take Liam home after practice. "Appreciate it," Liam says.

Conversation in the truck cab is muted on the way to the orphanage since all the occupants are tired. Bryson knows the way, so there's no need for directions. Before long, they pull up in front of what used to be a railroad hotel but is now the area's only orphanage for boys. It's a soot-stained edifice on the wrong side of the tracks. "Thanks so much," Liam says, happy to untangle his long legs and swivel them out of the truck. "See you tomorrow."

"Sounds good," Ryan smiles.

Liam goes to the front door of the building and lets himself inside. Only then does Bryson turn the truck's steering wheel toward home.

Over the weekend, the dreary weather is ideal for the Johnston High School students who need to catch up on school work or with virtual friends whom they haven't hit up in a while. But on Monday, they're forced to deal with reality again. For seniors like Ryan Walters and his friends, it's not that tough since most only have one or two required courses left to finish. The rest of their classes are easy electives.

Ryan's favorite subject is history, and it's his last class before lunchtime. Often, he stays behind to ask Mr. Dickens questions, but not today. When the bell rings, Ryan gathers his course materials, stuffs them into his bag, and goes to the cafeteria. He looks for Melanie and finds her at a table reserved for seniors. She has started eating, so he drops his bookbag on the floor next to her and then joins the line for students in the free and reduced-price lunch program. After filling his tray, Ryan goes back and takes the seat next to his girlfriend. She and her well-to-do friends are having chicken fried steak with all the trimmings. Ryan's spaghetti, topped with a watery red sauce, is not as appetizing. Melanie waits until her friends get up to go, then slides a piece of steak she's been saving onto Ryan's plate. "That's not necessary," he protests.

"Oh, hush."

Ryan holds a forkful of food in front of his mouth. "We need to talk," he says quietly.

Melanie nods. "See you outside." She stands up and leaves her tray for a slave to get.

A few minutes later, Ryan joins Melanie behind the school in an area the students call "the corner." It used to house Special Education but is now abandoned and camera-free. Still, Ryan looks around nervously. He takes Melanie's hand and leads her between two modular classroom buildings. They find several goths there vaping. "What are you two doing here?" Jeff asks.

"Must be slumming," another goth says, glancing up from his phone.

"I'm doing a project for biology," Ryan jokes. "Trying to determine if goths are animal, vegetable, or mineral."

"Hilarious," a girl with a dog collar around her neck sneers.

Ryan leads Melanie farther back among the decrepit buildings. "So, what's up?" she asks.

"I'm worried about Gerry," Ryan says.

"Really?"

"I think she's trans."

"Omigod."

"Yeah, and she's not bothering to hide it."

"Then it's only a matter of time before she disappears."

Ryan glances at their surroundings—cracked walls, broken windows, doors falling off their hinges. "Just like the kids who used to attend classes here."

"We have to do something," Melanie says fervently.

"Yes, but what?"

"I don't know. Can't you shut her up?"

At the far end, Jeff peers around the corner. "Uh-oh, they're coming," he hollers, then runs off. The other goths scatter, leaving Melanie and Ryan alone. "Which way?" she asks.

"Let's hide," Ryan suggests. He takes Melanie's hand, and they go into one of the classrooms. Outside, several four-wheelers driven by soldiers pull up. "In the closet," Ryan points. Hastily, the pair heads for the rear of the dirty building. Ryan opens the closet door and then closes it behind them.

In the dark, Melanie wraps her arms around Ryan. He holds her close and can feel her heart thudding. They kiss, and at that moment, the closet door is flung open by an armed soldier. Behind him, another guard holds the leash of a snarling attack dog. "What have we got here?" the first one wonders. "Looks like a couple of lovebirds."

"I'd shore like one of them kisses," the other man says, licking his lips. The Confederate uniform he wears is too small for his bloated belly. "Best take 'em to the office, though."

Raymond Dunsford doesn't stop tapping on the keyboard of his desktop when Melanie and Ryan are brought into his office with zip ties around their wrists. Dunsford is the high school's principal and has seen it all. But when he finally looks up to find the mayor's daughter in front of him, his face blanches. "Found these two swappin' spit in one of them old trailers back yonder," one of the soldiers says. "They thought they was smart but all we had to do was foller their footprints in the dust."

"Take off those restraints," Dunsford snaps. He reaches for his phone while the soldiers clumsily cut off the zip ties. "Good afternoon, Mayor," the principal says. "How are things downtown?" Dunsford wrinkles his brow as he listens, then says, "That's great news. However, I called because of a situation that's come up with Melanie. She was caught in a restricted area with a boy." Again, Dunsford listens as Melanie's father talks. After a moment, he says, "Yes, sir, I'll keep them in my office 'til you get here."

CHAPTER TWO

SCORCHED EARTH

Mayor Montgomery is in the Huntsville International Airport terminal, watching people pass through Internal Passport Control. Finally, he spots Wolfgang Schmidt, the man he's meeting. Schmidt holds his passport up to the scanner and, moments later, strolls into the reception area. Montgomery rushes over. "Welcome to Rocket City." He holds his hand up in a Hitler salute. Schmidt returns the gesture, and then the two men shake hands.

"It's wonderful of you to meet me," Schmidt says.

"My pleasure."

"I can't wait to see what you have to show me."

"You will be impressed, I'm sure."

The mayor's long black limousine is out front. When the driver sees his owner come out of the terminal, he opens the passenger door. Soon, Montgomery and his guest are comfortably seated. The car enters a line of vehicles leaving the airport. It's slow going because of the army checkpoint up ahead. When they get there, soldiers surround the limo and peer through the tinted windows. An officer recognizes Montgomery and waves the car through.

"How was your flight?" Montgomery asks once they are on their way.

"About what you'd expect from a commuter," Schmidt answers. "Got bounced all over the sky. Say, am I seeing things, or is the name of the high school we just passed Joseph Johnston?"

"Yes, that's right, why?"

"Where I live in Georgia, that's the most hated name ever."

"Still?"

"Well, he burned down half the state, didn't he?"

"That was over 160 years ago."

"So? I mean, why name a school after him?"

"I see your point."

"If Johnston had been any sort of general, he would have stood up to Sherman instead of retreating and burning everything in his path."

"I agree, but his scorched earth strategy is how we gained our independence."

"Yes, but at what cost?"

"I can't argue, *Herr* Schmidt. Many people feel as you do." Abruptly, the limousine slows down, and the mayor hastens to change the subject. "Look, we're entering the security zone for the labor camp."

"Great, how long now 'til we reach the industrial park?"

"Oh, that's another two miles after we get past this checkpoint." Montgomery takes his internal passport out. "May I?" he asks, holding out his hand. Schmidt furnishes the requested document as the limo rolls up to a gate manned by several bored-looking Confederates.

Once past the checkpoint, the skyline of the main camp comes into view. To one side are cooling towers for nuclear reactors; on the other side are factory buildings which, from a distance, seem to rise to the height of the towers. Beyond them, tenement-like barracks stretch to the horizon. "This is the first one of these I've seen," Schmidt says.

"Oh, you haven't been to Andersonville?" Montgomery asks.

"Why go there?" Schmidt shrugs. "It's a death camp, not a labor camp."

"Oh, right."

The limousine zigzags through a series of concrete barriers and then stops at the main gate. Immediately, guards in gray uniforms surround the vehicle. Two of them hold dogs who eagerly sniff the tires. Another slides a mirror under the car. The guards are supervised by a lieutenant whose cap is decorated with the CNP swastika. He goes to the passenger door and raps on the window with a baton. "Out," he commands.

Montgomery and Schmidt stand by the car and wait confidently while the captain scans their passports using his phone. Meanwhile, an inspector rifles through the interior of the vehicle. A camp guard searches the driver. This is all routine for the mayor who has visited the place many times. Idly, he watches an army blimp zigzag back and forth above the camp. Then, the Confederate officer returns the passports. "To what do we owe the pleasure of your visit today, Mr. Mayor?" he asks.

"*Herr* Schmidt plans to locate a factory here." Montgomery nods toward his companion.

"Great," the lieutenant enthuses. He turns to the German. "What will you produce?"

"Avionics," Schmidt replies. "We just received a ten-year contract from Focke-Wulf."

"Their factory is over there." The officer points.

Schmidt turns his head to look. "We've been shipping them from Georgia. With this new contract, that no longer makes sense."

The lieutenant's phone beeps, and he peers at the screen. "You're cleared," he says.

"Thanks," Montgomery replies. He and Schmidt get back into the limo. Soon, they pass through the main entrance under the watchful eye of cameras. A sign greets them inside: "Work Will Make You Free."

"Nice touch," Schmidt says. "But no worker ever gets out of one of these places, do they?"

"Not that I know of," Montgomery laughs. He presses a switch to lower the partition separating the driver's compartment from the cabin. "Robert, turn right into the next parking lot."

"Yes, boss," the driver replies.

Cameron Vinson, Director of Business Development for Toombs Labor Camp, is waiting in front of the Administrative Headquarters when his guests emerge from the limousine. "Good day, Mayor," he says. "And I presume this is *Herr* Schmidt?"

"That would be me," Schmidt acknowledges. "I'm the CEO of Red Lion Avionics."

"Well, we're excited to have you here," Vinson smiles. "The gate guards texted me a heads up. Would either of you gentlemen like to use the facilities before we go to the site?"

Montgomery casts an inquiring eye toward Schmidt who gives a negative shake of his head. "Looks like we're good," Vinson says. "So, let's take a ride to the industrial park and see what you think of the available lots."

Vinson ushers the visitors into an SUV and then gets behind the wheel. Once out of the parking lot, they pass a massive hangar belonging to Focke-Wulf. "They've got a mile-long runway behind that," Vinson explains.

"Impressive." Schmidt stares out the window.

A few minutes later, Vinson turns onto an access road. After going less than a mile, he parks on the side. It's a mild, late winter afternoon, so the men leave their coats in the vehicle when they get out. "This is the best lot we have." Vinson points to a cleared tract. "It's been graded for proper drainage and is zoned for general industrial use. The river is only half a mile away."

Schmidt steps onto the property and looks around. Towering pines border the cleared land. "It's perfect," the German says. "Tell me. Has the one next door been sold?"

"Not yet," Vinson answers.

"Would there be a discount if we take two?"

"I'm sure we could work something out."

"What can you tell me about the workforce here?"

"Oh, the usual," Vinson explains. "Abolitionists, Jews, political activists, and sexual deviants. Many are highly educated, experienced workers. An algorithm is used to match the skill set of each inmate to your job requirements."

"We only use slaves at my plant in Augusta," Schmidt comments.

"Oh really? That's a lot of capital to tie up in a depreciating asset. Leasing camp labor is more efficient. Plus, you get a tax break."

"That's what my finance guys told me."

"If you like, we can head back to my office and review the details," Vinson offers.

"All right."

When the three executives enter the admin building, Rebecca Walters is at the front desk. She hastily gets to her feet. "Good afternoon, gentlemen," she says without expression.

"We'll be in the conference room," Vinson snaps. "Get coffee."

"Yes, sir."

Presently, the men are seated at one end of a conference table, holding mugs of steaming coffee. Then Rebecca reappears with a platter of cinnamon rolls. "I just got these out of the microwave," she explains. "They're piping hot."

After their time outside in the cold, the men are happy to warm their bellies. "She's a jewel," Schmidt says between bites. "What's she in for?"

"Rebecca's 1/16th Jew on the maternal side," Vinson explains. "The Service got her off a local farm. Of course, they confiscated the land."

"I didn't know they were picking up the 1/16ths."

"Have been for over a year," Montgomery interjects. He uses the edge of his fork to scrape the last bit of icing from his plate.

"I have complete dossiers on the two lots we discussed," Vinson says, pushing his plate aside. He slides a binder over to Schmidt, who flips through it attentively. Rebecca reenters the room and unobtrusively tops off the men's coffee mugs.

Schmidt closes the binder. "Everything seems to be here," he says. "My lawyer will have to review the contract, and I know our engineers will want soil samples plus a substrate analysis."

"I can get those for you by the end of the week if that's all right."

"Perfect." Schmidt looks pointedly at his watch.

Montgomery takes the hint and stands up. "Let's get you back to the airport."

Vinson walks out to the parking lot with the two visitors. After some pleasantries, he sees them off. Once back inside, he goes to Rebecca's desk. "Those cinnamon buns were a great suggestion," he smiles. "I'll bring more for the next client meeting."

Rebecca looks down. She gets nervous when her boss acts friendly. "I'm glad you thought so, Mr. Vinson."

"Yeah, right." Vinson is irritated by Rebecca's formality. "Just get hold of Greg and tell him to round up soil samples for 86B and 92C. I'll also need ground radar images and a substrate analysis on each."

"Yes, sir," Rebecca replies and reaches for the phone. She's glad to have Vinson acting like his regular self once more.

With so much to do, the last hour of work flies by for Rebecca. She's startled when the whistle blows, signaling it's time to go. Hurriedly, she packs her things and then rushes to the parade ground. It's a mile from the office, so Rebecca is among the last in her section to fall into formation. By now, the sun has gone down. However, the camp's lighting system illuminates the area like a sports field.

Precisely at six o'clock, the tedious evening count begins as the camp commandant, General Garland, watches from his tower. First, the section leaders walk up and down the rows of inmates using handhelds to read QR codes tattooed onto each worker's forearm. Once everyone is scanned, the data is uploaded to the cloud. Then, instead of being released to the barracks as usual, the inmates are ordered to form a square. At this, a groan goes up. "Silence," Garland bellows. His amplified voice echoes off the concrete barracks nearby.

Sullenly, the inmates follow the commands of their section leaders. When they finish, the commandant's tower is in the center of a square formed by six-deep ranks of inmates. A Confederate Army light-duty truck drives between two sections and pulls up in front of the tower. In the back are two gray-clad soldiers and a woman whose hands are zip-tied. One of the soldiers smashes his rifle butt into the woman's back. She tumbles over the tailgate, falling heavily to the ground. Laughing, the two men jump down. They grasp the woman's arms and drag her to the tower stairs. When she hesitates rather than take the first fatal step, a soldier jabs her with his bayonet. She begins climbing as the back of her blouse turns red.

At the top, the prisoner is brought to the front of the platform. A soldier drapes a noose around her neck. After securing the rope end, he pulls the loop tight. General Garland steps to the microphone again. "Sabotage will not be tolerated," he shouts. "This wretch tried to pass off faulty welds, but once again, quality control was up to the task." He nods to the soldiers, who shove the victim over the side. At this, a collective gasp goes up from the workers. They don't want to look but know the cameras will see if they turn their heads. Feeling sick, they watch their colleague's body twitch until it's still.

Meanwhile, at the airport, Montgomery accompanies Schmidt

inside to check the flight monitor. "Looks like you'll be leaving right on time."

"That'll make the wife happy," Schmidt says. "She hates it when I come in at all hours and wake her."

"Mine's the same way," Montgomery laughs.

Schmidt raises his hand and clicks his heels. "Farewell. Hope to see you again soon."

"I'll look forward to it." Montgomery returns the Hitler salute.

On the way home, Montgomery tells Robert to stop by Liquor Express. "Wait," he says, then enters the establishment. A few minutes later, Montgomery comes out clutching a brown paper sack. "Home," he orders.

"Hi, honey," Dorothy Montgomery says when her husband comes in. "I was beginning to wonder about you."

"Pour me a stiff one." Montgomery hands Dorothy the sack. "I had to squire a German tycoon around all day, didn't get a thing done at the office." Montgomery wrenches his tie off and then settles onto the couch. "But it was worth it." He reaches to take the whiskey tumbler Dorothy offers. "Guy's full steam ahead to build an avionics plant at the camp."

"Oh honey, that's great news."

"For sure. Now, how was your day?"

Dorothy sits next to her husband. "It was wonderful," she exclaims. "Had bridge club and caught up with all the gossip from around town."

"Anything I should know?"

"Well, it's hush-hush, but if you promise to keep it quiet, I'll tell you."

"I promise."

"Gloria's divorcing Sam. She's going to take him to the cleaners."

Montgomery knocks back half his drink and then winces when the alcohol bites his throat. "So, she finally caught him with that house slave, huh?"

"How did you know about it?"

"Oh, he's been bragging about her forever. Says she's light enough to pass for white."

"If you knew, why didn't you say something? Gloria's a friend."

"Figured what she didn't know wouldn't hurt her."

"Nice the way you guys stick together."

"Sorry, honey." Montgomery puts an arm around Dorothy and kisses her. She leans into him, but after a token meeting of the lips, Montgomery pulls away. "Mel in her room?" he asks to cover the awkwardness. It's clear his wife no longer interests him.

Dorothy fusses with her hair. "Where else would she be?" she snaps.

"Just making sure." Montgomery takes his empty glass to the bar and reaches for the whiskey bottle.

"Sam's going to disappear one day," Dorothy says. "Fraternizing with slaves is illegal. So is miscegenation."

"Yeah, but everyone does it," Montgomery shrugs. "A little money usually hushes things up."

Upstairs, Melanie's in her room, staring longingly at a video Ryan just posted on TikTok. In it, Cynth, Jace, and another cheerleader are at Jaybird's, sitting on the tailgate of Ryan's pickup, slurping lime slushes and making faces. Melanie licks her lips, remembering the tangy but now foreign taste. She's been grounded since her father came to get her from the principal's office. Right now, Melanie would give anything to be at the drive-in with the others. She likes the video and then flops face down onto her bed.

After posting the video, Ryan watches the number of likes climb into the stratosphere. He sees Melanie is online and texts her a greeting. When she doesn't answer, he slides his phone into the back pocket of his jeans. Since the pickup's tailgate is fully occupied, he leans against the truck and idly chews on a plastic straw. Jaybird's is rocking this evening with the outdoor speakers cranked up. He taps his foot in time with a country tune. Nearby, another soccer player gets out a can of snuff and fishes around in it for just the right size pinch. After depositing it inside his lip, the boy offers Ryan some. "No thanks," Ryan grimaces. He doesn't dip and can't understand why anyone would.

A Mercedes limo pulls into the drive-in and stops in the middle of the driveway. Several cars queue up behind it, but no one honks. That's not polite. Eventually, the limo pulls to the curb opposite the take-out window. An officious-looking gentleman in a three-piece suit emerges from the back while the driver holds the door. A blond-haired boy follows the man into Jaybird's. "That's the German kid I almost got into a fight with the other day," Ryan exclaims. "His name's Dieter."

"Thought we ran him and the others off for good," Liam comments.

"Apparently not," Ryan frowns. *Something's up*, he thinks, but is at a loss for what to do. Then Fred Pryor, the Jaybird's manager, comes outside and beckons Mish, who has just delivered a tray to some customers. She roller-skates over and, after a few words with her owner, follows him into the restaurant.

"I don't like the look of this," Ryan mutters. He starts for the restaurant entrance, but Liam grasps his arm. "Stay loose," the goalkeeper says. He glances meaningfully at a pole-mounted camera.

Ryan struggles to get free, but Liam's grip is like an alligator's. He watches helplessly as Mish is led out of the restaurant by the well-dressed man. Her hands are zip-tied, and the roller skates are gone. Dieter walks behind, smiling broadly. His eyes scan the lot until they come to rest on the Johnston High School students around Ryan's truck. "Told you!" he shouts as Mish is forced into the limo.

With a superhuman burst of strength, Ryan breaks Liam's grip and starts for the German. But Liam stretches out his lanky frame, dives, and catches his friend's ankles. The two soccer players lie face down on the pavement and watch the limo drive off. "What'd you do that for?" Ryan demands. He kicks his feet free of Liam's now relaxed grip.

"That was Dr. Reinhold von Kluck, head of The Space Flight Complex," Liam whispers. "I've seen his picture in my newsfeed. Do you want to be videoed attacking him?"

"Guess not, but what about Mish?"

"We'll figure something out," Liam says under his breath. "But not here."

Liam and Ryan are not the only ones upset by Mish's sudden sale. Word about what happened gets around quickly. At the Montgomerys' the following morning, Versa's eyes are red from crying. She's at the stove, but her pancakes lack their normal airiness. In the dining room, Montgomery presides as usual. "More syrup," he demands, then leans back as Parker tilts the bottle. "Whoa," Montgomery shouts, "too much! What's gotten into everyone this morning?"

"Versa's daughter got sold," Melanie explains.

The mayor raises his fork and his eyebrows at the same time. "So?" he says, chewing on a soggy mouthful of pancake. "Slaves get bought and sold every day."

"But Mish and I grew up together."

"Exactly. She's as old as you. That means she's well past the age to be sold."

"How would you feel to come home one day and find that I've been sold down the river?"

"Don't be ridiculous. You're white."

"Yes, I'm white and Mish is Black. One goes to college, and the other gets raped by her horny owner."

"Now you're talking like an abolitionist."

Melanie glares at her father spitefully. "And why not?"

"You'll disappear."

"Why worry? You'll get me out. You're the mayor." Melanie waves James off and reaches for the butter herself.

Montgomery gasps. "Stop that."

"I don't need James to butter my toast," Melanie insists. "I can do it myself. Besides, look at him. At his age, he should be retired."

Montgomery laughs. "Don't tell me you still believe that fairytale about slaves retiring. The only place they go to retire is up a chimney." Standing behind Melanie, James remains impassive. He's used to being talked about by white people like he's not there.

Melanie glares at her father. "Is that what happened to Fran?"

"It's what happens to all of them when they're done working."

"You told me she was going to a retirement home for Blacks."

"Yes, and I told you there was an Easter Bunny. You outgrew that, and you'll outgrow this other nonsense. Now, it's almost time for the bus. Get ready."

CHAPTER THREE

RESISTANCE

A n owl screeches in the darkness, and the three Resistance members freeze. "That was close," Bryson exclaims.
"Must be in that tree yonder," Gary says.

Harper crawls up behind them. He's dragging a set of heavy-duty bolt cutters. "Let's get on with it," he whispers. "My nerves are shot."

It's only a short distance now to the chain-link fence surrounding a cellphone tower. Mercury vapor lamps illuminate the installation, and the men hesitate to crawl out of the darkness into the glare. Harper and Gary scan the vicinity, looking for any sign of life. Bryson unslings his rifle. "Get the one on the shed first," Harper whispers.

"No problem," Bryson mutters. He inserts a round into the chamber, then slides the bolt forward and locks it. Squinting, he lines up the target. The muzzle blast shatters the night, and a surveillance camera mounted on the roof of a maintenance shed explodes.

"One down, three to go." Gary smiles nervously.

Once the remaining cameras have been destroyed, the men approach the fence. "Case-hardened steel," Harper comments. "But no match for these babies." Though it's a frosty, early spring morning, Harper's face is soon sweaty from working the bolt-cutter levers. Eventually, he slices through enough links to create a gap in the fence. While Harper catches his breath, Gary pushes a gas can through the gap and follows it into the installation. Bryson and Harper crawl in behind him with their equipment.

Once inside the restricted area, the men get to their feet. Gary walks over to the tower and, after adjusting the straps on his backpack, begins climbing the ladder. The other two go to the maintenance shed. Harper grasps the padlock on the door and looks at the logo. "It's a Chinese job," he mutters. "Piece of cake." Again, his muscles bulge, and the bolt cutters do their job. Bryson enters the shed and throws a circuit breaker to shut off the main cable. "We've got at most half an hour now before The Service gets a helicopter up here," he says.

"Yeah, and your single-shot hunting rifle ain't no match for what they'll bring to the party," Harper comments.

"That's all they allow us civilians anymore, just bolt action."

"That's 'cause they're afraid of us." The two men bump fists in solidarity and then go back outside. Bryson slides a flask from his back pocket and unscrews the cap. "Tennessee's finest," he says and offers the whiskey to his friend, who shakes his head. Bryson swigs a double measure for himself.

"Gary should be on top by now." Harper looks up anxiously, but it's pitch-black beyond the cone of light at the tower's base.

"This is always the worst part. I hate waiting."

"Me too."

At this hour, it's tranquil on the mountaintop, but the men's nerves are too high-strung to appreciate it. They shove their hands into their pockets and stamp their feet against the chill. After what seems like an eternity, the lower portion of Gary's body appears in the light, and then the rest of him. He strolls over to his comrades, smiling happily. "Got the motherboards out of both DPSs, wrecked the transponder, then severed the main cable in several spots on the way down."

Bryson is already splashing gasoline around the shed. He fashions a torch out of some rolled-up paper, then waits for Gary and Harper to crawl back through the fence. Once they are out, he lights the torch and tosses it into the shed. Quickly, he steps back as the fire ignites with a *whoosh*. Cradling the rifle, he crawls out of the restricted area. Without a word, the saboteurs melt back into the forest.

A couple of hours later, Bryson is back home, sitting at the kitchen table with a beer, when Ryan comes in to make breakfast. "That's not good for you," Ryan says, opening the refrigerator door.

"You're wrong, son," Bryson says. "It's not drinking that hurts you. It's stopping."

Ryan gets some bacon frying, then breaks several eggs into a bowl. "Spoken like a true alcoholic," he comments. "Guess you were out with The Resistance last night."

"Yep, and all I can say is that I'm getting too old for it." Bryson drains the dregs of his brew and tosses the empty into a trash bin. "Two points," he crows.

"So, when can I start helping?" Ryan asks.

Bryson emits a satisfying belch. "Soon," he says. "I mean, graduation can't be far off."

"Two months is all," Ryan declares. He slides a plateful of bacon and eggs in front of Bryson, then sits across from him. "Now get some healthy food in you," he demands, before digging into his own breakfast.

"Thanks, son." Bryson douses his eggs with hot sauce, then slides the bottle across the table to Ryan.

Ryan grimaces. "Not for me." He pushes the stuff away. "But Dad, you know, sometimes I wonder why you're willing to have me join The Resistance. Most fathers wouldn't want their son risking his life."

"True, but what sort of life have you to look forward to?"

"That's what I'm wondering. I mean, why haven't we talked about college or anything?"

"There's no point," Bryson says. "You're going to be rounded up soon and sent to a labor camp like your mother."

"Just because some great-grandmother was Jewish?"

"That's all it takes nowadays." Bryson forks scrambled egg onto a piece of toast. "They've picked up all the 1/16ths by now. Next, they'll be going after 1/32nds like you."

"I don't get it. Southerners aren't prejudiced against Jews."

"No, but after the World War, when the Confederates were recruiting German scientists to come here, The Leader agreed to round up all Jews. Otherwise, the Nazis wouldn't have come."

"Why didn't you tell me this before?"

"Didn't see any need to worry you 'til now," Bryson says between mouthfuls. "Wanted you to have a carefree childhood, at least."

"So, how is it you know everything?"

"It's all there on the dark web," Bryson points to his phone, "the *New York Times*, *Washington Post*, and other reliable sources."

"You can be shot for that."

Bryson goes to the refrigerator and gets another beer. "So, what?" He pops the top.

Shaking his head disgustedly, Ryan returns to his room.

On the other side of town, Mish is also getting ready for the day. Her room is in the dormitory-like slave quarter at the rear of Gruenen Walde, a housing compound for senior Nazis. Once she's dressed, Mish walks to the von Klucks' house and lets herself in the back door. She's greeted by Dachsie, the von Klucks' dachshund. As always, the pooch wags her tail excitedly until Mish kneels. Then Dachsie rolls over and waits for Mish to rub her belly. Afterward, Mish gets the dog leash, and the pair go outside. As Mish strolls along behind Dachsie, the hound sniffs one patch of grass and then another. Finally, the persnickety purebred picks the perfect location and squats.

Back inside the house, Mish bids good morning to Dr. von Kluck, who is leaning against a kitchen counter holding a cup of coffee. She fills Dachsie's water bowl and then goes into the pantry for a can of dog food. Behind her, the pantry door clicks shut. She turns to see von Kluck approaching. "That dog gets more love from you than me, your master," he complains. "How about a kiss?"

Grasping the can, Mish retreats until her back is against the pantry shelf. "Sir, the only person I love is my mother. Now, thanks to you, I never see her."

Von Kluck smiles benignly. "I'd be happy to fix that for you, *Fräulein*, if only you'd be nicer to me."

"Must I remind you that fraternization with slaves is against the race law?"

"Who would know? Unless you report it to the authorities."

"Most assuredly, sir, I would report it. I've held off documenting incidents like this up to now for the sake of Dieter and Frau von Kluck. But you should be warned."

Momentarily defeated, von Kluck turns and opens the pantry door. "You'll come around," he says over his shoulder. "In the meantime, you can forget about getting any passes to see your mother."

In the darkened pantry, Mish allows herself to break down. Sobs wrack her body as images of her previous life gliding in-between and around cars at Jaybird's flash through her consciousness. She feels the weight of a tray in her hand and lifts it over her head. Looking up, Mish sees it's only the dog food. A laugh forces its way through the tears. She leaves the pantry and serves Dachsie her breakfast.

Mish's replacement at the drive-in is still getting used to the job. She's timid and seems scared of the customers. The Johnston high schoolers have tried to help. They are patient when she messes up orders and joke with her like they did with Mish. However, the slave never smiles. "It's her first job," Ryan tells Liam that afternoon while waiting for their burgers. "Can't be easy for her to be thrust into a public service job after growing up in the quarter."

"Mish was just as shy at first," Liam points out. "But she blossomed after a while."

Ryan glances at a nearby camera. He turns his head to the side and whispers, "I can't stop thinking about her with that Nazi."

"Me either," Liam mutters.

"Let's talk tonight at the soccer park."

"Bet."

The high school soccer season is over, but that only means travel ball is back. That night, the Huntsville Sports Complex is a beehive of activity. A steady stream of cars comes and goes, keeping the parking lot full. Some vehicles are driven by parents, others by students who, past the magic age of sixteen, drive themselves.

For the players on the Huntsville Rangers, the worst part of training is the team run. Dale Phillips, the coach, leads it before every practice. Still, it's not so strenuous as to prevent chatter between breaths as the players do their laps. "Did you hear about Messi?" one boy asks the group.

"Yeah, he wants to transfer," Liam answers.

"What's up with that?" Gerry inquires.

"He and Beckham are tight," Coach Phillips pants. "I'm betting he turns down the Saudis and goes to Miami."

"No way, he's too good."

After the run, Ryan leads the stretches. "Down the middle," he orders, then begins to count. The players are supposed to chant each number back, but several continue talking. Phillips isn't having that. "Y'all count," he demands. "If not, we'll do five more laps." Immediately, the slackers join the chorus. Satisfied, the coach begins putting down cones for a shooting drill.

An hour and a half later, the team circles up a final time. "One, two, three," Ryan shouts, and the players all holler, "Go Rangers!" That's the end of practice, so Liam and Ryan are free to walk off the field together. Before reaching the parking lot, they slip into a shadow between two fields where there are no cameras. "So, what are you thinking about Mish?" Liam asks.

"Dad showed me how to get onto the dark web the other night," Ryan says. "You'd be amazed. The newspapers in the North criticize the government, they have competing political parties, and every four years, there's an election to determine who the new leader will be."

"Wild, but what does that have to do with Mish?"

"I found out about a US government program to resettle escaped slaves," Ryan explains. "It's run by abolitionists who allow runaways to stay with them until they have jobs and housing. They even pay for college or job training."

"So, Mish would have a real future?"

"Right, but first, we'd have to get her away from von Kluck, through the Autonomous Zone, and across the border."

"You know the penalty for aiding a runaway, right?"

"Yeah." Ryan draws a finger across his throat.

"Correct, so nothing doing until we develop a solid plan."

"Of course," Ryan agrees. "Now, let's go. Coach might be waiting for you."

The parking lot is thinning out as players change their footgear and leave. Liam and Ryan wait beside Coach Phillips' SUV until they see him come across the parking lot with another coach. They're both talking and gesturing animatedly despite the bulging ball bags on their backs. Then, the liftgate on Phillips' vehicle clicks and slowly rises. He waves goodbye to the other coach, approaches the SUV, and swings the ball bag into the back. "You ready?" he asks Liam.

34

Ryan watches the coach drive off, glad someone else is ensuring Liam gets home. It's nearly closing time for the park. The lights on the fields blink off one after another as Ryan goes to get into the pickup.

The lights at the labor camp where Ryan's mother is incarcerated will stay on all night. That's done to discourage visitation between barracks by the inmates. In addition to the pole-mounted mercury vapor lamps, spotlights operated by tower guards probe the shadows. Still, it's pitch-dark in the shaft where Rebecca is toiling. She scrapes earth from the tunnel face and dumps it into a bucket. Once the container is full, she yanks on a rope. An inmate at the tunnel mouth drags the bucket away. Rebecca wearily begins to fill another one.

Rebecca's shirt is soaked with sweat when her turn at the tunnel face ends. The shaft is only wide enough for one person at a time, so her replacement waits while Rebecca crawls toward the entrance. The would-be escapees have made good progress on the tunnel over the last few months, and reaching the beginning takes her a while. Finally, Rebecca finds herself where a down-shaft joins the main tunnel. With relief, she gets to her feet. "Are you all right?" Cindy Blackburn calls from above.

"Yeah, just let me catch my breath before I climb up," Rebecca pants.

The fresh air at the tunnel mouth smells wonderful. After a few breaths, Rebecca places her foot on the ladder and begins hauling herself up the rungs. Cindy offers a hand as Rebecca nears the top; she then pulls her friend up. "Drink this." She holds out a canteen of water.

"Thanks." Rebecca chugs water as she gazes at the familiar surroundings. They are in a shed full of groundskeeping equipment. Nearby, another woman sits on the concrete floor next to a homemade accordion bellows. She wears a pink triangle on her tunic to denote her crime—she's a lesbian. Two more inmates are in a corner, shoveling earth into empty fertilizer bags. Like Rebecca, they have Stars of David sewn onto their shirts.

"Hang on to the canteen for me," Cindy says, putting on a pair of work gloves. She goes to the hole and gets on the ladder.

Rebecca watches her friend vanish and then has one more sip of water. She turns to the woman on the floor. "Break's over, Micki. You need to start pumping."

"No problem." Micki begins pushing and pulling on the bellows to pump air into the tunnel. It's funneled through a duct the tunnelers made using empty ration cans.

Once Rebecca sees the bellows going, she too goes to the ladder. Her job now will be to pull the buckets of earth Cindy hollows from the tunnel face back to the entrance. This promises to be another long, weary shift. The only good news is that she can rest the next couple of nights while other tunneling crews take their turns.

What to do with all the red clay dug out of the tunnel each night is the escapees' biggest challenge. Their solution is to conceal stockings full of earth beneath their clothes every morning before going to assembly. Once the inmate count is completed, each tunneler jerks a string to untie the knot holding the sock closed. As they stride busily about doing their morning chores, dirt dribbles onto the ground with each step. This approach avoids leaving telltale heaps of earth in the maintenance shed or around the compound.

But that morning, after working in the tunnel half the night, Rebecca's standing in formation when she has a coughing fit. She tries to be still, but spring pollen is aggravating her throat. With alarm, she feels dirt trickle down her leg from the stocking hidden under her pants. Thankfully, she's in the rear rank, but if the block warden notices the pile forming around her ankles, she and the other tunnelers will be caught. Casually, Rebecca shifts her weight, moving her foot forward and back. With an elbow, she draws her neighbor's attention to the problem and gets help dispersing the dirt.

A few minutes later, the block warden strides down Rebecca's rank, scanning the inmates with a handheld. Fortunately, the Confederate is focused on the count, and as she hurriedly passes, unknowingly helps to scatter the evidence. Rebecca sighs with relief. Once morning assembly is over, she joins the other inmates strolling toward the bathhouse and casually empties the sock.

After washing up, Rebecca gets into line at the commissary. Diane Benson, one of her roommates, comes up behind her. "Thank goodness it's Friday," she says sarcastically.

Rebecca plays along. "Yeah, can't wait 'til five o'clock rolls around."

"Got to get the party started."

"Oh, yeah."

At the head of the line, a Confederate soldier scans each inmate's QR. Another one hands each person a box. The label on it reads: "Minimum Daily Ration." It contains each inmate's food for the day. Diane and Rebecca chat as they wait their turn. Then, they collect their MDRs and head back to their barracks.

Inside the grim tenement, the two inmates climb several flights of stairs, pausing occasionally to catch their breath. Finally, they get to the right floor and proceed down a hallway to their room. Out of politeness, Rebecca knocks on the door and pauses momentarily before entering. Alice Shapiro, another roommate, looks up from the table and smiles as she raises a spoonful of oatmeal to her lips. "That looks good," Rebecca says.

Alice laughs. "Are you joking?"

"Yep."

Diane hasn't made her bed yet. While she takes care of that, Rebecca uses the microwave to boil water. Her stomach lurches at the idea of another oatmeal breakfast, but she's determined to keep up her strength. That means ingesting calories, appetizing or not.

Once her cereal is ready, Rebecca sits across from Alice. Now it's Diane's turn with the microwave. Currently, there are just the three of them in the room. The fourth bunk is not in use.

It doesn't take long for the women to finish breakfast. They store the lunch and dinner portions of the MDRs in their lockers and then leave. Outside, they split up to go to their workplaces.

A little before eight o'clock, Rebecca enters the camp's administrative headquarters. She goes to her desk in the business development section and sorts the mail. Afterward, Rebecca starts coffee brewing. Soon, the aroma of Colombia's finest fills the air. It's ready by the time Vinson comes in.

After a few minutes in his office, Vinson comes out holding a mug. Rebecca rushes to fill it. "Great job on the Red Lion contract," Vinson smiles. "I just checked my mail and found an envelope from them with the signed agreement inside."

"I saw their logo on the envelope and hoped that's what it was."

Vinson picks up the creamer and splashes some into his coffee. He lays a chocolate bar on the counter, turns, and goes back into his office. Hastily, Rebecca uses a paper towel to wipe the counter and conceal the candy simultaneously. With her heart pounding, she goes back to her desk. Somehow, she restrains herself from casting a guilty glance at the overhead camera.

CHAPTER FOUR

SPECIAL TRANSPORT

Melanie is sprawled on the stern lounge of the Montgomery family's boat, wearing a scanty bikini to maximize her tan. "Somebody needs to do something about all these barges," she complains as one goes past. It's stacked high with containers, putting the Montgomerys temporarily in the shade.

"Those barges are the lifeblood of the Confederate economy," Montgomery explains. He turns the bow of the ungainly pontoon boat into the wake left by the huge vessel.

"You need to put on more sunscreen," Dorothy tells Melanie.

"All right," Melanie agrees. "Come get my shoulders."

Montgomery backs off the throttle as the surface of the river slowly calms. While the boat drifts downstream, he reaches into the cooler. "Those barges are heading for New Orleans, the same place this beer came from."

"I thought the Tennessee River went north, into the Autonomous Zone." Melanie rolls over so Dorothy can slather lotion onto her back.

"So, you stayed awake during geography class," Montgomery laughs. "Sure, the Tennessee flows north into the AZ, but eventually, these waters we're on will enter the Mississippi."

"So how do these barges, with all that valuable cargo, get through the AZ?"

"It's simple," Montgomery says. He tilts the beer bottle back and, after several chugs, replaces it in the cupholder. "They pay off the pirates."

"Oh, hush," Dorothy says. "The child doesn't need to hear about all that ugliness."

"Why not? She's old enough now to know what kind of world we live in."

Abruptly, Dorothy goes and unsnaps the canopy. "Let's put up the top," she says. "We're all getting sunburned."

"Sure, but we don't have to unroll the screens." Montgomery gets up to help. "The bugs aren't that bad this early in summer."

Unbeknownst to Melanie, Ryan is also on the river. He and Bryson are farther upstream, bobbing up and down in a skiff. "I think I'm getting seasick," Ryan complains. He watches his father cut a worm in half and winces as blood squirts from the creature.

"Don't be a sissy." Bryson threads a piece of worm onto his hook.

"What makes you think the fish will be biting on a holiday with all these boats churning the water?"

"Who cares if they're biting? It's Crossing Day. That means beer, barbeque, and fishing."

Ryan watches his bobber skim across the surface, then disappear. He yanks back on his rod, but the fish gets away. "I never did get why Crossing Day is such a big deal." He reels in his line and looks at the bare hook in disgust.

"Crossing Day commemorates the most important day on the Confederate calendar," Bryson explains. He reaches into the bait can and then passes Ryan the other half of the worm. "On this day in 1864, Sherman was trying to get his starving army across the Altamaha River to the Port of Darien, south of Savannah. He had half his men over when Johnston attacked those who were left. It was the first Confederate victory in over a year. Sherman lost half his men, their wagons, and all his artillery. The next day, he surrendered."

"I know all that," Ryan says impatiently. "Just don't get why we celebrate that more than the Armistice."

Bryson snatches his rod back and hooks a fish. It's a feisty bluegill that puts up a good fight before he swings it into the boat. "Son, the Armistice was only a truce," Bryson says. "The Confederates prefer to honor the Battle of Altamaha Crossing 'cause it was a victory."

Over the next few hours, more fish are added to the Walters' stringer. Toward evening, Bryson decides they have enough. "We got us a nice mess of fish," he says. "Now we need to go home and clean 'em."

"Ugh," Ryan grimaces. His father yanks the starter cord, and after several tries, the little motor sputters to life. Ryan reaches for the rope and hauls in the anchor. It's a coffee can filled with red clay. The rope is attached to a wire clothes hanger embedded in it.

That evening, after a nice fish dinner, Ryan washes the dishes. His father sits at the kitchen table with his phone. "Hey, come here and dry," the boy says. Bryson lumbers out of his chair and grabs a dish towel. "So, how did you and the others come to join The Resistance?" Ryan asks.

"Tradition," Bryson explains. He takes a plate from the dishrack, dries it, then puts it away. "Highland people never had any truck with slavery. That goes back to before the War for Southern Independence."

"In history class, we were taught that Southern people were a hundred percent united against the Yankees."

"Pack of lies," Bryson snorts. "Sure, the Confederates eliminated most of the Unionists in the flatlands. Ran 'em off, took their land, and worse. But up here in the highlands, we fought back. A few of us still do."

Ryan fishes around in the soapy water. All that's left is a saucer. He runs a sponge over it, then puts it in the rack. "Crossing Day's over," he says. "It's been great, but it's back to school tomorrow. I'm going to bed."

"Goodnight, son." Bryson finishes drying the last dish. After putting it up, he sits and again picks up his phone.

The next day, at Johnston High School, Ryan goes to the guidance office to pay for his cap and gown rental. "So, tell me," Mrs. Lansdale asks, "have you changed your mind about going to college?"

"Maybe I'll take a class or two at Calhoun," Ryan answers. "If I'm not too busy helping my dad."

"With what? I thought they took y'all's farm."

Ryan thinks fast. "We're going to buy stuff at auctions to sell online," he improvises.

"Good luck with that," the guidance counselor says dubiously.

With everything set for graduation, Ryan has little to do at school. His grades are high enough to exempt him from finals, so he's done with his courses. After visiting guidance, he kills off the remainder of the morning in the communications center and then goes to the cafeteria for lunch.

Once he's filled a tray with free and reduced-price food, Ryan looks for Melanie. She's nowhere to be seen; however, there's a vacant seat at a table where several soccer players have gathered. "Sorry, that place is reserved," Liam says as Ryan puts his tray down.

"For who?" Ryan demands to know.

"For anyone but you, ha."

"Yeah, right." Ryan drops into the chair.

"So, who's going to the prom?" a boy at the end of the table asks.

"Not me," Liam says. He's trying to open a ketchup packet but can't get his thumbnail under the tab.

"Here, let me do that." Gerry takes it from him, pries the lid off, and passes it back.

Liam spreads the ketchup on a hotdog and takes a bite. "Proms are so lame."

"I wanted to go as a single, but they told me I had to wear a dress," Gerry says. "No way."

"Well, Melanie and I will be there for sure," Ryan declares. "Her dad finally agreed."

"How are you gonna pay for the tux?"

"I saved up."

"I hear a Memphis showband will be performing," a freshman soccer player says enviously. "Wish I could go."

Ryan raises a forkful of baked beans to his lips and chews mechanically. It's always beans and franks for the poor kids on Wednesdays. That's his least favorite meal. "I'm gonna go home and rest up before practice," he says, rising from his chair.

"Don't you want the hotdogs?" the freshman asks.

"Nah, take them." Ryan passes his tray over. The franks are unnaturally red and have a vague, unappetizing taste. Nevertheless, the boy happily makes room for them on his plate. *Guess he doesn't get much to eat at home*, Ryan thinks.

Outside, Ryan tries to remember where he parked the truck. Finally, he locates the vehicle, tosses his bookbag onto the passenger seat, and fires up the diesel motor. Leaving school, he switches on the radio, hoping for entertainment to break the monotony of the familiar route home. Instead of music, Ryan hears a public service announcement featuring the harsh voice of General Van Dorn. "Loyalty is the glue that holds our nation together," The Leader is saying. "Not loyalty to the state, the government, or the army, but to me, personally. Why, if I were to take my gun, go out onto the sidewalk, and randomly shoot the first person to come along, no one should question it. That's loyalty." There's a moment of silence. Then, an excited voice comes on. "Folks, why walk when you can ride? You got bad credit, no credit, you say? Well, I say, no problem! Just bring me a recent paycheck stub, and I'll put you into one of the fine used cars here at SELL 'EM ALL MOTORS. We're located at the corner of Holmes Avenue and Warner Street downtown." With a snort of disgust, Ryan changes the station.

At the sports complex that night, the Rangers must wait to get onto their field. The club's U-15 Elites are scrimmaging the U-16 Classics on it, and the game is running over. Coach Phillips has the team warm up and stretch behind a goal. Afterward, he leads them on a run. By the time they return, the scrimmage is over. Phillips gives the players a breather while he sets up cones for a defensive drill. Practice time is valuable, so he doesn't allow much of a break. "You guys over by the water," he shouts. "Get that portable goal."

Liam and Ryan take one more gulp and then jog toward where Phillips is pointing. Gerry joins them. "You guys need some muscle power," she says.

"We got all we need," Liam brags. He sprints to get to the goal first and grabs an end. Gerry beats Ryan to the other end, so he's stuck in the middle. They hoist it and start back toward their half of the field.

"Hey, put that down," a boy on the other side of the field shouts. He and several teammates run toward them.

"Just what we need," Liam says. "Germans!"

Ryan untangles himself from the sagging net and faces the approaching boys. They're attired in Blitz training uniforms. "That goal is ours," one of them says.

"Not true," Ryan replies. "It belongs to the park authority. Anyone can use it."

"But you took it off our half," the German blusters.

Liam lowers his end of the goal, and Gerry drops hers. They join Ryan in facing the Blitz players as more team members from each side hurry to the confab. "It can be used by whoever gets it first, bozo," Liam tells the German. "That's the way it's always been."

"What's this bozo name? *Was ist das denn?*" The German looks to his teammates for an answer.

"I believe he's calling you a clown, Fritz," Dieter explains, breaking into the circle around the portable goal.

"*Das geht nicht,*" Fritz growls. He balls his fists menacingly but hesitates. Liam is a foot taller.

Dieter steps between the two boys. "Let's all chill," he smiles. "No need to stress. There's another one over there." Dieter points to a portable goal lying on its side at the end of the neighboring field.

"Sure, but why should we be the ones to have to carry it from there?" Fritz wonders.

"Because they got to this one first, bozo," Dieter laughs. "Come on, boys, I'll race you to it. Last one does twenty push-ups."

Immediately, the Blitz players take off running, each trying to overtake Dieter, who has a head start. "Is it my imagination, or was Dieter actually being helpful just now?" Ryan asks. He grabs the end of the goal before Gerry can get there. Now she's stuck in the middle as Liam hoists the other end.

"I still don't trust him," Liam says. "Not after what happened with Mish."

"Hey, what's taking so long?" Phillips hollers. "I want that goal right here." The three Rangers speedwalk, hoisting the portable goal above their heads.

For soccer players, training is the next best thing to a regulation game. They know that even though much practice time is devoted to physical fitness and tactical instruction, coaches usually end each session with a match-related activity, meaning two goals, goalkeepers, and opposing teams, each trying to score. So it is this night, and later, when Gerry, Liam, and Ryan leave the field, they excitedly rehash the scrimmage. "Did you see the ball Kerry chipped into the corner for Sid?" Ryan asks.

"Sure, I see everything from where I am," Liam explains. "It was spot on."

"What about Sid's cross?" Gerry interjects. "He put it right on my head. Goal!"

Gerry is limping slightly. When the three friends reach the parking lot, her father, who is waiting by their car, notices. "That was a reckless slide tackle," he comments.

"Had to do it," Gerry smiles.

"Well, let's go home and get some ice on that knee." Before turning to go, he glances at Liam. "Nice save on the shot by Sean. I thought it was going in."

"Thanks." Liam smiles. As he and Ryan continue walking, they find themselves among a crowd of Blitz players leaving the park.

"Hey, guys," Dieter says.

"Hi," Ryan replies. He and Liam speed up to get away from the Germans.

Dieter follows. "Don't be sore about that portable goal," he says. "Fritz gets a little over-the-top sometimes."

"That's not what we're mad about." Ryan turns to face the German.

Liam stops beside Ryan and looks down at Dieter. "Yeah, Mish would still be working at Jaybird's if not for you."

Dieter scuffs the ground with his foot. "Yeah, I was a jerk that time. Because of me, Mish is now in danger. She's a great girl. I'd do anything to help her."

"Do you mean it?" Liam scowls.

"I swear."

Ryan gets out his phone. "What's your number?"

The two boys exchange phone numbers. "I'll hit you up tomorrow," Ryan promises. "We have a couple of ideas in mind."

"Sounds good." Dieter looks past Ryan to where vehicles are queuing to leave the park. "Don't want miss my ride," he exclaims and takes off running.

Coach Phillips is waiting by his SUV when Liam and Ryan get there. "Where have you been?" he frowns.

"Sorry, Coach," Ryan says. "Anyway, I'll drive Liam home."

Phillips' frown turns to a smile. "Great, thanks." He climbs into his vehicle before Ryan can change his mind.

"I've got a couple bucks," Liam says. "Let's go to Hardee's and eat like we mean it."

Twenty miles away, at Toombs Labor Camp, Ryan's mother and her friends wouldn't know what to do with a freshly cooked cheeseburger. Their bodies have become so accustomed to freeze-dried or canned food that anything else would make them sick. Now, after a dinner made by mixing desiccated potato flakes with hot water, they line up in the bathhouse. The cinderblock building is crowded with women inmates waiting to shower or use one of the toilets before curfew. There is no privacy, and for that reason, the bathhouse is one of the few places in the camp with no cameras. Instead, women guards push through the crowd to intimidate the inmates and discourage loitering. They temporarily squelch conversations as they pass, but once they're gone, the low murmur of voices picks up again.

Alice is just ahead of Rebecca in line. After a guard strolls by, she pulls a paperback out of her apron and reads. Every few seconds, Alice glances around to check on the guards before returning to the book. *It's pathetic*, Rebecca thinks. *We act like frightened bunnies.*

As if reading Rebecca's mind, Alice tucks her book away. "Are you going out again tonight?" she whispers over her shoulder.

"Not 'til later," Rebecca says softly.

"It's scary what you're doing."

"I'm surprised you and Diane aren't taking part. Don't you want to get out of here?"

"Yes, but I dread going to Andersonville. I'd rather take my chances here than risk going up one of those chimneys in Georgia."

"Don't you want to see your children?"

"Sure, but tunneling is too risky."

"Everything's a risk around here. Like what you were doing a minute ago."

"What, waiting in line?"

"No, reading. Where did you get that book?"

"Traded for it."

"On the black market, right?"

"Of course," Alice whispers. All around them, there's a lull in conversations as a hatchet-faced guard passes by. She dangles a nightstick from a lanyard, occasionally flipping it up and twirling it.

Rebecca waits until the Confederate is gone, then murmurs, "If you're caught with contraband, they'll put you in the cooler."

"It would be worth it." After glancing around, Alice slides the book out of her apron and shows Rebecca the cover. It's faded and torn, but the author's name is legible—J.R.R. Tolkien.

"Omigod! How much did you pay?"

"I saved the can of peaches we get on Sundays for ten weeks."

"Wow, you were desperate."

"No worries. When I'm done, I'll trade it to someone else and get what I paid back."

The line inches ahead as several women come out of the shower room. Diane is one of them. She spots her roommates and comes over. "I had to wait an hour for my turn to shower."

"Yep, we've been here almost that long, just to use a sink," Alice says.

"I hate this place," Rebecca exclaims.

"All I can say is it beats the alternative," Diane says, "a free, all-expenses-paid trip to Andersonville."

Rebecca is on the tunneling crew this evening. To avoid suspicion, she goes through her normal pre-bedtime routine in the bathhouse, then returns to her room and gets into bed. There she lies, waiting until the Focke-Wulf shift changes at midnight. When the aircraft workers begin leaving their rooms, Rebecca goes into the hallway and then mingles with a group of women as they plod downstairs. It's eerily quiet in the stairwell. Just the rhythmic slap of hundreds of cheap canvas sneakers on the concrete. The inmates are too depressed to talk.

Once she's outside, Rebecca heads for the bathhouse along with several shift workers who are making last-minute pit stops before their assembly. Instead of going inside, Rebecca takes advantage of the no-cameras-in-the-bathroom policy to sneak behind the building. Now comes the most nerve-racking part—getting to the maintenance shed.

She must low crawl more than a hundred yards across a field that is regularly crisscrossed with searchlights.

Dropping to her knees, Rebecca takes a deep breath and then applies her chest to the ground. She will keep it there, slithering along like a snake the entire way. After a light beam passes, she starts crawling using the insides of her knees and elbows for locomotion. *Got to keep my butt down*, she thinks with her face only an inch above the ground.

It's stop-and-go all the way as searchlights continuously probe the shadows for black-market activities or worse. Trigger-happy Confederates in the guard towers hope to relieve their boredom by finding something to shoot in a cone of illumination. But finally, Rebecca makes it to the shed. She finds the door ajar thanks to Micki, who once worked as a locksmith and long ago figured out the combination padlock. "Any trouble?" she asks.

"Just my nerves," Rebecca answers.

"Same here, but for whatever reason, once we start working, the anxiety goes away."

Rebecca goes to the corner and takes hold of one of the pallets on top of the tunnel entrance. "Then you and I might as well clear these away while we wait for the others."

"Might as well," Micki smiles.

Before long, the tunnel entrance is clear, and the other would-be escapees are present. "This is going to be a big night," Cindy says. "We've been angling toward the surface for the last month. According to my calculations, we'll break through tonight."

"But we're not going out, right?" Rebecca asks.

"That's correct. We need to see where we are, then cover the exit up again until everything's ready for the escape."

"Still, it's exciting." Micki goes to the ladder. "I'm going down first."

"Wait." Rebecca reaches into a pants pocket. "I have something here that will give us some extra energy."

"Where did you get that?" Cindy exclaims. She and the other tunnelers stare reverently at the chocolate bar Rebecca is holding.

"Vinson," Rebecca frowns. She divides the bar and passes the pieces around.

"Oh, is he still hitting on you?" Cindy takes a dainty nibble of dark chocolate.

"I'm going to eat mine after we're done tonight," Micki says. She stores her portion in a jacket pocket, then goes to the ladder and begins her descent. Rebecca sits behind the bellows and grasps the handles. As she works, her share of the chocolate melts in her mouth.

Four hours later, it's Cindy at the tunnel face who gets the team's first breath of free air. It pours into the small hole she has made in the forest floor. Through it, she gazes up at a tangle of pine branches. Above them, the dark sky is dotted with bright stars. But that's enough. She blocks the hole so it won't be noticeable. Excitedly, she backs out of the tunnel to tell the others.

There are three other tunneling crews. Once all would-be escapees have been informed of the breakthrough, the wait begins for the next overcast, moonless night. Nervously, the tunnelers arrange, then re-arrange their escape kits. Each has a carefully reproduced map of the surrounding area, hand-sewn civilian clothes, a rudimentary compass, and a forged internal passport. Day by day, as the moon wanes, the tunnelers look to the sky for hints about the weather. "Red sky in the morning, sailor, take warning," Rebecca mutters one morning, gazing at the rose-colored dawn.

"What does that mean?" another inmate asks. They are all standing in formation, waiting to be counted.

"Oh, it's an ancient belief seafarers had about weather forecasting. They thought that if the sunrise had a reddish tinge, a storm was coming, but if the sky was that color in the evening, it foretold a pleasant tomorrow."

"What nonsense."

Rebecca sees their section leader finish with the front row and round the corner. "Actually, there's scientific wisdom in many of those ancient beliefs," she whispers, then holds out her arm with the QR code facing up.

By the end of the week, conditions are right for the escape. There's a new moon and a thin layer of clouds to cut down on starlight. "I'll miss you guys," Rebecca tells Alice and Diane who have risen from their bunks to see their roommate off.

"I wish you would reconsider while you still have a chance," Diane pleads. Her face is a mask of concern.

Rebecca makes light of it. "'Better to die on your feet than to live on your knees,' somebody once said, but I don't remember who."

"Here, take this." Alice slips a necklace into Rebecca's hand. It's a simple chain with a Star of David.

"Oh, my goodness, where did you get it?"

"I made it."

Rebecca hugs Alice and kisses her cheek. "I'll treasure this in honor of my grandmother even though I'm a Christian. Help me put it on."

Wearing the necklace, Rebecca shares a last hug with Diane. She takes her escape kit and slips out the door. In the company of shift workers, Rebecca exits the building and then dodges behind the bathhouse. It's time for her to make the harrowing crawl to the maintenance shed.

Nearly a dozen escapees are waiting half an hour later when Rebecca arrives. A few nervous grimaces are the only greetings she receives. "Now it's just Micki," Cindy says. She's the one who made the schedule, giving each escapee a set time for the rendezvous.

The doorknob rattles, and the inmates jerk their heads in that direction. "It's only me," Micki whispers unnecessarily. She's visible thanks to the rays shining through the window from a security light outside.

"I'll take the bellows," Rebecca says as the others drag pallets off the tunnel entrance.

As soon as the way is clear, Laura Masterson goes to the ladder. She's the leader of another tunneling crew. "Give us fifteen minutes, then your group can come," she tells another inmate.

"Got it."

Laura's head disappears into the hole, then others in her crew follow. Rebecca energetically works the bellows until she, Cindy, and Micki are the only ones left. "Let me take over for you," Cindy offers.

"Nah, I've got this. Y'all go ahead."

Rebecca watches her friends disappear into the hole. Now she's alone. As she pumps air into the tunnel, Rebecca can't help darting glances at the door. She fears that a phalanx of gray-clad guards will burst in at any minute to arrest her.

As time passes, with only the squeaking of the bellows to keep her company, Rebecca grows more confident. Then, the scent of the forest rises from the opening. It's a combination of peat, loam, pine, and decay. *They've reopened the tunnel*, she thinks. Her heart beats faster as she releases the bellows, picks up her escape kit, and goes to the ladder.

Soon, Rebecca is on her hands and knees, crawling through the tunnel. It's pitch-black, but that's not a problem since all she must do is go forward. Over the past year, her knees have grown callused, so there is little discomfort, only anxiety. Finally, Rebecca reaches the source of the fresh air that has been blowing in her face. She sticks her head out of the opening and, in the pale light of dawn, sees several pairs of feet clad in prison-issue sneakers. Close behind them is a dirt road that's partially overgrown with weeds.

After extricating herself from the hole, Rebecca sees her fellow escapees staring at her with their hands behind their backs. "Why haven't you guys changed into your civies?" she asks.

Abruptly, Rebecca is grabbed from behind. Her arms are roughly jerked back. "They won't be needin' civilian clothes where they're goin', you neither." The soldier fastens a zip tie around Rebecca's wrists.

"Won't need any clothes at all," a Confederate sergeant behind Rebecca says. He prods her with a nightstick until she's lined up with the other escapees facing him. "Now, I'm Sergeant Campbell in command of this here detail," he announces. "Y'all best listen up 'cause I'm jest gonna ask ya once. Who all was in on this with you?" Campbell gazes at the inmates placidly while smacking the palm of one hand with the nightstick. Rebecca winces each time it strikes flesh. She watches, mesmerized.

The sergeant seems to be a paragon of patience as he waits for a reply. Then, a Confederate Army deuce-and-a-half truck maneuvers up the dirt road and into the clearing. Several female inmates are pushed off the back. Like the escapees, their hands are bound, so now they lie on the ground helplessly. One of them rolls over on her side, and Rebecca gasps. It's Diane.

A soldier jumps off the truck and kicks one of the inmates on the ground. "On your feet," he growls, then lowers his bayonet to make his point. The other Confederates similarly motivate the others. Rebecca sees that Alice is among them. She recognizes another as one of Micki's roommates.

With the new arrivals lined up alongside the escapees, Campbell addresses the prisoners. "Now we can do this the hard way or the easy way," he says while slapping his palm with the nightstick. "Who's gonna give me the names of everyone else who was in on your stupid plot?" He stares at the women expectantly, but silence reigns. No one answers him.

Abruptly, Campbell strides down the line of women and then randomly stops in front of one. He jams the tip of his nightstick under the woman's chin, forcing her to look up. It's Diane. "Do you have any names for me?" the Confederate asks her. Without waiting for a reply, he viciously kicks Diane's legs from under her. As she lays on the ground with her hands tied, the soldier clubs her.

"Please stop," Diane begs. "Please, please." But the sergeant is not done. He steps back and aims a kick at Diane's stomach. When she curls up to protect that area, he kicks her in the head. Mercifully, Diane loses consciousness.

Recognizing that his victim is now impervious to pain, the sergeant strolls farther down the line. He stops in front of Rebecca. "You're the ringleader, aren't you?" He holds the nightstick up threateningly, then hesitates. An army staff car is bumping up the road with an insignia plate on the front displaying two stars. It comes to a halt behind the deuce-and-a-half. General Garland gets out. He pauses to take in the scene, then strides up to Sergeant Campbell. "If you kill them all here, how can I make an example of them?"

Campbell snaps to attention and salutes the general, still holding the nightstick. "Sir, I'm just trying to ensure we have all of them."

The general ignores the salute, leaving the sergeant standing at attention, foolishly holding the nightstick to the brim of his field cap. "I'm informed that these here are the entire kit and caboodle. Are you saying my intel is faulty?"

"Sir, not at all," Campbell protests.

"Security's been watching and listening to them for weeks, ever since the ground radar picked up the tunnel. We know everyone who was in on it or knew about it."

"Yes, sir."

The general points to Diane. "Throw that one aboard the truck and then get the rest loaded. Morning assembly is starting. I want to parade them in front of the other inmates."

With relief, Campbell drops his arm and turns to bark a series of orders to the soldiers. Two of them grab Diane and hoist her into the truck. The other prisoners climb onto the vehicle's first step with their hands still tied. They are shoved the rest of the way aboard by the Confederates.

Once all the prisoners are loaded, two soldiers lift and lock the tailgate. They back away as the truck turns around, then get in the rear of an SUV. Sergeant Campbell grabs the passenger seat while the rest of his squad climbs aboard a three-quarter-ton utility truck. Once everything is ready, the little convoy leaves the clearing with Garland's staff car in the lead. The general sits in the back, scrolls through the contacts on his phone, and initiates a call. Despite the early hour, it's picked up on the second ring. "What can I do for you, General?" a feminine voice asks.

"I'm getting a transport together with some would-be escape artists," Garland says, "and would like to make an example of them. Could you bring your team to the parade ground this morning for assembly?"

"Yes, sir."

"We can show the inmates what it's like to be prepped for Andersonville."

"Great idea, General."

The corners of the general's eyes crinkle as his face lights up in a smile. "I'm happy you think so, Sarah."

Farther back in the convoy, there are no smiles as the prisoners contemplate their predicament. It's a rough ride sitting on the truck floor, getting jounced every time the deuce-and-a-half hits a rut. By now, Diane has regained consciousness. She stares blankly out the back at the receding scenery. Rebecca clings to her wrist, feeling her pulse. "How is she?" Micki asks.

"Faint breathing and a weak pulse. It's a bad concussion."

The dirt road runs along the outside perimeter of the camp. The convoy follows it to the main gate and gets waved through by soldiers who recognize General Garland. From there, it's only two miles to the parade ground, where inmates are already filing in for morning assembly. When they arrive, Garland orders the staff car driver to park beside his tower. The other vehicles pull up nearby and the soldiers dismount. They quickly get into squad formation. As Garland approaches, the Confederates snap to attention. "At ease," the general commands. "Sergeant, get the prisoners down and line them up over there." Garland points to the front of the tower.

"Yes, sir."

A flatbed pickup truck arrives followed by a staff car bearing Medical Corps insignia. Garland strolls over to the driver's side of the car. "Morning, Sarah," he smiles.

Dr. Sarah Fisher is the camp's chief medical officer. She's young for the position but well-qualified and, more importantly, well-connected. It doesn't hurt that she's beautiful, even in a white smock and flat nurse's shoes. "It's going to be a lovely day, Phil." Sarah returns the general's smile. "Should I get the chair down?" She points to a customized wooden armchair on the flatbed.

The general steps back so he can see the chair. Then he swivels his head to take in the entire scene. By now, the inmates are in ranks, and section leaders have begun the count. The escapees are lined up nearby. They seem to be in shock. "Come to think of it, Sarah, I like the chair as it is now, where everyone can see it," Garland says. "Just have your team remove the tie-downs and center it."

"Yes, sir." Sarah relays the general's orders to the soldiers with her. Then she turns to her driver. "Move my staff car over there," she snaps, pointing to where the other vehicles are parked.

The morning count of inmates is still dragging on. So, once everything is arranged to the general's satisfaction, the soldiers, except those guarding the prisoners, are given a smoke break. They cluster beside Garland's tower, passing packets of cigarettes around. Several prefer to dip, and they, too, don't mind sharing their favorite brand with buddies. "This here comes from Virginia's finest leaf," a corporal brags, holding out a tin of snuff.

"Pshaw, Virginia ain't got nothin' on Carolina when it comes to tobacky," Campbell says.

On the other side of the tower, Sarah shakes a long cigarette out of her pack of Virginia Belles. She reaches into her pocket, but Garland gets his lighter out first. "Thanks," Sarah exhales.

"So, how's the smallpox experiment going?" Garland whispers.

Sarah gasps. "How do you know about that?"

"Oh, come on," Garland laughs, "I'm cleared for Ultra, same as you."

"My bad," Sarah grins. "Should've known. Still, it would be a disaster if social media learned that we are doing medical experiments on inmates."

"Just on the Jews, though, right?"

Sarah takes a long drag on her cigarette and then briefly turns her head to exhale. "Well, we've actually been trying some germs on the homos and trans people as well," she admits.

"Serves them right," Garland declares.

"I'm glad you understand," Sarah smiles. "But some of those bleeding hearts online wouldn't."

A gray-haired Confederate colonel approaches Garland and salutes. "Colonel Jackson reporting, sir."

"Are your people finally done with the count?" Garland returns the salute.

"Yes, sir."

"Well?"

"All present and accounted for, except that bunch." Jackson nods toward the prisoners.

"Then form a hollow square centered on the flatbed and be quick about it."

"Yes, sir."

The colonel turns and goes to issue commands to his subordinates. Immediately, bullhorns begin blaring marching orders to the inmates. They have been well-drilled over the years, and it doesn't take long to change formation. With the flatbed pickup and his tower now surrounded, General Garland goes up the stairs. Meanwhile, Sarah gets her prep kit and clambers onto the back of the truck. The soldiers put out their cigarettes. Following orders from Campbell, they line up beside the prisoners. "Fix bayonets," the sergeant orders.

Using bayonets to discourage dissent, the soldiers march the escapees to the rear of the flatbed and form them into a line. On the tower platform above them, General Garland speaks into a microphone. "This morning, we found these inmates outside the wire," he shouts. "They are ungrateful scum who didn't appreciate all we provided. Plentiful food, comfortable lodging, rewarding jobs, and the opportunity to live. Instead, they have chosen a one-way trip to Andersonville. Now you will see how we prepare those who are no longer fit to be among us for their end."

The general nods to Campbell, who goes to Rebecca, who heads the line of escapees. "Strip her," he says to the soldiers on either side. There's little that Rebecca can do to shield herself as the Confederates cut off her prison uniform. With her hands still tied, she is tossed naked onto the back of the flatbed like a rag doll.

Sarah looks down at her. "Get up," she orders.

Rebecca struggles into a half-kneeling position but, with her hands bound, has difficulty getting to her feet. Losing patience, Sarah bends down, grasps a length of Rebecca's hair, and yanks. When Rebecca shrieks, Sarah kicks her. With that, the would-be escapee manages to stand. "What do we have here?" Sarah reaches for the Star of David that Alice made and pretends to admire it for a moment before brutally snatching the chain off Rebecca's neck. "What trash," the doctor declares. She tosses the necklace onto the ground to lay beside some cigarette butts.

Tears of shame roll down Rebecca's cheek as she nakedly faces the assembled prisoners. One of Sarah's assistants climbs onto the truck and cuts off the zip tie binding Rebecca's wrists. He and Sarah force Rebecca onto the chair and tighten straps around her feet and hands. With Rebecca immobilized, Sarah uses clippers to cut her hair.

Once she has hacked Rebecca's hair off, Sarah puts the clippers aside and opens a plastic container. She fishes around for a grommet and washer, then gives them to her assistant to hold while she uses a hole punch to pierce Rebecca's ear. Ignoring Rebecca's cries, Sarah's assistant presses the grommet pieces together with a pair of pliers. Next, Sarah threads a key ring through the bleeding hole and affixes a metal tag. Stamped on the tag is TLC LOT 148.

As Rebecca looks out over the sea of faces surrounding her, she can read pity in the inmates' eyes. However, their faces remain expressionless for the cameras. Rebecca hopes the ordeal is over, but Sarah takes out a scalpel. "You won't need this where you're going," she says, lightly tapping Rebecca's QR code with the instrument. Then Sarah deftly slices the tattoo off of Rebecca's strapped-down arm. Rebecca is too shocked to cry out. She looks down and sees blood already welling in the wound. Curiously, there's no pain.

Sarah's aide kneels to unstrap Rebecca's feet and hands. Standing, he grasps the escapee's arm and jerks her out of the chair. Now, the numbness wears off. Pain hits Rebecca with a rush. She staggers and then falls off the back of the flatbed. "Get the next one up here," Sarah orders.

Less than an hour later, twenty-three bald, naked, bleeding women are lined up in front of the inmate formation with tags hanging from their ears. "The next stop for these morons will be their last," Garland hollers into the microphone. "So let this be a lesson. Appreciate what you have here and forget what's on the outside. You are dismissed."

Morning assembly has taken longer than usual, so the inmates must rush to eat, take care of their morning business, and get to work. Rebecca and the other prisoners are shackled. They can only shuffle their feet while being herded back to the truck.

Once all the prisoners are again aboard the deuce-and-a-half, the driver puts his vehicle into gear. He follows Sergeant Campbell's SUV off the parade ground and onto the main drive. The utility truck full of soldiers brings up the rear as the convoy proceeds toward the labor camp entrance. Soon, the would-be escapees leave the facility for the second time this day. They will not be back.

Even though summer is well on the way, it's chilly this early in the morning. The naked prisoners feel cold riding in the back of the canvas-sided truck. The metal floor is cool to the touch, and finding a comfortable way to sit is impossible. At least they are spared the jostling that made their ride on the dirt road such an ordeal. That's because the convoy has turned onto the Dixiebahn, a smooth, limited-access highway that allows unlimited speed.

The prisoners are lost in their thoughts, so there's little conversation. Diane is stretched out, either asleep or passed out. *Probably because of the concussion*, Rebecca thinks. *I should probably check on her, but what difference would it make?* Instead, Rebecca gazes out the vehicle's rear and watches the trees on either side fly past. A black speck way back in the passing lane quickly grows larger, and then, with a *whoosh*, a low-slung sports car speeds past. The Confederate Army vehicles stay in the right lane with their emergency flashers on.

Traffic slows early that afternoon as the convoy approaches Atlanta. Even with five lanes, backups are constant. Diane is awake now and sits by the tailgate. She's oblivious to the stares and honking horns of passing drivers who are either shocked or titillated by her appearance. "Diane hasn't a clue about what's going on," Micki comments.

"Wish I could say the same," Rebecca grimaces.

Cindy has her back against the side of the truck and her knees tucked under her chin. "I'm sorry I talked y'all into escaping," she says.

"Oh, come on," Micki replies. "No one talked me into it. I was right there with you all along, maybe even before you."

"Ditto," Rebecca says. "But I never guessed we were endangering our roommates as well."

"Me neither," Cindy says. "I tried to get mine to come dig with us, but they refused. Now they're in the same boat as us anyway."

"Yeah, it's too bad about the others," Micki says. "But sooner or later, everyone ends up at Andersonville." Micki has been sitting cross-legged, but now one limb is cramping. "Ouch," she says and gingerly tries to straighten it.

Once again, conversation dies as the women get a last look at the jagged skyline of the South's biggest city. On the outskirts of town, they pass a massive soccer stadium surrounded by acres of parking. "Home of the Atlanta Fire," a sign reads. Everyone knows the team's name refers to the decision that Confederate General Joe Johnston made during the War for Southern Independence to evacuate all the residents from Atlanta before burning it to the ground. When the Yankees entered the city, their leader, General William Sherman, found none of the provisions or accommodations he had hoped for. The Confederate cavalry had cut off his supply line from Tennessee, so his army was in dire straits.

The convoy is now beyond city limits, however progress remains slow as the vehicles merge with heavy traffic heading south toward the bedroom communities around Macon. Every exit along the way features the usual conglomeration of fast-food joints, motels, convenience stores, and chain restaurants. Between exits, the monotony of one housing development after another is occasionally broken by the sight of a still-working plantation. On them, slaves can be seen in the fields, tending to young cotton plants.

It's been a traumatic and exhausting day for the prisoners aboard the deuce-and-a-half. Now, despite their discomfort, most drift off into a fitful sleep on the blood-smeared truck bed. Rebecca lays on her side, cradling her head on the uninjured arm. She's at peace with the situation and prepared to die, knowing that she tried to find freedom rather than meekly accept years of slavery. Her only worry is how Bryson and Ryan will take the news of her attempted escape and subsequent execution. *I hope they'll be all right,* she frets.

Sometime later, Rebecca is jarred awake when the truck hits a rough patch of pavement. She sits up guessing that they have turned off the Dixiebahn. Aside from the three-quarter-ton utility truck, no other vehicles are behind them. Rebecca scoots closer to the canvas opening in the back, careful not to wake Diane, who has fallen asleep again. *She shouldn't be allowed to sleep with a concussion,* Rebecca thinks as she looks at her former roommate, *but at this point, what harm can it do?*

Rebecca shifts her gaze to take in the orderly rows of pine trees lining the road. They are grown to feed the South's paper mills and lumber yards. Most of the wood will end up in products bound for China. Rebecca watches the dark shapes flash by on either side, then recede into the distance like the wake of a speedboat. With the sun barely above the horizon, the road is in the shade. It's dark and tranquil. For a moment, she feels alone in the woods and free. The anxiety that has been raging inside her fades. But that changes a short while later when the truck lurches to a halt at a brightly lit checkpoint. Immediately, the convoy is surrounded by gun-toting guards who demand to see Sergeant Campbell's identification and the cargo manifest. A German wearing the black uniform of the Security Service takes the paperwork to the back of the deuce-and-a-half, followed by Campbell. "Is this all you got?" he asks, peering inside.

"It's a special transport," Campbell explains. "Not the normal shipment."

"Got it," the SS guard says. "You're good to go." He returns the manifest and disappears back into the guard shack. Campbell regains his seat in the SUV and waits until the barrier is lifted. A sentry waves the convoy through the checkpoint. Now they are on the Andersonville Parkway, lined with a razor-wire-topped chain-link fence. An awful stench fills the air.

After another mile, the convoy is forced to zigzag through an array of concrete barriers before arriving at the entrance to a walled compound. A fifteen-foot-high gate guards the entrance. It swings open, and the convoy enters the facility. The SUV goes a short distance and stops in front of a row of retractable one-way metal spikes. An SS officer emerges from a concrete-block guardhouse holding a soft drink. Campbell gets out of the SUV with the shipping manifest. He strolls over to where the German is waiting. "We've been expecting you," the officer says, throwing up a Hitler salute. "Sieg Heil."

Campbell casually touches the brim of his headgear to acknowledge the salute. He passes the manifest and his ID to the Nazi, who briefly scans the documents before returning them. Campbell replaces the ID in his wallet. "Sorry, we're late. The Atlanta traffic was horrible, even in the middle of the day."

"It's always like that."

"So, are they gonna process these now?"

"Not likely." The Nazi tilts back his head to drink. He shakes the can to ensure it's empty, then turns and tosses it into a trash can. *"Tor!"* he brags.

"Just lucky," Campbell snipes. "So, what's the holdup?"

"Look for yourself."

Campbell turns his head in the direction the officer is pointing and sees a long line of cattle trucks waiting outside a massive building. It looks like a steel plant with several furnaces belching smoke at one end and a row of loading docks at the other. Trailers full of people are backed up to the loading docks. One of them is slowly emptying out. Campbell returns his attention to the Nazi. "I count eleven transports waiting to unload."

"If you say so."

"The same thing happened last time," Campbell complains. "We waited three hours, and the line didn't move. Had to unload them in a corral to be processed later."

"You should have come this morning."

"No one told me that. What chaos. I thought you Germans were supposed to be efficient."

The Nazi brings his phone up and scrolls with his thumb before pausing. "According to my information, this lot escaped from your labor camp. True?"

"Yeah, that's right," Campbell admits.

"Permit me to suggest that you Confederates do a better job with your facilities and not worry so much about how we Nazis manage ours."

Campbell decides to give up the argument. "OK, well we can't wait, so which corral can we use to unload?"

The Nazi scrolls his phone again and then holds it up so Campbell can see. "You can have 18B. Here it is on the map."

"Oh crap, that's all the way to the end."

"Tough." The Nazi laughs. "Take it or leave it."

Campbell turns and goes back to the SUV without saluting. He expects the Nazi to call after him, but nothing happens. "What a jerk," he mutters.

"Where to now?" the driver asks, moving his lips around a lit cigarette.

"Wait one." Campbell reaches across and honks the horn impatiently. When nothing happens, he hits the horn again. Slowly, the tire-puncturing spikes that block the road recede into the grating. "Go right at that light." Campbell points to a blinking caution light up ahead. "Then it's another five miles until we get to where we can drop this load."

The convoy heads toward the central processing building and then turns onto a service road. As they proceed, the revolting odor in the air grows stronger. Campbell knows what's causing it, from previous trips to Andersonville. He doesn't want to look but can't help eventually glancing out the passenger side window. *No matter how many times I come here, it's still unbelievable*, he thinks as his senses recoil from seeing hundreds of old, naked, Black people milling around in an open corral. He stares at their dirty, emaciated bodies. *No telling how long they've been there*, he wonders. The retired slaves always get processed last.

Another corral comes up on the driver's side. Young children inhabit it. *Retards*, Campbell guesses. Even though he's been bombarded with public service announcements about the need to rid society of dead weight, it's hard for Campbell to accept the propriety of leaving kids outside without clothing or shelter. He tries to put it out of his mind. *The last thing I need is to go soft*, he thinks. *First, I'd be out of a job; second, I'd be here in one of these corrals waiting to get processed.* He shudders at the thought.

The Nazi administration enforces strict segregation of the corrals. In addition to the ones for retirees and retards, the convoy passes others that hold abolitionists, Resistance members, and insubordinate slaves. Just before the road dead-ends, they come to the lot reserved for runaways. A sign on the gate reads "FUGITIVES 18B," so Sergeant Campbell knows they're at the right place. He goes to the entrance, scrolls through his phone to find the relevant QR code, and holds it up to the scanner. With a clanking noise, the gate slides open so the convoy can enter.

Once inside, Campbell exits the SUV and makes his way to the utility truck at the rear of the convoy. "Un-ass the vehicle," he orders. While his troops grumpily comply, Campbell fires up a smoke and looks around. The corral is situated on a lot that slopes down to a creek before rising on the other side. Shelters have been dug in the muddy bank of the waterway. Now, a trustee clad in a ragged orange jumpsuit emerges from one. She scrambles up the slope to where the sergeant is standing. "Good day, sir," the woman says. She's deeply wrinkled, and her skin is bronzed by the sun.

"Don't call me sir," Campbell snaps. "I work for a living."

"Yes, Sergeant," the trustee meekly replies.

"And get downwind of me. You stink."

Campbell turns to his squad, who have finally dismounted from the utility truck and await orders. "Get them wretches off the truck and remove the shackles. We got to get the hell out of here."

The soldiers are as anxious as Campbell to put Andersonville in the rearview mirror. They quickly get the prisoners down. Once the shackles have been unlocked, they toss them into the back of the truck. A few minutes later, the women are left standing on the packed red earth of the corral, watching the convoy leave. "I'm Jesse," the trustee says. "Welcome to hell."

"Where's a bathroom?" Micki asks. "I've got to go."

"There's no facilities of any kind here," Jesse says. "Go in the creek." She points downhill.

"What about clothing and shelter?" Rebecca asks.

"Your best bet is to sleep in one of the caves dug into the bank over yonder." Jesse points toward where she came from. "As for clothing, only trustees are issued these jumpsuits."

"How do you get to be a trustee?"

"By volunteering, but they only accept you if you're young and look healthy."

Micki and several other women who visited the creek climb back up the hill. "The water is filthy," one complains.

"Yeah, it runs through the other corrals before it gets here," Jesse shrugs. "So, it's an open sewer."

The day's heat is dissipating now that the sun has gone down. In the twilight, the women huddle together, uncertain about what to do next. "I thought they would kill us as soon as we got here," Diane moans.

Rebecca glances at her friend, relieved she has finally said something after being silent all day. She tries to smile, but the hideous bruises on Diane's face and body make Rebecca grimace instead. "Come on, let's you and I find a place to lie down for the night." She takes Diane's hand.

If anything, the noxious odor that pervades the place is worse down by the creek. Some of the women try to cope by holding their noses but find breathing through their mouths even worse. With one hand, Rebecca leads Diane to a small cave on the other side of the waterway. Looking in, Rebecca's happy to find several burlap bags that previous prisoners must have used to sleep on. She kneels to rearrange the items into a bed while Diane waits. Then, both crawl into the hole and stretch out.

Gazing up at the earthen ceiling, Rebecca decides to chat with God. "Lord," she whispers, "I'm thankful you've given me such a good life. I was blessed with loving parents and, later, a wonderful family of my own. Now, all I ask is a quick death."

"Amen," Diane murmurs.

The two prisoners try to relax, but with dusk comes mosquitos. Before long, one of the little vampires is dive-bombing Rebecca's ear. She tries to swat it but only cuffs herself. Then something furry brushes against her leg. Rebecca hurriedly sits, only to bonk her head on the cave's low ceiling. She catches a glimpse of a rat nonchalantly waddling away.

Hastily, Rebecca lies back down and shifts her gaze outside. Through gaps in the fence, she views a sliver of the moon above the tree line. Fireflies flicker among the leaves, but then she sees a pinpoint of manmade light. One of the Nazi tower guards is smoking.

Pitch darkness descends, slamming the door on what has been the worst day of Rebecca's life. Beside her, Diane is breathing deeply. Rebecca almost envies her friend's concussed state. *I'd love to just zonk out like that*, she thinks. However, the temperature has dropped along with the sun, adding to her general discomfort. Rebecca is not used to being unclean, but now portions of her body are encrusted with a combination of dried blood and red earth. Rebecca's wounded arm and pierced ear throb with pain. Her stomach growls. Miserably, she settles down for a long, restless night.

There are few worse places on the planet to meet the sunrise than Andersonville, Georgia. Whatever goodness can be ascribed to humanity has been left outside the death camp gate. As the naked and wounded prisoners emerge from their caves, their only hope is to be promptly killed. They dread being left in limbo.

That's why excitement ripples through the members of TLC Lot 148 when a Confederate truck pulls up outside the corral. A soldier hops down from the passenger side and goes to the back while the driver opens the gate. "Have they come to get us?" Micki asks hopefully.

"Nah, it's just the morning feed," Jesse replies.

"Great," another prisoner exclaims. "I'm starving."

Now, both soldiers come into the corral carrying lumpy burlap bags on their shoulders. They unceremoniously drop them inside the gate and turn to get one more load. Then they stroll back to their vehicle, and the gate slams shut behind them.

Micki longingly watches the vehicle depart while the others go to see what's for breakfast. Consternation ensues when it turns out that the bags only contain ears of corn. They don't look very appetizing, however, the prisoners aren't picky. Several begin ripping off the outside greenery. Once Cindy gets hers unwrapped, she tries to sink her teeth into the corn. "This is brick hard," she complains.

"You have to gnaw on it awhile," Jesse explains. "Keep trying; you'll get the hang of it."

"Where do we go to fetch water?" Alice asks. "I'm thirsty."

Jesse points to the creek while munching on a few niblets she has separated from the cob she's working on. "That's all there is," she says between chews. "We drink from it, wash up in it, and use it for a bathroom."

"No way," Diane moans.

"Oh, just wait 'til that Georgia sun starts broiling down in a couple of hours," Jesse smirks. "You'll be happy to have any drop of water you can get."

Rebecca has succeeded in getting some nourishment out of her ear of corn. "What I don't understand is why they feed us at all?"

"From what I hear, they didn't used to," Jesse replies. "But the administrators got tired of having to drag prisoners out of corrals who were either dead or too weak to walk. Either way made processing impossible, so those cases were a total loss."

"How so?"

"Organ death occurs rapidly after people die, and processing is all about harvesting organs, tissue, and blood. That's why they need you to walk into the plant."

"So, they make money by killing us?"

"Boatloads."

With hands on hips, Rebecca looks skyward in disgust. She hopes an alien spaceship might come down and snatch her away. However, there's no help to be found above. Only buzzards riding updrafts in long lazy circles above the camp. The tops of chimneys can be seen in the distance, belching greasy black smoke into the cloudless Carolina-blue sky.

Reluctantly, Rebecca redirects her attention to the grim reality around her. "Do you mind if I take one of these?" She picks up an empty burlap bag. "I'll use it as a blanket. It got downright chilly last night."

"Me too!" Micki snatches a sack while other prisoners rush to get the last ones. With the bags all spoken for, the women begin drifting back toward their caves.

"Wait," Cindy calls, "let's clean up the mess."

"Are you serious?" another member of Lot 148 scoffs. "Look around you." She turns and walks away.

"I'll help." Rebecca bends to pick up a soggy corn cob. Alice and Micki get busy also, and soon, the four friends have a burlap bag full of leftovers. Cindy empties it into the creek as they go back toward their shelters. "We've got to stick together," she says. "No telling how long we'll have to wait to be processed."

CHAPTER FIVE

CRASH AND DASH

"**O**h, Johnston High, we truly see the beauty of your majesty," Melanie sings. Ryan is in another row, also belting out the Joseph Johnston High School alma mater. They are in the cavernous school gym, with 243 other seniors, having graduation practice.

"All right, front row, turn to your left and begin to file out," Mrs. Lansdale hollers through a bullhorn. Sullenly, the students do as instructed. It's their third run-through, and they are tired of the rigmarole. "Hey, I'm supposed to be somewhere soon," a boy walking behind Ryan complains.

"School's almost over, so you should be good," Ryan replies.

The line of students passes through the open front doors of the gym and proceeds onto the lawn, where family and friends will join them on graduation day. They mill around in the bright sunshine, happy to escape the confines of the gym and Mrs. Lansdale. She's still inside, prodding the last few rows of students.

Melanie finds Ryan in the crowd. Taking advantage of the babble of voices around them, she whispers, "I've been thinking, and now I want to go with y'all."

Ryan looks around to spot the nearest camera and turns his back to it. "No way," he says, "far too dangerous."

"I don't care."

"Listen, I have nothing to lose, but you do."

"Like what? A life that I despise? I'd end up exactly like my parents—they can't even go to the bathroom without a slave to hand them the toilet paper."

Ryan winces. "Oh, come on."

"Well, slight exaggeration," Melanie smiles. "But you and I, in fact, all our friends, know that the whole system is rotten. Most of our parents are disgusting. They've been spoiled their whole lives and now won't even lift a finger for themselves."

Ryan changes the subject. "Have you been able to accumulate any supplies for us?"

"Yep, I've been taking cans of soup and vegetables out of the pantry one day and bags of rice or noodles the next," Melanie replies. "Our family has so much food. No one will miss it."

"That's great, thanks."

"Yeah, it's getting to be quite a hoard, enough to feed all of us." Melanie is back on topic, and now Ryan sees that further resistance is hopeless.

"Truth be told, I want you to come," he says.

Melanie takes Ryan's hand and squeezes it. "All will go as planned," she says. "You'll see."

Behind them, Mrs. Lansdale is standing in the auditorium doorway. She raises the megaphone to her lips. "That's all for today," she hollers. "We'll have one more run-through the day before." With that, a collective groan goes up from the students scattered about the front lawn. Hastily, they make their escape.

On his way home, Ryan thinks about how nice it would be to have Melanie seated next to him. But thanks to her father, that can't be. Mayor Montgomery has partially lifted the restrictions on Melanie, but only for the prom.

An eighteen-wheeler rumbles past, then tucks back into the slow lane where Ryan has been loafing along. As on almost every big rig nowadays, there's a plea for driver applicants posted on the back. "Highest pay in the industry," it promises. "Home most weekends." Ryan immediately segues into a daydream about life on the road. *Melanie and I could both get commercial driver's licenses,* he fantasizes. *And buy a truck in installments. While one of us drives, the other will rest in the cabin.* Ryan pictures himself at the controls of his Xbox playing FIFA online while his girlfriend drives. *I could get really good*, he thinks.

The daydream is so good Ryan almost misses his exit. Tires squeal as he cuts the wheel and flies up the ramp. His heart races as adrenaline courses through his body. *Idiot!* he accuses himself. People get killed like that.

Shakily, Ryan drives the rest of the way home. He finds a new-looking four-door sedan parked in front of the house. Ryan goes inside to find Bryson alone at the kitchen table with a half-full whiskey bottle in front of him. "Whose car?" he asks.

"It's a rental, me and the guys picked it up this morning."

"For Resistance work?" Ryan pulls out a chair and sits across from his father.

"Yeah, we used it today and will be out with it again tomorrow."

"You shouldn't be drinking if you're doing dangerous stuff tomorrow."

Bryson glances at the whiskey bottle. Sunlight slanting through the kitchen window causes the amber liquor to glow enticingly. "I was thinking the same thing but then I found this in the mailbox when I got home." Bryson slides an envelope across the table.

Ryan picks up the envelope and studies the return address. It's from the Confederate Department of Labor in Richmond. Inside is a letter stating that Rebecca Walters has opted for early retirement and is awaiting processing at Andersonville. "Oh no," Ryan's face blanches. He rereads the letter, hoping there is some mistake. Tears well in his eyes. "Mom, oh Mom, what are they doing to you?" Ryan's shoulders quiver as he sobs.

Bryson pushes the bottle across the table. "Now's as good a time as any to start down the road to perdition."

Through blurred eyes, Ryan sees the whiskey in front of him. He raises the bottle toward his lips, but the fumes reach his nostrils before he can drink. "No thanks," he shudders. "I'm going to my room."

Sleep doesn't come easy for Ryan that night. He's too agitated with thoughts of his mother. It was bad enough when she was locked up in the labor camp. But at least there was a glimmer of hope then. Now, even that is gone. He tosses and turns until finally drifting off. But at the first blush of dawn, one of Bryson's roosters sounds off. As Ryan awakens, the bad news of the night before hits him like a physical blow. *Please let it all have been a bad dream*, he prays.

Slowly, Ryan makes his way to the bathroom. He's surprised to find the door locked. *Dad's hangover must be too bad for him to sleep*, he thinks, and heads for the kitchen. The letter from the labor department is still on the table. So, it wasn't a dream, Ryan realizes. Hatred of the Confederate government rises within him. *Mish isn't the only one who needs to escape*, he concludes. *We all do.*

Down the hall, Ryan hears the bathroom door open and guesses Bryson is now in his bedroom getting dressed for the day. Ryan's determined to get some food into his father, so he pops a couple of frozen waffles into the toaster. While they cook, he starts coffee brewing.

In no time, the first batch of waffles is ready. Ryan takes two more out of the package. "Not for me," Bryson says, coming up behind him. "I'm meeting some friends at Hardee's."

"Is it safe for you guys to go there?"

Bryson searches in the cupboard for his favorite mug, "No place is safe," he mutters.

"It's in the dish rack," Ryan points.

After filling his mug, Bryson sits across the kitchen table from his son, who has a paper plate full of waffles. "We're planning a really big job," Bryson confides. "That's what the rental car is for."

"Sounds dangerous."

Bryson nods. "We're dedicating it to Rebecca."

"She'd probably prefer that you lay low and stay safe." Ryan butters a waffle and tries a bite. *Too bland*, he thinks and reaches for the jelly.

"Your mother never believed in playing it safe. Neither of us did."

"Then I guess you won't disapprove when I tell you what me and some friends are up to."

"That all depends."

"We're going to help a slave girl we know escape."

"Sounds like a noble endeavor, but you should know that few ever make it to the United States."

"Why's that?"

Bryson blows on his steaming coffee thoughtfully. "Mainly because of the Autonomous Zone," he says. "You have to pass through it to get to the North."

"So what," Ryan shrugs. "According to what I learned in history, the AZ is only a hundred miles wide. It was created at the time of the 1865 Armistice."

"Correct, but what they didn't tell you is that nothing has changed in the AZ since the War for Southern Independence. Pro-slavery and anti-slavery guerrillas still fight each other there. They raid each other's settlements while raping, plundering, and murdering. No one is safe."

"Why doesn't the government do something?"

"The treaty President McClellan and Jefferson Davis signed to end the war specified a demilitarized zone where the armed forces of neither the North nor the South can enter."

Ryan pops one more waffle into the toaster. "Not even police?"

"Not even police," Bryson echoes. He glances at his watch and abruptly stands. "I've got to go."

A chill foreboding comes over Ryan as he watches Bryson tilt his weather-beaten ball cap onto his balding head and turn toward the door. "I love you, Dad," he blurts out.

Bryson looks back over his shoulder. He's not demonstrative and rarely shares his feelings, but the warm smile he gives his son before going out says it all. Soon, the slamming of a car door and the crunch of gravel signal his departure. Only then does Ryan realize he never asked Bryson about the "really big job" he mentioned. The anxiety he felt earlier returns.

Gary and Harper are already at Hardee's when Bryson arrives. The latecomer waves to his friends and then goes to the counter for a loaded biscuit and some coffee. "Cotton's gone up another ten cents," Harper announces when Bryson slides into the booth.

"I believe you've mistaken me for someone who cares," Bryson mutters.

Gary nervously glances at a wall-mounted camera and then looks imploringly at Bryson, who decides to cooperate with the dumb farmer act. "How about soybeans?" He raises his voice.

Harper energetically scrolls his phone. He stops to peer intently at the screen. "Down twelve cents so far this morning."

"Oh really?" Bryson has another bite of his sausage and egg biscuit.

"I'm done with soybeans," Gary pitches in. "Gonna lease my land to a fella to install solar panels."

"Wave of the future," Harper comments. "One of these days, people will be starving and wondering what happened."

"Can't eat a solar panel," Bryson laughs.

"You 'bout done with that?" Gary asks impatiently. He and Harper are long finished with their breakfast.

Bryson takes a last bite of his biscuit, then folds the wrapper and uses it to funnel the crumbs into his coffee. "Waste not, want not."

"Tight as a tick," Harper laughs. "Always was."

The three men go outside and pile into the rental car. After depositing his coffee in a cupholder, Bryson pushes the starter. The electric motors whirr reassuringly. "Why do I always end up in the back?" Gary complains.

"'Cause you're as slow as molasses." Bryson reaches to turn up the volume on a Travis Tritt song. "Now that's country music," he declares.

"Thought he was dead," Gary says. "Never hear nothin' new from him anymore."

"That's 'cause he's done said it all."

"Hey, we got more important stuff to discuss," Harper insists. "Like where we goin' anyhow?"

"How 'bout Little Dippers again?" Bryson suggests.

"Nah, we followed him around yesterday," Harper says. "Never did stop anyplace good."

"Make it Two Guys and a Hose," Gary orders. "And let's hope for better luck."

Bryson reaches for his phone and sets the GPS. "Take the next right, darlin'," Tammy Wilson purrs.

"What in the world was that?" Gary asks.

Bryon waits for a gap in the stream of traffic and then exits the Hardee's parking lot. "I pay extra to have Tammy's voice giving the directions," he explains. "I'm a huge fan, so it cheers me up no end."

"She can sure sing," Gary comments. "No doubt about that."

A gasoline tanker goes by on the left. "Why don't we go after that?"

Harper asks. "It would make a bigger bang than one of them septic service trucks."

"Hazmat carriers all have transponders," Gary explains. "They are tracked by The Service using drones. The first out-of-route turn we'd take, and next thing you'd know, a swarm of black helicopters would be all over us."

"So, they don't care about a tankful of sewage?"

"Not as far as I know," Gary says. "Hey, that's it up on the left." Bryson slows, then pulls into a convenience store and parks facing the Two Guys and a Hose driveway. The three men settle back to wait. Soon, they are scrolling through their phones. "Here, look at this." Harper passes his phone to Bryson.

"Unreal," Bryson exclaims. "Messi sure lives up to the hype."

"Too bad he ain't playin' real football," Gary scoffs.

"Oh, put a cork in it," Harper says. "You don't like soccer because the Germans brought it over."

"That's reason enough, ain't it?"

Harper takes a round container out of the center console, unscrews the lid, and gets a pinch of snuff. "All Germans aren't bad," he says, with his lower lip bulging out. "Just them card-carrying Nazis." He passes the tin to Bryson, who immediately redirects it to Gary.

"Hey, looky yonder," Bryson exclaims as a septic service truck emerges from the Two Guys and a Hose driveway. He pushes a dashboard button, and the car's motors hum. As they're leaving the parking lot, an abrasive ringing noise fills the cabin. "Hey, buckle up," Bryson snaps. Sheepishly, Harper fastens his seat belt.

Ten minutes later, the septic truck turns into a trailer park outside Huntsville's city limits. Bryson parks across the street and holds a pair of binoculars to his eyes. "Don't look good," he mutters. "I count three cameras just on the main drive. No doubt more on the side streets."

The truck driver pries the lid off the first septic tank while his partner unravels the hose. "They'll be in there all mornin'," Bryson complains.

"Might as well go for coffee," Gary decides.

"And a donut?" Harper ventures.

"Suit yourself."

As it turns out, the two guys are still hosing out the trailer park that afternoon. By then, the rental car is littered with empty cardboard coffee cups, wadded-up donut wrappers, and half-full spit bottles. Harper has his seat tilted back and is dozing. "Where do I go to resign from this here Resistance?" Bryson asks. "It ain't nothin' like I 'spected it to be."

"Once you're in, the only way out is toes up," Gary grins. "Hey, it looks like they're finally leaving."

Sure enough, the septic truck is returning down the trailer park's main drive toward the highway. Bryson pokes Harper to wake him, then adjusts the steering wheel before starting the motors. He waits for the Two Guys' truck to turn and one more car to pass before falling into line. Eagerly, The Resistance members watch to see where their quarry goes next. They let out a collective groan when the septic truck stops at a Waffle House. "How can they think about eatin' after what they've been doin' half the day?" Bryson wonders.

"A man's got to eat even if he's got turdy hands," Harper jokes. "I'm goin' back to sleep."

"I've got a bad feelin' about today," Bryson complains. "It's looking to be another washout."

After nearly an hour spent dawdling over lunch, the two guys return to their truck and get back on the highway. "They're heading out of town," Gary says excitedly. "This could be good."

Bryson lags behind the septic truck as it picks up speed. He's hoping they won't figure out they're being followed. The farther they get from the city, the more variety there is in the scenery. Instead of apartment complexes, shopping malls, fast-food restaurants, and convenience stores, they begin to see rolling farmland sprouting either solar panels or spring crops. Yet, suburban sprawl is even found here, mainly in the form of single-family housing developments. When the Two Guys' brake lights finally come on, it's to turn into one of these.

Twin fieldstone pillars guard the entrance to the development, which is fronted by a wall made of the same material. Between the pillars is an unfinished guardhouse. A sign beside the highway reads, "Coming Soon, Homes from the low 400s." Bryson waits until the septic truck has disappeared around a bend in the road leading into the site. Then he cautiously follows, eyes darting first to the right and then left. "It's raw," he says hopefully, "not much infrastructure."

"Meaning no cameras," Harper exclaims.

"And no light poles to hang 'em on either," Gary smiles.

The dirt road they're on has been leveled and built up on the sides. Concrete curbs at some of the crossroads and regularly spaced manholes indicate that a drainage system is being installed. That's confirmed when Harper gets to where the septic service truck is parked. An array of concrete drainage pipes is stacked nearby.

The two guys are out of their vehicle, getting ready to pump out several port-a-johns. One of them glances over at the men in the rental car, then returns to stretching out the hose. Behind him is an office trailer, mounted on cinderblocks, bearing the logo of a construction company. "Where's all the hard hats?" Bryson wonders. Aside from the two guys, the site is deserted.

"It's past four on a Friday, and turkey season started today," Gary remarks. "Need I say more?"

Harper lowers his window and spits a stream of brown juice. "Hard to believe there ain't no security up here with all this equipment around."

"Ain't no one gonna steal a dozer that's useless lessen you got the code," Bryson says. "This is what we've been hunting for." He takes a stocking mask out of his pocket and pulls it over his face so only his eyes are showing. While Harper and Gary mask up, Bryson gets out of the car and goes to the trunk for his rifle. Then, the three Resistance members stroll over to where the two guys are kneeling with their hose. One of them looks up at the intruders. "Oh, come on, you've got to be kidding," he exclaims.

"We ain't lookin' to hurt anyone." Bryson holds the rifle with the barrel pointed toward the ground. "Just aimin' to borrow your truck for a spell."

The worker gets up and rubs his hands on his uniform pants. The name Bubba Warner is embroidered on his shirt. "You in The Resistance?"

"That's right," Harper allows.

Bubba glances at his partner. "Jack, these boys mean business," he says. "Best give them the keys."

"Left 'em in the ignition." Jack stares wide-eyed at Bryson. "Didn't expect no trouble up here."

Harper steps up onto the passenger side of the septic truck and peers inside. Sure enough, the vehicle has an old-fashioned ignition. The keys are dangling from it. "Come on," he says to Gary.

"Hey, how are we supposed to get back to the shop?" Bubba asks.

"I'll take you," Bryson says. "After we're done."

"And when will that be?" Jack demands.

"You'll be the first to know." Bryson swivels so that the barrel of his rifle is now pointing at Jack's sewage-splattered boots.

"All right, all right. Take it easy, man!"

The breeze picks up, and there's a rumble of thunder as Bryson watches the septic tanker drive off. He glances at the sky and sees an angry cloud bank approaching. "Is that office open?" he asks.

"Who knows?" Jack snaps.

Keeping the septic crew in view, Bryson backs toward the office trailer and up the stairs. He tries the door, but it's locked. Rain begins pelting down. "Let us inside the car," Bubba shouts.

Instead of answering, Bryson steps back and raises the rifle. He waits until another peal of thunder sounds, then pulls the trigger. "Found the key," he announces and kicks what's left of the office door open. Hastily, he reloads.

After shepherding the two septic workers into the trailer and seeing them uncomfortably seated on metal folding chairs, Bryson settles his butt onto a desk. "Put your phones over there." He uses the rifle to point at a side table.

Bubba immediately does as ordered. However, Jack doesn't move. "Mine's gone," he says. "It was in the truck."

"Oh really?" Bryson smiles. He goes to the table and picks up Bubba's phone. Returning to the desk, he uses his thumb to find the recent calls. Near the top is one to a Jack Dougherty. Bryson calls that number, and moments later, a ringtone emanates from Jack's pocket. Bryson allows it to ring until Jack takes the phone out and dismisses the call. "Seems like you misremembered," Bryson says, "'bout your phone being in the truck."

Frowning, Jack places his phone on the table.

"We're gonna be here awhile; might as well get to know one another," Bryson suggests. "How long have you two been in the septic business?"

Bubba glances at his partner. "Must be nigh on ten years now."

"Don't seem near that long," Jack comments.

"Guess it's true then."

"What?"

"Time flies when you're having a good time."

Jack guffaws. "Yeah, right."

"How about you?" Bubba asks Bryson. "Do you have a job other than stealing trucks?"

"I was a farmer once, but the government stole my land."

"That ain't no excuse for what you're doing now," Jack insists, "terrorizing innocent folks like us."

Bryson shrugs. "Can't make an omelet without breaking some eggs."

It gets quiet in the trailer as the two septic workers ponder the meaning of Bryson's words. Rain drums on the metal roof. "I need a smoke," Bubba says. "Mind if I light up?"

"Go right ahead." Holding the rifle, Bryson goes to stand by the open door. *Nothin' like second-hand smoke to make you appreciate fresh air*, he thinks.

Several miles away, Harper and Gary are also appreciating any unpolluted air that comes their way. Anything's better than the noxious odors emanating from the sewage they're dumping onto Harper's cornfield. "If this don't make for a bumper crop, nothin' will," Harper says through the bandana he has tied over his nose and mouth.

"I'm fixin' to blow lunch," Gary complains.

"Can't say I didn't warn you 'bout eating so many donuts."

The flood of gray water coursing out of the truck tank slows to a trickle and then stops. "Whew, let's get away from here." Gary climbs into the passenger seat, leaving Harper to close the valve. Once that's done, they take the truck to Harper's barn. "Where did you stash the nitrogen fertilizer?" Gary asks.

"Come on, I'll show you."

Gary follows Harper inside his barn. A wall of hay bales is stacked at the far end. "Behind those," Harper points.

"Oh no," Gary exclaims.

"Yep, we'll have to move them to the other side." Harper pulls a dusty trailer out of an unused horse stall, then goes into another stall and fires up his ATV. He hooks the trailer onto the four-wheeler and drives to one end of the hay bale stash as Gary watches. "Hey, wake up. You need to get on top and help me lower them onto the trailer."

Gary snaps out of his daze and begins climbing. Once he's in position, the two men wrestle one of the bales onto the trailer. Harper moves it across the barn's dirt floor. "One down and nineteen more to go."

"Then let's get 'er done." Gary moves to the next bale. Now that he and Harper are in sync, it doesn't take long until they've moved enough hay to see some fifty-pound fertilizer sacks stacked against the barn wall. An hour later, they've finished moving the bales. Harper puts the trailer back and then parks the ATV. "I'm gonna back the truck in," he says. "It'll make loading it easier."

Gary goes over to read the label on one of the bags. "How do you know this is the right kind for a bomb?"

"Bryson got the recipe off the dark web," Harper replies. "And Control verified it. That's who gave us the other stuff."

"You mean the detonator."

"And timer."

"Oh, right."

Harper opens one of the barn doors while Gary gets the other. Outside, darkness has fallen, and the thunderstorms have moved off. Here and there, stars can be seen through the low-hanging clouds. "Looks like the rain missed us," Harper says. He strolls over to the septic truck and gets inside. Promptly, the overused motor sputters, coughs, and catches on. Harper backs into his barn and then rejoins his partner.

"This ain't gonna be easy," Gary complains, eyes fixed on the wall-high stack of fertilizer.

"True, but we got all night." Harper climbs on top of the tank and opens the hatch. Meanwhile, Gary shoulders a fertilizer sack. He steps onto the truck's running board and pushes his load far enough up for his partner to grasp it. Harper uses his knife to slit the sack open and dumps the contents into the tank. "Next," he says, tossing the empty aside.

Before long, Gary is panting, and his shirt is soaked with sweat. "Let's switch," he suggests.

"Get me two more," Harper insists. "Then we can trade places."

"Deal," Gary grunts as he hauls another sack to the truck. "Just one more," he mutters.

The two men exchange places several more times over the next couple of hours until the last fertilizer disappears into the septic truck's tank. Afterward, Harper bends to lift a floorboard and reaches for the shoebox hidden below. "This is what will make it go bang."

Carrying the box, Harper climbs into the truck's driver's seat and starts the motor. Once Gary is aboard, Harper drives a short distance to a fueling station, where he keeps the diesel for his farm equipment. "How do you know how much to put in?" Gary asks.

"It's in the recipe." Harper climbs down from the cab and unlocks the pump. "Get on top. I'll pass the nozzle to you."

"Isn't it your turn to be on top?"

"I have to watch the meter."

"Oh, right."

It's tedious listening to the ancient electric pump chug while the dial on the fuel meter slowly turns. But finally, the diesel fuel to fertilizer ratio meets Bryson's recipe. Harper shuts the pump off. He gets his box of goodies and joins Gary on top of the tank. First, he buries a blasting cap in the dark, gooey mixture they've created. Then, he connects the blasting cap to a timer. "It'll either blow sky-high or fizzle out," Harper says. "One or the other."

Gary replaces the hatch cover on the tank and tightens the clamp. "How much time do we have?"

"One hour and counting."

"Then let's go."

With Harper behind the wheel, the two Resistance members head for their target. It's an electric substation in a rural area south of the city. "Text Bryson and tell him we're thirty minutes out," Harper says.

"Copy," Gary replies.

When Gary's message comes through, Bryson is busy opening the back of Bubba's phone. Before checking the message, Bryson removes Bubba's battery and puts it on the desk next to Jack's. The two septic service workers remain asleep on the floor. One is lightly snoring.

Bryson clicks the back of Bubba's phone into place, then reads Gary's message. Immediately, he grasps the rifle and slides off the desk. He pockets the two batteries, looks around, and then goes out.

Adrenaline is one of God's miracles, Bryson thinks as he pilots the rental car back down the dirt road. *Without it, I'd have trouble keeping my eyes open at this hour of the mornin'*. He turns onto the main highway and pushes down the accelerator. A glance at the speedometer shows 64 miles an hour. *Only nine over*, Bryson thinks and sets the cruise. *The cops won't pull me for that*. He chews his lip anxiously as time drags past. The road is empty, other than an occasional eighteen-wheeler. Bryson checks the odometer every few minutes, willing it to turn faster. Finally, Tammy speaks up, "Slow down, baby, you've got to turn left at the next crossroad."

Bryson does as he's told. This puts him on a rough-and-tumble farm road. He wonders how long it's been since they paved it. Ahead, a doe nibbles grass on the roadside. Bryson slows, ready to slam on the brakes. But the deer only gazes at him placidly, ruminating. Around the next curve, Bryson sees Harper and Gary in his headlights. They're standing in the middle of the road. The septic truck is behind them, parked on a dirt driveway that leads to a cluster of lights a short distance away.

Bryson stops next to his co-conspirators and lowers the window. "You boys out stargazing?"

"Had to do something while we waited for you," Harper replies.

"Sorry, the barista was slow tonight."

"You wouldn't know a latte if it bit you in the butt."

"Hey, I don't want to spoil your fun, but that truck is fixin' to blow," Gary says.

"'Spect we better get on with it then," Harper concedes.

"Everyone understand the plan?"

"You call it a plan? I call it crash and dash."

"Pretty much covers it," Gary admits.

"OK, I'm on it." Harper turns toward the truck. "Don't leave without me, you heah?"

"Wouldn't think of it." Gary waits until Harper's behind the wheel of the septic tanker, then climbs into the back seat of the rental. "Follow at a distance," he tells Bryson.

The substation is less than half a mile down the weed-infested driveway. Harper gets the tanker up to speed as he approaches the chain-link fence surrounding it. Inside, the transformer and a looming transmission tower are lit up like a sci-fi movie set. The faster Harper goes, the less control he has over the jouncing, bouncing tanker. He grips the wheel and presses the accelerator to the floor. *Just hope I don't get electrocuted* is his last thought before impact.

Time slows to a crawl for Harper. The next couple of seconds seem endless. First, the airbag explodes, knocking him back in the seat and blinding him. When he tries to escape the whiteness, he finds himself immobilized by the locked seat belt. All the while, he's being rocked worse than the best roller coaster he ever rode.

It's distinctly anticlimactic when all motion abruptly ceases. The airbag shrinks, and the seat belt releases its grip. Harper sees that the front bumper of the septic tanker has pushed the chain-link fence up to the concrete foundation of the transformer. Shakily, he tries to open the door, but it won't budge. Fighting against a rising tide of panic, Harper undoes the seat belt. He's getting ready to slide over to the passenger side and try that door when Gary appears at his window.

Standing on the running board, Gary waits for Harper to lower the glass. "We got to go."

"I can't get the door open."

Gary reaches inside to unlock the door. "Come on."

With all three Resistance members now in the rental car, Bryson heads back up the dirt road. When they reach the highway, he turns toward Huntsville. A few minutes later, as they approach the city, The Resistance members see the lights of The Space Flight Complex flicker and then go out. A long moment later, they hear the *BOOM* echoing in the foothills. "Appears what I learned back in high school is correct," Bryson comments.

"What's that?" Gary asks.

"Electricity travels faster than sound."

"Well, live and learn."

The headlamps of an oncoming car appear in the distance. Bryson looks for a place to turn off. However, trees grow right up to the roadside. "Dang," he mutters. "Just have to brazen it out."

"Go the speed limit and no faster," Gary instructs.

The men all know that any vehicle out in a rural area at this time of night will raise the Security Service's suspicion. Sure enough, blue lights begin dancing in the grill of the patrol car as the two vehicles pass, going in opposite directions. Looking in the mirror, Bryson is almost blinded by strident red brake lights. He slams on his own brakes. As the rental car comes to a stop, he grabs the rifle.

By the time the patrol car completes its one-eighty, Bryson is out of the rental and has dropped into the prone position. He aims at the approaching vehicle's front driver's side tire and is pleased moments later when it explodes. The driver reacts poorly and loses control of his cruiser. Screeching tires, metal crunching into trees, and tinkling glass break the forest silence. Bryson quickly rises and returns to the rental car. After stowing the rifle, he gets back behind the wheel.

"Shouldn't we go check on them?" Harper wonders aloud. He's still dazed.

"There's no time." Bryson floors it, and the rental leaps ahead. "We're fixin' to have our hands full."

"For sure," Gary concurs. He grabs a handhold as the car rockets through the gears.

Trees flash by on either side as Bryson forgets all about the speed limit. "I'm making for the airport," he says. "We can ditch the car and then melt into the crowd inside the terminal."

"Sounds like a plan," Harper agrees. The faint sound The Resistance members have been hearing gets louder until it's a full-throated roar. That's the only warning they get before a hail of bullets cuts across the car's trunk, demolishing the rear window. In the back seat, Gary reflexively brushes broken glass off the back of his neck.

"Where did it go?" Bryson asks.

Gary half-turns, then cranes his neck. The sky is lightening, but he still can't see anything. So, he twists fully around and, kneeling on the back seat, sticks his head out of the hole where the window used to be. A black helicopter is hovering above. As Gary watches, it peels off into a shallow turn to come up behind them again. "We got a whirlybird on our tail," he hollers.

"Then get the rifle," Bryson instructs.

The gun is with Harper, who has been reloading it. Now, he passes it back. As the helicopter comes around, Gary pokes the barrel out of the back and hopes for a shot. However, the pilot now flies parallel to the car, allowing his door gunner to try his luck. Puffs of white smoke emerge from the machine gun barrel as bullets ricochet off the car's hood. "He's trying to disable the engine," Harper says.

"Not much chance of that," Bryson scoffs. "This baby has two motors. If one goes out, the other one will still provide plenty of power."

Gary turns back around in his seat and lowers the side window. He aims the rifle at their tormentor and squeezes off a round. "Looks like I scared him off," Gary brags when the chopper increases its distance.

Up ahead, a country store's LED sign advertises low gas prices, boiled peanuts, and cold beer. "In two miles, turn right at the light, sugar," Tammy says.

But the Security Service has other ideas. A kamikaze drone streaks up the road behind the car. It flies through the back window and explodes. Instantly, the vehicle becomes a cartwheeling mass of burning wreckage. The helicopter pilot glances at his door gunner. "That's how it's done," he says over the intercom. Then, he unmutes his radio mic. "Topper One, this is Mongoose, over."

"Come in, Mongoose."

"Problem eliminated, Topper One. You can send a clean-up crew to grid coordinates Charley Foxtrot 145710."

"Roger that, Mongoose. Topper One out."

"Over and out."

CHAPTER SIX

ORGAN DEATH

T he burlap robe Rebecca has fashioned from empty feed bags makes her skin itch. Still, she's happy to have something to wear. Looking around in the faint light of morning, she sees other members of Lot 148 also sporting the latest fashion. *Hope I don't look as bad as they do,* Rebecca says to herself. But her wish is in vain. Like the others, she's lost weight over the last week. Her dirty hair hangs limp, and her eyes glitter with fever.

"It's from drinking the water," Jesse explains.

Micki shambles up to the group. "I can't stop going to the bathroom," she moans.

"Me either," Alice says. "I'm having one cramp after another."

"Hey, good morning," Rebecca says to Diane, who has just come up the hill from the creek.

"What's good about it?" Diane asks. "It was all I could do to get up for breakfast."

Rebecca puts her arm around her roommate. "We must eat to keep up our strength."

"Why?" Diane asks. The bruises on her face have turned from black and blue to purple and yellow.

"So, where is the food?" Micki wonders. "It's past time."

"Maybe there won't be any today," Jesse says. "Could be they'll come for us now."

"That's what you've been saying all week," Rebecca complains.

Jesse glances at the line of chimneys in the distance, all belching smoke. "Obviously, they've been busy."

"Tell me something," Rebecca asks. "How come you know everything?"

"Used to work on the line—central processing."

"How did you end up here with us?"

Jesse gazes up at the sky. Tears flow down her cheeks, creating muddy streaks. "Couldn't take it anymore," she moans. "So I asked to be processed."

"You're going with us?" Rebecca asks.

"Yep, beats watching lines of people walk into the building all day, every day, and killing them."

"That's what trustees do?"

"That's right, and then we help with dismemberment." Jesse wipes her eyes with her filthy sleeve.

"Ugh!"

Diane turns toward the creek. "If they aren't gonna feed us, I'm going back to my hole."

"Oh, come on, stay and talk with us awhile," Rebecca pleads. "Makes the time go by faster."

"Can't eat conversation," Alice mutters. "I've got to lie down before I faint."

Diane and Alice start to leave, but then they all hear a truck arrive. It's a livestock carrier. An SS guard climbs down from the passenger seat and opens the gate so the driver can back the trailer into the corral. "Oh my," Micki exclaims.

"If you want to be processed, get on over here," the guard hollers. "I promise you, it's painless."

There's a burst of activity by the creek as women come out of the caves and begin wading across. Most are clad in burlap bags, although some are still naked. Their filthy skin is covered with rashes, sores, and bug bites.

"You'll have to leave them rags here for the clean-up crew," the guard tells the prisoners. She waits while they strip, then lowers a ramp. The women begin streaming up it into the carrier.

"Is it true about being painless?" Rebecca asks Jesse as they wait to climb aboard.

"Yes, that part is true."

Once all the prisoners are on the carrier, the guards raise the ramp. Soon, the truck is on the way to Central Processing. Rebecca looks at the sky through the grating. Billowing clouds sail across it like tall ships. It seems unreal to be going to her death on such a beautiful day. *Heavenly Father*, she silently prays. *How can you allow so much evil in this world?* Rebecca has thought about this question for a long time. The only answer she's been able to come up with is to blame the devil. *The forces of darkness in the universe must be just as powerful as God*, she thinks. *It's up to each of us to choose which side we're on.*

The line of trucks outside Central Processing is short today. That's a blessing because June in South Georgia is like the dog days of summer anywhere else. Nothing prevents the sun from broiling down through the wire mesh truck top. Some of the women hold up their hands to gain a brief respite. "I'll be glad when this hell is over," Diane says.

"Me too," Micki pants. "Anything's better."

"If you had told me when I was young that I'd be happy to go when my time of death rolled around, I would have called you crazy."

"That's what they depend on," Jesse explains. "By making death preferable to life, they keep us docile, and processing runs efficiently."

An empty truck leaves one of the loading docks. Now it's Lot 148's turn. Their truck lurches forward, moves a hundred yards or so, and then the driver backs into the vacant dock. The bedraggled women in the trailer breathe a sigh of relief, glad to be in the shade of the warehouse-like processing building. The sound of children wailing comes from the trailer next door. Rebecca and Micki go to that side and peer through the mesh. "For pity's sake," Micki exclaims. "Some of those children don't look over five years old."

"Just when you think it can't get any worse, it does," Cindy moans. "There's got to be a special place in hell for a government that would put kids through this." Slowly, the children are shepherded off the carrier by orange-jumpsuit-clad trustees. Once it's empty, the truck leaves. Shortly afterward, another cattle carrier backs in. This one's loaded with elderly Blacks.

It's afternoon when the ramp at the rear of Lot 148's trailer is lowered. "Let's stick together," Rebecca tells her friends as the women file out.

"Sure," Alice replies.

"I'm so sorry I got you into this mess."

"Oh, forget it. We should have all been working with you on that tunnel."

Micki and Cindy come up from behind. "It was a beautiful tunnel," Micki says wistfully.

"An architectural wonder," Cindy smiles.

There's a holdup at the entrance to the facility while trustees straighten the line. Then, a woman wearing a black SS uniform comes out of the building. She holds a bullhorn to her lips and shouts, "If you are ready to be processed, turn left when you enter the building. Those who want to live and work here as trustees must go to the right. You will be given a physical exam to determine suitability."

"What do you think?" Alice asks.

"I don't recommend it," Jesse declares.

"Then I'll pass," Cindy says.

"Me too," Rebecca agrees. "Stick a fork in me. I'm done."

"Let's say the Lord's Prayer," Diane suggests. The friends reach for each other's hands and bow their heads.

A few minutes later, the double doors at the entrance are pushed open. One by one, members of Lot 148 are allowed to enter. All of them go to the left. While Rebecca waits in line to be processed, she looks around. They're now in a cavernous hall big enough to hold a jumbo passenger jet. It's like a factory with several assembly lines—only in this case, they're disassembly lines.

Diane is the first member of Lot 148 to be processed. She follows instructions and lies face-up on a conveyor belt. A white-coated medic quickly finds a vein in her arm and starts an intravenous anesthetic infusion. The process takes less than a minute. As Diane's eyes roll back in her head, the conveyor jerkily moves her deeper into the building. "Is she dead now?" Rebecca asks Jesse.

"No, Diane's comatose. They want her heart to keep pumping oxygenated blood throughout her body until they're finished. She'll be taken to the ophthalmology station now to have her corneas removed. That's where I used to work. Had to disinfect the surgical area, then receive tissue from the surgeon, place it in a vial, and put it in the cooler."

The line moves steadily forward as more inmates take their turn on the conveyor. "So, when does death occur?" Rebecca asks.

"Not until they've taken all transplantable items," Jesse replies. "The last is the heart. At that point, the donor is brain-dead. They drain the blood, and what's left goes into an oven."

"Bye, y'all," Micki says over her shoulder as a trustee leads her to the conveyor. "Proud to have known you."

An SS guard comes over and scowls. "Pipe down," he orders.

Jesse starts to say something but thinks better of it. She's now at the head of the line. An orange-jumpsuit-clad trustee comes over and takes her arm. "You're the wisest one among us," the trustee whispers.

"We can only do what we must," Jesse replies. "Don't know where I'm going, but it's got to be better than here."

Alice and Rebecca are all that's left of Lot 148. A trustee comes for Rebecca, but Alice cuts in front. "Please," she begs. "I don't want to be left alone."

"Sure." Rebecca doesn't want to be the last either, but can see how distraught her friend is. "Remember what Jesus said to the thief who was crucified beside him," Rebecca whispers. "'Today you will be with me in paradise.'"

Alice crosses herself. "Thanks, I feel calm now, almost peaceful."

The trustee takes Alice's arm and leads her away. All of Rebecca's friends are gone. Alone, she is prey to the cold grip of fear. *What if there is no God?* she wonders. *What if there's nothing ahead for me but the pitiless void of oblivion?* A trustee approaches and then pauses to cast a weary glance at a wall clock. She looks tired. "Tough day, huh?" Rebecca empathizes. She's back to being herself again, more concerned about others than her own plight. Moments later, as the needle is inserted, Rebecca asks Jesus to forgive her sins.

Prayers are also being said in Johnston High School's gym this day, where the senior class has assembled for the last time. The students bow their heads for the invocation and then settle back in their chairs to hear speeches. As valedictorian, Melanie is first up. "Greetings,

Rebels!" she calls from the rostrum. A chorus of whoops from students and parents alike greets this opening. "I stand before you today with more questions than answers," Melanie says into the microphone. "More perspiration than inspiration. What makes me sweat, you wonder? The answer is my concern about the future. As I look into my crystal ball for hints, what I see is stagnation. We graduates must deal with an economic system that creates jobs for slaves and prosperity for agribusiness investors while relegating most others to social welfare. Meanwhile, we fall farther behind the rest of the world in education, technology, manufacturing, and infrastructure. As international pariahs, there is no escape. Our citizens are not welcome anywhere and cannot obtain exit visas from the government, even if there was some place to go. You may say we should relax and be happy with the guaranteed minimum income, but only the hardest hearts can witness how our fellow human beings are treated and be content. Slaves work from dawn to dusk under the broiling sun, tending to cash crops that only bring money to the few. When slaves get old, they disappear, and everyone knows what that means. Everyone knows what it means when kids with learning disabilities vanish, when gay or trans people are snatched up, never to be seen again."

Melanie pauses for breath. At that moment, Principal Dunsford steps to the podium and shoves her aside. "Honored guests," he says into the microphone, "students and faculty. Please be assured that those comments were not included in the speech that the school administration approved."

Someone in the student section boos. More students let loose with shrill whistles and hoots. A girl in the front row stands. "Let her speak!" she shouts. Other students leap to their feet. They clap their hands rhythmically and chant: "Let her speak, let her speak."

Dunsford turns and picks up several folders from the table behind him. "These are your diplomas," he shouts. "Do you want them or not?"

Slowly, the tempest dies down as the students realize that all their hard work might go into the trash. "Get her off the stage," Dunsford orders one of the soldiers guarding the podium.

The gym quiets, and Melanie is led back to her seat. As the soldier walks away, the girl next to Melanie nudges her. "Well done," she murmurs. Melanie smiles, and they bump fists.

As Dunsford launches into a laudatory introduction of the next speaker, the dignitaries in attendance again relax. They applaud enthusiastically as the Dean of Calhoun Community College steps forward. She starts strong, but soon, her sing-song diction and oft-repeated views about the value of STEM majors have the audience fidgeting. Students furtively feel for their phones through their graduation gowns. But knowing Mrs. Lansdale has eagle eyes, they reluctantly leave them where they are. It's agony to sit without a screen to gaze at, but finally, the commencement address is over. Following Mrs. Lansdale's hand signals, the students queue up for the last act of their high school career. For the guests, the awarding of diplomas is a tedious process. The students, however, come to realize that every step forward is bringing them closer to a point of no return. Belatedly, they try to hang on to each moment. This makes the time go by faster. All too soon, they each receive their walking papers.

Outside the gym, students form groups and cling together like survivors of a catastrophe who are elated to still be alive. It's hard to tell if their happiness is based on giddiness about the future or hope that things haven't really changed. The moment is shattered when parents and friends burst out of the gym's double doors, searching for graduates to congratulate. Among them is Mayor Montgomery, who strides up to his daughter and, ignoring her classmates, gets into her face. "Where did you learn all that nonsense you spouted today?" he seethes. "Who cares about a bunch of gays, retards, and used-up slaves?"

"I do," Melanie declares. "They're human beings, just like us."

Inspiration strikes as the mayor sees Melanie's friends all nod their heads. "I know where you're getting this garbage," he scowls. "It's those online chat rooms you and these other delinquents hang out in." The mayor holds out his hand insistently. "I'm going to end this," he says. "Give me your phone."

"I left it in my locker," Melanie lies.

Montgomery angrily grabs Melanie's arm and jerks her toward the school.

"Ouch, you're hurting me," she cries and tries to pull away.

Nearby conversations cease as curious faces turn to see Huntsville's mayor battling his daughter. Realizing the optic isn't good, Montgomery releases Melanie's arm. "I'll sort you out at home later," he hisses.

As Montgomery stalks off, Melanie's friends relax. "He should be canceled," one says.

"I'm on it." Melanie hitches up her graduation gown and pulls out her phone. She rapidly taps on the screen, then looks up with a smile. "Deleted."

"Great idea," another cheerleader says. "My mom has got to go." She and several more students reach for their phones to follow Melanie's example. However, Ryan remains motionless. He loves his father and would never ghost him. He'd give anything to be in contact with Bryson, but every time Ryan tries to call him, he gets a message saying the number is out of service.

Now that the ruckus caused by Mayor Montgomery is over and the excitement of graduation is wearing off, Melanie tunes back into her boyfriend's distress. "Still no word, huh?" she murmurs, taking Ryan's hand.

He looks down and shakes his head. "He's never been away this long."

"Have you filed a missing person report?"

"No, he told me never to do that, not under any circumstances."

The sad faces around Ryan are in sharp contrast to the happy expressions prevailing outside the gym. Not everyone knows what's going on with Ryan. One of their classmates glances up from her phone. "Everyone's going to Jaybird's," she says, "to celebrate."

"I could use a blue raspberry slush," a soccer player exclaims. He glances toward Ryan. "You comin'?"

Ryan dredges up a smile for his friend. "You guys go ahead. Maybe I'll stop by later." With relief, several kids leave the group and head for the parking lot to find their cars. That only leaves Ryan, Liam, Gerry, and Melanie.

"I think the Security Service probably picked Dad up," Ryan whispers.

"Why?" Liam asks.

Ryan looks around nervously. The nearest light pole with a camera is on the other side of the field. Nevertheless, he covers his mouth to talk. "Dad's in The Resistance. Last time I saw him, he said he was going out on a job."

"Bryson's in The Resistance?" Melanie asks. "And you never told me?"

Ryan meets Melanie's accusing stare. "I was sworn to secrecy, sorry." He tries for a kiss, but Melanie turns her face away. "Honestly, it was just as much for your protection as anything." Ryan tries again. This time, Melanie relents.

"The Service doesn't play around," Liam says. "If they have your dad, it's not good."

"I got a registered letter from them yesterday," Gerry says. "Just looking at the return address made me gulp."

"What did it say?" Liam asks.

"They want me to come in for an interview. I'm supposed to bring toiletries and a change of clothes."

"So, what got you onto their radar?" Melanie asks.

"I'm guessing my mother turned me in."

"What for?"

"I told her I'm tired of being treated like a girl."

"That couldn't have gone over well."

"And asked if I could change my legal name from Geraldine to Gerald."

"Oh my, Gerry," Liam moans. "Looks like we've got a problem."

"More than one," Ryan elaborates. He looks around nervously. "We should go somewhere to talk."

"Yeah, I need a drink," Liam declares. "And I don't mean blue raspberry slush."

Ryan shrugs. "There's plenty to drink at my house."

"Then let's go," Gerry agrees. "But I want y'all to stop referring to me as she."

"Better make mine a double," Liam winks. "Can I have a ride?"

At Ryan's house, the four friends get comfortable on the worn furniture in the living room. Melanie helps Ryan distribute adult beverages, and soon, each graduate holds a cold beer. The athletes aren't used to the bitter taste, so only a few tentative sips are taken. "Did you tell Bryson about our plan with Mish?" Liam asks Ryan.

"Why do you ask?"

"If The Service has him, he'll be tortured."

"He'd never talk. Besides, I just gave him the general idea, no details."

"All right."

"What's all this about Mish?" Gerry asks.

Liam looks first at Ryan and then at Melanie. When neither objects, he turns back to Gerry. "We're going to help her escape from von Kluck and get to the North."

"Wow," Gerry exclaims, "that's wild!"

"We've been hoarding canned food, rice, cereal, and stuff like that for weeks," Melanie elaborates.

"Aren't you afraid of getting caught? Fugitives are sent straight to Andersonville."

"I know. But Mish needs help, and we have nothing to look forward to here."

Liam turns toward Gerry. "You don't either. Once The Service gets hold of someone, they never let go."

Gerry wrinkles his brow in thought. "Guess I'd better go with y'all," he says after a pause.

Ryan finds some music on his phone and then goes across the room to switch on a Bluetooth speaker. As the room fills with sound, he regains his seat. "Let's review the plan," he suggests.

Later, on her way back from Ryan's, Melanie stops at a dollar store to pick up a prepaid phone. Sitting in the car, she enters her most important contacts. Afterward, she hides the device in her bookbag. When Melanie gets home, she's not surprised to find her father waiting. He approaches with his hand out, and she nonchalantly tosses him the phone her parents gave her. It lands in Montgomery's outstretched palm, but he bobbles it. Only quick reflexes prevent it from hitting the floor. "I'll keep this until you've learned your lesson," he scowls.

"What lesson?" Melanie asks, then bites her lip. *Why do you always have to push his buttons?* she asks herself.

Montgomery steps closer. "Start by learning who earns the money around here. I pay for your upkeep and can cut you off anytime."

As her father talks, the air fills with a sweet, alcoholic mist. *How many has he had?* Melanie wonders.

"Yoohoo, dinner is served," Dorothy Montgomery calls.

Melanie follows her father into the dining room. She's surprised to see a new slave standing behind her chair. "What's your name?"

"I'm Dwight, Miss."

"Where's James?"

At the head of the table, Montgomery smirks. "James retired. From now on, Dwight will fill in for him."

"You bastard," Melanie shrieks. "You did it."

Montgomery pounds his fist on the table, rattling the dishes. "That's right, I did, and now maybe you'll understand that I'm the boss around here."

In a blind rage, Melanie looks for something to throw at her father. She seizes her water glass, but as she's taking her arm back, she notices Versa in the kitchen doorway. The cook is holding out her hand like a traffic cop. With her eyes she's begging Melanie not to do it. Slowly, Melanie calms. She sips the water and then glances at her mother, who seems frozen with shock. "May I be excused, Mom?" Melanie asks. "I'm getting a migraine."

"By all means," Montgomery interjects. "Go to your room."

Once outside the dining room, Melanie circles back to the kitchen, where Versa is busily icing a cake. She turns from the stove when Melanie enters. "Thanks for stopping me just now," Melanie says.

"Girl, there isn't any use in makin' things worse. The labor camps are full of young people like you. Parents turn their children in as abolitionists, and that's it."

"Dad wouldn't do that."

"Wanna bet? I heard all about the speech you made at school today. How long do you think it'll be 'til your father has The Service breathing down his neck about you? If it comes to a choice between his job as mayor and you, best believe it'll be you who gets thrown under the bus."

Melanie pauses to think over what Versa's saying. "Guess you're right," she finally admits. "And that ties in with what I came to tell you."

"What's that?"

"Don't tell anyone, but I'm leaving. Me and some friends. We're going to rescue Mish from von Kluck, and then all of us will escape from the Confederacy."

Reflexively, Versa places a hand over her heart. She uses her other hand to reach behind her for a kitchen chair. "That's crazy," she gasps. "You'll all be killed."

Melanie pulls up a chair next to where Versa is seated. "We have a plan," she says. "It's going to work."

"You're only a child," Versa moans. "What do you know?"

"I know that Mish is in danger and that me and my friends have no future here. We're getting out. We'll send word to you when we reach the United States."

Versa reads the steely determination in Melanie's eyes. She realizes there is no point in arguing. Melanie is like a fledging ready to spread her wings. "Go then," Versa says. "With my blessing." She goes back to the stove and hastily dips a spatula into the icing bowl. "Now, if I don't get this cake ready for dessert, it'll be me who's in trouble."

Upstairs, Melanie throws herself onto her bed. It's been a long, emotionally exhausting day. Her eyes fill with tears as she thinks of James and about leaving Versa and the life she's known. Not surprisingly, Melanie cries herself to sleep. Sometime during the night, she gets up to turn out the light and changes into a nightgown. Then she goes back to bed.

By habit, Melanie reaches for her phone first thing in the morning. At first, she's baffled to be looking at an Android screen, but then she remembers what happened to her good phone. *Omigod*, she thinks. *Ryan and them still have my old number. What if they send an incriminating text, and Dad gets it?* Hastily, Melanie texts her friends, asking them to update their contacts with her new number. As confirmations come in from Gerry and Liam, she starts to relax. But her anxiety rises as the minutes pass with no response from Ryan.

Ryan can't reply to Melanie because he's asleep, dreaming of the big bass he's always wanted to catch. He sees the fish's unmistakable shape in the clear water and casts his lure. The sky above is cloudless; however, a peal of thunder rumbles through his dream. Foggily, Ryan realizes it's not thunder he's hearing, that he's home in bed, and someone's pounding on the front door. He stumbles to his feet and peers through a window to see a nondescript black car in the driveway. A burst of adrenaline burns the last of Ryan's morning fog away. He dons a pair of soccer shorts, throws on a T-shirt, and goes barefoot to the door.

"I'm Lieutenant Ferguson, Security Service," a husky man announces once Ryan wrests the door open. "This is my partner, Agent Boyce."

"Good morning."

"Are you Bryson Walters?"

"His son," Ryan answers.

The other SS agent pushes past Ryan into the house. He looks down his nose at the shabby interior. "So, where's Mr. Walters at?"

"I don't know," Ryan shrugs.

"You're his son, but can't say where he is?" Boyce sneers.

"Or won't," Ferguson says menacingly.

Ryan improvises. "He's probably sleeping it off in a ditch somewhere."

"What makes you say that?"

"He's a binge drinker. Doesn't touch a drop for months at a time, then something sets him off, and he goes on a bender." Ryan points to the beer cans littering the living room and the almost empty bottle of whiskey on the table.

"Then I guess you don't mind if we have a look around?"

"Go right ahead." Faking nonchalance, Ryan goes into the kitchen and gets a cereal box from the cupboard. He hears the back door slam as the other agent goes to look outside. Meanwhile, Ferguson is opening and closing closet doors and searching under beds.

After a while, the two agents return to the kitchen to find Ryan slicing a banana for his cereal. "Don't eat anything until I'm done with you," Ferguson orders. He unwraps a sealed box, opens it, then puts on rubber gloves. Removing a glass tube from the box, Ferguson places it on the counter next to Ryan's cereal bowl. "Spit in it," he orders.

"What for?"

Ferguson slams his hand on the kitchen counter. "We can do this here or downtown."

"I know my rights," Ryan says bravely. "You need a warrant."

"All right, we'll get a warrant," Ferguson growls. "And put you in a holding cell while it's processed."

Ryan gulps. He knows that few who go into SS headquarters ever come out. He goes to the refrigerator for milk. "Tell me what you need this for, and maybe I'll waive my rights," he says over his shoulder.

Ferguson looks at his partner, who shrugs carelessly. "Oh, all right," Ferguson sighs. "Your father was listed as the driver for a rental car that was picked up at the airport last week. It was supposed to be returned on Saturday but is still missing. Meanwhile, there was a fiery one-car crash just south of the city. Parts of the vehicle were scattered along the road, and the vehicle identification numbers were obliterated. Likewise, the remains of the occupants are unidentifiable. We suspect whoever was in the car had something to do with blowing up a power station. We have recovered tissue from the wreckage. Now, I need your DNA to help me determine if anyone related to you was in that car, specifically Bryson Walters. If so, I'll know the wreck is the missing rental car, and Mr. Walters was one of the terrorists. If not, we can look elsewhere."

"OK, now I get it," Ryan says. "I'll be happy to cooperate and prove that my father is no terrorist. It doesn't surprise me if he and a few of his buddies rented a car to go drinking instead of cramming into one of their work trucks. They're probably in Panama City right now, passed out drunk. Guess that's why the rental car hasn't been returned." Ryan picks up the glass tube and spits into it.

"Again," Ferguson demands.

Once Ryan has expectorated to the agent's satisfaction, Ferguson seals the tube and then puts it back into the box. He tosses his gloves into the sink and looks at Ryan. "Don't go anywhere," he orders. "If this links to any of the samples we collected from the wreck, it means Mr. Walters was in The Resistance. That makes all his associates and family members persons of interest." Ferguson grins at Ryan mirthlessly. Then he and his partner go out the door.

From the kitchen window, Ryan watches the black car become smaller the farther down the dirt drive it goes. Even after the last of the red dust kicked up by the vehicle has blown away, Ryan remains frozen. *Maybe if I just stand here and never move, time will stop, and Dad will still be alive*, he thinks. However, the awful truth cannot be suppressed. *He's dead*, Ryan concedes. He thinks back to their last conversation about how his parents didn't believe in playing it safe in the face of injustice. Ryan turns away from the window and picks up the whiskey bottle. "Here's to you, Dad," he toasts. "You died bravely, just as you lived. May I follow in your footsteps." Ryan tilts the bottle back. His eyes water as the liquor scalds his esophagus. Then he turns and hurls the empty at the far wall. It hits with a satisfying thud and shatters. Ryan goes to his room to pack.

CHAPTER SEVEN

TRACKING APP

Moonlight glistens off the rippling surface of the Tennessee River as Melanie and Gerry carry provisions to the Montgomerys' pontoon boat. It's spooky in the deserted marina. The floating dock creaks as they go from one section to the next. Although no one else is there, Melanie and Gerry talk softly. "I'll get the cooler," Gerry says. "You can start unloading water if you like." Gerry points to the back of his truck, where gallon jugs of distilled water are nestled.

"Uh-oh, someone's coming," Melanie whispers. The two friends turn and watch headlights flicker through the trees that line the way into the marina. Gravel crunches as a pickup appears at the security gate. "Relax, Ger, it's Liam and Ryan."

"Why aren't they moving?"

Melanie starts toward the gate. "No doubt, Ryan forgot the code."

Ryan is out of the truck pushing buttons on the gate's digital lock. He looks over when Melanie comes up to the fence. "Two-five-zero-three-one, right?" he asks.

"No, wrong," Melanie smiles. "Try five-two-zero-one-three."

This time, the lock clicks, and the gate springs open. "I'm dyslexic," Ryan shrugs.

"You're not dyslexic. You just never listen when I tell you something." Melanie goes back to help Gerry.

Meanwhile, at Gruenen Walde, Mish is taking Dachsie for her last walk of the day. At least, that's the way it appears. However, Dieter is waiting behind some trees as she comes down the sidewalk. Dachsie wags her tail when she spots her second-favorite person. The pooch has no objection when Mish passes her leash to the boy. "I'll take her to the car," Dieter says. "Try not to be too long."

Mish hastens along the walkway, past a series of cookie-cutter mansions. She skirts around the tennis courts at the rear of the compound, then crosses a pedestrian bridge to access the Gruenen Walde slave quarter. It's a three-story building laid out much like a college dormitory. The fob on Mish's room key electronically unlocks the front door. Once inside the lobby, she glances at a camera to give the facial recognition software a good look. Now she's clocked in for the evening.

Inside her room, Mish hurriedly strips the bed. She stuffs a pillowcase with clothes from her dresser, then opens the window and tosses it out. Mish has practiced using bedding to make a rope ladder. Now, she firmly ties two sheets and the blanket together. After anchoring one end, she dangles the rest out the window. With hands on hips, Mish takes a last glance around her hateful room. Then she clambers onto the windowsill, takes hold of a sheet, and begins lowering herself. Mish knows the makeshift ladder will be short of the ground, so it's no surprise moments later when she finds herself hanging in mid-air. It's frightening to look down and see nothing but inky blackness below. "Don't worry," Dieter whispers, "you've got this." Mish lets go and makes a controlled landing on the ground. Dieter pats her on the back. "Come on," he whispers.

Mish snatches up the pillowcase. She follows Dieter as he darts from one shadow to the next. Instead of using the exposed pedestrian bridge, they cross the creek by balancing on a fallen log. After that, it's only a little farther to where Dieter's car is parked. He pops open the trunk, and Mish climbs in with her pillowcase. Pitch-black descends with the trunk lid. Moments later, Mish feels the car moving. Shortly, it comes to a stop. "Evening, sir," someone says. Mish recognizes the voice of one of the gate guards she often talks to when walking Dachsie.

"Hey, Donald, how's it going?" Dieter asks.

"Oh, all right, just boring."

"Well, you've only got what, maybe two more hours?"

"That's right."

"Then what?"

"Go home, watch TV, and crush a twelve-pack."

"Sounds like a plan."

"Nothing else to do at this hour. I hate swing shifts."

"I see your point."

"So, what's all that stuff on the back seat?"

"Camping gear. Me and some buddies are going for the weekend."

"Sounds like fun."

"Yeah, and speaking of that, I better get moving. Don't want to keep them waiting."

"Got it. Well, have a good time."

"Thanks."

The pounding of Mish's heart slows as the car picks up speed. Something is reassuring about the *clop-clop* sound made by the tires hitting cracks in the pavement. In the darkness, there's nothing for her to do but relax and get into harmony with the vibration and gentle swaying of the vehicle.

Half an hour later, Dieter pulls up to the security gate at the marina. Confidently, he enters the code Melanie gave him. With a click, the gate slides open. Dieter spots Ryan's truck and heads for the space beside it. After popping the trunk, he goes to help Mish out. Her eyes are closed, and she's not moving. Momentary panic gives way to relief when Mish stirs and comes awake. "Oh, hi," she says. "I must have dozed off."

"Glad you got some rest. Now we've got work to do." Dieter offers Mish his hand and helps her climb out of the trunk.

"Where's Dachsie?"

"Front passenger seat."

Mish goes to open a car door while Dieter unloads gear from the back seat. Soon, Dachsie is busy exploring. She sniffs a tire, then barks at Liam, who comes over from the dock.

"Hi, Dieter." Liam and Dieter shake, then simulate a hug. "What can I do to help?" Liam asks.

"You can get that stuff from the back seat."

Liam goes around to the other side of the car. He opens the back door and looks inside. "Why does Mish need two sleeping bags?"

"One is for her, the other is for me," Dieter explains. "I decided to come."

Liam frowns. "That's not what we planned."

"Yeah, but I thought about it and concluded that it wouldn't take long for them to figure out who helped Mish past security."

"What about food and water for you?"

"I brought plenty." Dieter reaches for a tote and drags it out of the car.

"And I suppose the dog is along for the ride also?"

"Mish wouldn't leave without her."

Liam shoulders a duffel bag and carries it toward the dock. "It's all good," he says over his shoulder, "come on."

Dieter follows Liam onto the dock while carrying the tote. When they get to where the Montgomerys' pontoon boat is moored, they go up the gangway and look for a place to put their loads. "Food goes aft," Melanie says, pointing toward the rear of the craft. "You can stow your clothing and camping gear behind the seats."

"Hey, you two haven't met yet," Ryan exclaims. "Dieter, this is Melanie."

Dieter waves. "Very nice to meet you."

"Guys, Dieter has decided to come with us," Liam explains. "He doesn't think he'll be safe here after they find Mish gone."

"It's all right by me," Melanie says. "Welcome aboard."

"And here's the star of the show," Dieter announces as Mish tentatively crosses the gangway with Dachsie nipping at her heels.

"Y'all are crazy," Mish says. "Risking your lives for a slave girl!"

"We love you, Mish," Ryan says earnestly, "and besides, we're all sick and tired of this rotten system. Slavery, cameras spying on us everywhere, the Security Service, The Leader, and well, everything."

"Oh, you brought a pillow," Melanie exclaims. "Why didn't I think of that?"

Mish sets the pillowcase on a boat seat, reaches in, and pulls out a pair of jeans. "This isn't a pillow, it's my suitcase."

Gerry laughs. "That's one way to do it."

"Hey, we need to ditch these vehicles," Ryan says. "And our phones."

"What for?" Gerry asks.

"If they find our rides here, how long would it take them to figure out we're on the boat?" Ryan asks. "And using a cellphone, even turning one on, would be like telling The Service, here are my GPS coordinates, come get me."

"That's right," Dieter agrees. "Might as well walk around with a target on your back." He takes his phone out and hands it over. Ryan drops it into a bag and then collects the rest. "If you need anything else from your vehicle, get it now," he says. "Then we'll take them someplace where they won't be noticed for a while."

Dieter rushes back to his car to finish unloading. After emptying it, he gets behind the wheel and flashes the lights to let Ryan know he's ready. Ryan leads the way out of the parking lot in his pickup. Dieter and Gerry follow in their vehicles. They go back to the main highway and then drive ten miles to a twenty-four-hour Walmart Supercenter. In the parking lot, Ryan gets out. Approaching Dieter's car, he motions for him to roll down the window. "Park as close to an entrance as possible, then come get in with me." Nearby, Gerry is standing beside his truck. Ryan goes over and makes the same suggestion he gave Dieter. "You got it," Gerry says.

Presently, all three teenagers are crammed into the cab of Ryan's pickup. "Let's go to the dollar store we passed on the way," Ryan says. "They have ConFedEx drop boxes. I want to ship our phones somewhere and hope that throws The Service off our trail."

Dieter moves his knee so Ryan can shift gears. "Any idea where?"

"I'm thinking South Florida," Ryan explains. "That's 180 degrees opposite the direction we'll really go."

"The Seaquarium is way south. My parents took me once to see the orcas. It was cool."

"All right, that'll work."

A few minutes later, Ryan pulls into the dollar store parking lot. He gets out with the bag of phones and goes inside. At the ConFedEx kiosk, he gets a shipping label and enters a fictional return address. Then he uses his phone to look up the address for the Miami Seaquarium and puts that down for "addressee." *As good a place to send them as any*, he muses. *Always wanted to see it.* Ryan makes sure each phone is turned on and puts them into a cardboard shipping container. A stack of multipage store ads is on a stand nearby. Ryan wads some of the flyers and stuffs them into the box so the phones won't rattle. He follows the idiot-proof direction to affix the label, pays, and then seals the box before depositing it.

Outside, Ryan takes a deep breath to settle his nerves. Reflexively, he reaches for his back pocket, only to find it empty. It's unsettling to be without his phone. He feels untethered, like a helium-filled party balloon released into thin air. *There's no going back now*, he realizes. His heartbeat quickens.

When Ryan gets back to the truck, Gerry and Dieter are sitting on the back bumper. "When's the next pickup?" Gerry asks.

"Tomorrow morning, eight o'clock. I ordered three-day delivery, meaning the shipment will be trucked, not flown. The Service might follow the phones all the way to Florida."

"Once they catch on, they'll return and check the store video."

"Yeah, but we'll be long gone by then." Ryan opens the driver's side door while the other two climb over the tailgate into the back. They settle onto the truck bed and lean against the cab. Ryan sticks his head out the window. "Plenty of room in here."

"Nah, we're good," Gerry replies.

Riding in the bumpy back adds to Dieter and Gerry's adventurous frame of mind. Soon, they're out of the suburbs and heading down a dark country lane. Looking up, Gerry marvels at ghostly cloud shapes backlit by the ambient light of the Milky Way. *Someone I don't know halfway around the world might be looking up at this exact moment and seeing this same sight.* Gerry's reverie ends when the truck lurches to a stop at the marina's security gate. Ryan taps on the keypad, but the lock stays locked. He sticks his head out of the window. "It's five-two-zero-one-three," Dieter tells him.

"Why did I think three-one-zero-two-five?" Ryan mutters.

"Maybe you're dyslexic," Dieter comments as Ryan finally unlocks the gate and drives into the marina parking lot.

"Everybody out," Ryan calls when they get to the dock.

Once Dieter and Gerry are clear of the vehicle, Ryan backs up all the way to the gate. "So long, baby," he whispers, then shifts gears and floors the accelerator. Tires spin, and gravel flies as the truck careens across the parking lot and down the boat ramp. A geyser forms as the front bumper crashes into the river. In a moment, the vehicle is floating. Ryan unfastens his seat belt and tries to open the door. Water pressure from outside keeps it shut. The current causes the pickup to rotate as it slowly sinks. "Go out the window," Dieter yells. "It's the only way."

Ryan rolls his window down. He sticks both arms out and then his head. By now, the cab is inundated. Thus, his hindquarters follow the rest of him out of the window with just a few well-placed kicks.

"Hallelujah," Melanie hollers when she sees her boyfriend's head break the surface. Ryan sloshes his way ashore and then joins the others as they watch the tailgate of his trusty pickup slowly vanish beneath the waves. "Sooner or later, they're going to figure out that we're on the river," Gerry says.

"For sure," Ryan agrees, "but if we'd left our rides here, it would have been sooner."

"So, what are we waiting for?" Mish picks Dachsie up and goes to where the boat is docked. The remaining teenagers follow her across the gangway. Melanie goes to the console to fiddle with the controls, then she turns the key and presses the starter. Immediately, the twin Mercury outboards begin to purr. "Get ready to cast off," Melanie orders.

Ryan and Liam go to untie the mooring lines. However, Ryan struggles with the knot. "Here, let me help you," Dieter offers. The German boy yanks on the knot, then pulls, and it comes apart. "They call it the sailor's knot," Dieter explains, "easy to tie and untie, but very strong."

"Pull in the gangway," Melanie shouts as the stern drifts away from the dock. At the bow, Liam finishes untying that line. Melanie shifts into reverse to back the craft away from other boats. Visibility in the darkened marina is poor, but thanks to a sliver of moon and the sparkling stars, Melanie can see well enough to avoid collisions. Once clear of the dock, she shifts into forward and slightly advances the throttle. Soon, they're out of the sheltered cove that's home to the marina. A breeze coming across the open water kicks up waves. They slap against the twin aluminum tubes that keep the large vessel afloat.

Now that the river's current is pushing them, Melanie shuts the motors down. As the boat drifts, the initial excitement felt by the passengers gradually dissipates. Tired of standing, Mish settles onto a lounge seat and puts Dachsie down. "What if she falls in?" Dieter asks.

"Dogs have excellent depth perception and, like humans, are reluctant to leap into the unknown," Mish explains. "So don't worry."

"I'm hungry," Ryan complains.

Melanie laughs. "You're always hungry." She's peering into the darkness, alert for unexpected obstacles.

"Who else wants a peanut butter sandwich?" Ryan shines his flashlight into a tote and takes out the fixings.

"If you're making 'em, I'll sure eat one," Gerry exclaims.

"Me too," several more voices concur.

A midnight snack of PB&J restores calm after the day's stress. Afterward, Mish unrolls the sleeping bag Dieter brought for her and stretches out on the lounge with Dachsie. Ryan, Liam, and Gerry lay mats on the deck. But Dieter is still too wound up to sleep. He joins Melanie on lookout duty. "Why aren't we using the motors?"

"We've got almost three hundred miles to go," Melanie answers. "And the supply of gas is tight. So, the plan is to drift with the current as much as possible."

"That's going to take forever."

"Yeah, and without our phones."

"Let me off," Dieter laughs.

"So, tell me," Melanie asks. "What made you decide to tag along?"

Dieter feels his face get hot and knows he's blushing. "I love Mish," he blurts out.

"I get that," Melanie says. She can't see Dieter's red face in the semi-darkness but can hear the passion in his voice. "Uh-oh, there's a snag up ahead." Melanie starts the motors and advances the throttle enough to get steerage. She turns the wheel, and they avoid the obstruction. Once the boat is back in the main current, Melanie shuts the motors down again. Total quiet returns for a moment until Dieter picks up the conversation. "I hope you don't mind me sharing. My problem is that Mish doesn't seem to feel the same way about me."

"Well, she probably blames you for losing her job at Jaybird's," Melanie points out.

"I know, and she should. When I first saw Mish, I knew I wanted to be with her. It seemed logical to buy her, but once she began working at my house and I saw how my father acted, it hit me how horrible it was for Mish and that it was my fault. I've tried to make it up to her ever since."

"Then you're on the right track and should just be patient. Mish has been through a lot. Imagine being bought and sold like a stick of furniture."

"It's unimaginable," Dieter exclaims. "You'd have to experience being a slave yourself."

Silence on the river returns as Melanie and Dieter contemplate the life they've left behind and the South's peculiar institution. As the night drags by, they watch for commercial shipping, sandbars, and snags. When potential trouble arises, Melanie uses the outboards to propel the vehicle closer to shore. Otherwise, she keeps it in the main current, and the boat drifts steadily along.

Finally, the sky lightens with a false dawn, signaling that the real thing won't be long. "We need to find a place to hide during daylight hours," Melanie says.

Dieter peers into the gloom. "It'll be easier to find a spot after the sun rises."

"You're right. Can't wait to stretch out and close my eyes."

"Me too."

"Thanks for keeping me company. Tonight, I'll show you and the others how to operate this boat so we can all take turns steering it."

"Good plan."

It takes another hour for the sunrise to brighten the sky enough for Melanie and Dieter to make out the shoreline. "What if we pull in between that island and the bank?" Dieter points to a brushy piece of land that seemingly rises out of the water not far from shore.

"Looks like a good possibility," Melanie agrees. She fires up the motors and turns the wheel. As they approach the shore, it turns out Dieter has found a good spot for a layover. So, Melanie tucks the boat in behind the island, and Dieter drops the anchor. Melanie unrolls her sleeping bag on the stern lounge while Dieter lays his camping pad on the deck near the others. "All I want to do is sleep," Melanie says.

"Ditto."

As the pontoon boat gently rocks, the crew dozes. Meanwhile, at the Security Service Headquarters (SSHQ) in Huntsville, Ferguson and his partner Boyce are wide awake. "Delete, delete, delete," Boyce complains, tapping on the keyboard of his desktop. "I spend half my life deleting useless emails."

"Same here," Ferguson says. "It's because we're copied on stuff that doesn't concern us."

"Play WDRM radio," Boyce says. A moment later, he's snapping his fingers to a tune from his favorite oom-pah band. "*Oktoberfest* is only four months away." He grins at Ferguson.

Ferguson's cell phone jingles, and he reaches for it, but a second later, a notification from the forensics lab appears on his desktop. As often happens when he's in the office, it's hard for Ferguson to decide whether to read the email on his phone or computer. He chooses the latter and eagerly reads the DNA analysis for Ryan Walters. "*Achtung!*" Ferguson exclaims.

"What's up?" Boyce asks.

"I'm looking at the DNA report on that kid from yesterday."

"And?"

"It says he's related to the driver of the car that was fleeing the power station explosion."

"So, his father wasn't off on a drinking binge after all."

"Nah, he was off blowing stuff up."

"Now we know the missing rental car will never be returned."

"Right."

"And we've identified one of the terrorists."

"That's also correct. But DNA from three separate people was found in the wreckage. We need to identify the others before we can close this case." Ferguson gets up and reaches for his holster. "Bet I know who can tell us who his dad's friends were."

"And if he lies to us again . . ." Boyce laces his fingers together and then cracks all the knuckles at once.

Somehow, in only one day, the Walters' house has taken on a deserted look. Maybe because the pickup that was often parked there is gone. Or that no one has weedeated the walkway lately. Bryson and Ryan were never into gardening, but in the past, pinecones scattered about the front yard and weeds growing in the flower beds gave the place a lived-in look. Now, the vibe has changed. When Ferguson and Boyce arrive, they immediately sense it. "Our bird has flown the coop," Boyce comments.

Ferguson gets out of the car. "Well, let's see what we can see." He walks up the rickety steps of the front porch, stands well back from the door, and then delivers a karate front kick. The wooden door flies off its hinges and into the living room. Boyce has his handgun out and follows it into the house, pointing the weapon this way and that. He goes down the hall and checks the bedrooms. But, just as the two men suspected, no one's there.

It's easy to tell which room was Ryan's, thanks to the soccer memorabilia. Ferguson pulls one of the drawers out of the boy's dresser and rifles through it without finding anything of interest. Boyce checks the closet. Methodically, the two men continue to search the house. They find nothing to indicate where their quarry has gone.

Back outside, the agents ponder what to do next. They're distracted by a cloud of red dust rising from the dirt road that leads to the house. The dust is coming from the wheels of a black luxury car. Presently, the vehicle slides to a stop. Huntsville's mayor gets out and angrily slams the door. He strides up to the porch but is taken aback to find two burly-looking characters there. "Good morning," Ferguson says.

Regaining his composure, the mayor starts up the steps. "Out of my way," he orders.

Ferguson continues to block Montgomery. He reaches for his credentials then dangles the badge at eye level for the irate Mayor to see. "I'm Lieutenant Ferguson, and this is Agent Boyce."

Montgomery gulps. No one wants a run-in with The Service. "Gla-gla-glad to meet you," he stammers. "Uh . . . what brings you boys out here this early in the morning?"

"We're investigating a crime. Now, what are you doing here?"

"Looking for my daughter," Montgomery explains. "I fear she has run off with the boy who lives here."

"I see."

"If you don't know, I'm Mayor Montgomery."

Unimpressed, Boyce chews on a toothpick while gazing around the barnyard. A rooster is strutting back and forth in front of the henhouse. Boyce tilts his ball cap back on his forehead and thinks, *Must be lots of eggs piling up in there.* He steps down from the porch. "I'm going to search those outbuildings."

Ferguson turns to watch his partner wander off. "So, is Ryan in trouble?" the mayor asks impatiently.

"I'll ask the questions if you don't mind," Ferguson snaps.

"Oh, sure."

"To start with, have you filed a missing person report?"

Montgomery is caught off guard. "No," he admits. "Didn't think of it. When she wasn't at breakfast, and I found her room empty, I jumped into the car and came straight here."

"Just as well," Ferguson concedes. "If she is associating with Ryan Walters, her disappearance will be added to my caseload anyway. Now, what I need from you is a list of all her known acquaintances."

"No problem."

"And what's her cellphone number? Finding someone is normally a piece of cake if they're carrying a cellphone."

Montgomery reaches into his pocket. "I confiscated her phone," he says, handing the device to Ferguson. "Will that make it harder to find her?"

"Yes, however, we can now see her contacts, read texts, and access her social media. If she's with Ryan Walters, and his number is in here, we can trace his movements and might bag both of them."

"Sounds good. I've about given up on the girl."

Ferguson turns on the phone. "So, what's the password?"

"I have no idea," Montgomery shrugs.

Boyce catches the tail end of the conversation as he climbs back onto the porch. "You confiscated her phone and didn't get the password?" He holds his cap in his hands. It's full of eggs.

"I was angry, didn't think of it."

Ferguson takes a notepad and pen from his pocket. "No worries." He flips open the pad. "We'll hack it. Now I need your daughter's full name, citizen registration number, and the number for this phone."

Once back at SSHQ, the agents open a box of donuts they picked up on the way. Boyce goes for a raspberry-filled kind, while Ferguson settles for an original glazed. They pry the lids off coffee cups and have breakfast while ruthlessly deleting extraneous emails. Both men focus intently on their screens, but that doesn't stop them from decimating the donuts. Finally, Ferguson grabs a napkin and uses it to scrub sugar off his fingers. "Hey, take this to the lab when you're done." He gets a clear evidence bag, drops Melanie's phone in, and seals it.

The only item now left in the donut box is a lemon-filled kind. Boyce prefers raspberry but takes it anyway. "Sure thing, boss," he says and disappears the donut in two bites.

"Tell 'em it's urgent, then stay there, looking over their shoulders 'til they crack it."

"Will do." Boyce takes the evidence bag and goes out.

Ferguson has a ten o'clock staff meeting coming up that he needs to prepare for. On the computer, he brings up a copy of the report he did for last week's meeting. He changes the date, adds the new case he's working on to his list, and then saves the document under a new name. With a sigh, Ferguson begins updating the old cases. After that, he recaps his progress thus far on the power station explosion. With only minutes to spare, he backs his work up to the cloud, prints it out, and then goes down the hall.

Captain Gerhard Tyson, the chief of detectives, isn't satisfied wasting Monday mornings with his staff meeting. Afterward, he invariably insists on taking his minions to lunch. They always go to the same Mexican restaurant. It features an assortment of that country's best lagers, so the luncheons are well-lubricated. This day, Ferguson anxiously squirms his way through the ordeal, wishing to get back on the job. But it's not 'til close to two that he makes it back to the office. Boyce is there chewing on a toothpick. A Styrofoam container that once held a Hardee's Thickburger rests next to his keyboard.

"Well, what have you got?" Ferguson asks as he settles behind his desk.

Boyce consults a notepad. "The lab had no problem hacking the girl's phone. Her most frequent contact is our friend, Ryan Walters.

But she's also been texting with Dieter von Kluck, Geraldine Downy, and Liam Larsen." Boyce turns the page of his notebook and then peers at it while wrinkling his brow. Ferguson drums on his desk with a pencil. "Are you going to tell me what they've been communicating about? Or do I have to drag it out of you?"

"Oh, sorry, the technician was talking so fast, I had to scribble to get it down. What I got here is that they were texting in some code, talking gibberish about a package they wanted to pick up before going on vacation."

"Did they say where?"

"Where what?"

Ferguson breaks the pencil in half. "Where they're going on vacation, dummy."

"Nah, they didn't say, but I got a good idea."

"Spill it."

"Florida." Boyce gets up and shows Ferguson his phone. "That's them there." He points to four green triangles that are steadily moving down the Dixiebahn. "The techie downloaded a tracker onto my phone. It updates the location of the cellphones belonging to Ryan and the other three every five seconds. They left town a little after eight this morning. The Montgomery girl is probably with them."

"Drat, they're already past Atlanta."

"Almost to Macon," Boyce drawls. "Want me to get a chopper on their tail?"

"Negative. I want them alive." Ferguson reaches for his mouse and then hunts for a travel request form in his PDFs. He starts typing with his partner looking over his shoulder. "What, two days?" Boyce complains. "I need to pack."

"Not until you send me everything we've got on Liam Larsen, Geraldine Downy, and Dieter von Kluck. I already have the files for the Walters kid and the mayor's daughter. She's an abolitionist."

Boyce gets busy on his desktop while Ferguson completes the travel form and forwards it to his boss. A few minutes later, Captain Tyson's voice comes over the intercom. "Hey, I got this travel authorization you sent."

"Yes, sir."

"So how does a trip to Florida tie into a case of sabotage here?"

"We got a trace on the son of one of the perps on the power station hit. My gut tells me he knows who else was involved; might even be an accomplice."

"So why not let the Florida office pick him up?"

"They shoot first and ask questions later."

"Too true."

"Me and Boyce will fly into Miami, intercept them, and bring 'em back."

"The Florida boys aren't going to like it."

"What they don't know won't hurt them."

There's a pause, and then a notification pops up on Ferguson's screen: "Travel Request Approved."

"Got it, thanks," Ferguson says.

"We never had this conversation." Tyson hangs up.

On the other side of the office, Boyce is searching through his desk. He looks up and sees that his partner is off the intercom. "Got any Tums?"

"Yeah, but not until I get those files."

"Just sent 'em."

Ferguson checks his inbox. Sure enough, an email with attachments is there. He opens a desk drawer and takes out a roll of antacids. "You should lay off the junk food." Ferguson cocks his arm and then launches a spiral. Boyce one-hands it. "I'm going to pack," he says, getting up. On his way out, Boyce bites a couple of tablets off the roll then puts the rest into his pocket. "Hey!" Ferguson complains. But his partner is gone.

Wearily, Ferguson checks on flights to Miami. He finds one that connects through Atlanta, and makes reservations. Next, he clicks on one of the dossiers Boyce sent. It's for Liam Larsen. Impatiently, Ferguson scrolls through the file until he finds the boy's emergency contact. Instead of a parent name, Liam's next of kin is listed as the Huntsville Home for Boys. Ferguson dials the number and asks to speak to the administrator. Shortly, a woman comes to the phone. Ferguson gets right to the point. "I'm with The Service," he says. "What can you tell me about Liam Gallagher?" Ferguson listens for a moment and then snaps, "Hey, I'm not asking for a reference. Do you know where he is?" After a pause, the agent speaks again: "So you have no idea where he went? What about relatives he may be with or friends? Does he have any regular visitors he may have gone to see?" Ferguson frowns as the administrator answers. "I see," he finally says. "Well, if you hear from him or think of anything that might be useful, call me." After rattling off his number, Ferguson slams down the phone. He opens the next file and dials. "Hello, you have reached Tom Downy," a voice says. "Please text me. I don't respond to voicemails."

After dashing off a text, Ferguson opens the last dossier. The name von Kluck sounds familiar. As he reads through Dieter's file, it clicks. *What's a German kid doing mixed up in this?* he wonders. *And the son of a big shot to boot.* Ferguson decides to interview von Kluck in person. He straps on his shoulder holster and jostles it until the heavy weight of the Glock settles into place. *Dealing with this joker isn't going to be easy,* he thinks as he goes out to the parking lot. Sitting in his car, Ferguson responds to a text from Downy. After some back and forth, Downy promises to send a list of Gerry's contacts. Only then does Ferguson start the car and ease out of his parking space.

Jerry Jackson, a Huntsville police detective, is at the Gruenen Walde security gate when Ferguson pulls up. He's talking with the rent-a-cop who works there. "Hi, Jer," Ferguson calls through his rolled-down window, "what's up?"

"The Eiffel Tower," Jackson replies.

"Very funny."

"Yeah, well, I need a laugh. We got a missing person, a runaway slave, and an upset VIP."

"Von Kluck?"

"None other."

"Want to introduce me?"

"Come on."

After the security guard raises the gate, Ferguson follows the detective's car into the German compound. They go up a hill and then turn into a cul-de-sac. Von Kluck's mini-mansion is at the end. Two men are standing outside. Jackson gets out of his vehicle and approaches them.

Ferguson hastens to catch up. They wait politely while the men talk. "*Das ist unmö*glich," the older one is saying.

"*Ganz genau*," the other man replies. He's wearing a black raincoat even though there isn't a cloud in the sky.

"Excuse me," Jackson interjects. "This is Lieutenant Ferguson from the Security Service. Lieutenant, please meet Reinhold von Kluck, Director of The Space Flight Complex, and this is Colonel Schlieffen of the SFC Police."

"My pleasure," Ferguson says with a slight bow.

Von Kluck is not so polite. "Tell me, Lieutenant," he scowls, "what do you bring to this clown show?"

"Pardon?"

"I've got two Huntsville cops turning my house upside down and another spreading fingerprint dust all over. It's a four-alarm dumpster fire."

Jackson shifts his weight uncomfortably. "We're only following procedure."

"Wasting time, more like it. I want my slave girl back."

"What about your son?" Ferguson asks.

"Who cares?" Von Kluck shrugs. "The brat has been eyeing the girl for months. Now he's run off with her. If you can't sort this out, I will ask Colonel Schlieffen to intervene."

"And, I couldn't help noticing, Lieutenant," Schlieffen raises his eyebrows, "that you still haven't answered *Herr Direktor's* question. What is The Service's interest in this matter?"

Ferguson turns to face the tall German. "We are investigating a Resistance ring," he explains. "*Herr* von Kluck's son, Dieter, might be involved."

"*Das ist Verruckt.*" Von Kluck points a finger at his head, indicating that Ferguson might be a mental case.

"If you think the idea's crazy, fine. Just give me a look at his room and a list of his friends, and I'll be on my way."

"Be my guest. You can't mess up my house more than it has been already."

Upstairs, Ferguson finds that Jackson's men have thoroughly

tossed Dieter's room, leaving nothing interesting. While he's rummaging through the pockets of a pile of clothes, Frau von Kluck comes in. "His friends are mainly other soccer players." She gives Ferguson a handwritten list.

Ferguson glances at the paper and then tucks it into a pocket. "Thank-you."

"Just between us," Frau von Kluck says, "I'd just as soon not have that slave girl back."

"Got it." The agent nods. "You'd be surprised how often I hear that."

Outside, Ferguson finds Jackson sipping a soft drink. "It's all yours," Ferguson says, getting into his car.

"Thanks for nothing."

Ferguson winds his way out of the neighborhood and approaches the gate. He pulls onto the grass across from the guard shack and gets out. "When's the last time you saw Dieter von Kluck?" he asks the rent-a-cop.

"That's what the other guy wanted to know."

Ferguson sighs. "OK, so what did you tell him?"

"He came through last night around nine."

"Did you notice anything strange?"

The guard scratches his head. "Said he was going camping with some friends. I wondered why they would be heading out after dark and not first thing in the morning."

"Did you see any camping gear?"

"There were a couple of duffel bags on the back seat, with a tote, cooler, and fishing rods."

"Anything else seem funny?"

"He was overly friendly, maybe nervous."

"Got it." Ferguson returns to his car and drives across town to the apartment complex he and his wife call home. She's at work, so he scrawls her a note and sticks it on the fridge. In the bedroom, Ferguson packs a carry-on for the trip to Florida. Then he heads back out the door. During the drive back to the office, Ferguson streams an opera passage by his favorite tenor. *Incredible*, the detective thinks and turns up the volume. Then it hits him why the von Kluck kid was nervous.

The slave girl was in the trunk, he realizes. *That's why the cooler and camping gear were on the back seat.*

Ferguson parks in front of SSHQ and goes upstairs. He finds that Boyce has returned to the office. The agent is tilted back in his chair, feet on the desk, furiously working his phone. "When's the last time you had those shoes resoled?" Ferguson gazes disgustedly at the holes in his partner's shoes.

"Been thinking about it." Boyce keeps his eyes fixed on the phone screen.

"What are you playing?"

"Blitzkrieg. I'm Rommel kicking the crap out of Patton."

"One day, the entire internet will crash because of you gamers."

"Then, they'll build another one. Drat!" Boyce tosses his phone onto the desk like discarding a card. "I was winning a minute ago, but my tank just got blown up."

"That only proves one thing."

"What's that?"

"Life sucks, and then you die."

"Ha-ha."

Ferguson's phone jingles with a notification. Eagerly, he unlocks the screen. "Well, it's about time," he exclaims.

"What?" Boyce asks.

"Our e-tickets. We're good to go." Ferguson gets to his feet and again struggles into his shoulder holster. However, Boyce isn't moving. He just started a new game. "Aw, don't you think we should wait 'til tomorrow?"

"No way," Ferguson snaps. "That kid lied to my face. I won't rest until I get the cuffs on him or see him stretched out cold. You can play that garbage on the plane."

"Whatever you say, boss."

By the time the two agents have managed to park at the airport, check in, and make it to their gate, the plane is boarding. They get in line, and it's not long until their tickets are scanned for the final time. Once aboard, Ferguson stows his carry-on in the bin above his seat row, then he clambers next to the window. "Where are they?" he asks once Boyce is settled into his aisle seat.

Boyce takes out his phone and, with a wrinkled brow, ponders the screen.

"Oh, come on," Ferguson says impatiently.

"Sorry, but it looks like they're not moving. Thought the screen was frozen."

"Maybe they've stopped somewhere for the night; ever think of that? I mean, they left eleven hours ago."

"Good point. Well, my screen isn't frozen. They're a little south of Daytona."

"That's all right by me. Hope they stay there until morning." Ferguson takes a true-crime thriller out of his bag and settles a pair of noise-canceling headphones over his ears. Soon, the plane is airborne. Once the "Fasten Seat Belts" sign goes off, a slave gets a drink cart going up and down the aisle. Often, he must pause to grasp a seat back because of turbulence. After everyone is served, the steward makes one more pass to collect the empty cups.

The flight terminates in Atlanta, and the little plane's passengers gratefully rise from their cheap seats to stretch out the kinks. "Whoever designed the interior of this plane missed his true calling," Ferguson comments.

"What's that?" Boyce gets Ferguson's bag down from the bin and then his.

"Creating torture chambers."

"Ha-ha, maybe we could hire him."

"Hush up." Ferguson puts a finger to his lips. He already regrets his little joke.

Once out on the concourse, the agents pause to get oriented. "Let's go that way." Ferguson points to a people-mover access a short distance away. Soon, they're gliding along, taking in the brightly colored advertisements for Georgia-based corporations. Stylishly dressed people throng the concourse, getting on and off the people-mover to patronize shops and restaurants. "This is a far cry from our piddly little airport in Huntsville, huh?" Ferguson says.

"And how." Boyce cranes his neck to stare at patrons decorously seated at a chic wine bar. "Wonder how much a glass of that bubbly would be." He licks his lips.

"If you have to ask, you can't afford it."

"Those jokers must all be rich. Hell, most of them look like foreigners."

"Atlanta's where many rich Nazis came after the World War," Ferguson explains. "They brought their wealth and manufacturing knowledge here and set up companies. Nowadays, buyers from Russia, Iran, China, and other countries that don't boycott the Confederacy come here to work deals with them."

"Man, I'm in the wrong business," Boyce complains. He's watching a silver-haired gentleman standing outside a duty-free shop holding a phone to his ear. Diamonds sparkle off the man's Rolex. "Look there. That dude's watch is worth more than my truck."

Ferguson glances in the direction Boyce is pointing, then gets off the people-mover. "Come on," he says and leads the way to where a crowd is standing beneath a forty-foot-high digital display. He cranes his neck to peer over the shoulders of the people in front.

"Our flight isn't up there," Boyce mutters. "Just ones going to Moscow, Pyongyang, Jeddah, and such."

A few moments later, the board flickers and a waterfall of fresh listings descends. "Those were the international flights," Ferguson explains. "These are domestic. Our flight to Miami leaves from Gate 9A. That means we've got to hustle. We're on the wrong concourse."

"Drat," Boyce exclaims. He doesn't like to hustle.

Eschewing the leisurely pace of the people-mover, Ferguson gets his feet into high gear and heads for Concourse A. Boyce grumbles along behind, lugging his carry-on as though it contains a set of barbells. Fortunately for him, Gate 9 is one of the first they come to upon reaching the correct concourse. When they get there, the first-class passengers are already boarding. Many of them are accompanied by slaves who carry bags or supervise children. A blue-haired lady is rolled aboard in her wheelchair by a female slave. All this takes time, and the out-of-breath detectives welcome a break.

Once the elite passengers and their accouterments have been settled, the slaves stand aside. They will buckle up in jump seats after the coach passengers have boarded. Ferguson and Boyce wait until their row is called, then get in line for the jetway. An agent is scanning e-tickets on phones at the entrance. Once that's done, they climb aboard the Focke-Wulf SuperJet and find their seats. "I'm not getting paid enough for this," Boyce mutters.

"For what?" Ferguson asks. "All you've done all day is play that dumb game on your phone."

Reflexively, Boyce pats his pocket to make sure his phone is still there. "I only play it to relieve the stress."

"Right." Ferguson glances at his watch. *Boyce has a point*, he thinks. *We've been going strong since zero-dark-thirty this morning.* He rests his head against the seat back and closes his eyes. *Wish I could tilt it, but that's a no-no 'til we're airborne.* Despite his discomfort, Ferguson is soon in la-la land. He sleeps right through the take-off. Afterward, even the clanking of the drink carts fails to rouse him. Boyce takes advantage by getting himself a beer, which he quickly quaffs.

In his dream, Ferguson is tramping along a North Alabama forest trail. It's a frosty morning, and he exhales clouds of vapor that seem to crystallize and then hang in the crisp mountain air. But something isn't right. The pine scent of the forest has been replaced by the nauseating odor of overcooked airline lasagna. It's all just a dream, Ferguson realizes. Reluctantly, he opens his eyes to see his partner slathering butter onto a roll. "Don't worry," Boyce says and points to Ferguson's pull-down table, "Your dinner's right there."

"You can have it," Ferguson shrugs. "All except the salad and brownie."

"You sure?" Boyce is already reaching for the entrée.

Several slaves who serve as stewards for the airline begin cleaning up after the meal. Others get the drink cart back into action for those aboard who want one more shot at a double. The downward slope of the aisle indicates that the plane is descending. So, the slaves must work fast.

Presently, the "Fasten Seat Belts" sign comes on. Banging can be heard in the galley amidship as cabinet doors are slammed shut and carts locked away. Stewards carrying trash bags go up and down the aisle, encouraging the drinkers to finish up. The captain's voice comes over the intercom with a squelch. "This is Captain Kincaid. Thanks for flying with us this evening. You'll be pleased to know it's a beautiful night in Miami, with the temperature at 87 degrees and falling. Tomorrow's high is forecast to be 96. We will land right on time and expect to be at the gate by 12:18. Thanks again for choosing Rebel Air. Please keep us in mind for all your future travels."

Upon arrival at the gate, the economy class passengers are again required to wait. They are happy to stand and escape the tight confines of their seats. But now they are crammed in the aisle, trying to get their carry-ons down without bumping into each other. Meanwhile, first class slowly empties. Once that's done, the remaining passengers are allowed to stampede off.

The island vibe at the Miami airport is in stark contrast to the all-business atmosphere in Atlanta. Rather than corporate advertising, the signs here are for reptile exhibitions, airboat rides, and greyhound racing. Instead of designer clothes, people dress like they're going fishing. However, Ferguson is not the laid-back kind. He hustles to exit the terminal with Boyce in his wake. Once outside, the agents are blanketed by humid, jasmine-scented air. Boyce breathes deeply. "I could get used to this," he says.

Ferguson sees a van approaching with the logo for their rental car company. "Wait until tomorrow around noon and see if you like it," he snaps. "Now come on."

Formalities are kept to a minimum at the rental car outpost. In no time, Boyce is behind the wheel of a cheap electric car. "Where to?" he asks with his finger on the starter.

"When's the last time you checked on the location of those kids?" Ferguson asks.

"While you were getting the car."

"And?"

"Still where they were."

Ferguson speaks into his phone. "Motels with vacancies near me." He peers at the screen.

"Yay, I thought you'd keep me up all night."

"Follow the signs for the airport exit," Ferguson orders. "Then turn right."

The area around the airport is crowded with motels, and it's off-season. Before long, Ferguson is coming out of the office of a Budget

Inn. He returns to the car and directs Boyce to an adjacent building where they can park outside their ground-level accommodation. While Ferguson waits, Boyce tries to open the door. Repeatedly, he holds a key card up to the lock, but the light blinks red every time. "Try the other end," Ferguson suggests. *Click*, and they're in.

Ferguson goes to the bed farthest from the door and lays his bag on it. If someone breaks in during the night, he wants Boyce to be first to deal with it. "I'm hungry," he says.

"Not me." Boyce pats his belly contentedly.

"Then you can take the first shower while I rustle up something." Ferguson sits on the bed and taps on his phone.

Boyce takes his shaving kit out. "Guess you can get me whatever you have as long as you're ordering."

"Thought you were full."

"Forgot that we have meal vouchers. You know what they say, 'Free food tastes better than food paid for.'"

"Oh, all right." Ferguson doubles his order and clicks "SUBMIT." When he looks up from the phone, Boyce has disappeared into the bathroom. With a sigh, Ferguson turns on the TV and then props several pillows against the headboard. He takes off his shoes and stretches out on the bed to watch some cable news.

The next thing Ferguson knows is that an urgent voice in the back of his head is telling him to get up. With a start, the agent opens his eyes. He must squint because of the sunshine filtering through the blinds. A glance at the bedside clock shows that it's almost eight. Boyce is snoring contently in the other bed. Ferguson jumps to his feet. He roughly shakes his partner and hollers, "Get up!"

"What the hell?" Boyce mutters. He scoots to the far side of the bed and pulls a pillow over his head.

Angrily, Ferguson grasps his partner's leg through the covers and drags him out of bed. "Ouch," Boyce hollers as he crashes onto the floor.

"Get your phone," Ferguson orders.

Thoroughly awake, Boyce does as he's told. "Now what?"

"Find them!"

Ferguson scrolls his phone and then taps some keys. "Oh no," he moans, staring at the screen. "They're here already."

"Are they moving?"

"No, they've stopped at an industrial park about twenty miles away."

"Get dressed."

Once both agents are ready, they go out to the car. "Where are we going for breakfast?" Boyce asks.

Ferguson looks at his partner incredulously. Then he remembers his uneaten dinner. He returns to the room and finds the sack of fast food. Back outside, he tosses it to Boyce. "You can have that."

"A cheeseburger for breakfast?"

"Shut up and eat. I'll drive while you track them kids and provide directions."

Boyce gets into the passenger seat. "Looks like they left the industrial park and are on the move." He has his phone in one hand and the burger in the other.

"So, where to?"

"Turn right, and then we should see a Dixiebahn entrance. We need to go south."

Ferguson gets the little car humming. The motor is surprisingly powerful. Tires squeal as he floors the accelerator. In no time, they're merging onto the interstate and angling toward the HOV lane. "Looks like they've stopped at an AutoZone," Boyce says.

"Could be they're having car trouble," Ferguson guesses.

Traffic is heavy on the overused road even though rush hour is ending. Looking out the window, Ferguson marvels at the sameness of the scenery that whizzes by. It's a steady stream of shopping malls, car dealers, motels, chain restaurants, and mega-sized convenience stores. The office buildings resemble bunkers with thick walls and small, glare-proof windows designed to keep air conditioning in and rays out. No trees other than decorative palms line the acres and acres of parking lots. "They're moving again," Boyce announces.

"Do we need to get off?"

"Not yet. They've gone to a hospital."

"Where?"

"Coral Gables, about ten miles farther down."

"Hope they stay there. I'm planning to put that Ryan kid into intensive care."

Boyce recenters his screen and concentrates on the triangles he's following. "Sorry, but they're on the move again. Now they're at a beauty salon."

"I don't get all these stops," Ferguson complains.

"Yeah, it doesn't make sense."

Even though the car windows are tinted, the sun outside is without pity. Ferguson puts his visor down. He pokes the touch screen to maximize the air conditioning. "How people lived here back in the day is beyond me."

Boyce squints at the orange furnace hanging in the sky. "The Seminoles must be hard-core."

"Yeah, we fought 'em for years, but they finally made us smoke the peace pipe."

"That reminds me, we should go to a casino while we're here."

"Don't you think we've got bigger fish to fry?"

"Speaking of fish, it looks like ours are going into the net."

"Oh really?"

"Yep, they're crossing a bridge onto an island. Only one way on or off."

"Hooray."

Boyce smiles happily. "Turn off at the next exit and follow the signs for Rickenbacker Causeway."

After paying a toll, Ferguson gets moving again. He and Boyce swivel their heads, marveling at the glorious water views on either side. Windsurfers, fishermen, and cyclists are out in force. Their vans and SUVs pack the parking spaces along the causeway. Meanwhile, picnickers in scanty bathing suits cluster in the shade of the palm trees to enjoy the sea breeze. "They just left a seafood restaurant and are on the move again," Boyce exclaims. "Only a mile ahead."

Ferguson's heart races as he presses down on the accelerator. They're on the island proper now and pass a soccer stadium that overlooks the bay. Boyce studies his phone, then looks up. "We've got them," he says. Turn into that parking lot on the right."

Hundreds of cars are packed into the Miami Seaquarium parking lot, but that doesn't bother Ferguson. He speeds to the reserved spaces nearest the entrance and screeches to a halt. Reaching under his seat, the agent grabs his gun. As he exits the vehicle, Ferguson tucks the 9mm into his waistband and pulls the tails of his shirt over it. "Have you got a bead on them?" he asks.

"They just went in there." Boyce points to a gate with a sign that reads, "Employees Only."

Ferguson takes off running with Boyce shuffling along behind. A uniformed guard bars the way past the gate but quickly steps back when Ferguson waves his SS badge. The two agents go down a walkway then take a flight of steps up to a door marked "OFFICE." Inside, a receptionist is chatting with a woman ConFedEx driver. They pause their conversation as the breathless men rush up to the counter. "Where are they?" Ferguson demands.

"They who?" the receptionist asks.

"The teenagers that just came in."

The driver backs away from Ferguson, hoping that whatever he has isn't contagious. Meanwhile, the receptionist slides her phone off the desktop. With her eyes still on Ferguson, she thumbs her phone—911.

"Wait a minute." Boyce picks up a parcel on the counter and looks at the shipping label. "This originated in Huntsville."

Ferguson snatches the box out of his partner's hand and shakes it. Angrily, he rips the tape off and opens the package. "Hey, that was addressed to us," the receptionist complains.

"Tough."

"I'm calling the law."

"I am the law." Ferguson dumps the package contents onto the counter and stares disgustedly at four smartphones. "Forget what I said about intensive care," Ferguson tells Boyce. "That kid's going to the morgue along with all his stinking friends. They'll happily go there once I'm done with 'em."

CHAPTER EIGHT

THE PIT

A t first, Ryan and his friends find life on the river to be a drag. They consider not having a phone to be a form of sensory deprivation. But as the days pass, they slowly decompress and begin to appreciate their surroundings. The lapping waves and gentle rocking of the boat soothe nerves jangled by years of digital overstimulation. It's relaxing to sit and watch the wildlife abounding in the canebrakes along the shore. The animals mainly come out at dawn or late evening. Members of the boat crew delight in being the first to spot a family of beavers working on their home or river otters at play in the current. They point out their sightings to each other.

The end of the first week finds the boat laid up for the day just inside the mouth of a stream that empties into the Tennessee. Tall oaks and maples shade the craft and hide it from view. For camouflage, the crew has piled branches and leaves on top of the canopy. Now, with the sun well up, the smell of frying bacon fills the air. "This is the last of it." Ryan adjusts the flame on a camp stove. "We each get one slice."

Gerry goes to the cooler and peers inside. By now, the ice has melted. Few victuals remain. "Good thing we brought plenty of freeze-dried food," he says.

"That will keep us going," Melanie comments. "But we'll need more gas for the motors to reach the Autonomous Zone."

Gerry holds his hand up to block the sun and gazes theatrically at the broad river. "I'm looking for a Texaco," he explains.

"Hilarious," Melanie drawls. "But if you want to see something unfunny, go look in one of those." She points to a row of five-gallon gas cans at the stern. "They're all empty."

"OK, so how do we go about finding a marina?" Dieter asks.

"It's simple." Melanie opens a storage compartment and gets her burner phone.

Ryan gives a start, then snatches the phone out of his girlfriend's hand. "Why didn't you turn this in with the others?"

"Relax," Melanie smiles. "It's a prepaid phone that's registered in a fake name. Besides, it's been off the whole time."

"I still don't like it," Ryan scowls.

"Don't worry, I'll only switch it on for a moment."

Reluctantly, Ryan hands the phone back to Melanie. "Keep it short," he orders.

Melanie turns the phone on and impatiently waits for it to boot up. Then, "Gas near me," she says.

Ryan looks over Melanie's shoulder. "Where are we?"

"Tennessee. The nearest town is Camden, about thirty miles away."

"What about gas?" Liam asks.

"There's a marina in Camden, but it closes at six." Melanie shuts the phone off.

"I don't like the idea of going there in broad daylight," Ryan says.

"It's either that or hope the river current takes us where we need to go."

"What's wrong with that?"

"The motors are needed occasionally to avoid hazards and keep us in the current. We'd have never gotten off that sandbar last night without them."

Gerry comes over with a box of Cheez-Its. He sits on a lounge chair and pops one into his mouth. "Even with the outboards, the boat wouldn't budge 'til we all got off."

"Man, it was weird standing on that sandbar in the middle of the river with it so dark you couldn't see the water, just feel it tickling your legs." Mish reaches over Gerry's shoulder and grabs the Cheez-Its.

"Hey!" Gerry complains.

"So, have we all agreed to take our chances and head for the marina now?" Melanie asks.

"Guess we'd better," Ryan agrees. "If we hadn't had the use of the motors to get off that sandbar last night, we'd have been sitting ducks this morning when the sun came up." No one disagrees, so while Liam and Gerry clear the brush off the canopy, Dieter and Ryan untie the bow and stern lines. When the boat is ready, Melanie starts the twin outboards. She steers for the middle of the river. Once they're in the main current, she shuts the motors down.

It's quiet other than the sound of waves breaking against the pontoons and the chatter of birds high in the trees along the bank. Ryan goes to the bow, where his fishing rod is propped against a rail. He picks it up, flips the bail open, and casts his lure, trying to land it behind a snag. *Bingo!* he exults when the spinner lands right where he aimed. A moment later, he feels a tug on his line and rears back to set the hook on a nice bass. Immediately, the fish leaps out of the water, shaking its head as if to say, "Not today, young man." As his line grows slack, Ryan's lure springs back toward him. All that's left is his memory of the sun flashing off the startlingly bronze sides of the smallmouth.

With a sigh, Ryan tries another cast, this time with no luck. Still, it's nice to be drifting under the azure sky, taking in the natural beauty all around. Ryan twists his head from side to side, marveling at the massive oaks and maples that line the shore. *This is a big improvement over traveling in the dark*, he muses.

As Ryan repetitively casts his lure out and reels it in, Liam comes up beside him. "The water is so clear, you can see all the way to the bottom," he exclaims.

"Yeah, I've been amazed by all the sunken logs lying down there."

"Oh, I learned about that in woodworking class," Liam says. "Those logs are left over from the nineteenth century when they cleared land for cotton fields. The plantation owners sold the timber to lumber companies. At one time, this river was choked with massive log rafts that were floated downriver to sawmills. Because of jam-ups, some of the timber got waterlogged and sank. Today, that wood is highly prized by artisans. Just one of those logs would be worth several thousand dollars."

"Wow, then why aren't people going after them?"

"Because it takes thousands of dollars of equipment and effort to get one water-soaked log out of the river to where it needs to go," Liam laughs.

Ryan rears back on his rod. The drag on his reel screeches as a large bass tries to escape. "You've got one," Liam exclaims.

"Grab the net," Ryan pants excitedly. He tries to keep the rod tip up, although it's being bent double by the fish. *Don't jerk.* Ryan remembers his father coaching him long ago. *Just maintain steady pressure.* Slowly, the fish tires, and Ryan brings it near the boat. Liam gets the landing net under the bass and hauls it out. "We dine tonight!" he exults.

Farther back in the boat, past the seating area, Dieter is at the console with one hand lightly resting on the wheel. With the outboards shut down, there is no point in trying to steer the large craft. His job is to watch out for any navigational hazards. Right now, the boat is drifting sideways, so Dieter must do a quarter turn to see where they're going. With the tall trees on either side, it's like traveling down a broad highway. Dieter's mind wanders as he reflects on how long the river has been rolling along like this. He imagines Native Americans in dugout canoes hundreds of years ago, seeing the same view he's looking at now.

Dieter shifts his gaze back to the mundane. The seating area in front of him is littered with damp towels, paper plates with half-eaten sandwiches, and various articles of clothing. A half-full bowl of dog food is being ignored by Dachsie who is curled up beside Mish. She and Gerry are seated in lounge chairs with a chessboard set up between them. Both stare intently at the board, oblivious to everything around them. "Is that a barge coming around the bend?" Melanie asks. She has come up from behind and is looking downriver through binoculars.

Slowly, the speck in the distance grows larger. Now Dieter can make out the white froth of a bow wave. "We need to pull over and hide," he says. "Looks like an island coming up to starboard. We may be able to tuck in behind."

Melanie zeroes her binoculars on the riverbank where Dieter is pointing. "Good idea," she says. Dieter pushes the starter, and the big outboards come to life. After adjusting the throttle, he steers the awkward craft toward shore.

The shade behind the island is a welcome break from the glare in the middle of the river. After securing the boat, Ryan and Liam get into swimsuits. They climb down a boarding ladder into the water. With a whoop, Ryan immerses himself. He resurfaces, sputtering while Liam tries to stay clear. The goalkeeper has his long arms crossed over his goose-pimpled chest and doesn't seem happy to be standing in the cold river. Ryan steps closer, reaching both hands into the water menacingly. "Don't," Liam begs, but it's too late. His friend's hands reappear filled with water that is soon hurtling in Liam's direction. As Ryan brings up more of the wet stuff, Liam reluctantly dives under. Moments later, Ryan's feet are jerked out from under him. Quickly, Liam is on top, pushing Ryan's head under the water. "Got you," he shouts.

Dieter also puts on a swimsuit. "You guys need to act your age," he admonishes from the stern. By way of answer, the river rats turn to splash the German. They windmill their arms, scooping up as much water as possible with each rotation. Dieter blinks his eyes clear of the deluge and analyzes the situation. Seeing that the water is up to Liam's waist, he chances a cannonball dive. The aquatic explosion momentarily disconcerts Liam and Ryan. Then, a three-way splash fight breaks out.

Copious splashing is hard work. Before long, the boys are breathing heavily. "Do you give?" Liam demands of the other two. That's all it takes for an alliance to form between Germany and Alabama. But the burst of energy this rekindles is short-lived. Soon, a tacit truce takes hold.

After catching their breath, the boys venture farther from the island. They tread water as the line of barges passes, pushed by tugboats. Each barge is loaded high with forty-foot containers. Most bear the logos of Chinese shipping firms. "Amazing to think that those were packed with goods and then loaded aboard a ship on the other side of the world," Liam says.

"Without them, we wouldn't have phones, TVs, microwaves, or anything," Ryan comments.

"I know the barges come up the Mississippi as far as the Autonomous Zone," Dieter says. "But how do they get past it to here?"

"Melanie's dad told her that the shipping companies pay pirates for protection," Ryan explains.

Dieter dives down to touch the river bottom. He lingers with his hand touching it, then kicks his way back to the surface. He sees Ryan and Liam swimming toward the boat. Mish beckons from the stern. "Come on," she hollers. "We've got to go."

The river is once again clear of traffic, so with the sun now glaring at them out of the western sky, the teenagers continue their voyage. By now, the cool of the morning has given way to early summer heat. This encourages the crew to seek shelter under the canopy. Before long, most are sprawled on their sleeping mats, reading or snoozing. It's Gerry's turn to be on watch at the console. With the motors off, there is no sensation of speed. To pass the time, Gerry picks out landmarks along the shore and watches them slowly pass by.

As the sun drops lower, Melanie grows more anxious. She long ago switched the fuel line to the last gas tank. It's been necessary, through-out the afternoon, to use the motors. So, it's a relief when they round a bend, and Mish, who is now at the console, points to a collection of ramshackle buildings tucked into a cove not far away.

With her binoculars, Melanie spots a wooden dock with a gas pump. Covered boat slips line the shore. Many hold pontoon boats, but few are as large as theirs.

Melanie relieves Mish at the console and starts the motors, keeping the throttles well back. They pass a boat ramp. A pickup truck towing a jon boat is backing into it. Melanie steers clear. Slowly, she brings the boat closer to the dock and then reverses one of the motors to snug up against a piling. Ryan loops the bow line around it and clinches a sailor knot. Liam is busy at the stern. Once the craft is secure, Gerry lowers the gangway and starts to cross. But Dachsie cuts in front of him and scampers onto the dock to sniff around. Now, the others can follow.

No one is tending the gas pump. As they wait for an attendant, the teenagers marvel at the solid feel of the dock. It's a novelty after more than a week on the water. "Where's Dachsie?" Mish asks.

"Over there." Dieter points to the riverbank, where the dog is in a standoff with an angry goose.

"Looks like she has her paws full," Gerry comments.

At the boat ramp, two grizzled old-timers wearing denim overalls and long white beards launch the jon boat. Afterward, one parks their truck while the other keeps the boat from floating away. "I'm going to the store and see what's up with the gas," Ryan decides. He sets off toward a wooden building on the shore surrounded by a gravel parking lot. The sign above the entrance reads "Camp Store." Placards advertising soft drinks, chewing tobacco, and headache remedies are plastered helter-skelter on the walls.

With nothing better to do, the others follow the team captain to the end of the dock and up a hill to the store. Inside, they find a gray-haired man counting currency at the checkout counter. The cash register drawer is open, and the tray is partway out. "We need gas," Ryan says. The man doesn't look up.

Liam comes in behind the others. Out of habit, he reaches into his back pocket for his phone. Of course, it's not there. He glances around the store and then wanders over to a display to see if the boiled peanuts are warm. "They's still hot," the man behind the counter says, looking up. He's wearing a white shirt with a black tie. The shirt is frayed at the collar. "Ah jest now shut 'er off."

"What about gas?" Ryan persists.

"Ahm busy, get it yourself and then come on back and tell me how many gallons."

Ryan goes back to the door and pushes it open. "I'll help," Gerry says and follows him out. The others scatter throughout the store, snatching up soft drinks, candy bars, and bags of chips. Peanut butter and jelly sandwiches get old fast.

A woman is sitting behind the lunch counter in the rear of the store. Melanie goes over to study the menu sign. "Is it too late to get a cheeseburger?" she asks.

The woman looks up from her crocheting. "Are you staying at the campground?"

"No, ma'am, we're on a boat. Just stopped for gas."

Dieter, Liam, and Mish come up behind Melanie, arms full of junk food. "You kids act like you're starving," the woman says. "Guess I can fire up the grill. Do you want French fries with the burgers?" A chorus of yeses answers this question.

The woman fusses with her cooking appliances for several minutes and then turns around. "My name's Dot," she says. Politely, the teenagers introduce themselves. They settle onto counter stools.

Dot gets hamburger patties and a package of fries out of the refrigerator. "Four cheeseburger platters, right?

"Uh, we have two friends gassing up the boat," Melanie explains. "Better make it six."

"Sure thing, honey." Dot quickly gets the meat sizzling on the grill. Judging that the fat in the fryer is now hot enough, she dumps the entire package of fries in. "Haven't seen y'all 'round heah before. Where you from?"

"Uh, Alabama," Dieter says.

"Do slaves eat at the same table as white people in Alabama?"

Mish jumps up as if bitten by a fire ant. She backs away from the counter and sidles toward the door.

Dot turns to Liam. "So, tell me, what are y'all doing this far from home?"

"Just doin' some fishing,"

"Last I heard they got plenty of fish in the state of Alabama."

Dieter clears his throat. "Oh, we ran out of gas for the boat and drifted downstream. Didn't mean to come this far."

Dot goes to the deep fryer, grabs the basket handle, and gives it a shake. Then she flips the burgers over. "Never seen one chile, let alone a whole mess, settle down at this counter and get nary a phone out. My guess is y'all are on the run and ditched your phones to keep from being tracked."

Liam glances at Melanie and then stands up. "We appreciate your hospitality," he says. "But we need to be going."

"Oh hush," Dot says. "And sit still. You don't see me calling anyone, do you?"

Nervously, Liam regains his seat. Dot pulls cheese slices off a stack and puts them on the burgers. Over her shoulder, she calls Mish. "Come back heah, honey, and grab your seat. Supper's almost ready."

At the dock, Ryan is by the pump, turning it on and off as Gerry fills each of the gas cans. It's a tedious process, but Gerry finally squeezes the last drop of fuel into the final tank. He screws the cap back on and then carries the nozzle across the gangway. Ryan replaces it and then looks at the dial on the pump. "Let's go," he says.

By now, the marina's owner has finished totaling the day's receipts. When Liam and Gerry return, he raises his eyebrows expectantly. "We got twenty-four and a half gallons," Ryan tells him.

The owner taps on an old-fashioned calculator and then peers at the screen. "That'll be $79.76."

Ryan looks around for the others and sees them at the lunch counter. "Hey, who's got money?" he hollers.

Melanie wipes her greasy fingers on a paper napkin and starts to get up. Dot places a restraining hand on her forearm. "Vern, they can pay for everything at once," she calls to her husband. "Send those other two over here. Food's getting cold."

While the teenagers concentrate on their sandwiches, Dot goes to the checkout and confers with Vern. "Them kids is heading for the AZ," she says. "Bet you anything they're tryin' to get to the North."

Vern glances at his watch, then flips the "OPEN" sign hanging in the window to "CLOSED." "I was wondering how come they're so palsy-walsy with that slave girl," he mutters. "We best get them on their way."

Of course, Gerry and Ryan are the last to finish their food. The others wait patiently, then once everyone is finished, they carry their purchases to the front counter to be rung up. "Add a twenty-pound bag of ice, please," Ryan says. Vern happily taps the keys on the register. When the total comes up, he looks from one teenager to the other as they reach into their pockets in search of cash. "I've got ten bucks," Ryan says. The others also come up with money, but the total is far short of what's needed.

"It's OK, I'll use this." Melanie takes out a debit card.

"Bad idea!" Ryan whispers, then bites his lip when both Dot and Vern dart glances at him.

Melanie hands Vern the card, then turns toward Ryan. "It's OK," she says quietly. "I'll explain later."

While Vern runs the card, Dot turns out the lights. Once the transaction is complete, the teenagers straggle out of the store. Dot and Vern follow. "Those burgers were delicious," Dieter says as Dot locks up.

"Yes, thanks so much," Mish smiles. "I was famished."

"Y'all are helping this slave escape, aren't you?" Dot accuses.

"If you knew the whole story, you wouldn't blame us," Dieter says defiantly.

"We don't blame you," Vern says. "Folks 'round here got no use for slavery. We pay an honest day's wage for an honest day's work. But you children don't know what's waitin' for you down this river."

"Best you go on back to your master and let your friends get on with their lives," Dot tells Mish.

"I didn't ask them to do this," Mish explains. "Next thing I knew, there they were."

"That's right," Ryan agrees. "We wanted to help her. But Mish isn't the only one who wants to escape the Confederacy. We all do."

Dot uses the hem of her apron to wipe tears from her eyes. "Then God bless you," she says and turns away.

Vern starts to go after his wife, then pauses. "The river flows north from here to the AZ." He shades his eyes and points. "It's less than a hundred miles. The border will be heavily guarded."

"Thanks," Ryan says. "Y'all have been great." He takes Melanie's hand and they stroll toward the dock. "What did you mean about it being OK to use your debit card?" Ryan asks. "That'll make it easy for The Service to track us."

"Yes, and so will video from the cameras scattered around this place. But we had to pay, and by the time they catch on, we'll either be safe in the North or dead."

"That's a cheerful thought."

"If you want to worry, think about how we're going to get past the guards and into the AZ."

"All right," Ryan agrees.

The boat crew gathers on the dock. No one is anxious to get back aboard the craft. The journey was a lark at first, but being confined on the boat has become tiresome. Finally, Gerry steps onto the gangway, followed by Liam. Dieter lets out a piercing whistle. After a wait, Dachsie comes out from underneath the store and trots over. Mish picks up the pooch and carries her aboard. The others follow. Once the lines are untied, Melanie starts the motors and pilots them out of the marina.

At another marina, back in Alabama, Mayor Montgomery is wondering why his pontoon boat isn't in its slip. Unlike his daughter and her friends, Mayor Montgomery wants very much to go boating. He invited the general manager of the Focke-Wulf factory and his family for an outing the next day. Now, after a long day's work, he has come to the marina to hose his boat down. But it's not where it's supposed to be. Angrily, Montgomery reaches for his phone. "Riverside Park Marina," he says and puts it on speaker.

After two rings, a voice answers, "Good evening, Mayor."

"It was a nice evening," Montgomery snaps. "Until I got to the marina."

"Uh-oh, what's wrong?"

"My boat's gone. I don't see it in any of the other slips."

"I'll be right over."

The park office is less than a mile away. So, it doesn't take long for the ranger, Ron Santmyer, to arrive on his four-wheeler. He joins the mayor in staring at the water where the boat should be. Together, they scratch their heads. "Noticed it was gone the other day," Ron mutters. "Figured you were using it. Haven't been back this way since."

"So, there's no security guard, no cameras?"

"Why bother? The gate is kept locked. The only way in is with the code."

"When's the last time that code was changed?"

Ron scratches his head some more. "Been a while," he admits.

"So, half of Huntsville probably has it by now!" Montgomery raises his phone. "Chief Fife," he tells it. Moments later, the voicemail for Huntsville's police chief comes on. Montgomery listens to the outgoing message impatiently and then snaps, "Chief, it's the mayor. I'm at Riverside Park Marina. Someone stole my boat."

It doesn't take long for several squad cars full of Huntsville cops to race up to the marina gate, sirens blaring. Ron goes to let them in, and the investigation begins. However, boat theft is not considered a major crime, so no one thinks to notify other law enforcement agencies, including the Security Service. Consequently, the next morning, while Ferguson drinks coffee and reads the police blotter from the day before, there's no mention of the missing boat.

Morning is Ferguson's favorite time to work. He can sort through his messages, make calls, and read reports without interruption. That's because the field agents don't usually come in until late. They specialize in night raids and are usually out into the wee hours kicking down doors. Often, noon rolls around before most of them turn up at headquarters.

So it is that Lieutenant Ferguson has the coffee and donuts to himself again this morning. He also was out late. However, the weight of responsibility plus his zeal got him up early to seize another day. Now, he's plopped behind his desk, sorting through emails. *I'm gonna come down with carpal tunnel*, he thinks as he clicks to delete yet another message. *Our spam blocker sucks.*

The cellphone next to Ferguson's mouse jingles a notification. *More spam*, he thinks. However, the text message is from Boyce. "Just got word the Bible-beaters in IR-2 are ready to sing."

"OMW," Ferguson types.

"Still home. Give me half an hour."

"All right, see you at The Pit in thirty minutes."

"Sounds good."

Ferguson reaches for a legal pad and then leans back in his chair. *So, the old goat's ready to spill his guts.* He begins jotting down notes for the upcoming interrogation. As Ferguson concentrates, he loses track of time. So, almost an hour goes by before he gives a start and looks at his watch. Hastily, he shoves his laptop and legal pad into a backpack, slings it over his shoulder, and goes out.

The Seymour Pitman Building is a grim turn-of-the-century stone edifice the SS uses to confine prisoners. It's located in an area of Huntsville that never caught on. That's because of the nearby wastewater treatment plant. It produces a dank odor that permeates the neighborhood, which is mainly comprised of tenements. Many have been abandoned and are now boarded up. It's good that most residents have left. This way, they don't have to listen to the screams coming from the basement of The Pit.

Ferguson runs into little traffic going across town at midday. However, accessing the government parking garage at The Pit and getting through security entails one delay after another. Still, his partner isn't mad when Ferguson finally gets to the reception area. Boyce is so engrossed in conversation with the pretty desk officer that he barely acknowledges Ferguson's arrival. "Honestly, if you like horses, you would love this movie," he tells her.

"Oh, I'm crazy about horses," the desk officer exclaims.

"Great, then why don't we go and see it this weekend."

"Let me see what my husband says."

Boyce puts his hand on the woman's arm. "Can't we just leave him out of it?"

The desk officer snatches her arm away and scowls. Judging that this is a good time to interrupt, Ferguson shoves Boyce aside. "Hey, Doris," he says.

Doris smiles with relief. "Good day, Lieutenant."

"I hear that our birds in IR-2 are ready to confess."

"Oh really? Well, come to think of it, I haven't heard any noise from down there recently."

"Yep, Haberman must have let up on them." Ferguson goes to a doorway and stares into an iris scanner mounted on the wall. A green light flashes and the door unlocks. Ferguson snaps his fingers to get Boyce's attention. "Let's go."

Entering Interrogation Room #2, the agents endeavor to avoid the vomit and human excrement on the floor. "Sheesh," Boyce mutters. He glances at the preacher and his wife and is sorry he did. They're both hanging by their wrists with shoulders clearly dislocated. She's missing both eyes, and the gore dribbles down her cheeks. His groin is a gaping wound, bleeding freely. Both bodies are covered with ugly purple welts. Behind them, Dr. Cecil Haberman is leaning against a counter, smoking a cigarette. "Break time?" Ferguson asks.

Haberman offers Ferguson his pack. "Yeah, want one?"

"I'll pass."

"Suit yourself." Haberman takes a final drag, goes over to the preacher, and stubs the smoking butt out on the man's chest. A faint moan is the only reaction.

"I hear we're having budget cuts," Boyce comments. "But they should at least get you an ashtray."

"Good one," Haberman says with a twisted smile.

Ferguson stands in front of the preacher. "I'm here to help you," he says gently. "All this will be over if you just answer a few simple questions." Patiently, Ferguson waits for a response. When the silence remains unbroken, Haberman steps forward and jolts the clergyman with an electric cattle prod. Another welt appears under his rib cage.

Ferguson tries again. "Just give me a name."

The preacher's broken body hangs listlessly. He's no longer conscious. Ferguson goes to the woman. "How can you do nothing while your husband suffers?" he asks. "Tell me what doctor you've been using. That's all I want."

The woman's mouth moves, and Ferguson thinks she's getting ready to say something. He bends in to better hear and so catches the full force of her expectoration. Oblivious to the spittle running down his cheek, he brutally kicks the woman and then kicks her again. Ferguson draws his arm back for a punch, but Boyce grabs him from behind and drags him away.

It takes Ferguson a while to calm down. Finally, his chest stops heaving, and the tenseness goes out of his body. Boyce gives him his handkerchief. "We're not going to get anything out of them," he says.

Haberman is holding a stethoscope to the preacher's chest. After a pause, he shakes his head, then goes to the woman and listens for a heartbeat. "Looks like your partner's correct," he tells Ferguson. "They're both *kaput*."

"I thought you said they were ready to spill the beans."

"He was going to talk to save her, but at the last minute, she ordered him not to."

Ferguson wipes the spit off his face, folds the handkerchief, and holds it out to his partner. "Keep it!" Boyce raises both hands and backs away.

"Guess I'll take that cigarette now," Ferguson says.

Haberman offers his pack. Boyce takes one as well. Presently, all three men are huffing and puffing. Blood flows across the concrete floor past their feet into a drain. "Phew, they need to hose this joint out," Boyce exhales.

"So, what were you trying to find out?" Haberman asks.

"The name of the doctor who was providing gender-affirming care for the kids they were sheltering."

"Trans?"

"Yeah."

"I can't believe a minister would help those creeps."

"He was ordained in the State Church, but we dug into his background and found that his family were Episcopalians going way back. Both him and the wife."

"Figures."

Boyce takes a deep drag and then blows a series of smoke rings. They slowly dissipate in the still air. "Let's go," Ferguson says disgustedly.

In the parking lot, the agents pause beside Ferguson's car to breathe fresh air. "What a week," Boyce exclaims.

"What a life."

"It's Friday. Let's go to my place and crush a twenty-four-pack."

Ferguson thumbs his remote, and the car door clicks open. "Can't, promised the missus I'd get home early and help pack."

"Oh, that's right, you've got vacation next week."

"Yep."

"Where?"

"Panama City, we rented a condo." Ferguson climbs into the vehicle and buckles his seat belt. "I'm not going back to the office."

"Good thinking. You need to take off and get some relaxation. I'll keep a lid on the nonsense while you're gone."

"Yeah, right," Ferguson says doubtfully.

CHAPTER NINE

DRONE BAIT

With the gas cans full and only a short distance remaining to the border, the teenagers are confident of making it to the Autonomous Zone. Still, they only travel at night when danger from snags, sandbars, and other obstructions dictate a slow pace. This evening, it's Ryan's turn at the helm. As the boat drifts in the darkness, his imagination roams. A distant splash might be a fish jumping or a beaver diving into the water. The hooting of an owl makes him wonder what the fearsome predator is hunting in the night. After two hours of this, Ryan's exhausted and ready when Dieter comes to take over.

Several hours later, the darkness gives way to a rose-colored dawn. Yawning, Melanie emerges from her sleeping bag to relieve Gerry. They are both at the console when something whirrs overhead. They look up and see a dark object outlined against the lightening sky. Slowly, it passes above them and then doubles back. "Get Ryan," Melanie gasps.

Gerry shakes Ryan awake. "Hey, we've got a problem."

"What is it?" Ryan is instantly alert.

"Drone."

Ryan comes out of his sleeping bag, holding Bryson's rifle. He keeps it beside him for security and to have something of his father's nearby. Now, he fishes around in his backpack for a bullet and slips it into the chamber. By the time the drone returns, Ryan's ready.

"Wait," Liam suggests. "Maybe it didn't see us."

"Then why is it circling back?" Gerry asks.

To dispel any question that the quadcopter is on to them, it hovers directly overhead. "Must have an infrared camera," Dieter exclaims. "It picked up our heat signatures."

Ryan draws a bead on the center of the drone, hoping to disable the flight controller. It's an easy shot, but the quadcopter darts to the side just as he squeezes the trigger. "Dang, I missed." Ryan quickly reloads, but there's no sign of the drone when he looks up again.

"It's gone," Liam says.

"Hey, what's the plan?" Melanie asks. "You can bet that the Border Patrol is loading into their boats to come after us right now."

"We should find a place to ditch this boat and then head north through the woods," Ryan suggests.

"Then what?" Melanie demands.

"Find a way into the Autonomous Zone," Ryan explains. "It can't be too far away now."

"So, we're just going to waltz right in, huh?"

Ryan folds his arms and glares at his girlfriend. "OK, tell us your plan."

"Guys, save the arguing for later," Dieter suggests. "This boat now has a target on it. We'll all sink with it if we don't get going."

Angrily, Melanie fires up the outboards. The others barely have time to grab hold of something before she advances the throttle. The boat lurches forward, and Ryan almost loses his footing. "Pack up," he shouts over the noise of the motors. "Take everything you need for up to a week in the woods."

While Melanie steers toward the north bank, Ryan shoves camping gear into his and Melanie's backpacks. Nearby, Dieter is squaring away the supplies he brought for Mish and himself. The others are busy as well, and the deck is littered with cook sets, bags of freeze-dried food, sleeping bags, mats, tents, and other necessities. The challenge is fitting everything into the limited space available.

Once he's finished with their backpacks, Ryan goes to stand beside Melanie. "Take the wheel," she says and gets her binoculars. "I'm searching for a place to pull in."

Ryan steers with one hand and puts his other arm around Melanie's waist. "Sorry if I was impatient with you just then."

"Forget it." Melanie turns toward her boyfriend for a kiss.

Dieter and Mish also have their backpacks ready. They go to the bow to unravel the mooring line. "Hey, look." Dieter points toward the riverbank.

Melanie shifts her gaze to where there's a gap in the undergrowth. "Yeah, let's check out that opening."

The boat rocks violently in rough water as they approach the bank. The turbulence is caused by a stream that cascades over a rock ledge before emptying into the river. "This will work," Melanie shouts, "brace yourselves." She shoves the throttle all the way forward, and moments later, the pontoons crash onto the rocky shore at the waterfall's base. Standing at the bow, Dieter is quickly drenched. But he manages to toss a line over a tree limb and make it fast. Liam secures the stern while Mish finds a place to deploy the gangway. She gathers Dachsie in her arms and descends to the rocky ground. Dieter follows with both their backpacks.

"Ruck up," Ryan shouts. "Abandon ship!" He shoulders his backpack and then turns to help Melanie with hers.

Meanwhile, Liam clomps past Ryan toward the gangway, accompanied by Gerry. "Where do you get all that military lingo?" he asks.

"Junior ROTC," Ryan says with a grin.

"It's so lame."

Presently, the entire crew is ashore. While Ryan peers at a compass, the others look wistfully at the boat that brought them this far. As tiresome as it was to be stuck on the ungainly craft, they are now reluctant to say goodbye to her. Impatiently, Melanie moves closer to Ryan to see the compass dial. "All I know is we need to go north," Ryan says.

"My idea is that we just need to go somewhere," Melanie counters. "Anywhere away from this boat. Half of it is still hanging out in the river. How long do you think it will take them to find it?"

"That looks like a trail." Dieter points to a trampled area off to the left.

"Probably made by deer coming down for a drink," Liam comments.

Ryan hitches up his shoulder straps and begins walking. "Let's see where it goes."

With Ryan leading, the teenagers fall into a single file like Boy Scouts. In no time, they're all breathing heavily as they shoulder their loads up a steep hill. The farther they get from the river, the dryer the ground and the better the footing. The path they are on meanders back toward the stream and then levels off as they come to the crest of a ridge. The sound of crashing water below signifies they are now above the waterfall. Ryan raises his hand for a break so he can consult his compass. "What have you got?" Dieter asks.

"This stream is heading roughly in the right direction," Ryan says. "We can follow it for a while."

"All right."

Once again, the group sets off with Dachsie often running ahead to scout before returning to check on them. They descend for a while but soon encounter another uphill stretch. Following the streambank means that they avoid the undergrowth on either side. But after being cooped up on the boat for so long without exercise, the teenagers tire easily. Frequently, as the day progresses, one or the other of the hikers asks for a break. Late in the afternoon, they pause beside a picturesque pool created by a beaver dam. By acclamation, they decide to camp there. "I'm going to have dinner before anything else," Liam says.

"Makes sense," Ryan agrees. "What do you want to eat?" he asks Melanie.

"What difference does it make? Freeze-dried food all tastes the same."

"Too true."

Ryan gets the clever little backpacking stove he and Melanie bought and screws it into a fuel cylinder. He carefully lights it, adjusts the flame, and then balances a pot of water on it. Melanie opens a pouch that purports to contain two servings of gourmet Thai food. Once the water is boiling, Ryan pours a measure into the pouch. "How long does it have to sit?" he asks.

"Ten minutes."

Looking around, Ryan sees that the other soccer players are also waiting for their food to be ready. "Guys, we're all out of shape," he calls. "Let's have a short workout."

"Great idea," Liam agrees.

"Twenty-five push-ups, go." Gerry drops to the ground, and the other soccer players count along with him. Melanie and Mish coach. "All the way down," they shout, or "That's only twenty, do five more."

Ten minutes later, after more calisthenics, the soccer players are breathing heavily. They cool down with some stretches, then find a log to sit on while they eat. Nearby, Mish and Melanie are almost finished with their pouches. "I can't handle any more of this stuff," Melanie says.

"Me neither," Mish agrees. Her dinner is supposed to be chicken and dumplings, but one is indistinguishable from the other. The glutinous mass in the pouch looks disgusting.

Mish goes to get a trash bag. After dropping her pouch inside, she brings it to Melanie, who does likewise. By now, the others are finished eating, so Mish also gathers their trash.

It would be nice to relax after dinner. However, there are many chores to be done. After rinsing off their eating utensils, the teenagers get busy setting up tents. Ryan brought a rubber mallet to drive in stakes so he and Melanie finish first. They see Dieter nearby pounding a tent peg with a rock. "Try this." Ryan tosses him the mallet.

While Ryan puts on the rain fly, Melanie rolls out mats and sleeping bags inside their tent. Once everything's ready, Ryan brings rocks from the stream to make a fire ring. "We're going to need wood," he announces.

"I've got you," Liam declares. He and Gerry have their home for the night ready. They go off in search of wood. Mish accompanies them, leaving Dieter to finish with their tent. Meanwhile, Ryan completes the fire ring and then looks for kindling.

It's not long before Mish and Gerry return with arms full of sticks. Liam hauls a log and then goes to get another. As the sun drops below the ridgeline, the day's heat gives way to cool highland air. "I'm going to put on my jeans," Melanie says.

"Me too," Mish agrees. The other campers scatter to search in their backpacks for warmer clothes while Ryan painstakingly builds the fire. Finally, he lights it and then goes to change as well.

"Where did you learn to build a fire?" Liam asks once the group has reassembled. They're seated around the ring, watching flames from the kindling lick against the bigger pieces higher up.

"My father taught me," Ryan answers. "He showed me how to make a mound with small bits of pine straw and leaf clutter, then add tiny pieces of wood until it's big enough. Only then can you start surrounding the mound with bigger and bigger twigs. Sticks and logs go on top."

"My father never taught me anything," Gerry complains. "He took my brothers camping and hunting but always left me behind. He said Mom and I could cook the venison they brought back."

"That had to be tough for you," Liam sympathizes.

"Yeah, Mother and I never got along. She swore she'd beat the tomboy out of me."

"Nice."

"I kept saying, Mom, I'm not a tomboy. I'm just a boy. She didn't get it."

Melanie scoots over and puts her arm around Gerry. "Well, we get it," she says. "And we love you."

"You know, our soccer team's the only real family I've ever known." Gerry blinks back tears.

"That's why soccer rules," Liam exclaims. "It brings people together, people from different countries, other races."

"I'm the only other race I see 'round here," Mish says. "And I never got to play soccer or any other sport."

"What about skating?" Ryan asks.

"That was for my job," Mish explains. "I had to practice for weeks before I could carry a tray. Every night I'd return to the quarter bleeding and bruised from falls."

"But you got good."

"Because I loved it." Mish sighs, thinking back. "The only time I felt free was on those skates. But now that's all over, thanks to him." Mish glares at Dieter, who's seated on a nearby log.

"You're right to be angry," Dieter hangs his head. "I blew it."

"Yeah, I should hate you, but I don't anymore. If it wasn't for you and *Frau* von Kluck protecting me from your father, who knows what might have happened."

There's an awkward silence around the campfire. Then Gerry speaks up. "Who wants a s'more?" The response is enthusiastic, so Gerry gets a bag of marshmallows and a pack of graham crackers from his backpack. Ryan goes to the woodpile and breaks off some sticks.

Before long, six marshmallows are slowly browning near the fire. But Ryan loses patience and moves his stick too close to the flames. He allows the marshmallow to burn for a moment, then blows it out. He uses a graham cracker to scrape the charred mass off his stick, then makes a sandwich using another cracker. "Mmm, good," Ryan smiles. But his happy expression fades when he bites into a burnt mouthful of marshmallow.

A minute later, Melanie pulls her stick away from the fire. The white marshmallow is now brown on all sides. Delicately, she makes her s'more. Mish copies Melanie's patient technique, and her dessert also turns out well. "First time I've ever made one." She wipes a smidgen of marshmallow filling from her lip.

"Oh, anyone can do it like that if you want to take all day," Ryan frowns.

Melanie bites into her now cool treat. "So, you've never been camping before?" she asks Mish.

"Ha, the only time slaves sleep out is when they're running away from Massa."

"I'd be running away all the time," Gerry says defiantly.

"You ever see someone tied shirtless to a post and whipped until every last bit of skin has been flayed off their back?" Mish throws her stick into the fire and stands up. "That's what happens to runaways when they get caught. They do it in front of the other slaves so everyone gets the message. Still, many try to escape. Mainly field hands on the big plantations. Sugar cane, rice, cotton, that's how bad it is. Dawn to dusk, seven days a week, men, women, and children, under the broiling sun, constantly beaten by white overseers with clubs." Firelight reflects off the tears coursing down Mish's cheeks. Smoke billows behind her. No one has anything further to say. One by one, the teenagers stand up to get ready for bed.

The fire appears to be out in the morning. However, closer inspection reveals an occasional wisp of smoke and, sometimes, a tiny spark. That's because Ryan covered the burning remnants with ashes before turning in the night before. Now, all that's needed to get the blaze going again is wood, but none is left.

"I'll go," Liam offers.

"Me as well," Mish pipes up. "Anything's better than standing around freezing."

Ryan is the only other camper who has emerged from his sleeping bag to brave the early morning chill. He gazes at the steep hillsides on either side, still gray and lifeless in the dim light. *We're going to need more kindling*, he decides and wanders toward the stream, picking up twigs as he goes.

Farther upstream, Liam and Mish are heading for the brush pile they found the day before. When they get to the right spot, it turns out they got all the good pieces of wood already. "I bet those branches we found yesterday were left in this pocket by the last flood," Liam says. "We can probably find another pile farther up."

"I don't mind walking some more," Mish smiles. "The more we walk, the warmer I get."

A short while later, they come to a bend in the stream where the current has deposited a likely collection of brush. Mish begins pulling sticks out of the pile while Liam hunts for logs to place on top of the fire. "What's that?" Mish asks, pointing to a white plastic cylinder that protrudes into the water from the opposite bank.

"I'm not sure," Liam says. He puts down a log he's hefting and moves closer to the water to get a better look. Mish joins him, and they both stare at the unnatural thing.

"There's more just past those trees," Mish points. "It runs down that hill into what looks like a meadow."

"Oh, now I see. That's PVC pipe," Liam says. "It's used for plumbing."

"What would anyone need plumbing for up here?" Mish wonders. "We're a thousand miles from nowhere."

"Let's find out," Liam suggests. "We can get across the stream by hopping from one rock to the next."

Mish puts the branches that she collected down in a neat stack. "Sounds good."

Back at the campsite, the rest of the teenagers are finally up. They stand around the fire ring, hoping for warmth. "Mish and Liam should have been back with the wood a long time ago," Ryan frets. He's gathered a pile of kindling but doesn't want to use it until some larger pieces of wood are available.

"I'm going to make hot chocolate," Melanie says. "At least I can warm my insides."

"Let me help," Gerry offers. "I want some, too."

Ryan kneels beside the tent he and Melanie share and reaches inside for the rifle. "I'm going to see what's taking the others so long."

"I'll go with you," Dieter declares.

"Thanks."

With rapid strides, the two soccer players make their way up the streambank. They try to minimize noise and be alert to their surroundings. The farther from camp they get without finding their friends, the more worried they become. Eventually, Dieter finds the tidy stack of wood Mish left next to the stream. "That isn't normal," he says. "Tree limbs don't make a neat pile like this when they fall."

Ryan looks where Dieter is pointing and nods his head. He shifts his gaze to take in both sides of the stream and spots the pipe. "That PVC doesn't fit the picture either."

"Let's see where it goes," Dieter suggests. The two boys wade to the opposite bank and follow the PVC pipe into a glade of waist-high marijuana plants. Water from the pipe flows into channels dug into the ground for irrigation. "Quiet, don't move," Dieter hisses. Ryan freezes, then slowly turns his head in the direction Dieter is looking. Liam and Mish are there, among the marijuana plants, looking at Dieter and him wide-eyed. A man is facing them, holding a shotgun. All Ryan and Dieter can see is the back of his hefty body, which is clad in denim overalls. Ryan brings the rifle up, takes a stealthy step, and then another. Dieter follows. As they approach the shotgun-wielding man, they hear him say, "I don't know how you young'uns got back in here, but this is your unlucky day."

"Mister, we don't care what you're doing," Liam pleads. "It's none of our business. We won't tell anybody if you just let us go."

"Can't," the man says. "This here's my livin'. Dasn't chance losing it. For all I know, you're lookin' to rip me off. Either that or turn me in."

Ryan points the rifle at the back of the man's head. He's close enough now to touch him. "Easy now," he says softly. "Got a gun on you. Get your finger off that trigger, or you're a dead man."

A red flush creeps up the back of the man's neck. "I told you our friends would be looking for us," Liam tells him. "Please don't do anything stupid. No one has to die today."

Slowly, the shotgun is lowered with the muzzle turned away. "Put it on the ground," Ryan commands.

After the marijuana farmer complies, Ryan steps forward and kicks the shotgun toward Dieter, who picks it up. "Hey, my pappy gave me that gun," the man complains.

"Cooperate, and maybe you'll get it back," Ryan says. "Now turn around."

The farmer faces Ryan, who keeps the rifle level. "How far's the AZ from here?" Ryan asks.

"'Bout four or five miles. Two hours at most to walk."

"Ever been inside?"

"Ha-ha, you jokin'?" The man turns his head to spit a stream of tobacco juice. Then he looks from Ryan to the other teenagers now clustered behind Ryan. "Oh, I get it. Y'all's runaways."

"That's right," Ryan admits.

"What happened? Daddy cut off your allowance?" the farmer sneers, showing off his tobacco-stained teeth.

"None of your business," Ryan snaps. "Show us how to get into the AZ, and we'll let you go."

"What about gettin' my gun back?"

"That too."

"All right, ah kin draw you a map."

"Wrong, you're going to take us." Ryan brings the rifle up for emphasis. The man holds both hands up in surrender. "Sure, sure."

Without turning his head, Ryan speaks to his friends. "You guys go break camp and tell Melanie and Gerry what's happening. I'll stay here and keep our new friend company."

"You got it," Dieter agrees.

"I'll bring your pack," Liam offers.

"Sounds good."

Behind him, Ryan hears the others head back the way they all came. The sun is well up now. It feels good on his back. The adrenaline that had his senses on high alert a few minutes ago is fading. His heartbeat is returning to normal. "So, we just gonna stand out here in the open and be drone bait?" the farmer asks.

"All right, good point. Let's find some cover." Ryan follows his prisoner out of the marijuana patch. They go up the hill and into the woods beside the stream. "Sit on that log," Ryan says, pointing. "You got a name?"

"Caleb."

Ryan leans against a tree a safe distance away and cradles the rifle in his arm. "Well, Caleb, I don't expect you're real happy right now, but if you help us, things could still turn out good for you."

"How's that?"

"We got some Confederate money with us. Not much, but some. When we get to the AZ, we'll let you have it. Won't need it where we're going."

"You said that true. Where you're goin', ya won't need nothin', 'cause you'll be dead."

"Not if we're careful. Travel by night and avoid settlements. It's only a hundred miles to freedom."

Caleb shrugs. "Might work," he allows. "Just remember, ya can't trust anyone 'round heah, and don't believe nothin' anyone tells you."

"Have you always lived in these parts?" Ryan asks to change the subject.

"Yep, been Frasers in these hills forever," Caleb says proudly. "We got a Bible at the house with writing going back hundreds of years. My pappy told us all about it like his paw did him. The first Fraser came to this country as a slave."

"You mean an indentured servant," Ryan corrects.

"Yeah, whatever you want to call it. He was freed after seven years workin' for another man with no pay. That's slavery, ain't it?"

"Absolutely." Ryan nods his head. "We covered it in history last year. In the early days of America, impoverished Europeans would sell themselves into labor for seven years to earn their passage here. Southern plantation owners bought many of them. The issue the planters ran into was what to do with the indentured servants after their time was up. At first, they gave them small parcels of land to farm. However, the planters didn't like sharing their valuable holdings, so, after a while, they started banishing the freed servants to the mountains where the land was worthless."

"You got that right," Caleb exclaims. "These hills are full of folks whose ancestors got here thataway."

"I believe you. In school, we learned that the planters finally solved their problem by stopping the use of indentured servants. Instead, they imported kidnapped Africans and made them permanent slaves."

"Yeah." Caleb shifts his tobacco chaw to the other cheek. "And they left my people up in these hills to scratch out a livin' from this rocky soil best we could. That's how come we never had no use for them high-and-mighty planters and their so-called Confederacy."

Ryan shades his eyes and peers into the glade where bright green marijuana leaves ripple in the breeze. "From what I can see, you got a nice little cash crop growing yonder, rocky soil and all."

Caleb grins. "A man's got to do what a man's got to do."

What has been a distant muffled sound slowly gets louder. Soon, it's distinguishable as the babble of happy teenage voices. Ryan sighs with relief as his friends finally appear around a bend in the trail on the opposite side of the stream. "Let's go," he tells Caleb.

"First, I need to get me a drink," Caleb says. "It's thirsty work sitting here jackin' my jaw with you."

"All right, but don't try any funny business," Ryan scowls.

Caleb holds his hand up as if he's saying The Leader Pledge of Loyalty. "I won't try anything, I swear."

Ryan follows Caleb to the stream and watches him kneel and then cup his hands in the sparkling water. The farmer drinks several hands full, then goes for one more scoop that takes longer than the others. Abruptly, Caleb rises and flings gravel into Ryan's eyes. In an instant, he tackles Ryan to the ground and tries to wrest the rifle away. Ryan clings to the wooden stock of his father's gun with grim determination. Whenever he feels his grip slacken, he remembers Bryson with it and becomes more determined. Meanwhile, Liam sees what's going on. He splashes across the stream and, using all his force, hurls Ryan's backpack at Caleb. It knocks the farmer sideways, and he loses his grasp on the rifle. Standing, Caleb turns to meet the new threat. "Ha-ha, just kidding," he says, raising his hands.

By now, Dieter is also across the stream. He points the shotgun at Caleb with a nervous finger on the trigger. "Easy, easy," Caleb says. "If you shoot me, you'll never find out about the AZ."

"Oh really?" Dieter raises his eyebrows. "What makes you know so much?"

Caleb grins. "How do you think we get our weed up north?" he asks. "The Yankees got to have it. We know how to get it to them."

"What's taking so long?" Melanie hollers from the opposite bank. She was with the last group coming up and didn't see what happened.

"We had some excitement," Ryan yells back. "I'll tell you about it later."

While Dieter guards the prisoner, Ryan takes the rifle to the stream and leans it against a boulder. He uses his hands to brush dirt off his clothes, then kneels by the water to rinse them. Emulating Caleb, he drinks a few scoops of water while he's at it.

Once Ryan's done, he goes to get his backpack. As he's buckling it on, Caleb calls to him. "No hard feelings, young'un, you heah?"

"You promised not to try anything," Ryan complains.

"Yeah. Ah also said not to believe anyone 'round heah."

Ryan goes to the boulder and picks up the rifle. "Guess I had to learn the hard way."

CHAPTER TEN

TILTROTOR

I t's a tanned and rested Lieutenant Ferguson who goes back to work after his vacation. Most people dread returning to the grind after a holiday, but Ferguson loves his job and is happy to get back at it. That is until he opens the office door and finds Boyce with his feet on the desk. The agent is holding his phone and rapidly tapping the keys. "What the hell?" Ferguson bellows.

Boyce glances over and is relieved to see his tolerant partner. "Just taking a little break."

"A little break, my butt. You haven't done jack since I left, have you?"

Boyce adopts a sincere expression while endeavoring to maintain eye contact with his boss. However, the device in his hands exerts a magnetic pull on his peepers. "Drat, I'm dead," he exclaims, staring at his phone in disbelief.

"Serves you right," Ferguson laughs. He hangs his shoulder holster on the hat rack and sits behind his desk.

"Couldn't you have stayed away another week?" Boyce asks. "I almost made it to level six."

"Forget that garbage. I want a complete rundown on what's been happening around here."

"The big news is that Lillian's pregnant."

"Lillian in dispatch?"

"That's the one. According to the ultrasound, it's a boy."

Ferguson fires up his desktop. When the home screen comes up, he enters the passcode. "They've been trying for a long time. Made no secret of it."

"Yeah, word is they finally went to a fertility clinic."

"TMI," Ferguson shrugs.

"Well, you wanted to know."

"What I really want to know is what's happening with our cases."

"Oh, well you'll be glad to know that one of those trans kids finally ratted out the doctor. The quack and those brats are all on their way to Andersonville."

"Good job."

Boyce knits his fingers together and cracks the knuckles. "Thank Haberman, he got it out of the sixteen-year-old."

"So, what else?"

"We got a couple of leads on them runaways, the ones who led us on that wild goose chase."

"Now you're talking." Ferguson gets up and paces back and forth excitedly. "Details," he demands.

"The mayor called. Says he found a charge on his daughter's debit card from a marina in Tennessee."

"And? What else?"

"His boat is missing."

"What boat?"

"A twenty-four-foot pontoon job."

Ferguson stops walking. With a frown, he holds a hand up and punches it. The clap resounds around the detective room. "So that punk Ryan and his friends were enjoying a river cruise while we were busting our asses in Florida?"

"Looks like it."

"So, what did you find out from the people at the marina?"

"I called, but there was no answer. Was just getting ready to try again." Boyce reaches for his phone.

"Call? On the phone? You mean you haven't gone there?"

"Tennessee? Are you serious?"

Ferguson takes hold of the back of Boyce's chair and spins it around so that the agent's feet are dragged off the desk. They crash onto the floor, taking Boyce's semi-supine form with them. "Hey, why did you do that?"

"We're going after those kids."

Boyce gets back onto his chair but keeps both feet on the floor. "Sure, whatever you say."

"If they get away this time, I'm gonna transfer you back to The Pit." Ferguson slams his hand on the desk for emphasis.

Boyce flinches. "You're obsessed with those kids," he complains. "Reminds me of *Moby Dick*."

"What do you know about *Moby Dick*?"

"Had to read it in high school. The teacher said it was full of symbolism."

"Like what?"

"Well, the whale, Moby Dick, represents slavery. It's white because of the good it does. Captain Ahab is always dressed in black. He's an abolitionist and is obsessed with destroying Moby Dick. But in the end, the whale triumphs."

"Very interesting. We can talk about it more on the way."

"To Tennessee?"

"Correct."

"How we gonna get there?"

"I'll rustle up a helicopter. Now you go to supply and get us full field kit for three days."

Boyce gets to his feet. "OK, but they'll want to know what it's for."

"Tell them we're going on a manhunt."

While Boyce is across the street requisitioning field equipment, Ferguson goes down the hall to his boss' office and raps on the door. Entering, Ferguson glances at Captain Tyson's computer screen and sees he's in the middle of a solitaire game. "Sorry to interrupt, Chief, but I have a priority request."

Tyson hastily minimizes his screen. "What's up?"

"We got a lead on the kid whose father blew up that power station."

"Isn't that kind of old news? Stuff's been getting blown up right, left, and yonder lately."

Unasked, Ferguson pulls up a chair and sits. "That's what I mean. We haven't found out what the kid knows about The Resistance. He might be able to identify other members of his father's cell. I bet they're the ones perpetrating these latest cases."

Tyson sighs. "So, what do you want?"

"A helicopter, plus clearance to operate in Tennessee."

"That all? Sure you don't want me to throw in a twenty-four-pack?"

"Would be nice."

Tyson doodles on a notepad while he cogitates. "Tennessee, huh? Think the brat's making for the AZ?"

"Him and his friends, including a runaway slave and Mayor Montgomery's daughter."

"Can't have that!"

Ferguson leans back in his chair. He can tell his boss is giving in. "I want to pick them up before they escape. We'll take the boy to The Pit and let Haberman teach him to sing. The rest can go straight to Andersonville."

"Good plan. I'll see what I can do for you. Check back in an hour."

"You got it."

Boyce is back at his desk when Ferguson returns to the office. "Where's our gear?"

"It was too much for me to carry. They're going to deliver."

"Have you requested video from that marina yet?"

"It's the next thing on my list." Boyce's fingers begin to fly over his keyboard.

Shaking his head, Ferguson settles onto his chair. "About time," he mutters.

Five emails came in while Ferguson was down the hall. He reads enough of each one to know they don't pertain to him, then deletes the lot. Someone knocks on the office door. "Come," Ferguson says loudly.

Two slaves wearing shackles shuffle in with rucksacks on their backs. Each has a stack of field equipment in his arms. Boyce gets to his feet. "Over there." He points to the conference table. The slaves drop the gear, unsling the rucks, and lean them against the table. Hastily, they back out the door, happy to get away from the SS agents.

Boyce goes to the conference table and begins sorting through the gear. "We got enough stuff here to start a war."

"Shut up and get ready," Ferguson replies. He's getting out of his civilian clothes and into camouflage-patterned field utilities. Once he's done lacing up the boots, he stuffs a sleeping bag into one of the rucks, then adds a poncho and three boxes of rations. In the bottom compartment, he stores hardware, including a lighter, flashlight, hatchet, can opener, heat tablets, and a LifeStraw. Ferguson rolls up a mat, straps it to the ruck, then hefts the load onto his back. *Not too bad*, he thinks.

By now, Boyce is also wearing camos and is about halfway done with his ruck. Ferguson sits and opens a box of 9mm ammunition. Like an automaton, he pushes one bullet after another into a magazine. Once it's full, he places it in an ammo pouch and starts on another. "Get over here and help with this," he snaps.

A half-hour later, the two men are ready to go. "All we need is a bird and our clearance," Ferguson says. Just then, the office door swings open, and Tyson strolls in. "I thought duck hunting season wasn't 'til December."

"We're going hunting, all right," Ferguson smirks. He slams a magazine into the butt of his pistol for emphasis.

"Well, I got you the mother of all whirlybirds," Tyson brags. "It's a tiltrotor."

"What's that?" Boyce asks.

"Takes off and lands like a helicopter but flies like a plane. So, it's much faster than a chopper."

"Sounds good."

"You'll also have a squad of Marines along."

"What for?" Boyce wonders. "We don't need help busting a bunch of kids."

"They're coming to protect the equipment, not you," Tyson laughs. "Tiltrotors are expensive."

"How did you swing it?" Ferguson asks.

"Let's just say I called in a few favors," Tyson says. "It'll be waiting for you at The Space Flight Complex."

Sure enough, when the SS agents reach the SFC Airfield, they find a dark gray tiltrotor waiting on a landing pad. The pilot is warming up the turbine engines while a squad of Confederate Marines smokes and jokes nearby. A sergeant sees the two tactically dressed men get out of their car and saunter toward him. *Even in camo, no one would mistake them for anything other than what they are*, he thinks. *Cops.*

Ferguson has his credentials out by the time they get to where the Marines are waiting. He holds the badge up to eye level so the squad leader can have a good look. "Fall in," the sergeant shouts.

The Marines with still-lit cigarettes pinch the burning ends off and then deposit the butts in their pockets. They line up and stand stiffly with their assault rifles. "At ease," the sergeant commands. The Marines shift from attention to a slightly more comfortable posture. Behind them, the rear ramp of the aircraft slowly lowers. Two crewmen come down to check it. One gives the thumbs up.

"All aboard," the sergeant commands.

Ferguson and Boyce wait until the last of the Marines have boarded, then follow them up the ramp. Inside the aircraft, metal ribs surround the occupants like the crash cage of a race car. The thin outer skin appears to be bolted onto this frame as an afterthought. Ferguson sees the Marines settling into uncomfortable-looking jump seats on either side of the fuselage. He flips one down for himself and sits with his ruck propped against his legs. Boyce sits beside him. Neither man attempts conversation. That would be futile, thanks to the piercing whine of the turbine engines. *The military could teach the airlines a thing or two about tormenting passengers*, Ferguson thinks.

The ramp comes up, and what had been a *whup-whup-whup* sound from the rotors becomes an indistinguishable roar. Shuddering violently, the aircraft lifts off the ground. It hovers briefly, then slowly pirouettes as the pilot points the nose toward the northwest. Ferguson glances out the porthole across from him but can see nothing but blue sky. The tiltrotor lurches as the nose drops. Ferguson can't help but grab hold of his seat as they accelerate. He glances at the Marines and is shocked to see most of their heads bobbing. Even asleep, they firmly grip their assault rifles, keeping them butt down between their knees.

Ferguson slackens his grip on the seat but doesn't remove his hands entirely. As the ground rushes by beneath the aircraft, it continues to shake, rattle, and roll. *I'm not sure I can take several hours of this*, he thinks. The tiltrotor contorts wildly as it hits an updraft. Ferguson swallows the bile rising in his throat. On top of everything, he's getting airsick. Dizzily, the agent leans his head back and closes his eyes. Next to him, Boyce is oblivious to everything but his phone.

Two hours later, Ferguson awakens with Boyce's elbow jammed into his ribs. "Wake up, we're going to land," Boyce announces. Angrily, Ferguson pushes his partner away. As the tiltrotor banks steeply, he sees what appears to be a trailer park out of the porthole. Their forward motion slows and then stops. The aircraft descends. A sudden jolt signifies that they are back on terra firma.

Without being told, the Marines are on their feet with weapons at the ready. As the back ramp descends, they rush down and encircle the craft to provide 360-degree security. The sergeant waits for the two SS agents at the foot of the ramp. Then, the three men cautiously scan the surroundings. They are in a field of fledgling corn plants. The still-turning rotor blades are wreaking havoc on the nascent crop.

Across a dirt road from the cornfield is an RV park littered with worn-out trailers. The glimmering waters of the Tennessee River are visible through trees that border the campground. Boyce points to a ramshackle wooden building set on a rise of ground near a boat dock. Ferguson nods, then turns toward the sergeant. "We're going to clear that building," he says. "Wait one."

"Yes, sir."

Something Boyce hates about his boss is that he's a speedwalker. So instead of his customary pimp roll, Boyce must adopt a purposeful stride to keep up. He's breathing heavily by the time they're halfway across the field. "You smoke too much," Ferguson says.

Dot and Vern are in front of the store, staring wide-eyed at the tiltrotor. It resembles a techno-mechanical monster from a sci-fi movie. Reluctantly, they tear their eyes away to focus on the two burly-looking men coming across the yard. "Good afternoon," the first one says and displays his credentials. "I'm Lieutenant Ferguson, and this here is Agent Boyce."

"Glad to meet ya," Vern says, although he's anything but.

"We're here to ask about some teenagers who passed this way about a week ago," Ferguson says with a fake smile. "Their parents are worried sick about them."

"Hmm," Vern stalls for time. "Uh, we've had lots of folks in and out of here since then."

"They were on a big pontoon boat," Boyce snaps. "Hard to miss."

With a sweep of his arm, Vern indicates the covered boat slips in the marina, "Half those boats are pontoons."

"How many of them were stolen?" Ferguson asks.

"None," Vern answers with alarm rising in his voice. "Wh-why do you ask?" he stammers.

"The kids we're looking for are runaways, and the boat they're using was stolen. Now, if you don't tell us what you know, you'll be charged as accessories."

Vern glances at Dot. "We don't know anything," she says bravely.

"Oh really?" Ferguson draws his pistol. "We'll see about that. You're under arrest."

"Get over there." Boyce points to the building. "Put your hands on the wall."

"Aren't you going to read us our rights?" Dot asks.

"Ha-ha," Boyce laughs. "You hillbillies have been watching too many re-runs. The Constitution's suspended, doncha know? We're under martial law. That means you don't have any rights."

"Let's just cut the crap, shall we?" Ferguson's smile is gone. "Those kids are wanted. We need descriptions and to know what they were up to. Tell us, and we'll be on our way."

"We get lots of folks stopping in here," Vern says defiantly. "How am I supposed to remember back nigh a week ago?"

"Maybe I can help you remember." Ferguson points the Glock at Vern's head.

"They're headed for the Autonomous Zone," Dot blurts out.

"And?"

"There was a total of six kids, male and female. Mostly dressed in shorts and T-shirts. One of the boys was very tall and athletic-looking. Rest were average height. One of the girls was a pretty blonde. Another was Black, possibly a runaway slave."

"They bought about eighty bucks worth of gas and a bunch of junk food," Vern adds.

"And ate cheeseburgers and fries at the lunch counter," Dot remembers.

Ferguson lowers the 9mm. "Now that wasn't so hard, was it?" He makes as if to re-holster the pistol. Instead, he launches a vicious backhand, catching Vern on the side of his head with the heavy gun. The old man's glasses fly off as he crumples to the ground. Blood gushes from a gaping head wound.

"Why?" Dot cries, dropping to her knees. "Why, why?" She bends over her unconscious husband, moaning.

"Shut the hell up, woman," Boyce snarls. He looks at Ferguson. "Are we going to bust them as accessories?"

"Nah, we got to get after those kids." Ferguson slides the Glock back into its holster. "Besides, we got all they know out of 'em already."

The tiltrotor pilot and his backup are outside the craft, knocking a pickleball back and forth when the SS agents return. The Marines are still in full tactical mode around their ungainly form of transportation. Ferguson goes to the sergeant. "The fugitives are ahead of us," he says. "But traveling much slower. With luck, we can catch up to them before they get to the AZ."

"Roger that."

Ferguson turns to Boyce. "Get with Confederate Border Patrol and see if they've got anything to report."

Boyce reaches for his phone and diligently taps out an email. He hits send and then glances at his boss for further instructions. Ferguson is thinking and doesn't meet his subordinate's inquiring eyes. A slow minute passes, and then Boyce's phone *plings*. "Well?" Ferguson asks.

"Says they sent a query to that section and will get back to us as soon as they have something."

Ferguson contemplates the ground at his feet and then comes to a decision. "Let's proceed upriver while we wait for a reply from CBP."

"Makes sense," Boyce shrugs.

Ferguson turns to the Marine sergeant. "Why don't you give your men a smoke break while I go talk to the pilots? It'll take them a while to start the turbines."

"Good idea, sir." The squad leader calls his command together. Presently, the Marines are busy satisfying their nicotine dependency and needling each other. Ferguson confers with the pilots.

At that moment, farther north, Ferguson's quarry is also having a break. The teenagers and their guide are under some trees on a ridge overlooking a picturesque waterway. "I thought we were done with rivers," Ryan comments.

"Can't you point that rifle somewhere else?" Caleb asks. "I'm too tired from walking to try anything."

"Yeah, right. Fool me once, shame on you, fool me twice, shame on me."

Caleb grins. "That's what my Pappy used to say."

"Mine too."

"So, what's the name of that river?" Melanie asks impatiently.

"It's the Cumberland," Caleb replies, "and you know what's on the other side?"

"Do tell."

"The Autonomous Zone."

"Yay, we made it," Mish exclaims.

"Not so fast," Dieter interjects. "How will we get across the river with all our gear?"

"Simple," Caleb says. "I'll show you, but then that's it. I got to get back to my farm."

Gerry gets to his feet. "Well, let's go, I'm ready."

"Not just yet," Caleb declares. "Look up at that big blue sky with nary a cloud. Then look at that wide open river. Once you're out on it, you're drone bait, and you best believe the CBP's got its beady eyes in the skies flapping their wings all up and down that border hunting for smugglers and runaways."

"So, what do we do?"

"Wait until dark. It's the onliest way." Caleb pulls the bill of his cap over his eyes and leans back against a log. In no time, he's snoring. The teenagers, too, search for a place to stretch out, confident that soon they will escape the Confederacy. They don't know that the CBP drone operator who spotted them while on the boat has found them again.

Now, the drone pilot enters the fugitives' current GPS coordinates into his log and refreshes it.

Aboard the tiltrotor, now heading north at full speed, Ferguson is wide awake. The CBP's latest message to Boyce arrived a few minutes ago, saying they have eyes on the runaways. Boyce got the GPS coordinates and is at the front of the aircraft now, sharing that information with the flight crew.

Nervously, Ferguson reaches for the handle of his pistol to make sure it's ready. *What's taking that fool so long?* he wonders with a glance toward the cockpit where Boyce is deep in conversation with the pilots. Finally, the agent comes back down the aisle, trying to keep his balance on the unsteady aircraft while avoiding contact with the Marines on either side. "I just got me a pair of tickets to the Stallions game next weekend," Boyce brags upon regaining his seat.

"To hell with that," Ferguson snaps. "Did they give you an ETA?"

"Yep, we're only ten minutes out."

"Good, what's the latest update from Border Patrol?"

Boyce fiddles with his phone and then looks up. "The kids still haven't moved."

"That doesn't make sense. Why do you think they've been sitting there all afternoon?"

"Beats me."

"I want to see for myself. Ask for a livestream."

"Copy."

The agents on the tiltrotor are not the only ones intent on the chase. At the sprawling CBP headquarters outside Nashville the drone pilot is also motivated. It's not every day that his work comes to the attention of The Service, which now wants to view his screen. The CBP pilot fantasizes about joining the Security Service and how that would impress his wife. Self-consciously, he double-clicks an icon to share his screen on the SS channel. With shaking fingers, he uses his joystick to maneuver the drone in for a closer look.

On the ground, Melanie is braiding Mish's hair. Liam can't sleep either, so he comes over to watch. Sunlight streaming through the trees flickers momentarily as a shadow crosses the forest floor. The whirr of a powerful electric motor sounds from above. Caleb sputters, snorts, and abruptly wakes up. "Drone," he exclaims as though uttering a curse.

Now, the ominous whirring above won't go away. It loiters threateningly. "They're on to us," Ryan exclaims. He looks at Caleb.

"Must have spotted us when we crossed that meadow this morning," the weed merchant mutters. "Thought about going around. Should have."

"Enough of that," Melanie snaps. Let's head for the river before the Border Patrol arrives."

"I'm with you," Gerry agrees. The teenagers quickly don their backpacks. Caleb has nothing to carry. He waits impatiently for the others. Once everyone is ready, they set out for the riverbank at a trot.

In the sky, less than ten miles away, Boyce is intent on his screen. Ferguson looks over his shoulder as the camera zooms in on a stand of trees near a blue line. Unnatural splashes of color flit among the forest's muted tones. "Drat, they're moving," Boyce says in disgust.

"More like running," Ferguson exclaims. "That idiotic drone pilot came too close."

Liam gets to the riverbank first, with Gerry close behind. They catch their breath while waiting for the others. Caleb is last, even with Ryan prodding him all the way. The marijuana farmer immediately goes to a brush pile and tears a tree limb away. "Help me," he demands and grabs another branch.

Gerry and Mish run to help while Liam struggles to shed his pack. Ryan holds the rifle, keeping an eye on Caleb. Soon, he's the only one not tearing debris off the pile.

It's not long before the outline of a log raft appears among the broken twigs and dry leaves. "Drag it to the river," Caleb commands. The raft is heavy, but the teenagers are motivated. Soon, the contraption is floating. "There's no way we can all fit aboard that," Liam points out.

"Nah, you'll have to swim and push it," Caleb explains. "It's for carrying loads and keeping people like me who can't swim afloat. I use it for smuggling weed."

"Got it." Liam wades into the river, holding his backpack, and places it on the raft. Gerry does likewise, while Melanie sticks a toe in the water. "It's cold," she comments.

Caleb points to the far shore. "When you get to the other side, keep going 'til you come to an old wagon road that heads toward them hills. After that, you got a four-day walk to another river. Get across, and you're a Yankee."

"Thanks for all your help," Dieter says. He unloads the shotgun and gives it to Caleb. Ryan hands the farmer a wad of Confederate money. As Caleb hurriedly departs, the teenagers finish piling gear onto the raft and then push off. Clinging to the sides, they kick industriously while paddling with their free arms.

Mish has the sense she forgot something and glances back where they were. On the bank, Dachsie meets her eyes with a questioning look. "Come on, baby," Mish calls, and the dog perks up. Seeing what's going on, Dieter issues a shrill whistle. With that, Dachsie torpedoes into the water and paddles toward the raft. Dieter meets her halfway and helps the hound get safely aboard, Then Mish and Dieter again join the effort to propel the clumsy craft. Inexorably, it gains speed.

While the teenagers hasten, the tiltrotor gradually transitions from flight to hover mode. Inside, Ferguson is on the verge of a heart attack. "They're getting away," he hollers. "By the time we find a place to land, those punks will be long gone." He elbows Boyce, hoping to jar a solution from him. However, Boyce only stares at his phone, wearing the expression of someone who has paid an exorbitant price to watch a bad movie. "We're almost there," he mutters. "Just another minute or so."

Ferguson brutally gnaws on his lip as the seconds drag by. He pounds on his leg impatiently while racking his brain for an answer. Though not a believer, the SS agent gazes heavenward for help. Strapped to the ceiling, he sees a yellow bag with the words LIFE RAFT emblazoned on it. Leaping to his feet, Ferguson opens the buckle to loosen the strap. The bag falls to his feet. Desperately, Ferguson stumbles to the front of the aircraft and taps on the co-pilot's shoulder. The officer is startled but recovers and turns to face Ferguson while pulling his headset away from one ear. "Hover over the river and drop the ramp," Ferguson orders.

"Roger that." The airman replaces the headset and then speaks to the captain over the intercom. The aircraft commander nods in acknowledgment.

Ferguson makes his way back to where Boyce and the Marine sergeant are waiting for him. "We're going to use the raft and life jackets to cross the river and nab the fugitives."

"That's a negative sir," the squad leader replies. "Me and my men are here to provide security for the aircraft. We can't leave it."

"No worries," Ferguson replies. "Me and my partner got this."

By now, the tiltrotor is hovering a few feet above the river with the ramp down. Propwash is blasting the water aside like Moses did the Red Sea. Ferguson motions to Boyce. "Follow me," he yells to make himself heard above the maelstrom.

"No way," Boyce shouts, holding up his phone. "I just watched them enter the AZ. We can't follow. It's against the Armistice, and we'd lose our jobs."

"I don't care about my job," Ferguson yells. "That kid isn't going to fool me again." Ferguson grasps the life raft, drags it to the rear of the aircraft, and yanks the cord to start it self-inflating. He returns to where he was sitting to retrieve his rucksack. Boyce is staring at him in awe. Marines on either side of the fuselage look on with the bored indifference enlisted men have for the antics of officers and idiots. Shouldering the ruck, Ferguson holds his free hand in front of Boyce with the middle finger raised. "You're fired!" he hollers while maintaining the one-finger salute. Then Ferguson marches back down to the edge of the ramp, kicks the now rigid raft into the river, and leaps in behind it.

On the far shore, the fugitives barely have time to unload their gear and help each other with their backpacks before the frightful flying object appears. They watch it hover for several minutes, then rise, rotate, and fly away. "Hey, there's someone in a raft heading this way," Mish exclaims.

"That can't be good," Gerry says, squinting.

"It's a guy. He's paddling like a maniac."

"Game on," Ryan exclaims. "Let's go." He leads the others through thick underbrush until he finds a game trail. It's narrow and tapers off toward the top, which requires much stooping and some crawling. Liam has the worst of it because of his height. He spends the next hour battling to push his way through branches. Daylight is fading when the fugitives come to where the trail dead ends on a rutted dirt road. "Caleb said to go that way." Ryan points.

"I'm dragging," Gerry complains. "We should look for a campsite."

"Dude, did you see the way that guy was paddling?" Dieter asks. "We need to keep going."

Ryan studies the rough and rocky way ahead. "We'll go until it's too dark to see," he decides, "and that's it. We can't afford for someone to turn an ankle or worse."

"All right," Gerry agrees.

Half a mile back, Ferguson is having no trouble following the path that was blazed by the teenagers. The underbrush has been trampled as though a herd of buffalo came through. His eyes gleam, and he licks his lips at the thought of finally coming face-to-face with Ryan Walters. But when the trail intersects a dirt road, he can no longer find signs of his quarry. The hard-packed surface of the thoroughfare is impossible to read. On a guess, Ferguson follows the road as it descends into the forest. He doesn't find any tracks. Panic rises in the agent's chest as darkness falls. He stops walking to take some deep breaths. Slowly, he calms, and reason returns. *Why would they be going downhill back toward the river?* he asks himself. *I've wasted half an hour on this.*

Turning, Ferguson heads back uphill. After stumbling several times in the darkness, he flips open a pouch on his tactical vest and removes a night vision device. He tightens the headband and positions the goggles over his eyes. There's no use in looking for clues on the trail because the optical equipment only gives him enough detail to avoid trail hazards. But confident now that he's on the right track, Ferguson strides purposefully into the greenish-tinged world he sees. As the agent walks, a plan takes shape in his mind.

In a thicket a scant mile or so ahead of Ferguson, Ryan and Melanie are struggling to put up their tent. "I can't see the hand in front of my face," she complains. "Whatever happened to starlight?"

"No moon out either." Ryan peers at the sky. "Must have clouds rolling in; might even rain." A rumble of thunder confirms Ryan's forecast. "I saw the flash and counted," he says. "The storm's about five miles away."

Without another word, the fugitives return to work on their homes for the evening. What had been a light breeze now picks up force. Gusts make it difficult to peg down tent flaps. Finally, Gerry and Liam finish setting up. They grab food to take into their tent and then fasten rain covers over their packs. "Good night," Gerry yells before he and Liam disappear.

The interval between lightning flashes and thunder gets shorter as the remaining teenagers prepare for bed. By the time Dieter crawls into the tent he shares with Mish, fat raindrops are splattering on the fly. "Where's Dachsie?" Mish asks.

"I thought she was with you." Dieter sticks his head out of the tent and whistles. Dachsie saunters over and sniffs inquisitively at the tent flap. Losing patience, Dieter grabs the dog and passes her to Mish.

Next door, Melanie and Ryan are already inside their accommodation. They sit on mats cross-legged, sharing a pouch of leftover chicken cacciatore. "This tastes just like Elmer's glue," Ryan complains.

"How do you know what that tastes like?" Melanie wonders.

"Boy in third grade dared me to eat a spoonful."

"Yuck, you're crazy."

Kapow! The flash and thunder come at the same time. For an instant, Ryan sees his girlfriend frozen in time with a spoonful of white glop halfway to her lips. "Man, that was close," she whimpers. The light is gone as quickly as it came.

Ryan takes Melanie's hand. "It's almost over," he whispers. But the sky now crackles as if Thor is ripping it. *KABOOM!* This explosion is louder than the last. "Hold me," Melanie whimpers. She puts the food pouch aside and reaches for Ryan. He clasps her shaking body in his arms as they fall over to lie on a mat. Tenderly, Ryan kisses Melanie's tear-dampened cheek. She turns her head so their lips meet.

There are no roosters nearby to rouse the campers from sleep. So, as the sky brightens in the morning, it's up to whoever hatches out of their tent first to get the others going. Because rain got into Dieter and Mish's tent overnight, they're the first to brave the day. Mish takes their damp sleeping bags out and spreads them to dry. Dieter rubs sleep from his eyes, then gets his backpack stove going. "Wake up and smell the coffee," he hollers.

Muffled exclamations are heard within the other tents, including a profane comment about Dieter's lack of consideration. The German chooses to ignore it. He opens a jar of instant and measures some into the bubbling water. Soggily, the others emerge from their cocoons, eager for caffeine.

Soon, more hot water is needed to pour into pouches of Quaker Oats. "Pass these around," Melanie offers after dumping some freeze-dried blueberries into her oatmeal.

"Yummy," Gerry smiles.

"We should spread all our gear out and let it dry," Mish suggests between mouthfuls of cereal.

"Bad idea," Ryan declares. "We need to finish eating and hit the trail. No telling where that guy who was following us yesterday might be."

"But I don't fancy having a wet sleeping bag again tonight."

Ryan shrugs. "If that's the worst thing that happens to us in the AZ, we'll be lucky. Now everyone eat up and pack up. We've got to go."

Even with steady pressure from Ryan, it takes more than an hour for the campers to finish eating, wash up, and then get their gear squared away. Liam and Gerry are the first to be ready, so they must wait patiently with heavy backpacks on until the rest load up. Finally, the grumpy teenagers leave the thicket and get back on the road. Again, Ryan and Melanie take the lead. The others straggle along behind.

The sun is well up an hour later as the fugitives pass a majestic oak. Dachsie follows her nose to the tree, barking furiously. Startled, the teenagers turn. They look back to see a man in a camo uniform come out from behind the oak. He's holding a pistol that looks like a small cannon. "Freeze, or I'll shoot!" Ferguson hollers. As the SS agent advances, Ryan starts to bring the rifle up. "I said freeze," Ferguson snarls. "Twitch a muscle, and it'll be the last thing you ever do." The agent looks over his sights at a spot between Ryan's eyes. "Slowly release your grip and drop the rifle." Ryan lets go of the gun. It thumps to the ground, and Ferguson kicks it away. "Somebody shut that dog up before I shoot it." Mish quickly scoops Dachsie up and shushes her.

"Ah . . . Lieutenant Ferguson, is that you?" Ryan hardly recognizes the agent in his field utilities.

"You remember, how special."

Melanie takes Ryan's hand, not liking the menace she hears in Ferguson's voice. "So, your father was off on a drinking binge, huh?" Ferguson scowls. "He had nothing to do with The Resistance, or so you told me."

"What difference does it make now?" Ryan asks. "He's dead."

"Yeah, him and a couple more traitors. But I need to know who his associates were."

Ryan shuffles his feet, kicking a pebble aside. "How would I know?" he says defiantly. "I can't believe you chased us all this way for that."

"Yeah, and for sending me on a wasted trip to Miami."

Dieter steps forward. "You mean to the Seaquarium?" he asks. "Sending our phones there was my idea."

"Then I'll start with you." Holding the Glock with both hands, Ferguson swings it to point at Dieter. "I'm taking Ryan back to Huntsville. The rest of you will die right here." Before Ferguson can pull the trigger, he's distracted by a troop of horse riders rounding a bend in the road ahead. The leader spots the cluster of people in his path and breaks into a gallop. The heavily armed riders behind follow.

Ferguson is torn between shooting Dieter or turning his firepower on the interlopers. While he's in this state of suspended animation, the troop leader arrives, trailing a long black whip in the dust. With an abrupt forward motion of his arm, the rider snakes the whip out. In an instant, Ferguson is wrapped in its coils. The pistol lies at his feet. "What are you waiting for, Billy?" the lead horseman says to a young man who pulls his mount up nearby.

The boy slides easily off his horse, strolls over to Ferguson, who's vainly struggling to regain his freedom, and picks up the gun. Gazing reverently at the shiny merchant of death, Billy lets out a low whistle. "Colonel, it's a 9mm Glock."

"Well, hasn't this been a heckuva good morning already?"

Ferguson is so angry he could spit. "I'm with The Service," he snaps. "Give me that gun back and stop interfering with the law."

"Law," the colonel drawls. "What law?"

"Whooee," another horse rider hollers. She's a tattooed Black woman holding a shotgun. "We got us a genuine SS agent."

"I'll believe it when I see it." The colonel dismounts and slackens the whip so Ferguson can escape its bonds. "You got any papers, boy?"

Twisting his head, Ferguson sees guns pointed at him from every direction. He starts to reach into a pocket for his ID but freezes when index fingers that had been casually resting on trigger guards suddenly curl around the triggers. "Slow and easy, bro," the Black woman suggests. Ferguson methodically undoes the Velcro fastener on a vest pocket and draws out his SS credentials. The colonel snatches the leather holder out of his hand and scrutinizes the ID. "So, what's The Service doing up here?"

"Came to arrest these criminals." With a sweep of his hand, Ferguson indicates the unhappy group of teenagers.

"Criminals? Are you joking?" A bearded horseman laughs. He's so large his horse appears puny beneath him. "Looks like a bunch of harmless runaways. We get them coming through here all the time."

"Don't hardly look like they're worth violating the Armistice over," the Black woman asserts.

Ferguson gulps. "I figured just to grab them and haul 'em back before anyone was the wiser."

"That's a stinking lie!" Melanie speaks up. "He was getting ready to waste us. All except him." She points to Ryan.

"Nice," the Black woman exclaims. "I say, let's do him instead." She points the shotgun at Ferguson with her finger twitching on the trigger.

"Hold off, Lyndsy," the colonel commands. "We can get more value out of him and these others on the hoof than in body bags."

"True," the bearded rider comments.

The colonel reaches into a saddlebag and pulls out a bundle of zip ties. "Secure the prisoners," he orders.

Immediately, the other riders join the colonel and Billy on the ground. Some keep their firearms pointed at the captives while others approach them. "Hold your hands out," the bearded man says to Ferguson.

"Like hell, I will."

Billy pulls the Glock out of his waistband and points it at the agent. "Come on, punk, make my day." The boy tries to emulate the fearsome expression of Clint Eastwood playing Dirty Harry.

Staring down the gaping barrel of his service revolver, Ferguson understands what terrified his past victims. Reluctantly, he holds his hands out. The bearded man deftly binds them. Another rider does the same to Ryan while Lyndsy approaches Mish. "I can't believe a sister would do this to me," Mish complains as Lyndsy pulls the zip tight.

"Honey, there ain't no black or white in the AZ, only alive or dead."

"Head 'em up and move 'em out," the colonel orders. Several high-pitched whistles erupt as the riders use horsewhips to encourage their captives into line and get them moving up the road. It's been a successful morning, and the riders cheerfully break into song:

Around her neck she wore a yellow ribbon,
She wore it in the springtime and in the month of May,
And if you ask her why the heck she wore it,
She wore it for her soldier who was far, far away,
Far away, far away,
She wore it for her soldier who was far, far away

After exhausting all the verses of the first song, the riders begin another. Their songfest continues as the column moves ever deeper into the Autonomous Zone. Around noon, the colonel pauses while crossing a brook to let his horse drink. In no time, the entire troop is spread out along the waterway, patiently waiting for their horses to have their fill. Several riders take the opportunity to drink out of their canteens. Others, including Billy, slide down to the ground with theirs and go to the stream for a refill. "What about them?" Billy asks the colonel, pointing at the cluster of prisoners.

The colonel shrugs. "Sure, take them some water if you want." Billy fills his canteen with the clear water and then offers it to Mish, who nods her head. Billy holds the canteen to her lips, and she uses her bound hands to tilt it to the desired angle. "Thank you," she says.

"No problem." Billy goes down the line of prisoners offering drinks.

Most gratefully accept. However, Ferguson, who is off standing by himself, just shakes his head angrily. "Suit yourself," Billy mutters. He tops the canteen off again and is about to loop the strap back over the pommel of his saddle when Mish speaks up. "Hey, can you spare some for the dog?"

Billy looks down at the wiener dog at Mish's feet. He takes the canteen, kneels before the pooch, and pours a measure into his hand. Dachsie eagerly laps it up, so he pours more. "C'mon, puppy, drink up."

"Are y'all pirates?" Mish asks.

"Heck no," Billy says disgustedly. "We're bushwhackers. Pirates are the pits."

"What's a bushwhacker?"

"Started out we were guerrilla fighters for the South during the War for Independence. Nowadays, we only fight to keep what's ours and maybe go after our enemies if they start something."

"What enemies?"

"Oh, we got plenty—renegade Indians, pirates, red legs, nothin' but scum the lot of 'em."

A sharp crack of the colonel's whip signals that the break is over. "Enough, you saddle bums," he yells. "Mount up."

Grinning mightily at their leader's manner of expressing himself, the riders settle back onto their horses. Billy and a couple of others round up the prisoners. In short order, the column is back in motion. Among the riders, high spirits give way to resignation as they plod along, watching for any signs of ambush ahead or snipers in the trees above. Besides that, their main preoccupation is chewing tobacco and seeing how far they can spit the juice.

Wispy clouds and fresh air left by the previous night's storm minimized the summer heat during the morning. However, the humidity has been building. As the afternoon drags past, the air grows heavier, and the cirrus gives way to cumulonimbus. Nervously, Ryan glances at the towering clouds on the horizon. "Looks like we may be in for more thunderstorms," he tells Melanie.

"Great," she scowls. "Whose idea was this anyway?

"Hey, we knew that the AZ would be rough."

"Rough is one thing. A bullet in the head is another. If this outfit hadn't come along, I'd be lying in the dirt back there feeding vultures."

Liam shortens his stride, so Melanie and Ryan can catch up. "That's proof God has a plan for us," he tells them. "Why else the miraculous rescue?"

"You call getting kidnapped by bushwhackers a rescue?" Mish replies.

"Oh come on, this beats a bullet between the eyes."

"As long as we're complaining," Dieter interjects, "I can't get the hang of walking with my hands immobilized. I keep trying to swing my arms, forgetting I can't."

Gerry has been bringing up the rear. Now he calls out, "If you guys would quit your bitchin' and look around, you'd see that we're coming into a settlement."

The colonel has been leading them up a wagon road that parallels the stream they stopped at a while back. As they enter a broad valley, the forest on either side gives way to agricultural fields surrounded by split-rail fences. Interspersed among the fields are tidy farmsteads featuring simple frame houses and large red barns. Hay appears to be a popular crop. The green pastures that begin at the valley floor continue up the rounded flanks of hills that border the settlement.

The column clears a rise in the ground, and a town appears a short distance away. Someone there must have spotted them because now a church bell begins tolling. "Straighten up the lines," the colonel shouts. "Dress right, dress." Riders who had been slouching in their saddles stiffen their spines and get into parade formation. As they approach town, well-chewed chaws are hocked into the dust.

The most impressive building ahead is a red brick church that appears capable of seating a large congregation. Outside is a well-equipped playground suitable for young children. Youth-size soccer goals are positioned on a nearby field. "Looks like folks around here are into soccer," Gerry says.

"Yeah, there's a stadium over there." Liam points with both hands.

The road turns into the town while the stream veers off to the left. Past the church, houses appear on either side of the road. Spurs jingle, and the *clop-clop* of horse hoofs striking the hard-packed road echoes between buildings. Front doors swing open as excited people rush out onto their porches. Many wave handkerchiefs. Some cheer the return of the troop. The column enters the business district where stores, restaurants, and bars predominate. Except for the courthouse, most are simple one-story wood-frame buildings.

There's a square with a fountain in front of the courthouse, which is a two-story white stucco building with an orange-tiled roof. Here, the colonel signals a halt and dismounts. Billy quickly gets down and, after securing his horse, takes the colonel's reins and ties his mount to a hitching post. As the colonel approaches the courthouse, a man runs out to meet him. "Colonel, good to see you back so soon."

"Thanks, Garrison. We ran into some good fortune less than a day's ride away. Now we're back with the booty."

The saddle-weary riders happily dismount and stretch their legs while the colonel and Garrison have a look at the prisoners. "We can bunk them in the jail until I get them sorted," the colonel suggests.

"Yes, sir. I'll get the keys and meet you at the entrance."

The colonel turns to issue orders. "Billy, you, Lyndsy, and Waylon take the prisoners 'round back," he says. "Everyone else needs to take care of the horses. Once we're done here, I'll meet y'all at the stables. Now, let's get this done so we can all go home."

Lyndsy, Billy, and the bearded man, Waylon, herd the prisoners onto a brick sidewalk that circles the impressive building. They follow it around back to find the colonel waiting beside a locked basement door.

After a short wait, the door swings open, and Garrison appears behind it. Lyndsy prods Ryan, and he goes down the stairs expecting the worst. But rather than a dark, filthy hole, the jail is a well-lit, tidy room with white-washed fieldstone walls. Each cell has a cot with a mattress and a wooden chair. Lyndsy escorts Ryan to one that's all the way down the center aisle and pushes him inside. While Billy covers Ryan with the Glock, Lyndsy uses her knife to cut through the zip tie, binding his wrists. With his hands now free, Ryan hastily sheds the heavy backpack. Lyndsy grabs a strap and drags it out of the cell. "Hey," Ryan complains.

"Shut up," Billy snaps. Keeping the pistol level, he backs out of the enclosure and locks it.

Lyndsy and Billy return to where Waylon is guarding the other prisoners. "Let's go," Billy says, pointing at Mish. She looks behind her and sees Dachsie romping with several other dogs on the courthouse lawn. "Now," Lyndsy insists and pokes Mish with her horsewhip. Reluctantly, she goes downstairs into the jail.

Presently, seven cells are occupied. "I've ordered grub from the cafe, and it'll be here shortly." Garrison says as Billy and the other bushwhackers depart. "Now, does anyone here have a medical issue or anything I need to know about?"

"I urgently need to make a phone call." Ferguson waves his phone. "But I can't get any bars in here. Could you let me outside for a minute?"

Garrison stares at the SS agent wide-eyed. *Looks like we got a psycho*, he says to himself. "Sure, we'll be happy to help," he tells Ferguson. "Now, just stay calm, and someone will be over to assist you shortly." Garrison secures the back door and then returns up the aisle, past the cells, into the main courthouse.

The day's trek has worn out the prisoners. Most stretch out on their cots, but not Ferguson. He impatiently paces back and forth at the front of his cell.

"No one is coming to take you outside, so you might as well relax," Ryan says from the cell next door.

"What do you know about it?" Ferguson snaps. "I should've shot you when I had the chance."

Ryan points to a lantern burning brightly on the wall. "See anything funny?"

Ferguson glances at the light and then does a double take. "That's a real flame in there."

"It's a coal oil lantern," Ryan says. "And so are all those." With a sweep of his arm, Ryan indicates the other lanterns hanging from fixtures on the jail wall. "Think they'd be using those if they had electricity? No electricity means no phone service."

Ferguson's hopeful expression fades as he searches the baseboards for electrical outlets. Finding none, he settles onto his cot, a picture of dejection. "These people are backward," he mutters.

"Didn't you learn about the Autonomous Zone in school?" Ryan asks. "Hardly anything has changed here since the War for Southern Independence. It's an Armistice violation for either side to smuggle stuff into the AZ. Punishment of those who get caught is severe." As he talks, Ryan wanders close to the bars separating his cell from Ferguson's. Suddenly, the SS agent springs from his cot, reaches an arm through the bars, and grabs Ryan by the throat. "Got ya, punk." Ferguson tries to drag Ryan close enough to choke him with both hands, but Ryan plants his feet and leans back, trying to break the larger man's hold. Slowly, Ferguson loses the tug of war. In desperation, he transfers his grip to the collar of Ryan's T-shirt and yanks. Thinking fast, Ryan ducks his head and throws both arms out. Ferguson stumbles backward, holding a Johnston High School Soccer T-shirt and nothing more.

Melanie shakes the front door of her cell in frustration. "You pig," she shouts at Ferguson. "Sick bastard!"

Shakily, Ryan backs onto his cot. "I'm OK," he tells Melanie. "Guy's got a grip like an anaconda."

"You'll wish I was only a snake by the time I'm through with you." Ferguson wads Ryan's sweaty T-shirt up and throws it at the boy.

Mish and Dieter have cells across from each other near the back door. "Hey, what's going on down there?" Dieter hollers. "What's the commotion?"

"The SS guy tried to kill Ryan," Gerry hollers back. He's across the aisle from Ryan and saw everything.

"That's crazy," Mish exclaims. "We should be working together on an escape, not murdering one another."

A wobbly cart comes clanking down the aisle from the main courthouse, with Garrison pushing it. It's piled high with food for the prisoners. The cart stops at Melanie's cell, and Garrison removes the lid from a pot. He uses a ladle to fill a wooden bowl with stew. "One thing we got plenty of around here is venison." He puts a hunk of bread on top and slides the dinner through an opening in the cell door. "Thanks," Melanie smiles. Garrison fills a tin cup with water and passes that across as well.

Slowly, Garrison makes his deliveries down one side of the cell block and then back up the other until he reaches Ferguson's cell. The agent is lying on his cot, hands clasped behind his head. "Come and get it." Garrison holds a bowl up to the opening, but Ferguson ignores him. So, Garrison rattles a tin cup against the bars of Ferguson's cell, hoping to stimulate a response. Nothing. "Hey, my job is to keep y'all healthy until the auction," he explains. "Don't make it harder than it already is."

"What auction?" Gerry asks. "What are you talking about?"

"They didn't tell you?" Garrison raises his eyebrows. "Monday is Market Day. That's when y'all get sold."

Ferguson perks up. "That's nonsense," he sneers. "We're not Black."

"I keep forgetting that you're newbies," Garrison says. "If you come to get your food and eat, I'll explain how things are."

Ferguson goes to the cell door and accepts his supper. After watching to make sure the agent is eating, Garrison pushes his cart next to Ryan's cell and makes his last delivery. Leaving the cart, he strolls back to the middle of the cell block. "Now listen up," he calls. "You people trespassed onto land governed by Colonel William Stansfield. As a result, you are now his property and will be disposed of at auction the day after tomorrow. It doesn't matter if you're Black, brown, white, or red. In Bloody Bill's territory, you're either free or a slave, one or the other. Any questions?"

Mish is by her cell door holding an empty bowl. "Makes no difference to me," she says. "I've been sold twice already. What are we supposed to do with the dirty dishes?"

"I'll bring the cart back around to collect them," Garrison promises.

"This is wild," Melanie complains. "A month ago, I was being waited on by a house full of slaves. Now I'm going to be one."

Mish laughs. "So, you think you're too good to be a slave, is that it?"

"No human being should be property," Melanie declares. "I only meant that it's a shock to have the whole world turned upside down simply by crossing a river."

Garrison retrieves the cart and begins collecting dirty dishes from the prisoners. "What kind of work will we be doing?" Dieter asks.

"Depends on who buys you. Could be farm work, mining, woodwork, or just about anything."

"Are slaves ever freed?"

"Sure. Slaves with special talents can earn money on the side with their owner's permission and then buy themselves. Another way is to fight bravely in a war." Garrison pushes the cart beside Ferguson's door. "I need your bowl," he says.

Ferguson grins malevolently. "Come in here and get it."

"All right then, keep it." After stopping at Ryan's cell, Garrison again disappears up the hall.

"Hey, Ferguson, any reason why you're trying to make it hard on yourself and us?" Dieter calls.

"Shut up, punk," Ferguson replies.

"If you had any sense, you'd realize you don't have jurisdiction here."

"I'm not looking for jurisdiction. I'm after some payback."

"If I'd known sending our phones to Florida was going to get this maniac on our trail, I wouldn't have suggested it," Dieter tells the others.

The clicking of heels echoes in the hallway. Craning their necks, the prisoners see several men entering the cell block with Garrison. One of them is pushing a wheelbarrow. "Stand back," Garrison tells Ryan when they reach his cell.

Once Ryan has backed away from the door, Garrison unlocks it. "These are my deputies. They'll shackle you so you can wash up for bed and use the commode. Sit on the cot with your legs stretched out." One of the deputies gets a set of irons from the wheelbarrow while two others level shotguns on Ryan. Seeing no hope of resisting, Ryan follows orders. After his feet have been shackled, the boy is taken outside to a wooden building. Inside is a rudimentary toilet. A deputy waits while Ryan takes care of business. When he comes out, the officer takes him to a trough with a hand pump. A bar of lye soap rests on a board behind the trough. Without being told, Ryan works the pump handle. As he's washing up, Garrison comes over. "Which of those is yours?" he points to where the teenagers' backpacks are stacked.

"The red one, third from the top," he answers.

"You can get it when you're done and take it back to your cell. We searched them and took out anything that could be used as a weapon."

"All right, thanks." The prospect of getting his stuff back momentarily lifts Ryan's spirits. But grim reality comes crashing back moments later. As he's shambling back into the jail with the backpack slung on one shoulder, Dieter passes, hobbling the other way. "This sucks," he says.

"Bet."

It's well past dark by the time the last teenager has been taken care of. Garrison saved Ferguson for last. Now, he goes to the agent's cell with his deputies. "You can go hard, or you can go easy."

Ferguson has watched the other prisoners come back, freshly scrubbed, with their backpacks. "I'll cooperate," he promises.

"Fetch me the bowl."

Like a sheepdog following his owner's command, Ferguson brings the cup and wooden bowl to the opening and passes them to Garrison. Then he sits on the cot with his feet outstretched, waiting to be shackled.

The teenagers are all in bed later when Ferguson is brought back to his cell. "Wake-up time is six-thirty," Garrison announces. "A deputy will be on duty in the hall all night. If you behave, you won't even know he's there." Garrison turns one of the lanterns down while deputies see to the others. The prisoners are left in the dark.

"Does anyone have any ideas on how we get out of here?" Dieter whispers.

There's a rustle of bed covers, and his cot creaks as Ryan rolls onto his stomach. "I'm too exhausted to think about it right now," he sighs. "Let's talk tomorrow."

CHAPTER ELEVEN

MARKET DAY

I t's Market Day in Williamstown. The streets are thronged with farmers who have come to buy, sell, and socialize. Folks are dressed as finely as possible, considering the homespun nature of most dresses and suits. They arrived on foot, on horseback, or in carriages. Most rose in the darkness and traveled all morning to get to town. The more well-to-do came yesterday and had dinner at a restaurant before spending the night at one of the hotels.

As the hour approaches for the market to open, hitching rails all up and down Main Street are crowded with horses. Two- and four-wheel carriages jam the street. Slowly, restaurants empty as patrons finish breakfast and head for the town square.

In the Grand Hotel lobby, Colonel William Stansfield is enjoying a leisurely morning. He's seated in his favorite chair, perusing the town newspaper while smoking a cigar. In honor of Market Day, he wears an Edwardian-style white suit. A planter's hat rests on his knee. As they pass, ladies curtsy to the colonel, and men tip their hats. He returns their salutations with a wave of his cigar.

Outside the Grand, foot traffic pounds the boards of the town's raised sidewalk. Shoppers gawk at the goods merchants have piled in store windows. Tired of sitting, the colonel rises to his feet, dons his hat, and, with stogie in hand, joins the crowd. At the end of the sidewalk, he descends to the town square, now filled with vendors. Some have spread quilts on the ground and stacked their offerings on top. Others use tables, or they display merchandise on the backs of wagons.

With time to kill before the auction, Stansfield wanders through the market, pausing now and again to examine merchandise for sale. On display is a wide variety of products brought into the Autonomous Zone by intrepid smugglers. Bestsellers include solar generators, power stations, electric fans, DVD players, pirated movies, and sports equipment. At one table, the colonel is delighted to purchase several boxes of 9mm ammo for Billy's new pistol. "Stop by here when you're done there," the vendor next door pleads. "And I'll take your picture."

The colonel glances at the smuggler's array of photographic equipment and his makeshift studio. "Sorry," he tells the man, "I'm good."

The ammunition smuggler bags the colonel's purchase and gives him change. "You know, Colonel," he comments, "in some parts, they say a picture's worth a thousand words. But up here, a bullet is worth a thousand pictures."

"Ha, that's a good one," Stansfield smiles. The photographer is not amused.

On the next block, local artisans have set up their stalls. This is the colonel's favorite section of the market. He admires the creativity of his citizens, who make furniture, clothes, tinware, cook sets, farm implements, and baked goods. Farmers display a variety of produce. Still, Stansfield manages to keep his wallet in his pocket until a free sample of honey a beekeeper offers meets with his approval. He springs for a pot.

The crowd in the square thins as shoppers begin heading for the stock pens on the edge of town. Even those with no need for livestock or slaves are going to the auction just to ogle the big spenders. With a practiced motion, the colonel reaches into a waistcoat pocket for his timepiece and flips it open. A quick glance confirms that it is indeed nearing time to go. Still, he's in no rush. The goods he has to sell won't be trotted out until the end. Slaves are always kept for the grand finale. He decides to amble by the house and drop off the honey and ammo before going to the auction.

While the colonel kills time, the prisoners from the jail sweat in a corral next to the auction ring. Time drags for them as a succession of barnyard animals are graveled off. Lyndsy, Waylon, and the other guards aren't happy to be minding prisoners under the broiling sun. They'd prefer to be toasting each other with samples brought to the market by local distillers and brewers. The bushwhackers look on enviously as friends with lopsided gaits and goofy grins stagger by.

Finally, a draft horse is brought out of the corral and led into the show ring. The magnificent beast is greeted by *oohs* and *aahs* from the crowd. Excited bidding ensues, and the price quickly spirals upward. "Hallelujah," Lyndsy sighs. "They're on the horses. Won't be long now."

After several more workhorses are gavelled off, the first thoroughbred appears to thunderous applause. By now, the colonel is among the guests in the VIP section that overlooks the ring. He joins in the applause and gets into the bidding, only to cease raising his hand once the price enters the stratosphere. Good-naturedly, he shakes hands with the friend who outbid him.

More racehorses are sold, and then, the last thoroughbred is brought out. As the auctioneer delineates its ancestry, Lyndsy unlocks the slave corral. She and the other guards escort the prisoners to a holding pen beside the show ring. They wait as bidding continues. Cheers erupt when the racehorse goes for a record price. She is led off to meet her ecstatic new owner.

That's the cue for the bushwhackers to bring their booty into the ring. "Ladies and gentlemen," the auctioneer intones, "it's been a long day. However, as is so often the case, the best is last. What you see before you is a fine gaggle of intelligent, hardworking, healthy young slaves who are ready to work hard at any assigned task. In the interest of getting y'all quickly on your way to somewhere cool where you might wet your whistle, I propose to sell the entire parcel at once. Bidding will start at twenty thousand dollars and rise in increments of five. Now, do I hear twenty?"

The auctioneer looks eagerly out at the sea of faces and then up to the VIP section. No one raises a hand. "If they don't sell," the colonel says to his friend. "I'll just put them to work around my place until the next market."

At that moment, a man standing beside the grandstand raises his hand. Now, the bidding takes off. Before long, it's up to forty thousand dollars, but there's a pause at that point. The auctioneer uses a handkerchief to wipe sweat from his brow. He goes to a side table and pours himself a cup of water. In the sudden quiet, Melanie whispers, "This is humiliating."

"Because of the low price we're fetching?" Gerry asks sarcastically.

"You know what I mean," Melanie snaps.

"She means that we've sunk to the same level as barnyard animals," Mish explains.

Dieter looks out at the sea of excited faces in the stands. "I wouldn't treat a pig like this."

"Gonna become a vegetarian, then?" Gerry asks.

"And not eat barbeque?" Dieter frowns. "Forget it."

Lyndsy uses her horsewhip to brush Dieter's leg. "Hush," she says.

After another cup of water, the auctioneer returns to the podium. "Now I have forty. Do I hear forty-five?" He fruitlessly scans the crowd for a sign. "Folks, take a long look. A passel this fine won't be seen for many a moon." The auctioneer is disappointed to see so many hands tucked away in pockets or behind backs. "Forty going once," he calls and pauses. "Come on, friends, we can't let this travesty occur. Someone step forward now and get the deal of a lifetime." It's dead quiet for a long moment. Then the auctioneer says, "I have forty going twice." He raises the gavel, but before he can bring it down, a burly man wearing mud-splattered overalls and knee-high boots strides up to the ring. "We just had a cave-in," he breathlessly announces. "Lost my entire crew. Had to rush to get here."

"Sorry to hear about your troubles, Jim," the auctioneer replies.

"That's all right. Looks like you've got some replacements for me. What was the last bid on this lot?"

"Forty grand."

"I'll go fifty."

"That's more like it," the auctioneer enthuses. "Now, who'll say fifty-five?"

The auctioneer tries to rally the crowd, but the bleachers are rapidly emptying. In the VIP section, the colonel hugs his wife and accepts congratulations from friends. "I came across that bunch a scant half-a-day's ride from here," he keeps repeating. "Just proves it's better to be lucky than good."

When no further bids come, the gavel crashes down, and the auctioneer cries, "Sold to Jim Gavin for fifty thousand dollars." At that, Ferguson lunges toward the nearest guard, who happens to be Waylon. "Selling white people is illegal," he cries. "You're all under arrest."

Jim Gavin looks over from the checkout counter to see Waylon lay Ferguson out with one punch. "Easy lad, that's my property."

"You can have him," Lyndsy exclaims. "The sooner the better."

A tedious amount of paperwork is required to title the slaves and confer ownership on the Gavin Mining Company. As Jim works with the colonel and Williamstown's city clerk, the mine owner's two sons bring a dray powered by four draft horses around. The driver, a heavily muscled man with a dark beard, sets the brake on the rig. He climbs down, holding a gun. "Get to work, Levy," he says to his younger brother.

While the wagon driver stands guard, Levy, goes to Ferguson, who's stretched out on the ground. First, Levy removes Ferguson's shackles, which belong to the jail, and then replaces them with chains. One by one, he does the same for the other new slaves. "Now grab your gear and climb aboard." Levy strikes an authoritative pose, but his youth makes him less intimidating than his brother.

Dieter struggles to climb onto the back of the tall wagon with his backpack. So, Liam takes it from him and then passes it up. He does the same for the others, but when he tries to help Ferguson, who has finally regained consciousness, Liam gets cussed out. The irate SS agent manages to climb onto the wagon by himself. Liam follows, and now all of Gavin's new property is aboard.

Mercifully, the sun dips behind a hill, and although plenty of light remains, the worst of the day's heat is past. Jim signs the final documents at the checkout then shakes hands with Colonel Stansfield. Carrying a satchel, he climbs aboard the dray to sit beside the driver. The crack of a whip gets the draft horses going, and the wagon commences creaking and rumbling up the road.

Little suspecting that they'll soon be looking back upon their time in jail nostalgically, the slaves gaze disinterestedly at the courthouse as they pass. That is until Mish spots Dachsie lying on the lawn with several other dogs. "Baby!" she calls, and the wiener dog lifts her head. Tail-wagging, Dachsie rises and stretches before falling in behind the slow-moving wagon.

Gavin Mining Company is located four miles north of Williamstown. To get there, it's necessary to follow the main thoroughfare for an hour until it forks. At the juncture, the main branch goes off to the northwest toward the town of Smithland. A secondary road meanders to the right, leading to Gavin's coal-mining operation.

The dray is great for carrying heavy loads of inanimate objects where comfort is not an issue. But the wagon's un-sprung suspension results in a jarring ride for human cargo. As the wooden wheels react to each undulation in the road, their protests are transmitted from the axles, through the frame, and into the bodies of the passengers. Facing backward, Ryan tries to time each jolt and roll with it. He envies Levy, who's following the dray on horseback. The rider seems to have adopted Dachsie. Occasionally, he bites off a piece of jerky and tosses it to the dog.

A little past the fork, the trail is intersected by a mountain stream. "My butt is killing me," Liam announces as the dray is pulled down a short incline and then jounces across the rocky waterway.

"And I thought my mother was a bad driver," Dieter jokes. "Hang in there, guys, this can't last forever."

A half hour later, it turns out Dieter was prescient. The dray turns onto a wagon road that leads into a hollow. At the far end, smoke rises from the chimney of a large white house. Across the road from it, is what appears to be a stockade complete with a wooden palisade. As they get closer, a barn and several weather-beaten outbuildings are seen behind the house. Soon, a cacophony of barking signifies that they've been spotted by the guardians of the place. The mangy mutts are excited to meet Dachsie and eagerly sniff her posterior.

A hatchet-faced woman wearing a dirty apron comes onto the broad porch of the house, allowing the screen door to slam behind her. "Whatcha got there, Jimbo?"

"Replacements for the loafers who got buried in the mine this morning."

"How much?"

"Fifty grand."

"Ouch! Maybe you should think about shoring up that tunnel before you send this crew in."

"Maybe so."

Levy crosses a leg over the saddle and slides down from his horse, landing on the ground with a thud. "What's for supper, Ma?"

The woman shrugs. "Ask Simpson."

A middle-aged man with unkempt gray hair and a scraggly mustache is in the side yard washing clothes in a tub. "Hey, Simpson, you got any grub for us?" Levy asks.

"Just some corn mush."

"What about side meat?"

"Y'all haven't brought me any for three days."

"We'll go hunting tomorrow, promise."

"Hey, don't ferget that bunch." Ma points to the back of the wagon.

Jim turns his head and looks at his cargo with an expression like he's seeing the slaves for the first time. A light seems to go off in his head. "Get them down from there Frank," he tells the driver.

Ferguson is anxious to get off the dray. He moves to the back and dangles his chained feet. Levy holds his shotgun at the ready while Frank comes to help. "You got two shakes to get your behind off of there." He motions with a cap and ball Colt pistol for emphasis.

It's a long way down. However, Ferguson unhesitatingly jumps and makes a clean two-point landing. Then Ryan tries it but gets discombobulated on the way down and ends up lying on the ground. Forgetting his feet are chained, Ferguson tries to stomp his nemesis. He trips, and now he also lies in the dirt. "Where did you find these clowns?" Ma asks.

Liam climbs down the side. "Come on," he says to Gerry, offering his hand. Meanwhile, Ryan gets to his feet and starts taking the backpacks down. Without further mishap, the remaining slaves make it to the ground. Clustering together, they look this way and that to take in the bleak picture.

A waist-high wooden table comprised of boards slapped against a pair of trees is available for stand-up dining. Frank and Levy herd the slaves over to it just as Simpson comes down the rickety front stairs of the house, struggling with the weight of an iron kettle. Ma follows with a stack of tin plates and assorted utensils.

As the slaves stand facing each other across the two-foot-wide tabletop, Simpson slops mush onto the plates. A wooden spoon is set atop each repast, and then the plates are passed until everyone has a meal. Liam bows his head. "God is great, God is good, and we thank him for this food," he intones. "Amen."

Looking up, Liam sees that only Dieter and a couple of other slaves waited for him. The owner, his wife, and two sons are at the opposite end, furiously spooning mush into their mouths. Simpson stands off to the side, looking on with satisfaction as his culinary effort is met with enthusiasm. His feet are also chained together.

After eating, the Gavin family goes to the tub Simpson used earlier and rinses off their plates in the gray water. They beckon the slaves who come and do likewise while avoiding the washboard and a few soggy articles of apparel that still await scrubbing. Once the dishes are done, Ma carries the stack toward the house. "Bring me back the jug," Jim calls as she's walking away.

"Like hell I will," Ma snaps over her shoulder. "Remember last time?"

"Woman, if I ever needed a taste, it's after this miserable day. Now you fetch that jug, or I'll whale the tar out of you."

Embarrassed by the family squabble, Simpson busies himself with the washboard. After scrubbing each remaining garment, he wrings them out and takes them to join others on a clothesline. "How's that stuff going to dry in the dark?" Frank asks.

"Getting a head start on tomorrow." Simpson shrugs.

A sudden motion within a nearby tree distracts Frank from the inanity of Simpson's reply. Like a flash, he draws the Colt and shoots. There's a rustle of leaves above, and then the shattered remains of a squirrel drop into the tub. "What'd you do that for?" Simpson asks.

"Side meat," Frank grins.

The screen door swings open pushed by Ma, who sullenly descends from the porch carrying a stoneware jug. Jim is waiting when she gets to the bottom step. He pulls the stopper out and then flips the jug up to tilt a respectable measure down his throat. The mine owner smacks his lips as he replaces the stopper.

Not to be outdone, Frank rushes to Jim's side. "Share and share alike?" He holds his hand out for the jug, but Ma steps in between father and son. "Not 'til you and Levy put the slaves away and tend to the horses." She points to where the draft horses are restlessly swishing their tails.

"All right, Ma." Frank licks his lips, anticipating what awaits once the chores are done. "The quarter is yonder," he says to the slaves. "Get a move on."

After witnessing Frank's gunplay, the slaves are inclined to do what he says. They get their packs from the pile next to the dray and sling them over their shoulders. Simpson leads them across the yard while the brothers follow with their guns ready. There's a chain with a padlock on the palisade gate, but it isn't locked. The slaves enter the compound, which includes a long wooden hut, an outhouse, and a trough half-full of water from an ungainly hand pump perched above it like a wading bird.

Holding his pistol in one hand, Frank uses the other to toss his key ring to Simpson. The house slave bends to unlock the chains on his feet, then goes around and does the same for the other slaves. He hands the keys back to Frank, who turns and walks out of the stockade with Levy on his heels. They shut the gate and lock the chain.

The slaves are left looking at the shabbily constructed hut. "Home sweet home," Gerry sneers.

"It's not that bad," Simpson says. "Come in and claim a bunk. You have a choice of uppers or lowers."

Now, there's a rush to get inside and choose sleeping accommodations. However, meager piles of possessions left on several bunks give the new slaves pause. Simpson grasps the problem. "Poor souls," he says. "These are all the earthly possessions the previous crew left behind."

"Let's say a prayer," Liam suggests, and before anyone objects, he starts. "Father God, you who have brought us safely through so many trials, we come to you in prayer now not for ourselves but for your children who slept in this place last night but who will now be with you for eternity. Welcome them into your loving arms, we pray. They are now in a much better place than the one they left behind."

"Amen," Mish sighs. Several others chime in.

Simpson respectfully gathers the things from one of the bunks and then goes to another. "I'll put these in a safe place," he promises.

Once the bunks are cleared, the subdued slaves go about getting settled. "Hey, the mattress on my bunk is stuffed with straw," Melanie complains.

"You mean, you've never slept on a straw mattress?" Simpson raises his eyebrows.

"Heck no, and I don't intend to start now." Melanie drags the mattress off her bunk and stashes it underneath. Happily, she gets a mat from her backpack and unrolls it onto the wooden slats. Several others do likewise.

Ryan waits until Ferguson has begun unpacking at his chosen bunk. Then, he selects one on the opposite end of the hut. Ferguson looks up and smiles. "'You can run, but you can't hide,'" he says, quoting the boxer Joe Louis. "I'll sort you out when the time comes."

"Oh, give it a rest," Liam exclaims. "If you lay a hand on Ryan, you'll answer to the rest of us."

Gerry's across the way from Ferguson. "Do the math," he suggests. "It's six of us and only one of you. Bad things can happen in a mine, in case you haven't heard." Glancing around the bunkhouse, Ferguson sees only hostile faces. Discretion wins out over his normal belligerence, and he buttons his lip. On a shelf by the door, the only lantern flickers. Moments later, it runs out of oil, and the slaves are plunged into darkness. They feel their way onto their bunks.

It's been a stressful day for the new miners, and sleep would be welcome. However, concern about what the morning has in store induces anxiety that makes slumber difficult. Muffled sounds from across the way don't help. The volume increases as the hours pass. "What's that horrible noise?" Melanie murmurs in the darkness.

"That's Levy on the fiddle and his dad playing banjo," Simpson explains. "The percussion is Frank clogging on the porch."

"Omigod."

The Gavins' drinking bout continues into the wee hours. But that doesn't extinguish their work ethic. Soon after the first rooster crows, Frank and Levy stomp into the bunkhouse with a lantern. "On your feet," Frank shouts. A fine alcoholic mist fills the air.

Mish is used to being ordered about and quickly descends from her upper. She gets her toiletries bag out of her pack and goes outside. One by one, the others join her at the trough to freshen up. Liam works the pump handle for those who choose to wash their hair. "Brrr, the water's freezing," Melanie complains.

Neither Frank nor Levy appears to have done much about their appearance. They're in the same clothes as yesterday, haven't shaved, and the oil in their hair hasn't been changed. Frank wears the stoic expression of one who is miserably hungover and tries not to show it. "Hey, let's go," he snaps at Melanie, who's holding a make-up mirror and applying lipstick.

Once again, Simpson is responsible for the chains. After each of the slaves has dressed and put their toiletries away, he shackles their feet. "First chores, then breakfast," Frank announces. "Follow me."

While Simpson goes into the house to start breakfast, the slaves are escorted to the barnyard. They're greeted by a flock of agitated chickens that pace aggressively about, pecking at anything on the ground. Hastily, Levy enters the barn and fills a couple of buckets with feed. He hands one to Dieter and the other to Melanie. Reading their baffled expressions, he gives instructions. "Just walk around and scatter this stuff on the ground for the chickens."

"Got it," Dieter says.

Frank notices Ryan uncertainly looking around. "Go to the house and ask Simpson for some slop," he orders. Ryan turns to go while Frank leads the others into the barn. "Grab shovels."

"What for?" Ferguson demands to know.

"To muck out the stalls."

"You're joking."

Frank reaches for the pistol handle, which is poking out of his pants. "All right, all right," Ferguson exclaims. He joins the others sorting through a haphazard assortment of farm implements. Once they're suitably equipped, the slaves begin shoveling out the horse stalls. At first, they fear getting kicked, but the huge animals seem happy for the company. Liam reaches up to stroke one's neck. The beast whinnies and swishes its tail. Gerry pushes a wheelbarrow next to the stall, and the others get busy filling it with manure.

Once the horse stalls are emptied, it's the cows' turn. Meanwhile, Levy brings feed for the animals. "Good job," he says to Gerry as they cross paths. Gerry is steering the wheelbarrow outside to the manure pile while he's bringing in a load of hay for the horses.

Slopping the hogs is Ryan's job. He's getting to know the pig family, which consists of a mom, a dad, and two charming piglets. The adults seem most appreciative of Simpson's slop, while the youngsters focus on Ryan, whom they haven't met before. After emptying the buckets, Ryan pauses to watch the swine eat. "Hey, you," Frank hollers, "go into the barn and get a bucket and stool."

By now, the chickens have calmed down. They are still eating but have become picky about what they peck. Frank sees that Melanie's basket of chicken feed is empty. "Go with him," he says, pointing toward Ryan, who has just entered the barn.

Before following Melanie and Ryan into the barn, Frank calls Dieter over. "Go inside the henhouse and collect the eggs," he says. "Once you're done, take 'em inside the house to the kitchen."

"What do I put them in?" Dieter asks.

"That's up to you." Frank turns and goes into the barn. He finds Melanie and Ryan. Each holds a three-legged stool with one hand and a bucket with the other. "Why aren't you milking?"

"Uh . . . is that what this stuff's for?" Ryan asks.

"Oh, so now you're gonna tell me you've never milked a cow?"

"Actually, we found it more convenient to get our milk at Walmart," Melanie smiles.

Frank scratches his head thoughtfully. "Guess it's too late to get our money back," he mutters. "Oh, come on then, I'll learn you."

Since all the chores have been done except the milking, Frank has the entire crew in attendance for his tutorial. After demonstrating the proper milking technique, he gives each of the slaves a try. It turns out that Gerry and Dieter are the best. As their reward, once the buckets are full, they get to take the fresh milk to the house. The others leisurely assemble in the yard, glad to be done with the morning's chores.

When Gerry and Dieter come back out the front door, they carry platters of food. Jim follows with a pitcher and cups. Without being told, the others head for the makeshift table. The morning's exertions and fresh country air have stimulated their appetites. Simpson loads plates with scrambled eggs, grits, and biscuits. Once everyone has a meal, they dig in. No one asks where Ma is. Probably, she's still angry about last night's shindig.

As they eat, the slaves dart uneasy glances at Jim and his sons. "If the mine isn't in any better shape than the rest of this operation, we're in trouble," Dieter whispers.

"Can't wait to see it," Gerry winks.

At the other end of the table, last night's partiers cheerlessly chew their food. Levy is the only one who appears to be enjoying breakfast. He reaches for the last biscuit, but Frank smacks his hand away and claims it for himself. With the food now gone, Simpson takes Levy's plate and stacks it on his own. Then he goes around the table collecting the rest. "Guess it's time to go to work," Jim says.

"So, where's this mine?" Ferguson blurts out.

Jim glares at his property. "Speak when you're spoken to, boy."

"You'll see it soon enough," Frank chimes in.

A deeply rutted dirt road begins behind the house and traverses a hill before disappearing behind it. Jim leads the slaves up the road while Levy and Frank bring up the rear, carrying their firepower. After a ten-minute walk, the group arrives at the mine entrance. It's a rectangular hole in the side of the hill framed by heavy wooden timbers. There's a clearing in front of the opening the size of half a soccer field. The surface consists of hard-packed red clay, bearing signs of heavy use. Off to one side is a weather-beaten wooden building. Frank goes to it and opens the door. Standing aside, he beckons to the slaves. "Get the carts out along with all the picks and shovels."

The slaves get busy piling tools onto flat-topped mining carts. Once loaded, they drag the low-slung conveyances out of the building and over to the mine entrance. Meanwhile, Frank and Levy separate several wooden timbers from a stack near the building. "Hey, you," Frank calls. Liam turns to see who Frank's talking to, so he's the one who gets to load the timbers onto a cart. Ryan comes over to help.

There's a short wait outside the mine while Jim lights the wicks on several lanterns. "Let's go dig some coal," he says, once the flames are adjusted to his satisfaction.

"Aren't we going to recover the ones who got buried yesterday first?" Liam asks.

"Oh, we took care of that right after the accident," Levy answers. "In case any were still alive."

"And?"

"All dead."

"What about the bodies?"

"Buried yonder." Levy points to a mound of red earth at the edge of the clearing.

Liam turns to look. "All together?"

"That's right, and what's it to you, might I ask?" Jim says impatiently. "They was already getting ripe. We needed to get 'em underground. Now take hold of those carts and follow me."

Once inside the mine, it doesn't take long to find coal. Shiny black columns of it appear at intervals as they go deeper. "Hey, I'm no expert," Dieter calls from his place in line. "But we just passed a pile of coal. Why don't we dig it out?"

Jim has been leading the miners deeper into the earth. Now, he brings the group to a halt and turns to face them. "My kin mined this land for generations," he explains. "First, they dug the coal near the surface. When that was gone, they started this shaft. To avoid cave-ins, they wouldn't extract all the coal. They left some of it to support the mine roof. The last fools we had working here dug out one of the pillars. That's how they died. So, only dig exactly where we tell you. I ain't got enough money to buy more help right now."

The miners continue down the shaft until they come to the rubble-strewn cavity where the last group of workers met their untimely end. Frank grabs a shovel and uses it to scoop up a chunk of anthracite. He dumps it onto one of the carts. "We can start with this mess from the cave-in." He hands the shovel to Mish. The others take the hint and get shovels for themselves.

As the slaves clear chunks of coal off the mine floor, Frank takes hold of a wooden beam and drags it from the cart. Levy comes over to help. Together, they stand it upright. Once the beam is in place, Frank hammers a wedge into the gap to make it snug with the ceiling. This process is repeated as the morning's work progresses.

By noon, two of the carts are piled high with coal. The one that carried the timber is bare, and the walls where they're working are now shored up. It's cool this deep in the earth, but the miners are sweating. They've almost finished clearing up the rubble, but there's still a pile of it in a corner. "Get that coal," Frank points. "Then we'll haul this load to the surface."

An hour later, all the carts are full. Gerry and Ryan seize the handle of one they've been loading and yank. It barely moves. "Give them a hand," Levy orders. Dieter and Mish pitch in. Slowly, the cart moves up the steep grade.

Eschewing assistance, Ferguson grabs a cart handle and pulls. The cart moves a few feet, but it's slow going. Gerry and Liam are in a hurry to get outside and breathe fresh air, so they come up behind Ferguson's cart and push. Frank and Levy help the remaining slaves get the last cart going. In this manner, the morning's haul is transported to the surface.

At first, it's a relief to be out of the close confines of the mine. The clean country air is a welcome change from the dank, coal-oil-flavored atmosphere below. But with the sun directly overhead, the miners soon look hopefully at the shade trees that border the clearing. Jim notices their unease. "Levy, show 'em the picnic table," he orders. "Wonder what's keeping Simpson?"

As if in answer to Jim's question, the horse-drawn dray comes over a rise in the road. Jauntily, the powerful animals pull the empty wagon the final way to the mine. Ma is driving with Simpson beside her. Once the rig creaks and clatters to a halt, the house slave climbs down carrying several canteens, which he takes to the rudely constructed picnic table. As the water is passed around among the workers, Ma comes over with a basket. "Get the other one," she tells Simpson.

In no time, each of the miners has a sandwich, some pickles, and a carrot. Melanie lifts the top of her sandwich and looks. She elbows Ryan, who's beside her. "It's only tomato," she says.

"Yeah, but check out the bread," Ryan replies. He holds his sandwich up to his nose and inhales. "Mmm, smells like how my mom used to bake it." Ryan gazes wistfully at the thick-cut, yeasty crust and is transported to another time and place—Rebecca's kitchen. He envisions his beautiful mother spreading honey on a piece of her homemade bread and handing it to him for an after-school treat. Tears slowly roll down his cheeks.

Oblivious to Ryan's distress, the other slaves dig into their tomato sandwiches. In between bites, they slug down water from the canteens. Meanwhile, the mine owner and his sons have their lunch standing beside the dray. They wolf down their food, and soon, they're ready to get back to work. While Ma and Simpson gather the dirty plates, Frank and Levy enter the shed. Each comes out with a stack of burlap bags. "Let's go," Jim shouts. He leads the slaves back to the carts and hands Gerry one of the sacks. "Get a shovel," he says to Ferguson.

"Hell no," Ferguson replies.

"What?!"

"I've gone along with this joke thus far to see where it would lead," Ferguson explains. "But now I'm done. Either you release me right now, or I'll kill you."

Frank draws his revolver. "The only one doin' any killin' round here is me. Now do what you're told."

"I'm a Confederate agent," Ferguson sneers. "Kill me, and you'll have a sky full of black helicopters looking for payback."

"Apparently, this fool never heard of the Armistice," Jim comments.

By now, Ma and Simpson have stopped what they were doing to watch the confrontation. "Ain't no one comin' to help you," Ma tells Ferguson. "You trespassed into the AZ. Now, you're an outlaw just like us."

"But there must be some laws, some rules."

"Onliest rule here is the golden rule." Ma reaches into her apron and takes out an 1849 twenty-dollar gold piece. "Those who have the gold, rule."

Jim chortles. "So, what you got in your pocket, boy?"

Under Frank's watchful eye, Ferguson reaches into his pocket and takes out a wad of Confederate money. "Ha-ha," Ma laughs when she sees it. "This here is worth ten thousand of those. And there's plenty more where it came from."

"All right, now I get it," Ferguson replies. "You paid about seven thousand dollars in gold for each of us. Well, I'll give you ten thousand for me and another ten for him." Ferguson points at Ryan. "You can keep the rest of them."

"Mighty generous," Levy comments.

Ma glances at the wad of graybacks Ferguson holds. "That don't look like no twenty grand."

"Oh, give me a couple of days. I'll go get it and come right back," Ferguson promises.

"You missed your callin'," Jim drawls. "Should have been a comedian. Now get a shovel and start filling bags. I'm done with this nonsense."

Ferguson crosses his arms over his chest. "I offered you a fair deal," he says. "Take it or leave it."

The sudden silence in the clearing is broken by the click of the hammer on Frank's Colt being pulled back. "Oh, don't shoot him just yet," Jim tells his son. "Take him to the cooler instead. We'll see how he likes it."

"You heard the man." Frank motions with the pistol. "Let's go."

Ferguson hesitates, so Levy steps toward him with his leg pulled back for a kick. "OK," Ferguson exclaims. "I'm coming."

Frank follows Ferguson out of the clearing and down the trail. Hastily, Ma and Simpson fall in behind, carrying empty canteens and baskets full of dirty dishes. Without being told, the remaining slaves get busy shoveling coal off the carts and into bags. They are also unhappy about the drastic change in their life circumstances, but after seeing Ferguson's protest fizzle, none care to take up the argument.

That evening, a bone-weary mining crew heads back to the Gavin homestead. Hampered by chains, they shamble behind the dray, which is piled high with sacks of coal. Once they're back at the house, Jim drives the big wagon into the barn. Levy escorts the slaves to the quarter. After the chains are removed, he locks them inside and then goes to help Jim and Frank with the horses.

Before going into the bunkhouse, the slaves gather at the trough. Liam works the pump handle while, one after another, the neophyte coal miners make use of lye soap and a scrub brush to wash their hands.

More is needed, however, and being too exhausted to care, the slaves get out of their filthy clothes. Without false modesty, they scrub coal dust off each other's nude bodies and then take turns under the water spout. Once Dieter feels clean enough, he relieves Liam and cranks the pump handle so the goalkeeper can have his turn. Afterward, leaving their clothes in the trough, the teenagers go inside and happily get into fresh attire.

Feeling rejuvenated, Ryan lays on his bunk. "I can't believe we were up before dawn, mucked out the barn, then went and dug over a hundred bags of coal."

"Incredible day," Dieter agrees.

"All I can say is being a slave isn't all it's cracked up to be," Gerry comments.

Mish is sitting on the side of her bed, massaging her feet. "Yeah, welcome to my world."

"But seriously," Melanie interjects. "I wish my father and his slave-owning buddies were sweating in a coal mine right now while someone holds a gun on them."

"Yeah, or maybe picking cotton, chopping cane, tending rice shoots." Mish grimaces. "That's the sort of work that put my father in an early grave."

Melanie has been lying on her mat, but now she sits up to face Mish, who has the bunk next door. "When I was growing up, Dad told me that Black people were better off as slaves in the Confederacy than back home in Africa. Believe it or not, that was the garbage I was raised on."

"Africa was a Garden of Eden until European countries sent their armies to take over." Mish unrolls her sleeping bag and spreads it out on her bunk.

"He also told me white masters are kind and that slaves are happy."

"Anyone here feeling happy right now?" Gerry asks. He's in an upper bunk across the aisle.

The door to the bunkhouse swings open. Frank comes in, holding his revolver. "I ain't in the mood to mess with those chains," he says, pointing the gun at the restraints Levy piled by the door. "So, if any of you want to mess up at dinner this evenin', I'll just plug a hole in you."

"No worries," Liam replies. "We're too tired to run."

"Then I'll take you at your word."

A pleasant surprise awaits the miners at the stand-up dinner table. Fried chicken, biscuits, and corn on the cob with butter. Simpson beams as compliments rain down. No one asks why fewer feathered friends are pecking around the yard this evening. To further enliven proceedings, Ma sets a foaming pitcher of beer on the table. Jim and Frank quickly fill their cups while Levy ostentatiously sticks with water. The pitcher is not passed down to the slaves' end of the table.

From the corner of his eye, Dieter sees Dachsie following her nose down some real or imagined scent trail. He whistles, and the dog looks up. "Come here, baby," Dieter calls.

With her tail wagging, the pooch trots over to renew her acquaintance with the teenagers. She is also interested in food. "Poor thing must be starving," Mish exclaims.

"You know that dog?" Ma asks. "Well, don't worry. I've been feeding her twice a day along with the others. Was wondering where she came from." Dachsie recognizes Ma's voice and goes to her. Ma hands the mutt a piece of her biscuit and almost loses a finger when Dachsie snaps at it.

With twilight, the heat of the day dissipates. A cooling breeze rustles leaves while fireflies flicker among the trees. "It's a lovely night," Mish sighs. But just then, a ghastly moan wafts across the yard. It emanates from a rectangular structure between the house and the slave quarter. The box is covered with tin sheeting and appears to be no more than five feet high and maybe three feet wide.

"What's that?" Ryan asks.

Frank follows Ryan's eyes to where he's looking. "Oh, that," he shrugs. "We call it the cooler, but it's really an oven." He swills some brew, then plunks the cup down, beaming with satisfaction. The gunslinger now sports a white foam mustache.

"So, is that Ferguson moaning in there?" Liam asks.

"For sure."

"Isn't it time to let him out?"

Surprised, Frank turns to look at Liam. "What do you care?" he asks.

"Just sayin'."

"Well, don't." Frank pours another cup of suds and chugs it. "Take 'em back to the quarter," he tells Levy.

"I'll bring the washtub as soon as we're done in the kitchen," Simpson promises. He and Ma get busy collecting the used dishes.

The thought of sleep, blissful sleep, propels the teenagers back to their lodging. They change into pajamas, then go outside to complete getting ready for bed. Several are at the trough, brushing teeth, when Simpson arrives with the washtub. "One of you can do laundry in the morning while the rest handle the chores," he explains. Dieter pumps water into the tub while the others gather the dirty clothes to soak overnight. Then they drift off to bed. No one is awake later when the lantern flickers and then goes out.

CHAPTER TWELVE

YOUTH GROUP

Ferguson staggers toward the dray, bearing the weight of a sack full of coal. Standing on the back of the wagon, Ryan grasps the load and hauls it aboard. There's only room now for a couple more. Mish and Dieter bring one, and then Gerry and Melanie bring the last bag. Ferguson walks off, mumbling incoherently and waving his arms. *If that's what a week in the cooler does for you,* Ryan thinks, *then all I can say is "spare me."*

Breathing heavily, Ryan lifts his shirttail and uses it to wipe the sweat from his eyes. It's almost fall, but there's no let-up in the heat. Bravely, Ryan squints at the source. *It's like a peek into the pit of hell,* he marvels.

Nearby, Melanie sees where her boyfriend is looking and reads his mind. "The ancient Egyptians used to worship the sun," she smiles. "If you can believe that."

"I'd get down on my knees and worship an air conditioner if I could find one," Gerry exclaims. "Hey, help me take these shovels to the shed."

"The sooner we clean up, the sooner we eat," Dieter hollers. He's carrying the last of the unused burlap bags.

Before jumping down from the wagon, Ryan glances around to see what Frank and Levy are doing. Over the last month, the mine owner's sons have become lackadaisical about supervising the slaves, who now know what to do. Sure enough, the two guards are among the trees, enjoying the shade.

The crack of Jim's whip gets the wagon moving and costs Ryan his footing. He lands on his feet and belatedly joins in the clean-up. Afterward, the slaves follow the wagon toward home, taking care not to step into any of the piles left by the horses.

"Hey guys, is it my imagination, or are we getting off early?" Melanie asks as she shambles along next to Ryan.

"You know what today is, right?" Mish asks.

"Another day in paradise?" Gerry guesses.

Mish laughs. "Almost as good," she replies. "It's Saturday."

"Wow, already?" Ryan exclaims. "That means no work tomorrow."

"That is, unless you consider listening to those church ladies sing to be work," Gerry comments.

Liam's long stride has him leading the pack as usual. He looks back over his shoulder at Gerry. "Oh, come on, they're not that bad."

"No, and the sound of two cats yowling in the night isn't that bad either."

"Stop it, y'all," Melanie orders. "I need a day off, and some of you desperately need to be saved. I'm not naming any names." She giggles.

"If the shoe fits, wear it," Dieter suggests.

"That's like the pot calling the kettle black," Ryan laughs.

"Enough with the cliches," Melanie moans. "I'd rather go to church than dig coal any day."

"And how," Liam agrees.

When the procession reaches Gavin's place, Jim *whoas* the horses, and the heavy-laden wagon screeches to a halt. "Levy, get the help squared away while I take this load to town. Frank, why don't you come along?"

Ma rushes over, wringing her hands. "Not this week, you promised."

"Don't take on so, woman. We'll be back shortly."

Frank dodges around his mother and clambers up next to Jim, "Giddy-up," the mine owner shouts while Ma looks on in despair. Levy and the slaves keep their distance. They've seen this movie before.

A little later, at dinner, Ma stands at the head of the table. She doesn't expect Jim and Frank back until late and knows they'll both be drunk. In deference to Ma's somber mood, the slaves tamp their conversation. All except Ferguson, whose muttering is only interrupted by an occasional bite of food. Finally, Ma and Simpson rise to rinse their dishes. After they finish, the slaves follow. Then Levy escorts them to the quarter and unlocks their chains. Once he leaves, the teenagers can relax. "Talk about a dysfunctional family," Ryan exclaims.

"Compared to them, dinners at my house were a laugh riot," Melanie chimes in.

Mish and Dieter go outside to get their clothes off the line. When they return, Mish is holding a tie-dyed T-shirt. "What do you think?" she asks Melanie.

"For church? Sure."

"My choices are limited."

"Yeah, same here." Melanie lays a pair of black jeans on her sleeping pad and positions a lime green T-shirt on top. "Does that go?" she asks.

Mish comes over. "Totally," she says, thinking, *you wore the same thing two weeks ago.* Mish keeps that thought to herself. *None of us brought enough clothes,* she figures. *Who knew?*

With darkness closing in, the others retrieve attire from the clothesline. "Wonder what they have planned for youth group tomorrow?" Liam asks.

"Mmmnn . . ." Ryan answers, which is the best he can do with a couple of clothespins in his mouth. His hands are full of laundry.

Dieter overhears the conversation as he's heading back toward the bunkhouse. "My bet is on a jigsaw puzzle if it's raining and volleyball if it's nice."

"Safe bet," Liam laughs. "Man, we're in a rut."

"They mean well."

Inside, the slaves hurry to finalize their church wardrobes while light remains. With his kitchen chores done, Simpson comes in holding a platter. "Who wants watermelon?" he asks and is immediately assailed by everyone in the bunkhouse except Ferguson. Before long, only a couple of slices remain. "Take it outside, y'all," Simpson asks.

The teenagers comply and soon are happily spitting seeds into the trough. "Thanks, Simpson," Dieter exclaims.

"Don't thank me, thank Ma." Simpson wipes his mouth with the back of his hand, then negates the effort by burying his face in watermelon again.

"What I don't get is how nice things are here sometimes," Ryan comments.

Melanie daintily picks several seeds out of her slice. "You call digging coal ten hours a day every day except Sunday nice?"

"Of course not," Liam interjects, "but I think what Ryan's saying is that it could be worse."

"And I agree," Dieter says. "I mean, here we are with our bellies full, no one whipping us, and a free day to look forward to tomorrow."

Ferguson wanders out of the bunkhouse to see what's going on. Noticing his bewildered expression, Liam takes the last slice of watermelon from the platter and offers it to him. "You should have come earlier," he smiles. "This is all that's left, have it."

With a quick motion, Ferguson dashes the watermelon to the ground. "Trying to poison me, huh?"

"That's crazy." Liam looks at the mess on the ground. Pulp from the melon splashed onto his running shoes. "No one wants to kill you."

"Ha, I know your tricks. But don't worry, I've got your number." Ferguson aims a finger at Liam, pulling his thumb back like the hammer of a gun. "Bam!" he yells and drops his thumb.

Gerry sees Liam flinch and hastens over. "What brings you out from under your rock?" he asks Ferguson.

"Oh, leave him alone," Liam says. "He's harmless."

"Ha, days, minutes, hours," Ferguson mumbles. "That's right. You'll see."

Using a well-practiced soccer technique, Gerry grasps Liam's shirt and tugs. "You need to steer clear of him."

"How's he gonna get better if he stays to himself?"

"Maybe he isn't going to get better. Maybe he never was better. Nothing we can do about it."

Liam stops resisting and allows himself to be dragged over by the fence. "I love you when you're being cynical and world-weary," he says once Gerry stops pulling.

"And I'm wild about you as well." Gerry lets go of Liam's jersey and takes his hand. "Just remember, when you're with me, you're with a boy."

"This is very confusing."

"Yeah, I get that." Gerry rises onto his tiptoes to kiss Liam and then turns to follow the others back into the bunkhouse. Whistling a happy tune, Liam returns to the trough and begins working the pump handle. He keeps going until the last watermelon seeds have been flushed down the drain. Exhausted, he goes back inside. In the dark, he gropes for his bunk.

The slaves wake up in the morning happy to know they won't go to the mine. But that doesn't mean the cows don't have to be milked, the stalls shoveled out, or the animals fed. Cheerfully, they go about their accustomed chores and then go to breakfast. Afterward, the teenagers freshen up at the pump before getting into church attire.

Ferguson takes no pains with his appearance. When Levy comes in to do the chains, he tries to hide. The boy finds Ferguson under his bunk. "Let's go, you. When Ma says everyone must go to church, that means everyone."

The dray is waiting when the slaves get over to the house. Nonchalantly, they climb aboard and get settled for the ride into town. There isn't much to see on the way, only a steady stream of well-tended farm fields and an occasional house with the usual outbuildings.

Mornings are the nicest part of the day in late summer, and this one doesn't disappoint. A light breeze is blowing, and the sky is as blue as a boy's baby blanket. It's dotted with wispy clouds that, depending on the humidity, might coalesce into more interesting shapes later. "Sundays are the best," Liam exclaims. "The Lord had it right."

"You're always taking up for God," Mish comments. "If he's so powerful, why is there slavery? Why all the cruelty and injustice in the world?"

Liam dangles his legs off the back of the wagon and lets them swing in harmony with the jolting. "The way I see it, there are two forces at work in the world, God and the devil. So, just as some folks are filled with the Holy Spirit, others are possessed by demons."

"Are you saying that Ma and Jim are possessed?"

"We all are to some extent. Christianity is about recognizing that just as God is active in our lives, so is Lucifer."

"So, when I do something rotten, I can simply shrug and say, 'the devil made me do it'?" Gerry asks. He's been watching the familiar scenery go by while half-listening to the conversation.

"Christians don't simply shrug it off when they mess up," Liam explains. "They confess their sins and ask God to help them do better. The problem is that many professed Christians, like Ma and Jim, don't recognize when they're doing wrong, so how can they ask for forgiveness or mend their ways?"

"That doesn't make sense," Mish complains. "I know good from evil. Everyone does."

"Not true," Melanie interjects. "I grew up being waited on morning, noon, and night by Black people and never questioned it."

Dieter puts his arm around Mish. "And I used to think that buying and selling slaves was how it's done. I'm so sorry."

"But that's how the devil works, y'all," Liam says. "He makes evil seem normal."

"Speaking of God and the devil, I see the church ahead," Gerry says. "But I'm not sure I can handle any more preaching."

Jim slows the horses and then gets into line behind other conveyances waiting to enter the church grounds. After a while, it's his turn to park under the trees behind the building. He clambers down and then goes to help Ma disembark. Frank and Levy tether their horses at a hitching post and come over to unlock the slaves. Chains are not allowed in church.

Once everyone's ready, they stroll to the imposing red brick church building. Inside, antique pews are reserved for long-time congregants. Above them, a balcony contains rows of benches for servants. The Gavins' property climbs a steep flight of stairs to join other slaves already there. They look down at the colorfully dressed gentry of the town, who are meeting and greeting each other as if they hadn't done the same a scant seven days ago. Presently, there's a bustle up front while the choir files in. Spirited conversations in the pews taper off as the pastor steps forward to begin the service.

For the young members of the congregation, the service seems to drag on endlessly. The pastor is determined to cram a week's worth of salvation into his sermon. He is not concise. Meanwhile, to keep his job, the choir leader must feature prominent ladies as soloists. Their attempts to hit high notes produce painful grimaces in the pews. But all that is forgotten by the church youth once the last amen is said. That's when Youth Pastor Mike Switzer takes over. He's responsible for activities, which allows him to indulge his passion for volleyball. The young people are mainly interested in social interaction.

With a mostly clear sky and a hint of fall in the air, Switzer happily leads his group toward the volleyball court. As they pass the soccer stadium, Ryan peers through the fence at a cluster of players who are warming up in the center circle. "Is that Levy?" he asks.

Gerry darts a look in the direction Ryan is pointing. "Sure looks like it," he says. "I'd recognize those bowlegs anywhere."

"Bowlegged people are often fast," Liam comments.

Dieter pauses to gaze at the field. "Funny, we haven't seen any players out there before."

"Look, the lines have been freshly painted," Ryan points. "They must have a fall season."

A blast of Switzer's whistle reminds the Gavin slaves of where they're supposed to be. Hastily, they join the youth group. Most of the members are children of landowners but are too polite to lord it over the slaves. "All right, I'm going to give each of you a number between one and three," Switzer announces. "Remember your number."

After randomly assigning each player a number, Switzer continues, "It will be the ones versus the threes for the first game."

"Aww . . ." several of the twos moan as they go sit in the bleachers. Gavin's slaves are among them. It turns out that the threes are short one player, so Switzer assigns himself to their team. He's very competitive and is quickly immersed in the game. When no one else on his team seems eager, he volunteers to serve.

With the youth pastor's attention elsewhere, Ryan and Dieter look through the open stadium gate to see what's happening on the soccer field. "Hey, those guys can play," Dieter says. "Watch number ten."

Ryan watches intently for a few minutes. "I see what you mean, pass and move, pass and move, everything one- and two-touch, reminds me of Gerry."

"Welcome to my fan club," Gerry smiles. "Hey, Liam, check out that goalkeeper. He's as big as you."

Liam tears his eyes away from a religious tract he picked up in church. "Oh, that's Waylon. He was one of the posse that captured us. The guy is huge." Liam and the other Gavin slaves look on wistfully as the soccer players continue training. Then, cheering and clapping erupt on the volleyball court. The threes have defeated the ones. "Uh-oh, looks like it's our turn to play," Gerry says as the ones walk dejectedly off the court. "All right, twos, let's see what you've got," Switzer crows. He's practically thumping his chest.

Youth group is only supposed to last an hour, but today, as often happens, it runs over. Unhappy parents and slave owners drift over to see what's causing the delay. They stand on the sidelines and glare at the young pastor whose team is competing in the day's championship round. It's a lengthy battle, but finally, the threes prevail. "Ice cream for everyone next Sunday," Switzer promises as the grown-ups flood the court to claim children and property. Among them is Frank Gavin, who's in no hurry. That's because Levy still has another hour of soccer practice.

By now, the morning breeze is gone, and even though the worst of summer is over, the sun is still broiling. Under Frank's watchful eye, the teenage slaves find a shady spot a safe distance from Ferguson. He and Simpson are out of the sun beneath the dray, quietly conversing. For whatever reason, the two seem to have hit it off. Perhaps it's because Ferguson doesn't blame Simpson for the misery he's been through in the Autonomous Zone.

Under a tree, Dieter sits with his back against a fallen log with his legs outstretched. Seizing the opportunity, Mish lays on the ground using Dieter's thigh as a pillow. He lightly rests his hand on her shoulder. Before long, she's breathing deeply. The others go into deep relaxation mode as well.

An hour later, soccer practice is over. Levy returns, carrying a team travel bag. "Where do you guys buy your soccer gear?" Ryan asks him.

"At the market. Some of the vendors there sell sports equipment."

Ryan stands up to have a closer look at the bag. "So where do they get it?"

"Mainly smuggling, but sometimes pirates will make a haul, and some of that will appear at the market. But it's expensive." Levy reaches into the travel bag and takes out a pair of German soccer cleats. "These boots cost five hundred bucks."

Dieter looks over. "They're expensive in Alabama, too. Because of the embargo."

A group of soccer players strolls past. Several wave to Levy. One says, "See you next week."

"Yeah, see you then." Levy puts his travel bag on the dray and then goes to help Frank remove the feed bags from the horses. Ma and Jim walk over with a couple of other soccer parents. After they wind up their conversation, Jim helps Ma onto the dray. "Let's go," the mine owner says.

"I'm not in the mood to go through the rigmarole with the chains," Levy tells the slaves. "Me and Frank will ride along behind. Y'all behave, and it'll be good."

"You got it," Ryan promises. He and the other slaves quickly clamber aboard the wagon before Levy can change his mind.

Having rested, the slaves are in a mood to talk as the wagon bumps along the road home. "Tell us how you came to be here," Melanie asks Simpson.

"I'll be happy to, but tell me your story first."

Mish is sitting with her knees tucked up under her chin. "It's all my fault," she says. "I got to know these guys at the restaurant where I worked. That job wasn't bad, but then I got sold to a man who wanted more from me than an honest day's work."

"She means my father," Dieter admits. "He's a dirty old man."

"Now I get it." Simpson nods. "Your friends tried to help you get to the North."

"That's right," Ryan says. "But each of us had reasons of our own for wanting to get away from the Confederacy."

"OK, so now, what about you?" Melanie asks.

"Oh, I used to be a history teacher," Simpson says. "High school. I had to run for it after one of my students turned me in."

"What for?"

"We were covering the War for Southern Independence, and a girl raised her hand to ask why the Yankees attacked us. I told her it was the other way around."

"So, you made a mistake. Anyone can make a mistake," Liam shrugs.

Simpson is sitting with his back against the partition at the front of the wagon bed. From there, he addresses the teenagers like a teacher. "Problem is—it wasn't a mistake." He gestures with his arms. "The schoolbooks say Lincoln sent a navy fleet to attack Charleston, and the Confederates had to defend themselves. That's a lie."

"How do you know?"

"I went on the dark web and researched it."

Ryan raises his hand, and Simpson points to him. "My father showed me how to get on the dark web. There are millions of books there you can read for free."

"That's right." Simpson sways as the dray navigates a deep rut. He grasps the partition to steady himself, then continues. "What I found in those books is that only seven states seceded when Lincoln got elected in 1860. They were all Deep South states where slavery was, and still is, immensely profitable. The slave states farther north didn't join the Confederacy because of the election. They waited to see what would happen. As time passed without a reaction from the federal government, the Confederates began to panic. They knew the other slave states wouldn't join them unless the North started a war. Lincoln refused to do that, so the Confederates tried to provoke him by taking federal property in the seceded states. They seized numerous federal buildings, arsenals, forts, and so on. Still, Lincoln did nothing. In the meantime, pro-union newspapers, prominent citizens, and politicians throughout the South advocated reconciliation. That's why the Confederates decided to fire on the United States Army soldiers at Fort Sumter. They knew that Lincoln couldn't ignore an act of war, and he didn't. The next day, Lincoln called for an army to recapture the fort. Immediately, Tennessee, Virginia, and North Carolina seceded because they didn't want the Yankees to pass through their states to attack South Carolina. In this way, the rebels got the wealthiest, most populous slave states to join them. Otherwise, they wouldn't have had a viable country."

"Whew, too much," Gerry complains. "If I'd known this ride came with a history lesson, I would have walked."

Ignoring Gerry, Ryan raises his hand again. "So where does the story about a Yankee fleet attacking the city of Charleston come from?"

"Good question," Simpson smiles. "The best lies are always built on a kernel of truth. What happened in the spring of 1861 was that the Confederates in Charleston mounted gun batteries on land that surrounded Fort Sumter on three sides. They fired at a Union ship, *The Star of the West*, that approached the island carrying provisions for the Union soldiers stationed there. The vessel was hit several times and had to turn back. The Yankee commander of the fort then notified the Confederates that he would be out of food and water in two days and would have to surrender. He requested safety for his command as they evacuated. Instead, the Confederates opened fire. Afterward, they made up the story about a big Yankee fleet coming to attack as an excuse for starting the war."

"That's very interesting, Simpson," Melanie says. "Or should we call you Professor Simpson."

The dray lurches to a halt in front of the Gavins' place, and the slaves scramble to get off the wagon. "I want to hear more next time," Dieter says.

"Me too," Liam agrees. "If nothing else, the professor's lesson helped pass the time."

That evening, after supper, the teenagers mope while preparing for bed. The high spirits they had in the morning fizzle as the weekend expires. Quietly, they go about getting work clothes ready for the morning. Most are in their bunks early with nothing to do other than stare morosely at the ceiling while they wait for the lantern to run out.

The slaves are all up and bustling around the bunkhouse the next morning when Levy shows up. By now, their internal alarm clocks automatically awaken them at the accustomed time. After Levy fastens their ankle chains, the slaves shamble out to do their chores. It's chilly this time of morning, but they know better than to dress warmly. It will surely heat up later.

As always, Ryan goes to the house for the slop bucket. Then he goes to visit his friends, who are happily wallowing in a mixture of mud and excrement. That is until the pig patriarch spots Ryan and alerts the others. The swine have learned to expect good things from him. Each morning, they rush over to greet him with excited oinks. Ryan looks upon them as pets at this point and is happy to get reacquainted. He's always impressed with the father's dignity, the mother's tenderness, and the piglets' playfulness.

The slaves have become efficient at their chores, even milking. So, it isn't long before they are finished. As they're having breakfast, they get a welcome surprise. "No mining today," Frank tells them. "We're going to get more wood for shoring up the passageways."

"Where?" Ryan asks.

"Wait, let me guess," Gerry says. "Hmmm . . . the forest maybe?"

Liam laughs. "Brilliant."

"We still have to go to the mine," Frank explains. "The tools are in the shed."

Once they've eaten, the slaves line up to rinse their plates. They stack them on the table for Simpson. Then, it's time to start up the road toward the mine. As they stroll along, Ryan drops back to talk with Levy. "If you don't mind me asking, how did soccer become a thing in the AZ?"

"You'd have to ask someone who's been around longer than me," Levy replies. "All I know is that smugglers started bringing balls and other soccer gear to sell on Market Day. Runaways taught the folks who lived here then how to play and the game took off. At some point, leaders of the warring factions in the AZ decided that sports competition might be better for their communities than killing, rape, and pillage."

"So, soccer brought peace?"

"It brought periods of peace, but there's still a lot of bitter feeling between factions that sometimes explodes. Still, soccer does help. It's a war game, you know. Better a game than the real thing."

"I agree. So, how's the team looking?"

"Oh, all right," Levy shrugs. "About the same as last year."

"How did that go?"

"We ended up tied for third out of six teams."

"So, middle of the table, huh?"

Levy dodges to avoid a big pile of horse poop. "Yeah, we would have done better, however, our goalkeeper got injured late in the season. We had to put a field player in the net. Poor guy had no idea what he was doing."

"Ugh."

"Yeah, it was ugly."

"Will you have a backup for the starting keeper this year?"

"Nah, I mean, well-schooled goalkeepers are hard to find."

"You know, Liam is a keeper. He made All-State in Alabama last year."

"Really?"

"Hey, Liam," Ryan calls.

Liam's long legs have propelled him up the road ahead of the others. Hearing his name, the tall goalkeeper puts on the brakes. "Hi, guys," he says once Levy and Ryan catch up. Levy looks up at Liam as if seeing the sturdily built athlete for the first time. "I hear you're a keeper," he says.

"That's right."

"How long have you been playing?"

"Oh, pretty much since I could walk. Soccer is about all we had to do at the orphanage where I grew up."

"Always goalkeeper?"

Liam laughs. "Yeah, I was always the tallest, so I was the unanimous choice. Still, I got to play in the field occasionally and did a lot of technical skills training with the field players."

"What about goalkeeper-specific training?"

"Two-hour sessions twice a week once I started playing travel ball for a club."

The slaves at the head of the line come to a halt in front of the shed. "Hey Levy," Frank shouts. "Get up here."

"We'll talk again soon," Levy tells Liam. He rushes up to the shed and unlocks it. Hanging on the wall with other tools are a pair of two-handled cross-cut saws. Carefully, Levy gets one down. Gerry comes and takes it from him while he gets another one.

After the saws have been distributed, the slaves are directed toward a stand of tall pines on the other side of the clearing. Levy and Frank follow, carrying axes. Once there, Frank selects a tree and beckons Gerry and Liam. "We want it to fall into the clearing," Frank tells them. "So first, we need to take out a notch." He points to a spot on the trunk. "Begin cutting diagonally down starting here."

Before long, Gerry and Liam have worn their arms out, making a sufficiently deep cut. Frank motions to the next pair and shows them where to start. Half an hour later, Ferguson and Dieter are drooping, but Melanie and Ryan are ready. Before they start, Frank moves everyone to safety. He comes back and uses a mallet to knock the wedge out of the tree. Now, there's a notch in the trunk with the open end facing the clearing.

Frank directs Melanie and Ryan to cut directly across, and they make good progress. When they cannot do anymore, Mish and Dieter take over. Soon, the tree is creaking and groaning. "When I say go, y'all need to clear out thataway," Frank points. He watches the saw blade bite deeper, and the tree seems to shiver. "Go," Frank shouts, but he and the slaves only flee a short distance before turning to watch the majestic pine topple into the clearing. It lands with a crash, and the thud vibrates up through the soles of the miners' feet. "Now the work really begins," Frank says.

What Frank means is that trimming the tree, cutting it into sections, and hoisting the logs onto the dray is hard labor. This must be done each time a tree is cut down. For the slaves, the novelty of being outside instead of underground quickly wears off. As the day wears on, it becomes a struggle to keep up with Frank's demands. So, it's a weary crew at day's end when the slavedriver finally calls a halt.

It's been cloudy all afternoon, and now, as the slaves start home, a light rain begins to fall. From time to time, one or another slave will stick their tongue out as they plod along to catch raindrops. "This slave business truly sucks," Melanie complains. "How come we still don't have a plan to get out of here?"

"I'm usually too tired at night to do any scheming," Ryan says.

"That's what slave owners count on," Mish comments. "Exhausted slaves rarely have the energy to run off."

Gerry catches up with the others. "Remember what Coach Gorman used to teach us," he advises. "Always plan your work and then work your plan, because no plan is a plan to fail."

Ryan smiles. "We used to laugh when he said that."

"Well, I'm not laughing now," Liam says. "If we get caught escaping, it's into the cooler or worse. I wouldn't want to risk it unless we have a realistic plan."

Over the coming days, the slaves discuss ideas for an escape during breaks from mining. However, every plan runs into the same roadblock—the chains. "These things are medieval," Melanie complains as they're shuffling home toward the end of the week. "At first, my ankles were rubbed raw, but now they're callused. It looks awful."

"No way we could make a run for it with these things slowing us down," Ryan comments.

Liam turns his head to look back at the others. "Don't despair," he says. "Remember Daniel in the lion's den."

"Yeah, maybe one day there'll be a story about us," Gerry scoffs. "Teenagers in the bushwhacker's den."

"Hey, Levy, how's it going?" Dieter raises his voice to warn that one of the overseers is gaining on them.

"Thank goodness it's Friday," Levy exclaims as he speedwalks past Dieter to come alongside Liam. "Hey, I've been thinking about what we talked about on Monday. Maybe you should come out for the team."

Liam smiles broadly. "That sounds great, but are slaves allowed?"

"Sure," Levy answers. "In fact, that's one way you can earn money to buy yourself."

Liam slows down his pace to accommodate Levy's shorter legs. "That sounds good," he says.

"The colonel pays each player a thousand dollars per season, plus a hundred dollars for every game you appear in."

"Wouldn't I need Jim's permission?"

"Oh, that won't be a problem. He's a soccer nut."

Ryan comes up beside Levy. "What about Dieter, Gerry, and me?" he asks. "We all played travel ball in Alabama just like Liam."

"If you think you're good enough, there's no reason you can't try out."

"When?"

"I'm sure the colonel will let you join our training session on Sunday. That will give you a chance to show what you can do."

"All right, I'm in."

"Me too," Gerry and Dieter chime in simultaneously.

The soccer playing slaves contain their enthusiasm until they get back to the quarter. "Who'd have thought we'd have a chance to play on a soccer team in the AZ?" Ryan exclaims as they gather at the trough to wash up.

"What do you mean, 'a chance?'" Gerry asks. "For me a tryout automatically means making the team, no lie."

Liam works the pump as the others pass the soap around. "You guys need to chill," he says. "Remember where we are."

"Maybe it's absurd to hope, but I'd love to earn enough to buy my freedom," Dieter sighs.

"What about me," Mish asks.

"Sorry," Dieter says. "I meant our freedom!"

The exhilarated slaves don't get much rest that night. But the following morning, they come back down to earth. "Hey, I did the math," Melanie says. "It would take y'all at least five years to earn enough to buy all of us back."

"Ugh, no way could I do five more years of this," Ryan moans.

"Imagine what the slaves down south have to deal with?" Mish comments. "Grueling labor, day after day, with no hope of ever being free."

"When you put it that way, I'm ashamed to feel sorry for myself," Melanie says.

Mish goes to Melanie and hugs her. "I truly love you," she says. "Your heart's in the right place."

Even though regaining their freedom remains a distant prospect, the chance to touch a soccer ball invigorates the former players. "We've got a short day ahead," Ryan says while they're waiting for Levy to come with the chains.

"Yeah, we got this, y'all," Dieter chimes in.

Levy finally shows up. Once the shackles are applied, the slaves leave to perform their morning chores. Afterward, they shovel down a breakfast of corn mush, and then it's time to go to the mine.

The morning is overcast with a cool breeze blowing from the Northeast. So, the mining crew doesn't break a sweat on the way to their workplace. By now, mining has become routine for the teenagers. Like automatons, they load tools and mining timber onto the carts. Once again, they descend into the earth. As the slaves dig, Frank and Levy shore up the cavity they are hollowing out. "It's hard to say what's worse," Mish comments during the first water break. "Being a lumberjack or a miner."

"I'd settle for being an accountant," Gerry comments.

"Or maybe a barista," Liam suggests.

Mish sighs, "I loved being a carhop. Those days seem long ago and far away."

"Hey, let's go," Frank shouts. "Break's over."

As always on Saturdays, the slaves finish digging around noon. After they eat lunch, all that's left is to bag the morning's haul and put everything away. The short day leaves them plenty of time to scrub the coal dust from their bodies once they get back to the quarter. Afterward, they do laundry or rest on their bunks while waiting for Levy to return and chain their feet for dinner.

With her husband and oldest son again in town, Ma is downcast during mealtime. She stands at the head of the table with only Levy and Dachsie for company. It's depressing, so no one tries to start a conversation. After everyone has eaten and the table has been cleared, Ma takes Dachsie into the house with her.

Although Saturday nights are the province of the bushwhacker men, the following mornings belong to their women. Aside from a few contrarians, church attendance is nearly universal. It provides the opportunity to get right with the Lord, socialize with friends, and enjoy after-church activities. Chief among those is soccer. When the Bushwhacker team is playing at home, it's customary for folks to bring food baskets and spread blankets on the grounds to picnic before going into the stadium.

But the start of the soccer season is still a week off, so this Sunday, only the players' families and a few die-hard supporters stick around after church to watch the team practice. The volleyball court also draws spectators, mainly parents who must wait for their children.

Before Switzer gets things going, Ryan takes him aside and informs him of the tryout. The pastor is happy to release all the Gavin slaves to the stadium. It means he won't have to divide playing time among three teams.

When they come through the stadium service entrance, the slaves are met by Levy. "I told the colonel about you. So, come on."

Most of the team is already on the pitch in training uniforms. Several are playing an informal keep-away game while they wait. Nearby, the colonel is speaking with a boy. Ryan recognizes him as they approach. "Hey, Billy." He smiles at the kid who disarmed Ferguson a couple of months ago.

"How are you?" Billy says with a glimmer of recognition. That's more than the colonel shows. He gazes upon the slaves as if seeing them for the first time. "Coach, this is Liam, the goalkeeper I told you about," Levy says by way of introduction. "This one's Gerry, a striker, and the other two, Ryan and Dieter, are center backs."

"Welcome to Joseph Wheeler Stadium," the colonel says. "Home of the Bushwhackers."

"Thank you, sir." Ryan indicates the backpack slung on his shoulder. "Where should we go to change?"

"Back through the tunnel, you came down just now, then turn right. You got," the colonel glances at his watch, "eight minutes."

"Yes, sir." Ryan, Liam, Dieter, and Gerry take off running while Melanie and Mish start walking toward the stands. "Excuse me," the colonel calls after them.

Melanie and Mish turn to see what the gentleman wants. He strolls over to them. "Have either of you done any cheerleading by any chance?"

"All the way through middle and high school," Melanie smiles.

"That's good to hear. We're having cheerleader tryouts next week. I know the coach is looking to sign a few more."

"But I . . ." Mish starts to say before Melanie interrupts. "What she means is that we don't have any outfits to wear." Melanie gives Mish's arm a warning squeeze.

"No problem," the colonel says. "You can wear Bushwhacker cheerleader uniforms for the tryout."

Mish has caught on. Now, she smiles. "Sounds great, thanks."

Breathlessly, several soccer players run out of the tunnel onto the field to gather with the others. They are trailed by Ryan, Dieter, Liam, and Gerry. "Two lines," the colonel calls. Billy goes to the head of one of the lines wearing the captain's armband. "Let's go, guys. One lap around."

After the warm-up lap, Billy leads the team through some stretches. A short break follows. While the players are at the water pump, Billy notices that the Gavin slaves are wearing running shoes. "Guys, we have a closet full of proper soccer cleats in the locker room and plenty of training uniforms. At the first water break, you need to dash over there and find your size."

As with most teams, the first half hour of practice is devoted to fitness, speed and agility, and strength training. Once that's over, another break is called. The new players take the opportunity to run to the locker room. When they return, wearing practice uniforms and new soccer boots, there's still time for water. "It's great to be back doing familiar stuff," Ryan comments. He works the pump handle while his friends drink. Then Dieter takes the handle.

Having quenched their thirst, the soccer players wait on the sideline for the session to resume. Gerry and Dieter are beside Ryan, who points to the end of the field. "Liam's over there, warming up with Waylon."

"Yeah, and there's Ferguson and Simpson." Dieter points to the top tier of the ultra-fans section behind one of the goals. Sure enough, the two older slaves are up there together.

"I wonder what the professor finds to talk with that lunatic about," Gerry laughs.

"All right team, we're over here," Billy shouts. The players immediately jog across the field to where the colonel's assistant coach has laid out an array of colored field markers. "I need four of you lined up behind each of the cones. The last group of four to get set up does twenty-five push-ups." There's a mad scramble as players dash across the grass, each determined not to be one of the last. In no time, the set-up is complete without any tardiness. So, Billy chooses his own group to do the extra PT. "Now, one-touch passes, go," he yells once they're done.

The passing drill goes through several progressions over the next half hour. All are very familiar to the newbies since this is a standard pregame activity for many club teams. As the players work, Billy hollers, demanding faster play and better touches. Meanwhile, he sorts out six stacks of colored training bibs. "All right, hold up," he calls. "Even up the lines."

Once Billy is satisfied that he has six groups of four players, he passes out the bibs. There are now two blue, two red, and two yellow teams. After the players have donned their training vests, they have another water break.

There is no rest for the player-coach, however. While the others gather at the pump, Billy uses cones to mark two twenty-yard-wide grids. When the break is over, he puts one red, one blue, and one yellow team into each grid. The players are still talking and laughing when he yells, "Last team to take a knee is it."

In one of the grids, yellow is clearly last, so a blue player quickly plays a ball in for a red player, and that keep-away game is underway. However, in Billy's grid, a violent argument is raging as to which team was last to kneel. "Enough," Billy hollers, and it gets quiet. "I'll settle this. Now, the last team to take a knee and touch your nose is it. Go." This time, there's no doubt that one of the red players has difficulty locating his nostrils. The others unmercifully mock the miscreant. Then, the game starts with yellow and blue in possession. Still, it doesn't take long for a blue player to make a mistake and lose the ball to a red defender. That condemns his team to be the "monkey in the middle," and so it goes. This game is a favorite among soccer teams everywhere. It requires soccer intelligence and a high level of technical skill from every player. Billy is content to let it go on for a half hour while the keepers do their own training at the other end of the pitch.

Water is much needed by the time another break is called. Thirstily, the players line up behind the pump, using elbows and hips to keep their place and drive off attempted cut-ins. Gerry is right in the middle of the scrum. After all the pick-and-shovel exercise he's been getting, holding his own is no problem. After drinking, Ryan, Dieter, and Gerry find a spot on the suddenly popular bench. "That was fun," Gerry pants.

Billy comes over and grabs a seat next to Ryan. "You guys obviously can play," he says. "I talked to the colonel, and he agrees. We want you on the team."

"That sounds good," Ryan smiles. "So, tell me, how did you get to be the coach?"

Billy laughs. "It helps if your father owns the team."

"Got it, but you're not doing a bad job."

"Oh, I'm just copying the coach we used to have. He was a slave who had experience coaching a pro team in Georgia. We caught him trying to emigrate to the North."

"So, where's he now?"

"Director of coaching for a club in New Jersey. He used the money he earned with us to buy his freedom."

"Got it. So, what's next on your practice plan?"

"Eleven versus eleven," Billy gets to his feet. "Let's go," he hollers.

Billy waits until the entire team has assembled, then gives bibs to the starters, leaving the reserves to play in their gray practice jerseys. "All right, guys, we've been working on possession, so I want to see both teams build their attacks one pass at a time. Neither side will be qualified to shoot in this game until you complete six sequential passes. Everybody got it?" Billy glares at each player until he gets a nod or a yes. "Then let's go."

Seeing two full sides take the field is what the supporters in the stands have been waiting for. Up until now, they've been socializing among themselves. But as the scrimmage kicks off, they fully tune in to what's happening on the pitch. Soon, they're taking note of the new players on the reserve team. "'Bout time we get some fresh blood 'round here," a farmer comments after Liam saves a shot taken by Levy, the Bushwhackers' starting striker.

Liam delivers a throw to a midfielder, and the reserves link a series of passes together, ending with a shot by Gerry that just goes wide. For the next hour, the scrimmage continues with neither side gaining an advantage. Billy wants to end with a goal by one of the teams but finally must call a halt with no score. Ryan and Dieter have done a creditable job anchoring the reserves' back line. As they walk off the field, Liam, the reserve keeper, comes up between them. "Well done, guys. Come on, and I'll buy you a drink." Liam takes off running, and his friends follow. They beat the others to the pump. Quickly, Liam seizes the handle.

With impatient families of soccer players waiting, Billy keeps the cool-down and stretches to a minimum. Afterward, the players circle up, and the colonel calls the new players over. "We have some additions to the team," he announces. "This is Ryan, that's Gerry, and over there you have Dieter. I think everyone got a good look at Liam here, who'll be our backup goalkeeper." The existing players graciously applaud their new teammates. "All right, break it down," Billy calls. The players cluster together, arms raised. "One-two-three," Billy shouts. "Bushwhackers win!" the players shout.

The dray is unattended when Ryan and the others get there. The horses don't seem to mind being alone. They munch contentedly on whatever is in their feedbags. After a short wait, Melanie and Mish show up. "I'm totally bushed," Mish moans.

"How come?" Dieter asks.

"Oh, Melanie has been teaching me cheers."

"That's cool," Dieter says. He and the others hear angry shouting and look back toward the stadium to see what's going on. It turns out to be Frank angrily berating Simpson and Ferguson. The threesome comes across the church lawn, with Frank prodding the other two with his pistol. "Next time I have to come looking for you clowns, it'll be cooler time; I guarantee it."

Levy has been standing beside the church building with friends, but now he rushes over to help. "Get the chains," Frank snaps.

The slaves were hoping to ride home chain-free, but Simpson and Ferguson's tardiness has spoiled that. They're all hobbled and must climb aboard the big wagon that way. As usual, Liam helps his fellow sufferers before clambering up himself.

The last to show up for the ride home are Ma and Jim. As the driver and owner, Jim has no fear of being left behind. Before climbing onto his seat, he pauses to speak to Liam. "Great job in goal today," he crows. "I was bragging on you to my friends, and you didn't disappoint."

"Does that mean we get tomorrow off?" Gerry asks.

Jim scowls. "That fresh tongue of yours is gonna cost you one day."

Abruptly, he turns and climbs aboard the rig. Once Ma is settled on the passenger side, Jim cracks the whip. The dray jolts into motion.

Going up Main Street is the most interesting part of the ride home for the young people. Hotels and restaurants line one whole block. Bars are jammed with businesspeople who, judging by the revelry, did not get saved this morning. Farther along, barber poles beckon those in need of a shave while wooden Indians stand guard outside general stores, promising a wide selection of smokables. The boardwalk is thronged with folks still dressed in their Sunday best who are seeing and being seen prior to heading home for another week of drudgery.

Once outside the city limits, the tedious portion of the trip commences. "Hey, Professor, how 'bout another lesson?" Ryan suggests. "Any other myths about Southern history you want to expose?"

Simpson laughs. "Heck, I wouldn't know where to begin. You know, immediately after the Armistice, the ladies of the South formed groups to spread misinformation. They claimed that the War for Southern Independence was a 'Glorious Cause.'" That the states seceded and formed the Confederacy only to uphold the principle of states' rights. That it had nothing to do with slavery."

"Are you saying that isn't true?" Liam asks.

"Oh, it's a complete crock." Simpson settles back against the partition to pontificate. "I looked up the Mississippi Ordinance of Secession on the dark web. It clearly says that the state legislators voted to secede solely to protect their right to property in slaves. The ordinances from the other states that formed the original Confederacy are equally clear, most notably South Carolina's. And, if you need more proof, read Jefferson Davis' speeches. When he talked about states' rights, he was referring to a state's constitutional right to maintain the institution of slavery. His Vice President, Alexander Stephens, was even more explicit. He said that Negro slavery was the 'cornerstone' of the Confederacy."

"Wow, and it still is more than 160 years later," Liam exclaims.

Gerry stretches and simulates a massive yawn. "Is class over yet?" he asks.

"Just for that, I'll tell you one more example of Confederate propaganda that's still being pushed—the idea that Southern people unanimously supported the Confederacy."

"Well, I know that's wrong," Ryan says. "My father was in The Resistance. He told me it's a family tradition going way back."

Simpson nods. "Yes, armed bands of anti-Confederate guerrillas roamed the South throughout the war. The guerrillas were Southerners who were motivated by loyalty to the Union, opposition to slavery, or defiance of conscription. Poor white people who didn't own slaves were among the resisters. They referred to the conflict as: 'A rich man's war but a poor man's fight.'"

"It's funny you say that," Ryan observes, "because nowadays, back home, it's mainly poor whites who fly Confederate battle flags in front of their trailers."

The dray lurches onto the narrow road that leads to Gavin's place. In the distance, the chimney of the sprawling wood-frame house pokes up among the trees. Seeing they're almost there, Simpson wraps up his lesson. "That's right, Ryan," he says. "Folks are taught myths about the 'glorious cause' of the Confederacy in school. They take pride in it. Most never learn the truth."

The dray comes to a halt in front of the house. Gavin's slaves awkwardly disembark. "You must really miss being in a classroom," Ryan says as he shambles toward the quarter with Simpson.

"I miss many things about teaching," Simpson replies. "But the restrictions they put on what we could say ruined it."

With fall around the corner, the humidity and the temperature drop as the sun nears the end of its parabola. The usual Sunday night blues descend on the slaves, muting the dinner table conversation. Even Ma seems affected. She quietly stands near Jim with Dachsie curled up at her feet.

After the meal, Levy escorts the slaves back to the quarter. He removes their chains, allowing them to catch up on personal chores or find other ways to kill time before going to bed. As twilight descends, Melanie and Ryan sit on the bunkhouse steps. "Look, there's Venus," Melanie points.

Ryan follows her finger to what looks like a bright star that is strangely alone. "It's beautiful," he says, trying to remember back to grammar school and a video the teacher showed about the planet.

"Just imagine it hurtling through space, devoid of life, doomed to meaninglessly circle the sun into infinity."

Ryan shivers at the thought. He tears his eyes away from the space rock and blinks. "Is that Dachsie?" he asks incredulously. To prove she's not a mirage, Dachsie approaches and licks Melanie's hand. "How did she get in here?" Melanie pats the dog and scratches her head. Promptly, Dachsie rolls onto her back. She can't talk, but her posture says: "Rub my belly, please."

While Melanie obliges the hound, Ryan gets up and retraces the animal's path. He finds what he's looking for when he reaches the stockade fence. "Hey, Mel, come here."

Trailed by the dog, Melanie goes to where Ryan is waiting. "Look what that badger-hunter did." Ryan points to a hole in the ground that runs under the stockade's wooden palisade.

"Omigod," Melanie exclaims. "She must have been working on that tunnel all day."

Attracted by the noise, Mish and Dieter come to see what's up. Dachsie runs from one to the other excitedly. "We need to cover that hole up," Dieter says. "If Jim sees it, he'll flip."

"What about Dachsie?" Mish picks the wiener dog up and cuddles her. The pooch lolls her head contentedly.

"She's got to go. Ma will be frantic." Dieter pats Dachsie's head and rubs her ears. The dog licks his hand. Nevertheless, Dieter disentangles Mish from her pet, kneels, and ushers Dachsie back through the tunnel. While Ryan uses his hands to push dirt back into the hole, Dieter tosses rocks in. Melanie goes into the bunkhouse past Simpson and Ferguson, who are standing in the doorway watching. She gets the broom and goes back out to sweep sand, pine straw, and leaf clutter to fill up the tunnel. By the time they finish, the last vestige of daylight is gone. Melanie puts the broom away, then joins the others at the pump to wash up.

The following days are routine for the slaves, but on Wednesday, after lunch, Jim informs them that mining is over for the day. "Once we get the coal from this morning bagged, we're going into town."

Happily, Gerry and Liam go to the shed for bags. Levy stands nearby with his shotgun held casually in the crook of his arm. "What's going on in town?" Ryan asks him.

"The colonel wants Dad to bring us to soccer training. Mish and Melanie have their cheerleading tryout. If they make it, then we'll all be coming to practice on Wednesdays 'til the end of the season."

The highly motivated teenagers get to work bagging coal. By one o'clock, they are done. Jim will take the sacks to the wholesaler the next time he goes. For now, they are left piled by the mine entrance.

The slaves start walking back to the quarter. "I can't believe we get the whole afternoon off," Melanie exults once they're well ahead of Levy.

"Yes, but I'm nervous about the tryout," Mish says. "And my muscles still ache from the gymnastics we did Sunday."

"Mine too," Melanie smiles. "Cheerleading uses completely different muscles than mining."

Ryan speeds up to come alongside Mish. "Same with soccer," he says. "It's been a long time since any of us have run laps or done speed and agility drills."

"Don't worry," Gerry says over his shoulder. "You'll catch up with me after a while. For now, I'm the fastest one here."

Dieter's walking next to Gerry. "Oh really," he says. "We'll sort that out at the field later."

"Bet."

When they get home, the teenagers gather at the trough to aggressively scrub up. Once each has had a session under the pump, they go inside to get dressed. A short while later, Levy comes back to replace the chains. He follows the slaves across the road to where the dray is waiting in the shade of an ancient oak tree. One by one, the teenagers awkwardly climb aboard.

The front door of the house opens, and Jim comes out, followed by Simpson. Frank strolls over to meet them at the bottom of the steps. A pack of dogs trails him. They trot around the yard, noses to the ground, searching for a promising scent. "I'm goin' huntin'," Frank announces. "No need for me to come to town with y'all."

"What about me and Ferguson?" Simpson asks. "Why should we go? We're too old for soccer."

Frank glances at Jim, who's feeding the horses carrots. "They were nothing but trouble on Sunday, I can tell you."

"That's right, I remember." Jim pauses what he's doing. "Guess it's better to leave 'em here." Hungrily, a horse tries to stick her nose into Jim's jacket pocket. He steps back and slips the impatient mare another carrot. "Take them to the quarter before you go off," he tells Frank. "Leave their chains on and make sure to lock the gate." His pockets now empty, Jim climbs onto the driver's seat.

"Come straight back, y'heah?" Ma calls from the porch. She looks forlorn, standing there with Dachsie in her arms. But Jim ignores her. He uses the reins to start the horses, and the big wagon lurches into motion. Levy follows on his mount, alert in case any of the slaves decide to jump.

The horses seem to be just as delighted at having a light load this afternoon as the slaves are to be getting a half day away from the mine. It's all Jim can do to keep the team from breaking into a gallop as they cover the distance to town in record time. With relief, Jim manages to halt the wagon in front of the stadium. Levy hitches his panting horse next to several others, then takes the slaves inside.

Soccer training starts a half hour later. After the team's customary warm-up, stretching, and ball work routine, Billy decides to hold a full-field scrimmage. The small group of supporters in the stands is delighted to watch the practice match. They cheer both teams enthusiastically while the colonel paces the sideline, beaming happily. After the starters score late in the second half, he rewards all the players by calling for a shooting drill to end practice. The players love to shoot, and goalkeepers are always glad to have the work. Several cheerleaders who have finished practice and are heading for a stadium exit pause to watch.

After the shooting drill, Billy leads the team in a series of sprints. Training ends with the usual cool-down and stretches. Once they're done, the team circles up around the colonel. "Boys, I liked the intensity today," he declares. "We'll need it when the Red Legs come to visit on Sunday." The players applaud and then break it down. Cheerfully, they jog off the field and into the tunnel that leads to their locker room. Inside, Ryan and Dieter hastily strip and put their training uniforms in the laundry basket. "What do you think of the boots they gave us?" Dieter asks.

Ryan gazes ruefully at the redness on his heel. "They'll be all right once I break them in."

"You know what they cost, don't you?"

"On the black market? Yeah. About the same as a Maserati." Ryan slides the soccer cleats into his locker and takes a towel out. Steam is already wafting out of the shower room. Loud voices of players exchanging jibes ricochet off the tile walls. Levy comes out as Ryan and Dieter enter. "You need to pick it up," Levy says. "Don't want to keep Jim waiting."

It's glorious under the hot shower, but Ryan and the other slaves keep it short to avoid Jim's wrath. However, it turns out they could have stayed longer because there's no sign of Jim once Levy and the slaves get out to where the dray is parked. Only Melanie and Mish are there. "How did the tryout go?" Dieter asks.

"Piece of cake." Melanie gives the thumbs up. "Mish did great, so both of us made the squad."

"Well done!" Dieter looks around expectantly. "So, where's Jim?"

"Haven't seen him."

"Uh-oh," Levy says. "I bet he's at the Grand drinking with the colonel and them. We might as well get out of the sun and relax."

"So, tell me," Ryan says to Levy once they've all settled in a shady spot. "Do you have a shower at your house?"

"Are you kidding? Dad's too cheap to spend money on a solar generator. That's what powers the water heater and pump for the shower here. Colonel Stansfield paid for it."

"I thought y'all were rich."

"Dad is rich. He's also very tight when it comes to spending his wealth. Claims he doesn't believe in modern technology." More soccer players emerge from the stadium. "Nice goal, Levy," one says as they pass. "We'll need one just like it next week."

Levy gives the thumbs up. "I got you."

An hour later, a sporty buggy pulls up with a thoroughbred between the traces. Jim exchanges a few last words with the colonel, then alights and staggers to where his son and the slaves are relaxing. "Whew," he says to Levy. "The colonel darn near talked my ear off. You should've come got me."

"We've been doing all right here," Levy replies. He remembers the tongue-lashing his father gave him once before when he tried to drag him out of a bar.

"I'd have come back sooner if I'd known you was just gonna be lollygagging and wasting time here."

"What's wrong with that?" Gerry smiles. "Beats digging coal."

Jim scowls. "Why ain't they chained?"

"Uh, I had them under guard," Levy improvises. He picks the shotgun up from the ground nearby.

"Yeah, right," Jim snaps. "Now get it done so we can leave."

It's a glum trip back to Gavin's place. The alcohol Jim imbibed hasn't helped his already problematic personality. The slaves nervously stay clear of him. Levy keeps his horse well back from the wagon. The joy he and the others felt during the practice game is gone.

With no one next to him on the driver's seat, Jim converses with himself. Occasionally, he breaks into song. The slaves hope he's cheering up, but the scene they come upon once they get to the house ends any chance of that. On the porch, Ma is holding Dachsie and watching Frank whip Simpson, who's chained to a pole next to the cooler. With the regularity of a metronome, Frank snakes the long whip back and then brings it forward to snap off another sliver of flesh from Simpson's back. Nearby, Ferguson kneels in the dirt, his blood-soaked shirt in shreds.

Seeing his father arrive in the wagon, Frank pauses. He uses the hem of his shirt to wipe sweat off his brow. Jim unsteadily approaches. "What's all this?"

"I shot a deer first thing and brought it back. Was going to hang it up right away when a little birdie told me to go check on these troublemakers. Well, guess what? They was tunnelin' under the stockade fence."

"This I've got to see."

Leaving Simpson to moan on the pole, the two men go to the slave quarter and walk around the palisade to the back. Sure enough, the hole Dachsie dug has been expanded and is big enough now for a person to crawl through. "What were they digging with?"

"Empty cans, a piece of board, their hands."

"Must not like it here."

On their way back, Jim talks to Frank in a low voice. "Bad idea, Dad," the slaves hear Frank say.

Jim's response is, "Shut up and do as you're told."

Frank unchains Simpson from the post while Jim goes up the stairs and into the house. Moments later, he comes out with a cavalry saber, which he points at Levy. "Go to the barn and get a rope."

Presently, Jim has cut two suitable lengths of rope. While Frank fashions nooses onto the ends, Jim positions the dray under the oak. Then Frank climbs onto the back of the wagon. He throws one rope and then the other over a sturdy limb. Once the rope ends are secure, Jim goes to where Ferguson is kneeling and unlocks the chain. "Get on the wagon," he says, using the sword for emphasis.

Simpson sees Jim coming for him and looks up at Ma. "Help!" he yells, but there is no sympathy in Ma's expression. "We treated you good," she shouts. "Like kin. And this is the thanks we get? You can go to hell."

Once both would-be escapees are standing on the end of the wagon with their hands tied and nooses around their necks, Jim climbs up behind them. "Dad, for the last time, don't toss near twenty grand away just 'cause you're angry," Frank pleads. "We ain't got that much to spare buyin' new workers."

"Listen to Frank, please!" Liam shouts. He's with the remaining slaves being guarded by Levy who swivels his shotgun to point at the goalkeeper.

Jim gazes at Ferguson's bloody back and then at Simpson, whose knees are shaking uncontrollably. He puts his foot in the small of the house slave's back and kicks. Ferguson gets the same treatment. Now, both men dangle by their necks, kicking their legs spasmodically. "Never reckoned ole Simpson knew how to dance so good," Jim laughs. He watches a moment longer as the slaves' faces turn purple, then steps to the edge of the wagon and swings the saber to first cut down

Simpson and then Ferguson. Liam rushes over to loosen the nooses still clinched tightly around their necks. Nevertheless, neither of the troublemakers moves. They lie still for several minutes before beginning to stir. "Take 'em back to the quarter," Jim orders.

Dieter and Ryan grasp Simpson and get him to his feet while Gerry and Liam work on Ferguson. Once both can move with assistance from fellow slaves, they stumble to the quarter, followed by Frank and Levy. As his property disappears behind the palisade, Jim looks up at Ma. "Get the jug, woman," he orders. "Best be quick about it."

CHAPTER THIRTEEN

PENALTY KICK

A chill wind roils the waters of the Ohio River as it flows past Pirate Stadium in Smithland. Reflexively, Ryan tugs on the zipper of his Bushwhackers jacket. He and his friends are waiting for someone to open the service entrance. "What's that?" Melanie asks, pointing to a strange craft moving swiftly on the river.

"Looks like a mega centipede," Gerry says. "Or maybe the Loch Ness monster has a cousin."

The boat comes closer, and now it's apparent that ten people are on board working five sets of oars. A coxswain sits in the back, holding the tiller. "It's a small galley," Dieter says. "I read about those in a book about Mediterranean history. They were used for war."

"Guys, read the sign on the stadium." Levy points with his shotgun. "This is the home base for pirates who collect tolls from ships that pass through the AZ. They row to where the Mississippi and Tennessee Rivers meet with cannons mounted on the bow of their galleys to use on ships that don't pay."

"That one isn't armed," Ryan observes.

"No, they must be using it for transportation today."

"Why don't they have motorboats?"

Levy laughs. "I'm sure smugglers could get some outboards into the AZ for a high enough price, but where are you gonna get gas around here?" He sweeps his arm, indicating the lack of modern commercial enterprise.

"Got it," Ryan says. "So, what's that on the far shore? It looks like a cellphone tower."

"That's the United States, bro. Land of the free and home of the brave."

"Why so sarcastic?"

"Well, you know they don't have slavery over there," Levy explains. "Instead, most people work for companies owned by investors. The workers take the money they earn and spend it in stores owned by the same investors. This way, the rich can't lose, and the poor can't win. The system is rigged so that most workers only earn enough to keep the bare minimum of food on the table and a roof over their heads. Many don't even have that."

"Still, workers are free to try and better themselves," Dieter interjects. "They have hope."

"That's right," Levy agrees. "They hope to start their own businesses and maybe earn enough to become investors themselves. That's what keeps the system going."

Melanie comes over to stand beside Ryan. "It sounds just like the South. Most white people are too poor to own slaves, but many support the Confederacy because they hope to save enough money to buy slaves someday and use them to get rich. Most die dirt poor anyway."

Ryan shoves his hands into his pockets and hunches his shoulders against the cold. *Why did we have to leave so early*, he wonders. *We're the first ones here.* He stamps his numb feet, then glances for the hundredth time at the stadium entrance. His impatience is rewarded with the sight of a security guard opening the gate. Ryan quickly picks up his bag and joins the other Bushwhackers filing into the venue.

In the visitors' locker room, the Bushwhackers thaw. It's late fall, and most traveled to Smithland over forty miles of bad road in open-air carriages and wagons. "Hey, snap out of it and get ready," Billy shouts. "The colonel will be in shortly. He'll want to see everyone in their uniforms ready to warm up."

Reluctantly, the players get out of their warm-ups and change into soccer jerseys and shorts. The colonel comes in as some are still lacing up their boots. "Finish what you're doing," he snaps. "Then I want your undivided attention."

With his arms folded and his face tense, the colonel waits until all the players have gathered before him. "Guys, this is the last regular season game," he tells them. "We're tied for first place with the Pirates, so whoever wins this game will have home-field advantage for the championship match next Saturday. I don't believe in hyping games because we come to win every time we lace up our boots, whether it's an off-season scrimmage or the championship. My job is not to motivate you to play hard. You wouldn't be on this team if that were necessary. No, my job is to get you to play smart. Out of eleven games so far this season, I'd only give you a passing grade for executing the game plan in four. Sure, we won more than that, but some of those were due more to poor play by our opponents than stellar execution by us. So, if you want to win today, remember, finishing is up to your creativity in the box. To get there with numbers, we must get possession forward and keep the ball. It must rapidly go from the outside in, from the inside out, up, and back. Anticipate so you play early. After turnovers, pressure must be applied by the closest one or two players while everyone else recovers to organize behind the pressure. That's it. That's our game. Play it."

The players applaud, then form a tight knot, hands raised and touching. "One-two-three, Bushwhackers win!"

Despite all the pregame enthusiasm, it's a somber group that returns to the visitor's locker room two hours later. The colonel's short after-game speech says it all: "Team, we played well, but we lost. We'll sort it out at practice on Wednesday."

After a win, the players are all happy to hang out in the locker room and brag about their highlights. Losses are different. Now, all anyone wants to do is put Smithland and the Pirates behind them. Conversations among the players are limited to complaints about the officials or brutal play by the Pirates' on-field enforcers. The worst part is knowing they'll have to do it all again in a week.

During the interminable ride home, the Gavin slaves sulk. The soccer players and cheerleaders are bummed by the loss, while Ferguson and Simpson are disgusted about having to come along. It doesn't occur to either that they're to blame for their trouble. They huddle for warmth behind the partition that separates the driver's seat from the wagon bed. Both have mostly recovered from what Jim and Frank did to them, at least physically. Mentally is another story. Since the escape attempt two months ago, Ferguson has been even more scatterbrained. Simpson has withdrawn. The others take turns trying to bring him out of his shell with limited results. Now, with nothing else to do as the wagon jolts along, Ryan eases beside the house slave to try again. "Professor, you haven't given us a history lesson in months."

A light flickers uncertainly in Simpson's eyes. "Why talk about history when you're living it?" he mutters.

"What do you mean?"

"I got fired for teaching that slavery is cruel. Now I'm proof."

"In school, we learned that slave owners are kind, that slaves know their place and are happy."

Simpson shifts around to face Ryan. "Are you happy?" he asks. "Do you know your place? Or would you escape if you thought you might get away?"

"I'd escape."

"Yes, and during the War for Southern Independence, when Yankee armies invaded the South, all the slaves for miles around fled from the plantations. Nearly 200,000 became Union soldiers. Thanks to them, the Yankees almost won the war."

Ryan gasps. "I had no idea," he exclaims.

"It's in the official records at the Library of Congress in Washington, D.C. I found out on the dark web."

"So, the slave masters back then were all cruel?"

"Oh, human nature doesn't work like that," Simpson smiles. "There were kind ones as well as evil ones. Some Southerners inherited slaves and immediately freed them because they knew slavery was wrong. But others whipped their slaves unmercifully to get the last ounce of work from them. At night, Southern men would go to the quarter and drag Black women out to rape them. The mixed-race children borne by those slaves would be sold or put to work in the fields."

"The teacher didn't tell us anything about that. No wonder the Yankees were against slavery."

"It's hard to say what was the worst thing about slavery at that time," Simpson sighs. "But right up there would be the heartless separation of slave families that occurred when plantation owners sold off fathers, mothers, and children to different buyers."

Rebecca's image flashes across Ryan's consciousness. The hollowness he felt when she was taken away comes back with a jolt. He feels guilty for not thinking about either her or his father so far that day. "The more I hear, the more I think you should be proud for trying to teach the truth," Ryan murmurs.

"Yeah, well look what it got me." Simpson pulls his legs up and wraps his arms around them. He gazes forlornly at the dark shadows passing by in the night. His heart beats in concert with the *clop-clop* of the horses. Simpson's done talking.

It's late when the Gavin crew gets home, but Ma is waiting. She passes sandwiches around. The slaves take them to the quarter to eat. Afterward, they prepare for bed, knowing the roosters will be sounding off in a few short hours.

Even though Jim is an ardent Bushwhackers supporter, it doesn't occur to him to rest his soccer-playing slaves after the journey. Expecting that half a day's productivity will be lost because of midweek practice, he works them extra hours the next couple of days. The soccer season has been tough on productivity, and Jim's glad things will return to normal soon, win or lose. Still, he's in a bittersweet mood on Wednesday afternoon as they leave for the final training session of the season. After this, his social life, which revolves around the team and its supporters, will be over until spring.

If Ryan and his friends were expecting anything new from Billy for the last practice of the season, they are disappointed. Seems that he has limited recall of the previous coach's drills and can only repeat the same ones again and again. Still, every player gets lots of touches on the ball. That's the point. "The ball is the best teacher," Billy often says. He got that maxim from the previous coach as well.

The great thing about Billy's practices lately is that they always end with an intrasquad scrimmage. That's how it goes today. First warm-up, then some light PT, ball work, a passing drill, and then the intrasquad to wrap things up. Today, thanks to a last-minute individual effort goal by Gerry, the reserves get a win against the first team.

Luxuriating in the hot shower afterward, they talk excitedly while the starters half-heartedly mock them.

Mish and Melanie are waiting outside the locker room when Ryan and the other Gavin slaves come out. "Y'all were awesome today!" Melanie exclaims.

"Yeah, they were desperate to score toward the end, but couldn't," Liam exclaims. "Thanks to these two." He puts one arm around Dieter's shoulder and another around Ryan.

"They tried but couldn't get around us," Ryan brags. Happily, the teenagers share high-fives all around. They talk excitedly about the game all the way home.

The lofty feeling Gavin's soccer slaves have after their victory, plus excitement about the upcoming championship game, gives them a tailwind going into the rump of the work week. They spend a routine Thursday, and then Friday dawns sunny and cold. As the teenagers perform chores, their minds are elsewhere. They picture themselves on the morrow, taking turns holding the championship trophy aloft.

Without being pressed, the soccer slaves work extra hard at the mine this day. They hope to wear themselves out so they can sleep. By now, they are inured to hard labor. Swinging picks, pushing heavy-laden carts, and lifting bags of coal have hardened their athletic bodies so that their muscles are clearly defined.

That evening, the teenagers rush through dinner so they can get to bed early. In their bunks, they talk excitedly until the oil in the lantern runs out. Then, out of consideration for one another, they remain still even though anticipation makes slumber elusive. Lying on their backs, the soccer players visualize themselves scoring the game-winner. This is ambitious since none of them have cracked the starting lineup. In the darkness, some at least fall asleep.

Gavin's slaves are up Saturday morning before the rooster's first crow. After Levy chains their feet, they begin chores. In the pre-dawn darkness, the November chill finds avenues to penetrate their clothes. So, after breakfast, Mish and Melanie go and get their sleeping bags for the trip to Smithland. When Jim brings the dray around, they throw them onto the back before climbing up. Quickly, they unzip the bags so they can use them as blankets. The soccer players climb aboard, wearing their Bushwhacker tracksuits. They aren't very warm but look cool with the ferocious Bushwhacker emblem embroidered on the jacket.

The last slaves to board the wagon are the unhappiest. Slave life hasn't gotten any better for Simpson and Ferguson thanks to Frank, who makes sure that they are always chained. They stare balefully at their tormentor whenever he twirls his six-shooter or practices quick draws. It's hard to say which jumps higher whenever Frank snaps off a shot at a potential addition to the dinner menu.

Once all the slaves are aboard, the mine owner's sons climb up and sit on the back of the dray with their guns. Neither Frank nor Levy cares to ride horseback today. They're still saddle-sore from last week, and it's too cold.

With the dray fully loaded, the only missing ingredient is the driver. It always seems like Jim, knowing that the others can't leave without him, is the least concerned with adhering to the departure times that he sets. Today is no exception. So, all the passengers can do now is sit and wait. It seems interminable, but finally, the Gavin patriarch pushes the screen door open and comes out, followed by Ma. She doesn't usually go to away games, but today is an exception. She doesn't want to miss the championship final.

Ma waits until her husband is in the driver's seat, then hands Dachsie up. Jim holds the dog like it's a dead skunk until his wife gets seated. Happily, he hands the pooch back. With his entire entourage now present and accounted for, Jim cracks the reins over the horses' heads, and they're off.

It isn't long, though, until they must stop at the intersection with the main road. It's congested with a steady stream of horse-drawn conveyances carrying Bushwhacker supporters north. Jim waits for an opening, then gets in line. Thankfully, the column is moving at a good clip. As he giddies the horses along, Jim wonders what supporters for the other teams, who didn't make the playoffs, are doing with the free time they now have. Aside from the Bushwhackers and the Pirates, all the other teams in the league have finished their season.

Conversation is normally the best way to pass the time on a journey. However, with Frank and Levy aboard, the slaves are inhibited at first. Slowly, however, they begin talking among themselves. "Looks like this is going to be the biggest crowd of the year," Mish says as they top a rise that gives them a view of the long line of carriages jolting along the rutted dirt road behind them.

Dieter shields his eyes and looks back. His lips move as he counts. "Wow, must be a thousand or more."

"It's fun cheerleading when you have a crowd," Melanie smiles. "Some of those away matches this year were a drag when only the ultra fans came."

"Yeah, 'cause they have their own cheers and songs," Mish says.

Liam laughs. "Yeah, and most are filthy."

"Nothin' I didn't hear in middle school," Melanie declares. "Hey, how about braiding my hair?" she asks Mish, who has her sleeping bag pulled up.

"Sure, then you can do mine." Mish scooches behind Melanie and gets to work. Meanwhile, Ryan turns his attention to the pastoral scenery. It's the sort of fairytale landscape described in a Tolkien novel; forested hills dotted with brilliant green meadows. Ryan almost expects to see a Hobbit village tucked into a vale. Instead, they pass a steady stream of well-tended farms. "Hey, Levy," Ryan calls. "Maybe you can tell me something."

"What's that?" Levy says with his ear cocked.

"I thought the AZ was cleared of all inhabitants at the time of the Armistice. How did it come to be settled again?"

Levy has been dangling his legs off the back of the dray. Now, he turns and sits cross-legged, facing Ryan. "It's simple," he says. "Folks didn't like being run off their land. So, soon after the Armistice was signed, they started filtering back. Over the years, the population multiplied, and more land was cleared. When a couple gets married in these parts, the community comes together to get them a house built, barn raised, and a crop in the ground."

"What about slaves?"

"They usually get one or two, along with a horse, some chickens, and a cow."

Mish looks up and shakes her head in disgust. "Levy, you're a good soccer player but not much of a human being."

"That hurts." Levy grins to show he couldn't care less.

"Listen to you equating human beings with barnyard animals."

"So, what's the diff? We're all animals, mammals to be exact. It's just that some are superior to others."

"Because of race?" Mish uses her thumb to keep one strand of Melanie's blonde hair in place while she twists another.

"Nah, I mean, that's what they believe in the Confederacy, but it's nonsense."

With three strands ready now, Mish deftly weaves them together. "OK, so why are you a master and me a slave?"

"Because I've made better life decisions than you." Levy smiles smugly.

"Omigod," Mish exclaims. "Where's your compassion, empathy, Christianity?"

"Empathy don't feed the bulldog," Levy declares. "Does nothing for my bank account. Fact is, family comes first, and my family can make more money with slaves than without. And yeah, to me, a slave is on par with a horse or cow. That doesn't mean owners should abuse them. The colonel would string up anyone he saw mistreating an animal or a slave. He makes the rules, and we follow. You got the same system in the Confederacy. The Leader's orders are never questioned. That's the way it works."

"Not in the United States."

"Maybe not now. But from what I hear, their experiment with democracy is failing. Who knows how long it will last?" Abruptly, Levy turns back the way he was facing. Mish grits her teeth angrily and starts another braid. "Ouch, that hurts." Melanie gingerly pats her head.

Mish takes a deep breath. "Sorry," she whispers. "He gets me so mad."

'I know," Melanie sighs. "Hate to say it, but I used to be exactly like him."

"Yeah, but you saw the light. He's hopeless."

"Too true."

The never-ending trip to Smithland finally ends three hours later. At the stadium, a long line of drivers waits to park their rigs. "Let us off," Levy calls to his father. "We're already late." The boy leaps to the ground as the dray slows. "Come on!" Levy shouts. He waits while his teammates climb down. Mish and Melanie hastily put their sleeping bags aside and join the others on the ground. Hampered by chains, the soccer slaves shamble into the stadium. Levy follows, holding the shotgun.

Jim giddies the horses to reclaim his spot in the parking line. After a lengthy wait, it's his turn to enter the pasture and park. As the wagon comes to a halt, Frank jumps down. He beckons Simpson and Ferguson with his pistol. "Unharness the horses."

Sullenly, the two slaves unhitch the horses and then hobble them. The beasts nibble the grass at their feet while Jim fills their feed bags. "That'll keep 'em," Ma says impatiently. A swell of noise created by thousands of voices rises from the stadium. "They must be done with the introductions. Let's go!" Ma tucks Dachsie under her arm and starts for the stadium. Jim hurries to catch up while Frank escorts Simpson and Ferguson, who are slowed by their chains. Frank bites his lip with impatience as the crowd noise picks up again. He faintly hears the Bushwhackers' fight song and hums along.

> *Whackers will shine tonight,*
> *Whackers will shine,*
> *They'll shine in beauty bright,*
> *All down the line,*
> *They're all dressed up tonight,*
> *That's one good sign,*
> *When the sun goes down,*
> *And the moon comes up,*
> *Whackers will shine.*

Inside the stadium, play is already underway. Gerry, Dieter, Liam, and Ryan are on the bench with the other reserves. They watch intently but, during stoppages, shift their attention to the tumultuous stadium atmosphere. Especially entertaining are each team's ultra fans packed into bleachers behind the goals. Many are bare-chested despite the cold. Just about all of them sport faces painted in team colors. On the Pirate end, an ultra pounds a bass drum while others chant in rhythm: "Whackers suck, they're not great, all they do is masturbate."

The Bushwhackers' ultras at the other end are not to be undone. They stamp their feet and sing: "Two gay Pirates, underneath a tree, K-I-S-S-I-N-G, first comes love, then comes jail, who is going to pay their bail?"

An excited cheer followed by an excruciating moan comes from the Pirate side when, after a nifty combination play, their striker hits a screamer at the Bushwhacker goal. The shot just misses going inside the far post. It's their best chance so far, and the Pirate faithful want more. They stand and clap in unison. "Go, Pirates, go. Go, Pirates, go." More pressure follows, and in the fortieth minute, a poor clearance by a Bushwhacker defender results in an easy score. The stadium erupts as a cannon goes off. Not satisfied with the official pyrotechnics, Pirate supporters light flares in the stands. A pall of smoke rises above the maniacs.

In search of payback, the Bushwhackers launch an all-out blitz on the Pirate goal. Billy makes a devious run and times it so he's still onside when Levy passes the ball to him through two Pirate defenders. It's a clean breakaway, and Billy is one-on-one with the goalkeeper, who comes out and puts in a vicious tackle that has nothing to do with winning the ball and everything to do with putting Billy in the hospital. The referee approaches the keeper with a yellow card and then points to the penalty spot.

As Billy is helped off the field by a couple of Bushwhacker benchwarmers, Gerry is subbed in. He goes to the Pirate end, where the other Bushwhackers are clustered. "You take it." Levy points to the ball, which is resting on the spot. "You never miss in practice." Gerry goes and picks the ball up, rotates it so the logo faces the goal, then sets it on an attractive-looking patch of grass. He steps back and waits for the ref to blow her whistle. Moments later, the scoreboard reads 1-1.

With the time running out in the half, the Pirates try a long ball into the Bushwhacker end for their kick-off. They send a barbaric horde after it, but all is to no avail, as two blasts of the ref's whistle end the period.

No one outside the team locker rooms knows what occurs within during halftime. Suffice it to say, both sides come out for the second stanza ready to rumble. The tone is set early on by the Pirate coach. "Blow down that number 23," he shouts, pointing at Gerry.

Sure enough, a minute later, as Gerry darts upfield with the ball seemingly glued to his foot, a Pirate slide tackles him, studs up, to end his day. "Arr, Arrgh, Yarr, Gar," the Pirate fans cheer. However, the ref is not happy. Out comes another yellow card.

What started as a soccer match is now a war of attrition. Cheap shots, jersey grabs, slide tackles, and trash talk constitute the game within the game. Fearful of losing a player to a red card, both sides save their most dastardly deeds for when the ref isn't looking. However, the spectators have full view and, human nature being what it is, heap their opprobrium on the opposing side while finding no fault with their own.

Forty-five minutes isn't a long time, and as the half dwindles, it dawns on both sides that mayhem isn't a game-winning strategy. At last, they begin linking passes together on offense and working together on defense. Unfortunately, this newfound maturity isn't reflected in the stands, where the tension that's normal during a close game is exacerbated by historical grievance. In the eighty-first minute, things come to a head when Ryan, who's been subbed in, delivers a shoulder-to-shoulder challenge in the box, and the opposing forward trips over his own two feet. What's apparent to Ryan, his teammates, and the Whacker fans is opaque to the ref. She points to the spot, and now one side of the stadium is gloating rapturously while the other is frothing at the mouth. It's unclear who starts it, but the first projectile thrown onto the field is soon followed by more from both sides. Beer bottles, lunch buckets, canteens, and even a nasty cloth diaper rain down as the confident Pirate captain prepares to take the penalty. It's then that a half-full jar of moonshine fells Waylon, the Bushwhackers' normally indestructible keeper. As the colonel rushes onto the pitch, he pauses to turn. "Warm up!" he shouts at Liam.

Dieter takes a ball out of the team bag and, as soon as Liam gets his gloves on, hurls overhand throws at him. Meanwhile, the ref calls the coaches over. "Any more garbage gets tossed onto the field, and I'll abandon the match."

The coaches return to their sides and desperately wave their arms, imploring the crowd to chill. The deluge slows to a trickle and then stops. Satisfied, the ref motions Liam onto the field. The Pirate drum begins pounding again, as Liam takes his stance on the goal line and endeavors to make himself big. Behind him, Bushwhacker ultras hurl insults at the Pirate captain, who confidently tees the ball up for the penalty kick. The whistle blows, and Liam dives to his right, which turns out to be the correct guess. Clasping the ball to his chest, Liam raises a knee to protect his reproductive future. These precautions are insufficient to prevent the frustrated Pirate captain from kicking him in the face.

Immediately, the benches clear, and so do the stands. Blood-curdling war cries ring out from the Pirate fans while Bushwhacker supporters sound the rebel yell. They meet in the center of the pitch, and fists fly. It isn't long before those who delight in this sort of thing pull out their knives, chains, and guns. At the first shot, panic ensues among those who came to watch soccer.

At the goal, Ryan helps Liam to his feet. "That's got to hurt," he says as blood streams from the goalkeeper's broken nose. A gun goes off nearby, and they turn to see Frank aiming at a bald man swinging a sword. Ryan looks for Melanie but can't see her. Then Liam grabs his elbow. "Over there," he shouts. As more gunfire erupts, Ryan dives onto the ground, and Liam follows. They crawl on their bellies, hoping not to get stepped on. When they reach an opening in the crowd, they get up to run. But someone grabs the back of Ryan's jersey. He turns to look down the barrel of Frank's Colt. "Going somewhere?"

Over Frank's shoulder, Ryan sees the guy with the sword drilling holes in Frank's back with his eyes. He limps toward them, clutching his chest and spitting blood. Drawing close, the wounded warrior lunges. Frank winces. He looks down to see the sword point poke out of the front of his shirt. The hand holding the pistol droops as Frank's grip relaxes. Ryan snatches the gun away and then turns to see what's become of Liam. It's not hard to spot the tall goalkeeper's head bobbing among the shorter rioters some distance away. Ryan hurries to catch up. "They're over by that exit." Liam points to where Melanie, Mish, Dieter, and Gerry have gathered.

"Let's go," Ryan shouts to make himself heard above the mob noise.

"Thank God," Melanie exclaims when she sees Ryan and Liam

emerge from the combat zone. Together, the teenagers turn to join other panicked spectators running out of the stadium toward the parking field. Once there, they go to the dray, but none of the Gavins are present. As they wait, Ryan gazes across the river, where a stream of traffic is moving along a distant road. The cars are tiny; however, the semi-trailers are easy to spot. Seeing the modern world so near gives Ryan an idea. "Guys, this is our chance to escape."

"And get hung for our trouble?" Melanie exclaims. "No thanks."

"Look, I've got Frank's gun." Ryan holds the Colt up for emphasis. "He's dead, and this is a rare time when we are out in public with no chains and no guards. Let's go to the river and see if we can find a boat. All we have to do is make it across. If anyone tries to stop us, I'll shoot them."

"I like it," Dieter exclaims.

"Who else?" Ryan asks.

Five hands go up. Melanie's is the last. "All right, I'm in," she sighs.

Clanking chains announce the arrival of Simpson and Ferguson. Ma is right behind them. "What's going on?" she asks.

"We're leaving." Dieter goes to pry Dachsie out of Ma's arms. Mish comes to help. There's a tussle as they free the dog from the woman's desperate grasp. "I can't believe this," she cries. "After all we done for you. Taught you how to mine and all."

Dieter tucks Dachsie under his arm and starts down a path toward the river. "We're wasting time," he says over his shoulder. "Let's go."

"What about us?" Simpson asks. "Can we come?"

"You maybe, not him." Ryan nods toward Ferguson.

As Ryan hurries away, Ferguson tries to keep up, hampered by his chains. "I'm done with The Service," he pants. "Now that I've experienced slavery, I could never support the Confederacy again."

Ryan shakes his head and speeds up, but Simpson calls after him. "It's true," he shouts. "I've been talking to him. Ferguson has changed."

"No way," Ryan hollers back. "He's not coming with us."

After a hurried walk, the breathless group reaches the riverbank. "Hey, there's a pier," Gerry points. He sets off on a narrow trail that parallels the water. The others follow. As they get closer, what at first were indistinct shapes turn out to be pirate galleys. Gerry leads the way onto the pier and stops at the first boat. It's tied up front and back. "Where are the oars?" Liam asks.

Ryan looks inside the boat. No oars. He shifts his gaze to the next pier. "I'll bet they're in that shed," he points. "Dieter, you and Mish untie the boat. Gerry, come with me."

It turns out that Ryan's guess is spot on. He and Gerry find a jumble of oars in the unlocked shed. Holding the pistol in one hand, Ryan hoists a set of sweeps onto his shoulder with the other. Gerry grabs two more pairs. When they get back, the boat is untied. Ryan and Gerry distribute the oars. Behind them, Simpson and Ferguson come onto the dock to plead with Liam. "We need to stick together," Simpson begs. "Don't worry, I'll vouch for Ferguson."

"Do you sincerely repent for the evil you've done?" Liam asks Ferguson.

Ferguson's eyes light up. "I truly do repent." He crosses himself reverently. "May God strike me dead if I lie."

The rickety pier creaks as Levy comes stomping onto it. "Ma told me y'all were heading this way." As usual, Levy carries the shotgun cradled in his arm. "She wants her dog back, and I want my slaves. Jim and Frank are dead, so now I'm the boss."

Ryan aims Frank's pistol at the center of Levy's chest. "Drop the gun," he orders. "Now!"

For a moment, Levy hesitates, but as Ryan's finger tightens on the trigger, he thinks better of it. The shotgun clatters onto the dock. Quick as a cat, Ferguson pounces on it. Pulling the hammer back, he holds the barrel to Mish's head. "It'd be a real shame to scatter her pretty brains all over this dock," he threatens. "Simpson, get Ryan's gun."

Ryan is caught with the pistol pointed toward Levy. He has no choice but to relax his fingers and let Simpson have it. "Why are you helping him?" he asks.

"Oh, it's funny, but after I got to know Ferguson, it turned out he and I work for the same firm." Simpson aims the Colt at Levy. "Paybacks are a bitch," he says with an evil grin.

"Hold off on that," Ferguson snaps. "We can't afford to waste a bullet. Those things are murder to reload." Simpson lowers the pistol. "Get lost," he tells Levy. The miner is only too happy to turn and run back the way he came.

"The rest of you get aboard," Ferguson tells the slaves, using the shotgun for emphasis.

Once all the slaves are aboard the craft, seated on benches with oars in hand, Simpson pushes off. He sits beside Ferguson, who's at the stern, holding the tiller with one hand and the shotgun with the other. "Take the oars back, then each of you dip your oar into the water and pull your end to your chest," Simpson instructs. "All together, now."

With the pistol and shotgun pointed at them, the teenagers do as they're told. At first, their synchronization is off, but eventually, they settle into a coordinated rhythm. Ryan and Liam are sitting on the first bench facing Ferguson and Simpson. They're so close to the armed men that Liam's feet almost reach Simpson's. When they come to the middle of the river, Ferguson turns the tiller so the craft swings around and the prow points downstream. "Hey, you're going the wrong way," Ryan complains.

"Not if we want to go to Dixie," Simpson smirks. "With this current and you slaves rowing, we'll be on the Mississippi by morning and back under the Stars and Bars by tomorrow night."

"You told us you were a teacher who hated the Confederacy," Ryan pants. He and Liam take their oars back for another stroke.

Simpson laughs. "You're so gullible, you'd believe anything. Actually, I'm an SS agent, like Fergy. My job is to investigate teachers who use Yankee propaganda from the dark web in their classes. What happened is that one teacher I was after ran for it, and I chased her too far. That's how I got caught by the colonel and sold to Gavin."

Ryan finishes another oar stroke, then mutters to Liam beside him, "I was warned not to trust anything I was told here, but I blew it. My bad."

Liam looks across at Simpson. "So, you and Ferguson were working together the whole time?"

"Nah, I was in a different SS district than Ferguson and didn't know him before this. So, it took a while for us to get on the same page. Then we devised my cover story, figuring you abolitionists would eat it up.

Of course, I know all the lies that Yankees tell about the Confederacy and our War for Independence. That made it easy for me to pose as a teacher and repeat them to you. Fergy and I planned to kill you and the others one night and then smuggle Ryan away using the tunnel. Frank foiled that scheme, but now you've given us a Plan B."

Angrily, Ryan takes his oar back, dips it into the water, and then pulls hard in concert with the others. The craft surges ahead, and the slaves begin another backstroke. This time, when the others dip their oars into the water and pull, Ryan keeps his just above the surface. The oar accelerates through thin air with Ryan pulling so fiercely that he falls backward and lands at Gerry's feet. That's all right, though, because the broad end of Ryan's oar swings around to slam into Ferguson, who drops the shotgun as he crashes into Simpson. Liam reflexively kicks the shotgun away. He stands to plant a boot, studs up, on Ferguson's chest, and kicks. The SS agent does a backflip into the river. Meanwhile, Simpson regains his balance, points the Colt at Liam, and squeezes the trigger. Liam is frozen with fear, but the pistol clicks and then clicks again as Simpson desperately yanks the trigger. "Looks like Frank used all six rounds," Ryan says as he gets to his feet.

No one is rowing, and the galley drifts sideways in the current. On the southern shore, a pirate horde is rushing down the trail the escapees used to get to the pier. "We'll have company soon," Mish warns.

Ryan removes his oar from the gunnel and pokes one end into Simpson's chest. In the river behind them, Ferguson is windmilling his arms and splashing up a storm to stay afloat. "Can't be easy treading water with chains around your ankles," Gerry observes.

Simpson looks down at his similarly encumbered legs, then up at Ryan. "You're not going to push me in, are you?"

"Heck no," Ryan answers. "What do you take me for?"

Simpson smiles with relief, then screams as Ryan shoves the oar forward, propelling him into the drink. "You shouldn't believe anything anyone tells you in the AZ," Ryan comments.

By now, several pirate galleys are underway. Ryan fits his paddle back into the oar lock, and he and Liam regain their seats. "Pull me hearties, pull," Gerry yells.

The teenagers get the galley pointed toward the Illinois shore.

They need all hands to row the large craft, so no one's at the tiller. Consequently, they leave a zigzag wake behind. "They're gaining," Mish exclaims. "We've got to pull."

"You need to get that dog out of your lap," Dieter says. After the next stroke, Mish follows the suggestion and, with Dachsie now at her feet, puts in a powerful stroke.

Thanks to months of sweat and toil in the mine, the escapees have ample muscle power. Still, it's hard to compete with the fully crewed pirate galleys chasing them. Then, the pursuit tapers off. "Why are they stopping?" Melanie wonders.

"Keep rowing," Ryan shouts. "All together." As he rows, Ryan looks back to where the pirate boats are clustered. "Guys, they're fishing Simpson and Ferguson out."

"Ha-ha," Gerry laughs. "Guess they need some more galley slaves."

"They can have 'em," Dieter says disgustedly.

"I said pull," Mish hollers. "We're almost there."

A few minutes later, the boat scrapes bottom near shore. "Everyone out," Ryan orders.

Dieter jumps into the knee-high water. Mish hands him Dachsie and then joins the others who are abandoning ship. Before heading toward the riverbank, Ryan wades to the prow and tries to push the boat away from shore. The heavy craft doesn't budge. Gerry and Liam see what he's doing and come to help. Together, they shove the boat out into the current and then splash after their friends. Once everyone's together, they climb uphill to a grassy bluff overlooking the river. There, they pause for breath.

On the river, the pirates row after the empty boat. It doesn't take long for them to bring her alongside. Some climb aboard and take up the oars. The prows of all the galleys then swing around. "What are they doing?" Melanie wonders.

With perfect synchronization, the pirate paddle blades go back, dip, and cut through the water. "Looks like they're going back to their side of the river," Ryan says. "All they wanted was their boat."

Gerry begins jumping up and down. "Guys, we made it," he hollers.

"Yahoo!" Liam shouts. Immediately, everyone is indiscriminately hugging, kissing, hooting, and hollering like they just won a penalty kick shootout. Dachsie dashes around the conglomeration, barking furiously.

After a while, the celebration subsides. The teenagers share a few more handshakes, high-fives, and back pats. Melanie hugs Ryan tight. "Sorry to interrupt, y'all," Dieter says. "But what now?"

The teenagers ponder Dieter's question. In the sudden silence, they become aware of faint traffic noise. "Sounds like a highway over that way," Ryan points. "Let's go and follow it to the next town."

"Good plan," Liam agrees. "We need to find something to eat."

"I'm hungry too," Melanie sighs. "And I want to call my mother."

"Do you think she'd let me talk to mine?" Mish asks.

"Guys, food and a phone would be nice," Gerry interrupts. "But what are we going to use for money?"

"How about this?" Mish takes an 1849 twenty-dollar gold piece out of her pocket. "While we were getting Dachsie away from Ma, my hand accidentally went into her apron."

"You're a marvel." Dieter hugs Mish, and they kiss.

"Mind if I have a look at that coin?" Ryan asks.

Mish and Dieter break their clinch, and Mish passes the gold piece to Ryan. He briefly admires it, then flips it up like a soccer official. "Call it," he says.

"Heads," Liam exclaims.

The coin lands, and the teenagers circle around to see the profile of Lady Liberty staring hopefully into the future. "Heads it is," Ryan announces.

"Then let's kick off." Liam waits for Ryan to pick up the coin, then sets out for the highway. The others hasten after their long-legged goalkeeper.

The End

Also by William A. Glass. . .

AS GOOD AS CAN BE

Dave Knight is a wayward child growing up in a military family during the 1950s. His older sister wants to kill him but settles for regularly beating him up. Other siblings join in the mayhem while their alcoholic father contributes to the chaos with his unique approach to parenting. As the Knight family moves from one army base to the next, Dave develops a give-a-damn attitude, which often leads to trouble. In high school, he joins other delinquents in a series of escapades, some dangerous, others funny, and a few that would be worthy of jail time should they ever be caught. After barely graduating, Dave is drafted into the army and sent to guard a nuclear weapons depot in Korea. There, he gets into trouble with his sergeant and tries to avoid dishonorable discharge.

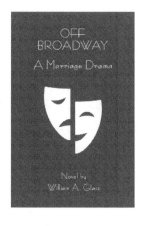

OFF BROADWAY: A Marriage Drama

Cindy and Dave Knight got married too young. Several years later, they're trying to make the best of it. He's a salesman on the fast track with a prestigious corporation. She's the indispensable assistant to a prominent Broadway producer. They own an apartment in Manhattan and enjoy knocking around the city together. However, Dave's erratic behavior and career obsession strain the relationship. Can it be saved?

Made in the USA
Columbia, SC
22 June 2024

37154573R00146